The Beethoven Years

The Beethoven Years

A Novel

Robert L. Shearer

iUniverse, Inc.
Bloomington

The Beethoven Years
A Novel

This is a work of fiction. All of the characters, names, incidents, organizations, and dialogue in this novel are either the products of the author's imagination or are used fictitiously.

iUniverse books may be ordered through booksellers or by contacting:

iUniverse
1663 Liberty Drive
Bloomington, IN 47403
www.iuniverse.com
1-800-Authors (1-800-288-4677)

ISBN: 978-0-5954-6334-3 (pbk)
ISBN: 978-0-5959-0629-1 (ebk)

Printed in the United States of America
iUniverse rev. date: 5/2/2011

For D.N.S.

who took the bullet that only grazed my brain

Author's Note

I would like to thank the following people for their help with the text of *The Beethoven Years*, and the companies that kindly gave permission for me to use certain published material. I am greatly indebted to Dr. Paul Beighley for his advice on the portrayal of bipolar disease and schizophrenia, and on the drugs used in their treatment; and to the model for "Dr. Wilmot" in Book IV of this work, Wende Anderson, Psy.D. She especially has my gratitude for her advice on the sections that deal with the doctor-patient relationship, as well as for her having not only read, but proofread, the entire manuscript. The author is also grateful for the encouragement of Mrs. Sylvia Radic, who was kind enough to proofread the work also. Of course, any remaining errors are my fault alone. I also thank my colleague Prof. Gabriella Baika for her advice on the French that appears in the novel, and especially for her help in translating into French the poem in Book I, Chapter Four.

Thanks also go to Alfred Publishing Company and Sony/ATV for their permission to quote from the song *Hey, Good Lookin'* by Hank Williams, Sr. in Chapter Three of Book II. I found I could not resist taking in its entirety an advertisement for an animé pornographic video, published by Astral Ocean/Asia Blue, and presenting it as a "libretto" on which the main character in Book I wants to compose an opera (the quotation appears in Chapter One there). Mr. Toshi Gold kindly allowed this on the reasonable condition that the website for his organization's online catalogue be given; it is www.asiablue.com, and Mr. Gold is at toshi@astralocean.com.

Because the actor James Woods appears as himself in Chapter Four of Book III, I sought his permission. His publicist, Ron Hofmann, and Mr. Woods himself, had no problem with this; I thank them both. The epigraph on the first page of the novel is a true quote, although the time-frame for my work is some years after the 1986 interview James Woods gave *Newsday* about his playing a schizophrenic for the television movie *Promise.* In the course of researching that role in Santa Monica (I move this to New York) he had gotten to know some people afflicted with schizophrenia, and it was one of those who had thought himself Beethoven. Although the initial inspiration for the novel came from that man's words as recounted by Mr. Woods, my main character is, however, solely the result of literary imagination.

Above all, I am greatly indebted to the research on the "Immortal Beloved" of the true Beethoven which was carried out and published by Maynard Solomon; as the reader will see, the novel turns on the provocative historical question of her identity, so admirably resolved by Prof. Solomon (and detailed in his *Beethoven*, Schirmer Books, 1977). I have used his research extensively.

As for indebtednesses of another kind, let me say that there are so many apt literary expressions that not only might one appropriate, but that one *should.* Donald Barthelme's account of an old-style printing press's plate "kissing the paper" in his "Our Work and Why We Do It" (*Amateurs*, Pocket Books, 1977) is transformed somewhat to apply to the structure of self-consciousness (in "Eastwind's" first convalescent dream, Chapter Ten of Book IV); another of that author's phrases, "a tourist of the emotions," was also irresistible. The last peroration of "Darrell Jimmy the Gentiles' Gentleman" is derived in some part from Jean-Paul Sartre's doctrine of *Le Regard;* and the content of "Hackensack's" imitation of Darrell Jimmy was inspired by a section of *The Diamond Cutter Sutra,* translated by F. Max Müller.

I have worked some of the reported and recorded remarks of Beethoven into the text, though sometimes in altered form; his tart response to the copyist Rampel, who somewhat fawningly had called him "gracious sir" – "Go to the devil with your 'gracious sir!' There is only one who can be called gracious, and that is God" – is a case in point in Chapter One of Book I. His remark to his friend Karl Holz – "I, too, am a king!" – appears in the work, though in the context of a schizophrenic's defiance of his psychiatrist; as well, excerpts from the Heiligenstadt Testament, the composer's impassioned account of his malady, are reworked a bit near the end of Chapter Two in Book IV. In places I have incorporated Beethoven's reference to his symphonies as his "children." And because it will certainly be mystifying to readers unacquainted with his Ninth Symphony, the *"vor Gott!"* that is quoted a number of times in the novel refers to the thunderous harmonic shift in the "Ode to Joy" section of that work's last movement, where, at measures ninety-three and ninety-four, the soprano "A" in an A-major chord maintains its uppermost placement but comes to beam out anew (and loudly) in an F-major setting.

Finally, a word about the use of dialect. Because "Ludi Vann" is a white man who takes himself to be black much of the time, he speaks, though inconsistently, in a kind of Ebonics (a term proposed by African-American academics in 1996), especially with his black friends. And while this dialect is, strictly speaking, neither primarily slang nor metaphoric in the sense of G.K. Chesterton's remark, "All slang is metaphor, and all metaphor is poetry," for me the allure of this gentle linguistic anarchy was precisely its character as a kind of poetry; no ethnic caricature is intended in the least.

Again, my thanks to the individuals and companies referenced above.

rls
Melbourne Beach, Florida
April 2011

The Beethoven Years

Quos deus vult perdere prius dementat.

Introduction: *con moto*

> I spent some time with a man who is working on his Ph.D. Before his illness was brought under control, he thought he was Beethoven. He said he looks back on that period as the happiest in his life.
> – James Woods, *Newsday*, December 1986

And it was, then. Blur to me now. But the breakthrough with Sepulveda has held now for over a year, and I find I can do it, can do it, can reach the level of belonging that a normal guy does, though the old patterns of his motifs and their development course beneath the medicated atmosphere in the electrical thunderstorm of my brain, but politely, they're tame now, background music, and I can say to Mr. Sands the boss, "Just fine, sir," and "Software has signed off on the design," and "Just a question of circuitry at this point," and he nods and I know thinks well of the future to which we both belong – those great words from which I still get a hint of brass in iambic proclamation: *belong* and *future*. Now.

These days I can spot the old newspaper seller without the flames shooting from around his head and his voice sounding in trumpets and trombones, can actually buy a newspaper and peruse the headlines and think: why, that's interesting. Didn't know for example that French Blow Up Atoll in Nuke Test, hadn't suspected Corpse in Attic Former Spouse, unapprised of Garbage Dumpster Babies Plan Reunion, all news to me at this juncture, now that this thing is under control – or nearly so; there are the dreams, still. But I can even work, as I do, with electronics and not have them speak my name, can design software and read schematics without circuits being the map of electrical Armageddon where Resistors finally would submit to the Transformer, positive and negative having been absolute terms for Good and Evil in the drama of electronic redemption and damnation. That's a relief. Electricity, that is to say, played a large part in my former life, if it was my life, but now even the vertical-eyed wall outlets with their censorious "oh!" mouths are more silent, though I admit I occasionally have to sing the jingle when I walk by them:

> *Götterfunken*, transformed di-ode to joy;
> Risperdal has whispered all,
> Functioning electro-chemical ploy!

Something Dr. Sepulveda suggested.

I have met the enemy and prevailed by ruling over it, by directing it through so many tunnels and hoops and coaxing it into fields where bloom the flowers of artificial light. And sound. Information. I make screens light up, I make organs sing, I dazzle the night of limitation with the fireworks of possibility, I have finished my doctorate and heard my calling. Though I am no longer he.

* * *

Finding out, or being found out, that I was not who I was is not exactly new to me. Let me go back, let me slow down a little. I shouldn't go on so.

I began learning my electronic skills in prison, in a program for what they called non-violent offenders, to the extent forgery fits that bill – though it seems to me forgery is, without blood, the most violent possible of crimes. It began with checks, but that soon became too easy; I perfected my method, which I got from the school of acting of the same name, at an early age, and practiced it stringently enough not to get caught: rather than simply trying to make my hand – wrist mostly – behave well enough to form someone else's signature, I was an innovator; I got to know the person, to learn his or her self-image, ambitions, tastes, loves, hates, and (this was the best part) I most importantly gained the craft of intuition into their darkest recesses, what they would deny to their last breath because life simply could not go on should this or that certain thought or fantasy get out. I once got fifty thousand dollars forging the signature of an older woman, my lover, by *being,* as I wrote her name, a vain aspirant to social status who adored Tony Bennett and hated Puccini ("Verdi-lite," she'd sniffed once), and whose darkest fantasy I knew to be that of "clean-up" in a sexual threesome involving representatives of the major races. A cosmopolitan woman. You laugh, but I actually *made myself into* that as I signed her name to the check I'd written to me. In court even she'd had a very hard time denying it was her signature. "It *is* my signature," she'd replied to my lawyer, who'd insisted it was, "but I didn't write it." The testimony of handwriting experts had not particularly aided the prosecution's case. I got away with that one. And the killer is: we returned to being lovers a few weeks later. "You're the me I know best," she enigmatically said one day, "a living mirror." "On the contrary," I'd countered, "I'm the you you don't know at all, the one who lives between the surface and the coated back of the glass."

Later escapades were to prove fatal to my career, at least with checks. But by then I had become fascinated with what I took to be the only question: what difference is there between an original and a *perfect* fake? In meaning and value? No, in *truth?* And so I was drawn to the areas where appearance could drift behind itself to take on the being of the works masters had made.

Oh, such lucidity! It comes with its side effect of drowsiness; calm mind, memories I almost never had.

I moved then to painting, and worked at it for years. Not a success; I had a teacher who could always tell. I considered engraving, but not for the sake of counterfeiting – a vulgar affair. I became a student of all the arts, but gravitated toward music, entering the music school at Emory a little older than most students. After several years of composition and theory, not to mention piano, I found a way. I composed a "Chopin" mazurka and sold it to a confederate in musicology who wished to make a name for himself with "discoveries" of lost music and letters of great composers. Needless to say, I had to learn Chopin's hand, but at that time I was suffering asthma attacks and undergoing bouts of morbidity, and (though not Polish) could work up a creditable *Żal* – this mainly involved getting a wince in my smile and much reading of the history of Poland – so I was able to make it convincing. Well, I admit I'm extemporizing a bit. But it was great *technical* training in the forgery of old manuscripts: how to make an ink that would test out as having come from a previous century; where I could still get paper with the right watermarks – a thorough education. As it turned out, my crony lost his nerve, though I kept the money he'd paid me. I didn't do it for the money, of course; it was really only the sincerest form of flattery raised a power.

And, oh did I learn my craft: manuscripts, diaries, documents; I became a master. I was brilliant at it; I had the gift. Look, you have to understand there is something primordial, sexual, Olympian to forgery of that sort. Is a genius of fakery a fake genius? Genius makes the work, but the greatness of the work makes genius. And if the greatness of the work is *in the work,* then to remake the work – rather, to *make* the work again – is to taste greatness, as if to *be* the genius-creator of it; that is, to overcome the disparity of reach and grasp, to break the vacuous bubble of temporal reflection that is only the ache of the knowing-self and the known-self endlessly switching places, an eternity of becoming: as if to arrive at oneself as another, to *be* oneself as another.

And I know now: the as-if was the anacrusis to the measures of madness in my life. The Anna crisis.

* * *

And then the day came when I discovered computers. I found the Internet. Suddenly, all the forgeries I had loved paled against the deep hue of promise, of the myriad of the possible. And I saw that hard artificial intelligence was the greatest forgery of all.

It fascinated me, it was profound for me, because it was the diabolical fakery of the human condition. The image of human cogitation artificial intelligence conjured for me was that of mockery, an insult to the daily suffering of abysmal self-awareness; a falsifier of ourselves. That was my perception.

And I thought, O wonderful.

Just out of prison, where the computer courses had been primitive, I got a parolee grant to get into graduate school: computer science, back at my old alma mater, no less, with a concentration in artificial intelligence. A man I took to be the ugliest, falsest human being to inhabit the universe, a founder of A.I. at M.I.T., bore down on me with his sick stare from a frame on my wall, like an icon of a saint. I'd had some ideas for software that would take me into the forgery of the human condition, lucrative fakeries, and I gained the methodology as though from an acolyte's devotion. It has served me well. At this moment, something I've developed has gotten the interest of the boss; it's served me very well.

I learned everything legal and illegal about computers. For a while I was fond of giving out the password to Fort Knox's accounting system (it was "srallod6771," "1776 dollars" backward. And it was only my seventeenth hack). But I was careful not to steal anything, not to leave any trail. I had bigger plans.

Because I knew there was something in me, something that whispered in my ear at an early age. At sixteen I had posed as my older brother, forged his signature as the co-signer of a car loan, then defaulted; it was the eldest crime, without, as I said, the blood.

In vain I sought a tattoo parlor that knew the mark of Cain. By then I was already in love with deception, fakery, false witness. And I know why now. In those days a deep notion held me – justified everything.

For I thought, Christ! Who couldn't see that the false side dictates the true side of the cosmos now? That in our time everything only *appears to be?* That the perfect fake is at once the original? End of story. The rest is pathetic grasping at foundational – *straws*. Straw houses are our only abodes. I was simply in tune with the cosmos in its world-forgery, and it made me a cosmic master. It taught me the legitimacy of evil. In those days. And I thought:

Evil: Good owes *everything* to it. Tell Good that Evil has left the building, its eyes would cut to the side; who turned out the lights, the dark backlighting? it would wonder.

Of course, all that could be said of Good's dependence on Evil could be reversed, I knew – the terms switched. But that was just it: in the passage of time, Good and Evil have always been wrapped up together, lovers whose identities merge. And what I came to think was, each comes to dominate for a while, each gets on top for a period. I saw the sickness of the twentieth century with its poison gas, death camps, atomic destruction, and I saw it was Evil's at-bat. Play ball, I'd said in my soul, and let me design some games.

And, oh, the scams I pulled, mainly from my bogus catalogue – Zephyr-Right's Deals (a name which delighted me in that it sounded, correctly, as "Zephyr-Right steals") – which offered outrageous items for sale; undelivered, they were embarrassing enough that no one filed any complaints. I did quite a business; it paid off some student loans.

That people took me at my word was mind-boggling at first, but it shored up my knowledge that what you appear to be for others is what you are, perception forging reality. It's all I had – it's all most of us ever have had. A master of the cosmos, I'd found everybody out, including myself. I lived to lie, I embraced falsehood and forgery that my practice might cast me, constellation-like, into a night whose gleaming lights could not be distinguished from those reflected from stars that had long since gone out of existence, sucked into collapse by the unwarranted heaviness of their being.

That was how I felt then. Maybe I was naïve.

But something came up.

One day I was attempting to sell a phony catalogue item that needed a German name. It was supposed to have been a dildo used by Eva Braun in the late stages of the war, when Hitler was too wracked with the knowledge of the imminent demise of the Third Reich to have been any good with his fleshly riding crop. That was the story; really, there are people who will believe things like that and send you their credit card numbers. I was trying to think of a name for it, something I was asking thousands for, conjuring the force and arrogance of Nazism – a name, maybe, with *"Panzer"* in it, as in *Der Panzerpoker,* say, or perhaps bearing Der Führer's fun-time gal's name, like "the Braun Bomber." Both those seemed a little lame.

At that time I was working on my doctorate at Emory and had the use of the various libraries. I went to the Hoke O'Kelley and asked for a book on German culture; the librarian found me something suitable. Looking like a serious student, I sat at a table, reveling at what I was really doing. I randomly opened the volume to a chapter on Goethe and kind of laughed; clearly, Goethe and dildoes were disparate universes. But I got curious about the "quotations" section of the chapter, and looked over the list of topics on which the great Romantic had expounded. I chose "Beethoven" and read the entry: "1812:" it stated, "Goethe says of Beethoven that he was 'an utterly untamed personality,' writing to his wife, 'never have I seen an artist with more power of concentration, more energy, more inwardness.'"

"Inwardness" stopped me. It was true. A man, a sufferer, a soul who wrestled with an inner angel that – maybe this was a kind of grace – wouldn't materialize to be the ectoplasm of the gaze of others. I was intrigued. No, rather, my knowledge of the daily whoredom our very appearance to the world entailed, was – piqued.

I began spending more time on Beethoven in the libraries, at his sonatas on the crummy upright piano in my apartment; eventually I immersed myself in his biographies – Thayer, among the standards, Solomon, among the later – any work about Beethoven I could find. I became fascinated with someone who rejected the whole outward image of himself, who had something inside that passed show, the sanctity of Hamlet's grief – pretty unthinkable in our evil, superficial time, I thought. He couldn't be forged because the world couldn't get past his deafness, couldn't get inside him.

I'm not romanticizing. Oh, sure, he sold the same composition to different publishers, he wrote crap for money once in a while, he tried to pass off the "van" in his name as "von," locating him among the nobility, he visited the brothels of Vienna, wooed other men's wives; he refused to defend his mother's honor against the rumor that he was the illegitimate son of Frederick the Great, for whom she had worked. He was irascible, wily, maybe a drunk. *But within . . !* An inwardness honed and purged to be the purest mettle, given to the fire of his own forge, vaporized into the absence the muse dreamt herself into.

It took me. I saw my fascination turning into obsession.

I know why now. Even though he was from a better time, the possibility that this inwardness was still open to us, even in our evil age, was a taunt, a rip in my otherwise whole-cloth cosmos, a universe of pure appearance stamping the ingots of Being, where the daily alchemy of value transmuted the shimmer of image into the gleam of truth, each of us spinning straw into gold – the old scam of a foundation for the reedy structure of our everyday world. He never fell to image because the inside never shows; that this was yet possible was the hole in my cosmology. But it became more than a gap; it became a sore.

I began hearing his music in my head, unbidden. I noticed one day that I walked in the rhythms of his measures. I considered the emptiness of my heart where there was no joy, only a kind of bitter glee, and I stopped walking one day, as I heard the last movement of his Ninth thundering in my mind; I stopped, stupefied: a man who had suffered the cruelest irony that God could have conceived – deafness for a great composer – had limned joy itself as divine! But it didn't make me happy; it wasn't some sort of movie-scene epiphany. No, it *hurt* with a confusion that came at me like the jagged edges of a broken beer bottle in a bar fight.

At first I loved him, naively, but that love matured into a passion I knew not where directed. It preyed on my mind.

*   *   *

But I'm getting nervous spouting off like this, telling you everything. Look, I've got work to do; something is really going my way here at the company. All I know is I'm no longer delusional. I've almost recovered, I know my name now. Recovery for me means covering the distance to myself. I'm on the way.

So enough. I'm tired of this first-person account. Shearer, you want to do the narrative, step in when it's needed? Would you? I really am pretty busy.

He says he'll do it. Wait...

He says he gets to jump around in time. Whatever.

All I know now is that I manipulate formulas, design schematics, write lines of symbols in calculated code to machines.

No more lines and dots in divine code to musicians.

BOOK ONE

Days of Dementia

Chapter One

Madness in the Beethoven Years

I the divine nigger for the Morse massa I jot and scratch but only as afterthought to thunderous harmonies in my headt, melody threading above and through time stitched in the hem of the garment as rhythms myriad, profuse, suggestive, but if time don't dance who can pay the Piper? The Piper demand his *dues,* muvvah. Demand, as I say, *tribute* else why you think tribu*lation,* great weary ache from pulling the worldt, you think clink-clank of chains be think-thank of mortals bearing destiny like perpetual brow-beadts enough for Him? But I say O froindes, *nicht diese* tones. *Nicht* 'em! He want spirit in dit-dit-dit-dah, Morse massa say that "V" for victory (political freedom, transcendence of death, fill-in-your-own-damn-blank), harmonies in thirds upper register for angelic voices so high only dogs hear truth, they try to talk it come out howls of demons…

Admitted, on page my notes look like clusters of fly shit but they not, you know what? They tiny, eensy-iny little black holes suck celestial ether through them, vibrate in pitch-black pitch, collapsing the gravity of the worl', like. My job 'scription be caging fly-away dots, constructing dialogue of points and lines that to the knowing eye become the known ear bursting in counterpoint and choirs… But not talkin' cart aheadt of horse here in that them dots, and them squiggles too, they ain't first in the order of things.

First be His thunderous voice the spirit speakin' to me 'bout the moodt of things, celestial weather, gossip of angels, the lates' in ontological fads, sayin' to me, you be he, you be he, you Ludi Vann you talk the talk for me whose authentic voice is silence, you a translator of silence, you who speak silence in the vernacular, you whom I done taught silence, whom I love most, as your affliction prove.

Well, that a big job. But he give it to me, and I walk the walk.

Silence, it hide in the sonority of brass, rustle in the silk of strings, it there in the nasal hair of reedts.

I walk through the throng of wounded also walking, also widh their version of what been done to 'em, each gotta stagger 'cording to the heaviness of the invisible crosses they bear, we congregate on da screets, we pool our eyes, exchange curses and promises. A black man sing, prophet in his own landt, which is: The Screets, pop. teeming widh us who acknowledge the whole universe because we can't appropriate any of the fucker, we hear the nigger sing

I am the alpha and the omega
The ultimate scene make-ah
I smile Shiva's crooked grin
You-got-to-end-where-you-begin.

Come, go gotha
You gotta go gotha
along with me.

Yeah, said grinnin' Shiva's grin
Dancin' Death's forward grine
Nobody's eyes saw my sin
An' I've hidden it from mine.

Come, go gotha

Ya gotta go gotha
along with me.

But nix these tones. I only sing along 'cause of my kinship with all black people, black is the color of silence, the nerve from my ear to my brain is black; white for that damn matter is all colors run riot in atonal confusion, Schoen-*bête-noire-ian*, the blandt cowardice of light keeping it from just damn declaring itself by withholding itself, ax me.

But nix these damn *Töne!*

Damn turn-na!

Damn tur-*nin'*. Toinin', toinin' wheel…

Turning turned, *mutatis mutandis.* I speak many dialects of silence. I am a chameleon of silence. I hear with my eyes, speak from them, one pique-ture worth a thousand words, looks could kill I'd outdone any serial maniac they fried; but looks could hold them in love, in compassion and forgiveness, that too I'd rate up there with my Master and his Son, and Fatboy of the Far East. I try to tell them of my love and compassion, of course it comes out in weird distorted harmonies of those who cannot hear themselves, scares them they hand me money not knowing I'm rich, live in constant tonal riches, a treasury of tones. Inside my head.

For how can I tell them I am deaf!? How can I say to them, speak louder! For I am deaf! Beethoven is deaf!

How do I know I am he? I can be no other, I have a proof that exhibits congruency on several points:

1. He suffered. I suffer.
2. He suffered. I suffer.
3. He suffered. I suffer.

Q.E.D.

Then too, I know Morse massa had a PLAN in mindt, I know he give me the affliction, his love, his voice (silence), I know 'cause I met Him. Still do, down on corner. 'Course He can't come oudt from behindt the burning bush, the cloudt on Mount Sinus, but ain't no cosmic injunction 'gainst DISGUISES, is they? So they be this look like to the nekkid eye newsseller, seen the flames from his headt, the infinite depth of his eyepools, the cosmic fury gentled down over the aeons omniscience in every hair of eyebrow, every wrinkle on foreheadt, singing black boy his man, dark seraphim attendant, "Yassuh, Mist' Godt." When not wailing. Tell me that ain't Massa Morse, street name: Augie Blick. Tell me he who bring the news ain't Godt. *But dint know it till he give me the affliction,* which he effected by means of subterfuge, i.e., by beckoning me over, shout in my face: "Every valley shall be exalted, every mountain laid low, and we shall be change in the blink of an eye, scientists affirm." Then he heldt up newspaper, headline shouting "One Dead in Murder-Suicide Half-Pact." And I fell into a rapture and had a vision:

I saw the body of an innocent man, eyes turned up in his head, knew it was I standing over him, not only observer of scene, but towering over his broken corpse like a cause he the effect of which, that is, I saw him Isaac-like to my Abraham who heard NOT the angel of the Lord calling off the hound of faith. I knew we shall both be changed when Augie blicks his fickle fick, our hearts white as snow, for I cleansed you of the world and am cleansed of the world, murderer and victim smiling into each other's eyes knowing they played their roles on the world's stage, just a goof to get to the Godhead... But I be blameless, blameless as Fate be bline, I not hearing His dog whistle to hound-of-faith: a silent tone to a hearing ear change in an *augenblick* to a piercing tone to a silent ear, a soprano "A," harmony of A-major, that in its constancy beamed out as His divine love/forgiveness in sudden *fortissimo* setting of F-major, *tutti*: *vor! Gott!*

That was the vision Fate granted me.

Sharp shooting pain in my ears, stillness on the aural plane, Augie Blick's divine mouth move and shout silence in my face stanching the blood with both His hands read my lips read my lips I speak the code.

I was *deaf.*

Thus knocked faith at my door.

* * *

REPORT OF OFFICER R. RIVERA, NYPD, #314562, Oct. 6, 1996.

Responded to call from A. Eisenhardt, owner of Abe's News and Books. Harassment by street person. Arrived approximately five minutes after dispatch. Homeless man on sidewalk looked to have been assaulted, hand to ears bleeding heavily. No I.D.

Complainant stated man approached him in a daze, was incoherent, seemed not to understand function of the establishment, raved and swore at him. Complainant shouted at him to leave. Man then grabbed receipt spindles from counter and pushed them into his own ears, collapsed on sidewalk. Complainant retrieved spindles, applied compresses. Ambulance called. Unit 21, Boucher and Brogdan, arrived approximately ten minutes.

Homeless man admitted to emergency room, Sisters of Mercy. Condition as yet undetermined.

* * *

From the files of Arnaud de Belmont, M.D., staff psychiatrist, New York State Hospital, Bellevue, New York:

The patient, a street person going by the appellation "Ludi Vann," medically treated at the S. of M. ER for self-inflicted injury: self-mutilation; ear-drums punctured by sharp objects. He is slowly recovering, but is still hearing-impaired to a debilitating degree.

History: paranoid schizophrenic episodes, including delusions. Webber and the staff psychologist at S. of M. agree on a diagnosis of Bipolar I Disorder, severe with psychotic features. He has been Involuntarily Committed twice before. Webber has started lithium therapy with him - results pending.

Because his hearing is minimal, we communicated by what he insisted on calling "conversation books." Our attempts at written communication were interrupted early when I scrawled that I preferred using the computer keyboard and screen, but that the system was down and couldn't function. He at that point responded in a hoarse, toneless voice that he was "down" too, in the sense street people use the term, but could still function. His diction was that of black English, though he is Caucasian.

Then to my amazement he got up and walked over to the unit, rummaged through my desk drawer (I thought it best to let him), found and bent a paperclip into a kind of screwdriver, undid the unit's cover and proceeded to inspect the tinny mazes and mysterious lumps, probing this and that connection; he turned the unit on and off until, suddenly, the screen came up and the keyboard worked. It obeyed all the commands, including those of the word processor program.

In the same uninflected voice he said something about a long familiarity with keyboards and his ability as an improviser. "Good," I typed, clacking at the keyboard, "let's key in our questions and answers." But he insisted on the ragged notebooks he'd brought to the session. As below:

CONVERSATION BOOK I

Belmont: *I want you to know our approach with you is a combination of chemical therapy and counseling, Ludi.*

Ludi Vann: ***Why are you do this***

Belmont: *We want to help you. You've been pretty sick. Don't be ashamed, we all have health problems from time to time, and the mind is no different.*

L.V.: ***Im not sick my minds afflicted OK but its a devine thing***

Belmont: *But we know you're suffering and we can help.*

L.V.: ***Im suffering but its a devine thing its no less than jesus what happened to him and be his message to us all***

Belmont: *Ludi, I know you're intelligent, and I know you'll appreciate me telling you that the imitation of Jesus is a psychiatric syndrome, it doesn't have to* [at this point he grabbed the notebook from me].

L.V.: **not imitating – suffering impossible!!! to fake as <u>life</u>**

Belmont: *Ludi, all I'm saying is that we can help you if you want. If you want to suffer, then it should be a rational choice, not a mental imbalance.*

L.V.: **its not my choice not up to me. God wheels man deals. God say, man obey. God great man frate**

Belmont: *How did you know how to fix my computer?*

L.V.: **God signs man rimes**

Belmont: *You must have spent a lot of time in electronics.*

L.V.: **lifeblood**

Belmont: *Lifeblood? In what way?*

L.V.: **everythings electricity God speaks electricity**

Belmont: *How is it that you learned electronics?*

L.V.: **Gods body. Wanted to be phsian phisycan doctr of Gods body. Know the secret bile and bituman corsing thru his temple**

Belmont: *The world.*

L.V.: **the wolrd**

Belmont: *Ludi, do you want help?*

L.V.: **for what**

Belmont: *To get over your mental condition. To live a better life.*

L.V.: **Im mad but let me tell you something I lived in a tree house off the N.J. turnpike few years. Farther back one is the more you know, knew the destiny of each car I could see for the next few seconds so long as their speed the hipnosis of mass to motion I saw the wreck about to happen, its necessity, knew ahead of time the bending of metal into metal but for drivers it was instantious, no foxkin idea. I had the mind of God for tiny eons, a world in** minatur. I was Laplace's Demon of freeway physics you dig. Moral – the farther out you are the more you see

Belmont: But are you happy?

L.V.: none of my business

* * *

Blake comes to me on the streets doesn't know he's Blake but I know because he sees the angels in the trees too. Saw a woman walking her dog that took a crap under one of those angel-studded trees, I broke out in harsh laughter to see one of the angels pull up his shining robe and drop turds near the dog who jumped up and back lady seeing nothing her eyes full of the world. Not obscene, chocolate the shit of angels as any chemical/metaphysical analysis would reveal. But we don't always agree Blake hating everything scientific/technical said to him who died the same year I did, Bill I'm personally happy with the Industrial Revolution, Bill, I used to destroy pianos until they made the fuckers with reinforced balls… Nor share I your disdain for Newton, Willie, poets and painters don't work in tonic and dominant, secondary dominants wherein the key of F equals mass times acceleration of C-major-seventh, always the attraction of harmonic bodies (see my Op. 7, first movement, closing theme, mm 111-127), nothing like that in "& every sand becomes a gem /reflected in the beams divine" know what I'm sayin'? Its truth a spiritual truth but not a musical one, the liability of poetry, while never the case for music, the worst music is at least the song of lying seraphim… O come on, Billy, you know that I consider music a higher revelation than all of philosophy, you don't have to get all… Bill! Let's go angel-spotting again!

(Now I know why the boy used the ampersand so much, I once wrote him a letter Dear Bill & how are you & I am fine & Adam's sin was he believed the image he saw reflecting in the polished apple the snake gave him & his squeeze Eve & I know you had your differences with Swedenborg but see his *Heaven & Hell* No. 160, yours forever, Ludi Vann, but never mailed it: "& every sand becomes a gem" – *Am,* per *sand.* O what *isn't* code?! Every day I know why I bear the affliction just yesterday discovered that LISTEN is the anagram and vice-version of SILENT.)

* * *

I walk through the sprawl of bums of drunks with their empty wine bottles fallen aside mute testimony half-note rests after the closing thunderclap cadence, elongated fermata of the long fermented. I once sat with them with their fallen bottles for some TV documentary there on the sidewalk, all of us in a row with backs to the grimy wall ("symbolic as hell, look, can you get an angle where we can pan down the row . . ?"). Well they got their angle somehow but they had to pay the bums and the director some wop or whoever the *fartiste* was gave each of us a Walkman thought it'd be "symbolic as hell" to have each of us wearing his Walkman "tuned to a different station." I took mine but when the panning began I was the only one not wearing the little headphones instead the camera caught the Fifth of my children roaring in my head leaping from my eyes blaring from my face… I walk through the sprawl of drunks I despise them I love them I exalt them told Belmont I want to behold the world entire in the elongated tear hanging from the eye of a drunk – no, not a perfectly round globe, for that belongs only to Gracious God – but the distorted, the pulled-out-of-shape, the tortured tear on the run excrescence of having-seen for there is the truest reflection of the world; all I would ask is its salt season the palate of those who would taste works of

REDEMPTION

ABYSMAL DEPTH

JOY JOY JOY!

Other than that they smell pretty vile.

But what of that now that Idiot Boy's got me the libretto for my opera, calls it *Leenawhora, or the Travail of Lazara the Living End* about redemption through cosmic penetration and also devotion to cyborg husband captured by cyberdroid torturing him in cybercell dungeon. I read the synopsis: "cyberhell, acid trip hell, laser fields of destruction, asteroid sex, transformers with hundreds of penisoids that fuck and pillage, Armageddon destruction, the most fantastically drawn females in bondage pray to videos, pussies that shoot lasers, vaginal energy fields, cyberpunks, yoda transformations, cockrems shoved into mouths, the bowels of 25th century hell, fingers turned into sex organs, 20-foot genitals, android orgy, spider women, rotating bestial organs…" which produces certain challenges thematically for the overture but what the hell I get three chances right?

* * *

Belmont: *Let's talk about your ears. Why?*

Ludi Vann: *I matched the high, piercing shreek, beat it.*

Belmont: *Where did this shriek come from?*

L.V.: *It was the tone of his hair the light flaming around his head. It made a great tinnitus in my ears.*

Belmont: *Whose? What head?*

L.V.: *Gracious God.*

Belmont: *You encounter God?*

L.V.: *Everywhere. Mostly the electrical sockets but sometimes He appears. In disguise.*

Belmont: *Tell me about the electrical sockets. God reaches you through them?*

L.V.: **Sings the AC electric, shoot into my brain.**

Belmont: *What does it sound like? What does he sing?*

L.V.: **Hums mostly, raw material for me to spin into cosmic melodic-harmonic drama in the** [unintelligible]. **But he give me the code too, breaks up the hum. Code come I know the sounds thru the key.**

Belmont: *So God is electricity?*

L.V.: **But only AC, alternating current. DC is His opposite, false AC. Useful but God's darker brother, the angel of homogeneity.**

Belmont: *Why is God AC?*

L.V.: **Because God is the self-cause, causa sui**

Belmont: *Ah, the god of the philosophers.*

L.V.: **of the Hebrews, I am that I am**

Belmont: *And yet alternating current.*

L.V.: **Alternating as He must between Himself as Cause and as Effect.**

Belmont: *Well, this is a new*

L.V.: **I am that I am. Look, that means that He already is in order to be.** [Here he merely looked at me; I wrote nothing.] **That means that God as God precedes Himself as the cause of himself, and the effect of that cause is the same self that existed – preexisted – as cause.**

Belmont: *So*

L.V.: **But He can then be isolated into cause, not the effekt, insofar as cause is primary and distink from effekt, and effec, not the cause insofar as the latter itself distink. So to pick up your "so" so if He the same thing in both ways He alternate. Now he Cause, but as the same he now Effect, you get the picture**

Belmont: *Because God is the self-cause he must alternate?*

L.V.: Because God the self-cause he got to come out of his own possibility of not being God, got to be a triumf over his non-existence – and the only way of triumf, successful self-cosmogony be to preserve that possibility of not-God at the core of God, see?

Belmont: Meaning God is also his

L.V.: His positive is negative, his negative positive

Belmont: Now, the first time you came under psychiatric care

L.V.: Fuck that shit I'm elucidating the divine nature as alternating positivity and negativity, you tell me that is not electricity alternating current!

Belmont: Now, did God appear to you the last time

L.V.: Lets stick with electricity doctor. Divine electricity.

Belmont: You think it's watching you?

L.V.: Fuck that standard form paranoia shit, OK? I'm saying you know electricity makes your brain and body work, makes the molecules hold together, hynotizes the atoms into them, galvanizes time into rust

Belmont: So

L.V.: So God be everywhere not separate from the world, God's body, pulsating with his self-founding alternating current the alpha that is omega like you ever see a sonogram of a fetus, doc, the tiny grinning skull belying the distendedness of time, no no, such irony can only unfucking fold. Music. Music made of time that justify its end from its beginning, its beginning in terms of its end – causa sui. God the fountainhead the godhead the source he thus can never speak except in music, you dig?

Belmont: No

L.V.: Because it all paradox if His positivity also his negativity, try speaking in paradoxes, what would your founder Froid the cold bastard think of describing Dora in paraxodial sentence after paradoxial sentence? He would not dig it, he would not dig it, Jack, not being no mystic. But music proves the world is not an error because the self-cause not no casual thing. Theorem: Where causal nothing casual.

Belmont: *So god is the electrical structure, alternating current, portending the self-cause, in all things.*

L.V.: words words words

Belmont: *and he speaks to you.*

L.V.: He speaks dreadfully and exaltedly to me

Belmont: *with electricity. Or in electricity.*

L.V.: I walk by the sockets they shriek, it all at first hellgrins from chorus of demons secretly enjoying their torment, Hammond orgasm, but its all His choir they send the code I translike decifer every buzz and hum and all the breaks between

Belmont: *You know God's meaning.*

L.V.: No one knows his meaning, doctor, what I scribble is only interpretation of

Belmont: *Of?*

L.V.: His meaningful silence, pregnant pause.

* * *

Belmont makes sure I take the poison that would kill Beethoven again but in subterfuge I'm able to keep him alive. Of course he/I died 1827 but what exactly made Beethoven himself needn't have been lost. But there is more to it than just transference or resurrection of "his/my energy" or unique atomic/molecular make-up that Nature brought out of herself into the same focus (lyric genius, devotion to a universe of tones made to vibrate out of the same time that turns the world), there's for example: even Beethoven (me) unto himself *then* both was *and* was aware *of* himself, existing as a gap, a hole-in-being within, thanks to the agony of consciousness… But behold: I shall tell you the secret of my madness and the concomitant truth of my identity as he:

My God-stricken mind is only the same gap between *am* and aware-of-am he experienced, pushed into the darkness of

A CLEFT
whose depth is a BOTTOMLESSNESS
borrowed and transformed into the infinite density
of SELFHOOD.

Or: I have burrowed up his ontological asshole to emerge as his mouth, his face, his brow contracted into will and woe…

* * *

You'd be surprised at who's here. Karl is here, glimpsed him yesterday in Central Park. But is SHE here? Is she now again, as even I am?

Belmont, Belmont's someone else too but who? Yes, even poor, twisted Belmont, CRITIC! CREECH! Everybody is somebody again, one day, even Belmont, even weird, suspicious, bent Belmont, something about him like he means well but got the paving contract on the road to Hell.

But everybody is somebody again, I got my assignment why is that a problem?

Yeah, besides Idiot-Boy there's Darrell Jimmy the Gentiles' Gentleman there's the dwarf we call Hackensack because he got the cough and the little sack he spit into, Dwarf have that distorted face and legs in diminution from real legs little high nasal voice, said to him once reading Nietzsche's great poem hey dwarf or sumpin' hey frawd because that his name backwards hey let's you an' me climb thisshere building you hangin' on to me you dig (like Nietzsche's snarf, so short he blow sand in his shoes with even the casualest fart), like in the poem, you've read *Sara Thrust It,* ain't you? we laughed at that. Darrell Genital the

Jimmying Gentleman he got the woman thing told him I used to think women carried purses because they got pussies but now convinced it the other way aroun', that, show me a purseless woman, said, I show you one gotta take it in the ass. So we took to checking incidence of purse-carrying by those whose double-X chromosomes had triumphed in the algebra of ecstatic spawn, we checked chicks as they strolled by but dint touch them for though there is the sex ack there is also the Involuntary Commitment Ack and they look nervous already just sideways glance. Several men slept-walked in a kind of lust trance to join us, DJ the GG held forth for our edification: "Gentlemen, in each woman is the Universal Truth of Return; indeed, it is why we adore the Source they hide between their legs and smile at us to seek, at the foundation of their torso and trousseau. The foundation, gentlemen: the altar of nature's own truth before which we kneel in order to enter. Or reënter, as Freud explains. But because they are only the particularization of the universal they violate it, degrade it, whore-ify it, gentlemen, in the moment of their orgasm, only to perish in their *petite mort* and thereby affirm it. But what of the universal here? I put it to you, gentlemen: the universal has appropriated the female, *not she it* – she who now lies limp beneath or beside the male, the male who finds only the failure of the universal to obtain, and whose most proper post-coital murmur can only be 'next…' Don Juan, to elicit an example from amorous history, gentlemen, was both Kierkegaard's despair and Nietzsche's tragic hero…" But if only to adore them just to see them of course I desire them but just to see them from the vanishing point of perspective, not necessary I touch them you look at fuckflix you see how *de trop* the male only there that the female shine forth in her truth, the Gentiles' Gentleman to the contrary notwithstanding, male left over, ugly appurtenance; the female mantis know something about gratuitousness of male, about cosmicity itself, she invite life into passion, the little death into the Big One, *is this the meaning of your longing,* O male mantis, how could your prayers have been answered thus? By the Law of Gravity expressly legislated for the mass of a guillotine blade by a Beckett-god for whom life and death are separated only by the cosmic arc of a swinging trap door…? Arc of Time, same as in the curve of their thigh… Yet I desire them, women, lie with them only seldom their choice not mine.

Darrell Jimmy showed me a poem told him I'd set it to music:

> *Nipple-kissed breast,*
> *Cunt-scented flowers,*
>   *Jasmine-gism:*
> *Tunnel of Love floats my boat.*
> *Ass so perfect its lobes beatify Euclid.*
> *O let me cage thy beauty,*
> *Make it sing on the perch of my cock!*

D.J. the G.G. go way back widh the woman thing, suffered from the tenth degree of nympholepsy before they gave him the testosterone-killers, *could not walk* down the street and not go nympholeptic when the New York Junior Ballet let out the girls he had to be restrained flailing arms and legs foaming at the mouth and spurting at the cock slain by beauty slain by beauty…

"Fucker has always had it bad," Frawd damn interjects.

"Cops hadda talk him back, you're okay now, take it easy, that's it, it's passing. Seizures got him to the E.R. but da young nurses…"

"How about male nurses, not uncommon these days? He's not a faggeroo, is he? Handles only his own pecker, don't he?" Piping voice.

"Here the details, you know, be unavailable. He once confessed to me that he'd numbed up his masturbatin' hand by holding it in the freezer compartment of his refrigerator first to make it other than his own to the touch but found the cold flesh anti-erotic."

"The things we do for love."

Alas, I allows, alas.

Frawd the dwarf know DJ a long time did a little piping for us as a riff on the Gentleman's peroration *re* the eternal feminine and its temporal failure while we watched women and what happened with his voice turned into a secret confirmation of who I be, said, "Gentlemen, I too have tasted the carnal fruits of pussy-love, yes with even normal-sized women, grunting and puffing between their legs, I too sought the temporary cosmicity of groove-reëntry, the launch of my astral body back into the womb. But here ontological significance intervenes, gentlemen. For what is this project-toward-pussy but the debased quest for the spiritual truth of Being? A substitute, gentlemen, for the ultimate. Therefore, lacking eternity, it's the valley of temporal repetition. It is, gentlemen, the Chinese food of cosmic arrival. Woman is the dead-end of truth. I say to my woman, 'Show more verve, Anna, you lousy substitute for nirvana,' but, as I say, gentlemen, it suffers a failure of ultimacy." We laughed and laughed at him we could see that El Drawfo was a perfect intimation of Darrell Jimmy the Gentiles' Gentleman, it was DJ's voice though an octave higher, his diction, style – but that *made* the little guy Darrell Jimmy; I saw DJ getting ripped from himself, he vibrated as Frawd appropriated his being, then faded like dust settling in the sunset. I was positively thrilled. 'Cause that's how it happened to me with *him.* The attenuated Darrell Jimmy, now no larger than four-feet-eight, went on, "Thus the teaching is that pussy is no-pussy and that is what is called pussy; that tits are no-tits and ass is no-ass and these are called, respectively, tits and ass.

That orgasm is no-orgasm and that cunt is no-cunt and that the cavern of the vagina is the emptiness of the universe, never filled. But that these things are called so." Yeah, yeah. We laughed and laughed. After a while Darrell Jimmy kinda got reabsorbed into himself, but his incarnation as Frawd was *epiphany*...

A woman go by seem not to belong to the race of angels with whom the divine promise reside, "Egad," says Darrell Jimmy, "there goes ugliness on the hoof. Although to say so is an unkindness."

"Shia, only to cloven bea'ts," says I. "Man, she a secretary at Ugly Stick, Inc. She da undersite o' desire, she disgus' widh da wad o' cum in you' handt…"

"She certainly is a rip in the fabric of illusion."

"Shia, she a hole in the veil o' Maya walk you' ass through to Buddhahoodt," I add, and sing:

I a Arhat now, baby,
Thanks to yo' ugly ass –
Saidt, yeah, a Arhat, mama,
You brought Nirvana to pass.

Well, now I be (clap-clap) *deliveredt fum sin*
Jus' by lookin' (jaw-drop) *at da shape you in!*
My desires at las' be purifiedt
(Pause, then frenzied:)
My libido done commitedt suicite!

Saidt I be a Arhat, fat mama,
Rescuedt fum da valley o' lus'.
Saidt yeah, a Arhat, pond'rous mama,
Seein' da temporal form o' yo' dus'.

"That is perhaps excessive," allows the Gentiles' Gentleman, "but your meaning has something of the clarity of a Eudoxian theorem applied within an Archimedian proof. Known as the "Sand Reckoner" in that he drew shapes in circles delineated on the ground, Archimedes often relied on his colleague's geometry, owing to the granular nature of his own diagrams, and of course, the occasional anthill. And here, gentlemen, I think we might appreciate the moment of existential angst the poor man must have had on such occasions: with all the pristine rigor of relations there in the sand bespeaking the order of the universe, suddenly a hole opens, disgorging little beings whose own cosmos was labyrinthine at best…"

DJ, see, done burnt out his brain with LSD back when he a student at Berkeley, but still know beautiful women when he see 'em, kep' his devotion.

But though they harbor the universe between their legs and its promise on their chests there is more so much more the rhapsodic heart of love. Idiot Boy says he seen her says she do the dance.

* * *

"So how did you become Beethoven? I don't suppose you can say you *heard* a call…" [Letterman audience laughs.]

Well, Dave, it's an interesting story. See, for a long time I knew I didn't exist. Before.

"Now, Ludi, who was it who knew that?" [Laughter from audience.]

Not me. [Laughter] I mean I was a hole with a center of gravity, a shadow of anti-matter bringing things into sepia relief, gliding against walls (flashing into chaotic bursts of color and line, eye beholding circumspect eye as I passed any mirror surface), bending over curbs. I eddied space, that's all.

"Didn't you have a name?"

I waited for my name to be called but the *Maitre deo* had laryngitis.

"Your name croaked out, hoarse."

A sibilance striving for a whisper.

PAUL SHAFFER: "You weren't written into the book of even temporary life?"

Invisible ink on a Saran Wrap page.

"And so?"

I knew the pointless charade would end when the great snake in my intestines arose into my throat to choke off my last lie. No, I was *elsewhere*, not here, gas grazing guts for eloquence. One day in the street I passed a Buddhist temple, poem like a six-pointed sutra came to me to set to music:

No primping
No preening
No sighing
No keening
Keeping the mirror well-dusted
Will keep you from getting busted

I knew that in a way, before the allure of *him*/me. But the writing in the dust on the mirror seemed to be spelling out a name. I tried not to look, imagined shattering the glass to shards, but found a RAGGED SLIVER gleaming in my mind that cut into me like a SILVER DAGGER; its light coalesced into a diamond with the density of rapturous absorption, its facets a fist that came to shake like an earthquake of the soul. Looking back on it now.

"Yes, but how . . ?"

The small boys came and told me they'd seen me somewhere in a distant city.

You're sure it was me?

It was you, they said.

Someone who looks like me?

Yeah.
Sounds like me?
Yeah.
Feels like me?
Yeah.
Someone to die my death, you say.
Sure. He's waiting.
I'm him?
The boys bent together in angelic harmony:

> And he's youoooooo-ou
> Ah ah oooh
> You-ooooo-ou
> Ah ah oooh

Little Anton gave me the benedictus nod then skateboarded away in his blond curls. With the others. I knew he was an angel then and went to Chicago.

Stayed in a flop house, slept under freeway bridges, made a cardboard for daytime, said "ELSEWHERE, PLEASE HELP" – people quizzically handing me change and a few bills.

Anton's brother-angel showed up, said he's very close now, New York, so took the grey dog thereto, spilled out on Forty-second, a man handed me a ticket from his overcoat, Olympia 567.

I found the hotel. Desk clerk wanted the word.
How many syllables?
Not polysyllabic.
How many letters?
Less than four but more than three.
How many vowels?
Less than three but more than two.
What language?
Silence, you'd call it.

What dialect?

Profound.

Hmmm. Does a pin drop?

If the seamstress is clumsy. Or palsied.

Done.

Then not only drops but resonates in C-minor, he said smiling.

If the word could be spoken, would a synonym of it be *Fate*, No. 5, Opus 67?

He gave me the key to 567.

Sabina was waiting in the room. She lay on the bed, naked, legs crossed. She gazed at me, then asked, "What are the three words?"

"I don't know."

She opened her legs. I sang her a love song.

Come on, baby, less do the gristle
Said, yeah, c'mon bay-be, less do the gristle
You toot my horn
I blow your whistle
'Roun' anna 'roun' anna upindown...

"You must interpret the oracle of my orifice," she said, when I had finished singing, "first. Cast the dregs of my delta. Read my lips."

I divined the source. I saw she was a runaway housewife from Des Plaines who in the previous lives I could read there had been:

a welder
an acquaintance of the Watergate Cubans
a pipe-fitter aboard the *Merrimac*
a turnkey in a prison
a seagull
a governor of Rhode Island
a hangman
a midwife

See, I look for the magical combination in women's past lives, search out the trifecta, be it though surrounded by other pasts (occasionally I read future lives); the trinity gotta be:

whore
Buddha
beloved

Being in that position of scrutiny I sought sixty-nine but was eighty-sixed. The exit led into a labyrinthine corridor.

"We need to take a break here, Ludi. You can finish your story when we come back…" [Commercial ensues.]

* * *

"We're back. My guest is Ludi Vann Beethoven… Now, Ludi, are you still composing?"

Well, gosh, Dave, I'm certainly not decomposing anymore. [Laughter, groans from audience.] But as I was saying:

I was in the corridor. It was black. Instinctively I felt for a thread, found a stiff string that burst into flames and burned away from me, illumining the maze as it twisted and turned and doubled-back – a fuse reaching its destination in an explosion which was the dream of a yogi, a vision of me in a subway station. Or maybe the yogi was dreamt by the stationmaster, the stationmaster dreamt by a chimney sweep, the chimney sweep by the chimney, the chimney by the smoke of the power plant where electricity is drawn from the whirling of magnets that are God's petrified brains around a coil wherein is distended His Infinite Nature, to supply volts to the third rail as I rode to the Fifty-seventh-Street stop. I whooshed out onto the street, telltale vortices of myself sucking along to Carnegie Hall.

I saw a poster behind the glass, Beethoven in his/my scowl, eyes penetrating into the hollow my soul had left. We stared at each other a long time, he the reflection of mine, mine his.

The boys, the angels, were *right!* There's the angelic consciousness for you.

Someone bumped into me to break the lock of his/my stare, said, "Gracious …!" (hint of jest, saving irony). I reached into his eyes: "Go to the devil with your 'gracious,' sir!" I said, shaking my fist, "there is only one who can be called gracious, and that is God." He fled. And I knew: I had to become deaf.

* * *

"Now, Ludi, if you're deaf, how is it we're having this conversation right now? You seem to be hearing all right."

I read the Braille of your breath, Dave, gauge the subtle temperature changes on my skin of each word, though that little gap between your teeth sometimes a powerful interference. Look, speech ain't necessarily sound. Consider sign-language monkeys being brought into the original sin of syntax, cementing their fate in semantics, at this very hour learning to stretch a skin of words over the abyss like a tympanum, or say trampoline in moments of poetic joy…

"And you were stone deaf when you composed the Ninth, right? Or was it more stoned than deaf?" [Audience snickers, hoots.]

You know, Dave, music is nigger. I don't mean just rhythm, it's nigger even in its most sophisticated and sublimated forms…

"Ludi, we don't talk like racists here…"

No racist. Some of my best homies are friends. No, I mean it's, you know, it *down*, knowmsayin'?

"Here we go, folks…"

And I have that blackness in me, Dave, the dark velvet lining an abyss grows like fungus as the lostness of the hours, you know, well, it done wrap itse'f 'roun' my ear muscles don' you dig? Full Nelson sh - - (beep!). Masked Marauder from da damn voidt.

"Whoa..." [Baffled chortling from audience]

So I compose outta my blackened aural nerve, okay?

"And so you wrote... the..."

You're f- - (beep!) – aye, Dave. But I rather... compiled it. I owe it all to my Sony and my Kurzweil.

"Sony recorder, Kurzweil...?"

PAUL SHAFFER: "Synthesizer. Sampling synthesizer."

The Sony was the first step, the Kurzweil did the rest. Me playing it like a Broadwood.

"You did your Ninth – electronically?"

Electricity God's own body in burning desire, Dave, honor to him in every keystroke.

"So you got your music by recording it? From where, Lincoln Center?" [Laughter from audience]

(No motherfucker I fucking wrote the fucking music they fucking play, get it? No, no... rather:) Actually, Dave, I appropriated existing sounds and keyed them into the synthesizer to create the Ninth of my children.

"Existing sounds."

Right, Dave. I had a neighbor who beat his wife who at the moment of excruciating pain hit a wretched and lovely F-sharp – sampled that, got moans off porn tapes, the screams of recorded victims. I stalked a woman for a year and a half because I knew that in the moment of her orgasm she would emit the purest B-flat, took another year to sample that soprano summit, succeeded with blandishments, rough charm, a promise (I said I'd make her famous in music), got her in a refrigerator box with the Sony going, and wasn't disappointed, Dave, wasn't disappointed in the least, it's a piccolo in my original score of 1823...

"Ludi, this is... this is..."

Sampled and sampled. At first it was a question of pitch, then turned to the rhythm of violence, the inevitable trochee of slam-bang, muggings, cries of PLEASE-don't in the modulation from major mode to fear/anguish mode – here I used fully-diminished seventh chord harmony punctuated with the shrieks of what originally was a choir of pubescent hillbilly girls, naked and greased, running for their venereal lives from their brothers. A true piquancy. Them little girls know sumpin' 'bout production of sound from the upper range of the vocal chords prompted by fear for the nether range of the torso, I tell you. Of course, getting the choir for the full chorus was difficult, the Women's Marathon people treating me as a pest – what do they know of genius? – but I got enough of the runners to wear those whistles with different pitches in their pussies, me darting in and out once the gun went off like a running coach/conductor with my mike directed at each cluster of gals of a certain pitch, jabbing at their crotches, the Sony drinking in the "scree-scree-scree" that tops the choir's sounds – AND, *Freu-de, schön-er Göt-ter-fun-ken…*

"Folks, we need to take another break here."

Wait, wait. Let me finish. So I put it all together at the Kurzweil, labored and labored, but a labor of love, put it all together in the key of D-minor, well, D-major for the finale. The chorus came out exceedingly well, Dave, a paean of pain – joy, joy… joy. Gotta tape here, just the last movement, it takes less than a second 'cause I recorded it at faster and faster speeds till finally it became just a single high pitch, a momentary screech. But my player here got the LSD on it – Long Sound Delivery – so you don't hafta be a damn dog to hear it, you wanna give a listen?

"Folks, we'll be right back."

[Sign on screen: Next: Martha Stewart]

Hee hee hee hee hee…

* * *

She do the dance, she a Shaker or maybe Quaker, moved here from Pennsylvania, but no less the Immortal Beloved. Bline Boy Eddy leads me to her, sayin', "You be thankful Ludi Vann I ain't no Helen Keller couldtn't also hear her way as I does now dat my eyes be petrifiedt eggs burnt-oudt suns not even hint o' 'lumination… jus'… jus'…"

"Rotten sulfur?" ax I. Can't hear him only see each word as the geometric theorem of function of mouth/lip shapes and jaw thrust; corollary: obverse anus in aspect and function (BBE mouth) contains Point "P," approximate center; intersected at Point "I" by ray of jaw-jut "R"; the word "Annie."

He be taking me to her, saying in his oracular manner, "I leads you to give da future somebody to play to, and dat ain' no shit. It da nex' thing, da followin' momen', it be Destiny, murderous Destiny dat be your damn curative when dey fin' oudt who you really be. Meanin', I knows you' name."

"I know it too, Beebee, it mean 'Thunder on the Mountain' in damn Chinee."

"Ain' no Ching can change a name."

"Why that?"

"'Cause a name like yo's can't be nothin' but a man's fate. No changin' dat."

"Damn man forges his fate as he crafts his evasions, ax me."

"Sheee-it, won't be no evadin' da Momen' o' Trufe. It tailin' you' ass dis very secondt, gonto catch up to you when you arrive in da future. Kick you' ass, like."

"So what kina dance she do, Beebee?" I ax, changing the subtext.

"Idiot Boy say she shake, she do da steps, bee's dance for the swarm to locate da spiritual honey," he say, and words and music come to me:

Well, we toin, toin, toin,
'Cause it a gif' to be simple,
A damn gif' to be free:
An' you will boin, boin, boin,
For no name can belong to thee.

And so I says to him, "She a spiritual being now, she my redemption to which you be white-canin' me, Bline Boy."

"Whut dis?" His cane has bumped into the half-eaten carcass of a rat, intact only in the hindquarters. "That's the rat's ass I don' give," I says, and go on:

"See, I be down widdat, widh spiritual being, I mean, *I the cat,* you don' think I suffer his despair? You know why I'm him, Beebee? Because Jewsus was all men, because I live to suffer as Jewsus did to release the spirit of men don' you know that's why he had to become flesh made to die? For their spirits? *Somebody got to be Beethoven* in his deaf-suffering jus' like Jewsus in his death-suffering. *Surd!* I cried, *surd* is to be deaf to God's inner harmony, to embrace the silence of His abyss, the *ab-surd,* you dig, to lie prone on the trampoline-tympanum stretched from birth pegged by death over the chasm of His absence, trembling with the tremulousness of making meaning *out of nothing...!* See, you gotta unnerstan', Beebee, it the divine work I do, interpreting the recalcitrant cipher of the world, reading lips, scribbling out the screeches of His electricity into diatonic aire-sculptures...

"Thus willed I deafness.

"Somebody, I tell you, Bline Boy, somebody got to do it. You don' think these the happiest years of my life living out his pain, his agony, you don' think I don' sag on the cross the damn nails in my ears shooting the nerve-harmony triangulatin' the next note from the three points of flesh, iron, and earwax? Vicarious pain the wors' kine."

"On da damn contrary, I sez," he rejoins, turning his dark glasses to my face.

"I knows the world is only half real…" says I, searching for grace.

Bline Boy ax, "Which half?"

"The half that kills you with promises."

"Which half be dat, Ludi Vann?"

"The one that tears out half your heart to stamp sorrow on the other half. The half made of time not made into music."

"Well, Ludi, you knows I go 'roun' widh a whissow on my lips," says he.

"What, like a damn referee?"

"Not dat kine o' whissow, now…"

"Deaf worse than bline. Widh deaf you only get a damn visual widh no harmonic to give it depth, you dig? Its silence drain the thirdt dimension, depth vacuumin' up toward the other two so as to listen closer, space be a hallucination of paper-thin height and width. You don' know what it like to see a damn Volkswagen start up an' not hear that jiggly whine testimony to German engineering, take the faith right outta you."

"You don' know what it like not be able to drive dat damn Volkswagen, Ludi. I drives a white cane."

"Shia," I responds, "I wears a sign say 'Shout.' Garage mechanics front me damn funnels changed a thousands oils, put in a bin marked 'Save for Ludi.' I come by, they jam small end into my ears, scream and laugh 'There you go. Now go compose a bagatelle for a bag lady hee hee.' Little shadow-kids seen me walkin' long widh two funnels stickin' oudt my ears, calledt me 'radar man,' like I a damn comic-book super-hero…"

Bline Boy laugh, say, "Shia, you an' me, Ludi, we damn complete da curdledt Micky Way, da galaxy o' Twis'."

"Long as I don' see no evil."

"Bline man, deaf man, shia, dat leave only *speakin'* evil…" he allow.

"My asshole is sealed."

* * *

Psychiatric Note No. 17. A. de Belmont, M.D.:

It's good to see improvement with "Ludi Vann." Of course there is much more distance to travel. We still have no real name for him, no record giving any other name than his absurd appellation. But the last sessions have shown some marked improvements. His hearing has improved, and now he only pretends to scribble across the pages of his "conversation books" as he actually speaks; of course, I'm obliged to play that game with him, moving my pen (ball-point retracted) over the sheets. But his manner and diction are quite improved as well; for that matter, the street English has been in abeyance for the last two sessions. Dr. Webber informs me that his medication is being changed to Clorazil, with increasing dosages.

I have noticed the patient to be more articulate, even artfully sarcastic. He recounted to me what I consider a fantasy about being on TV in his famous persona, devastating the show. It's obvious that he is aware of his intellect and as well the effect he has in using it. When I consider the meandering, badly-spelled diatribes from the early "conversation books" compared to what he is saying now, the change is dramatic.

However, the delusion of his being Beethoven persists. I do not consider his diagnosis to be full schizophrenia - which would preclude arguing with him - only schizophrenic episodes as far as that goes, and so, as a therapeutic technique, I argue with him about who he thinks he is. This session I asked him why he became the historical character he imitates. He was offended at first, and then, getting over it, suddenly replied, as I have it in recording:

I'll tell you why I became Beethoven. 'Cause of all the false notes I sounded in my previous lack of life. When I knew I was he they grouped themselves into exquisite harmony, self-redeeming melodies, a truth to emotions that had eluded me "before."

Belmont:

Could you give me some examples? That's a little abstract.

L.V.:

I used acronyms instead of words, words instead of meanings, meanings instead of feelings, feelings instead of truth, truth instead of the untruth, the untruth as my redemption, my redemption a flower on a cliff, the cliff an acronym for Cull Life's Illicit Fruits Forever… *da capo*.

A real tritone when I said…

Belmont:

A tritone? What's that?

L.V.:

It's the most dissonant harmony in music, an augmented fourth.

Belmont:

So, a real tritone when you said…

L.V.:

...when I repeated, "God's in his heaven, all's right with the world."

An A-flat in a C-major chord when I said: I forgive you, baby. A major seventh when I said, it's over, gal, I won't think of you…

The time I backed down from the right thing.

The time I stood up for the wrong thing.

Petulance that was envy.

Jealousy that was anger at my failure.

"Good will" that was self-interested in the most salacious of ways.

I loved my mother too poorly.

Belmont:

Let's talk about your parents. What about your father?

L.V.:

I loved my father too late.

Belmont:

Let's talk about your father, Ludi. What would you say your relationship…

L.V.:

BUT! BUT! ALL, ALL REDEEMED in the music of suffering, the exaltation of joy, the melancholy shadow of an A-minor chord ending a phrase that began in C-major… Because there's nothing so pure as motion, music moves through time, doc – music the gleaming of time's arcs and skitters in tones of clarinet sadness, keening, keening oboe solitude… the reed must itself be deaf for the instrument to speak…

Look, how could I not be him if redemption has transformed me thus? Q. E. and fucking D., doctor.

Belmont:

Tell me more about your childhood, Ludi. We've only touched briefly on that in the last sessions. What was your first musical experience?

L.V.:

When I was little more than an infant I heard what weren't even sounds to me then, more a knowledge in the air, when I heard them I wept openly, saying, how did the angels get here to say these things? How can they be here with the Knowledge, the bending of time into sounding shapes? Had I been older I would have called it the ether of Eden, not breathed but heard.

Belmont:

Did your parents play a role in…

L.V.:

My father said, what the hell are you talking about, what angels for God's sake? We had been passing a bar where what I would learn was "music" had been playing: the song *Aura Lee*. Thick harmony the net of God's love drawing us into his inner chamber where he speaks our true names, forgives us for repeating the false ones to everybody all the years.

Belmont:

And what true name would God speak for you, Ludi?

[Here Ludi stared back at me in silence, an accusatory look on his face. I saw no answer was forthcoming.]

So that was your introduction to music? Walking by a bar?

L.V.:

To be Beethoven is to know music is never music. The name "music" comes too late, too abstractly, doctor, it doesn't express the voices of angels whose vocal chords of divine ectoplasm resonate on a plane not accessible to human ears – but to some of the birds – mimicked best only by vibrating strings, air resonating through wood and brass. I resolved to make string and wood and metal sing out against their natures while remembering them in tone, tessitura and timbre, I resolved to make thunder and gossamer, the Almighty's power, the tears of angels falling to earth in infinitely shallow arcs… And the divinest of all – LAUGHTER, JOY, THE VALLEY OF DESPAIR ALSO THE MOUNTAIN OF TRIUMPH. See the Fifth of my children, doctor.

After these statements he refused to talk anymore. I was especially interested in his remarks about his father, but all attempts at getting him to elucidate further failed. There was no arguing with him about "his" music; about his identity. It makes me wonder if diagnoses aren't really just convenient hypotheses, self-justifying guesses. But I am encouraged nonetheless with the success of his medications.

I have spoken with the Society of Friends about getting him placed in a halfway house where he will be supervised in the taking of his new medication. As well, it may be possible to find a job requiring minimal skills for him, obviously not for the money, but for the dignity. There is therapy in that, too.

* * *

Bline Boy he bring me to where I be yesterday the day I saw Karl, my nephew.

"So dis where da cane quit, Ludi Vann," he say. "We be at Central Park. Dass all I kin do."

"Shia, why here?" I ax.

"Man, da cane like a divinin' rodt, you don' tell it, it tell you. All I knows is it quit."

"Shia, I guess it know it stuff."

"I gotta go now, Ludi. Da Nectah Espress due at my stop." And he tap away, retrograde-like, leaving me to survey the scene. Plenny o' people out today, and I look 'roun' trying not to see the cellphone users 'cause they make me listen in, conversations like "Where you at?" "Central Park." "How are your machines?" "My machines are in excellent repair. And your machines?" "My machines share the mechanical health the god of predetermined motion has granted to your machines," but can't help it look at a man on his phone staring at me, kinda an ironic look on his face, I hear the voice in his phone, a woman's voice quite lovely, saying, "Well, it's about time he showed up, why should I come back without him coming to me?"

I see the woman on the bench acrost the green, cellphone to her ear. I catch her fair form sunlight suffusing her hair grace abounding like a doe in spring.

And I know it her.

I shoot a look of thanks to the man and begin to make my way to where she sitting. Then I see I'm walking the side of an isosceles triangle towards her, she the apple-of-my-eye apex, *with someone else walking the other side.* O what hypotenuse of adversity let these lines arise whereby it, an unknown distance, come into fateful calculation, trigonometric truth? I walk a little faster, knowing velocity shrink space, then I stop, for suddenly I'm wondering will she love me again. But then he reach her and I see him put his arm 'roun' her, they kiss – familiarly, no passion.

O what thunderous dissonance!

I watch them walk away, side-by-side, and I follow from a safe distance. They leave the park, walk down Broadway. I stroll far behind they not suspect. They get to the old brownstone with "S. of F." above the door, haven't seen me, I walk by heart pounding lubricious eye follow them up the steps.

And I see the wedding rings.

* * *

"Who marriedt?" ax Bline Boy, when I toldt 'im.

"My baby-immortal, man! The Deathless Beloved you' cane done tappedt me to."

"Shia. She mus' be immortal she be here."

"And she knows she don't belong with no husband. She loves me. 'Dear Lady, My Beloved,' I wrote her, 'you are the inspiration for…' For… 'for my last sonata, the *Arietta* is for you…'"

"Not da *'Moonligh'?"*

"No, that's not her."

"Who dat one fo', den?"

"The… uh… the Guicciardi chick…"

"She da one down on Forty-secondt? Amana refrigerator box?"

"Hotpoint, I think."

"Shia, you mean Col'spot. Got da picture o' da ice-makah on da site."

"How couldt you know that, Bline Boy?"

"They's people knowahm bline, dey tells me shit; you da one thass deaf."

"That's her."

"I knows her, done Brailledt her face once."

"How was it?"

"Tear-duck pores, foreheadt o' nonparallel lines meetin' at a infinity o' woe. Da countess done fallen on hardt times."

"The count got bustedt. They started out together, mutual boosted shit. Jeans, T-shirts, espadrilles…"

"Shia. Mutual shoppin' cahts. Mutual sores…"

"That one time: mutual restraining orders. When she put the tampon-tongue on him."

"Yeah, yeah. But he hadt *two* black eyes."

"How couldt you know?"

"Shia, I kin ear-Braille da quality of a man's moans, Ludi. Can' see don' mean can' know."

"No, the Guiccardi chick and the count, they exemplify the distance between things, now."

"Dey reinvent space."

"They render 'rend.'"

"No moonligh' fo' da countess."

"She gets by, Beebee."

"By? Get by? By what…?"

"The cops. The psychiatrists."

[Bline Boy here gave out a great moaning wail:] "Yeah…! Yeah…! Yeeeeaaaahhh!"

Chapter Two

The Halfway House

Brett was not apprehensive initially, but when he noticed their charge seemed to harbor some unaccountable hostility toward him he spoke to his wife about it. She said, "He's harmless, Brett. There's a certain violence to him, but it's sort of… abstract violence."

"Annie, being a social worker doesn't allow you the luxury of a phrase like that."

"Belmont says that he interacts well with people who believe him. He has friends. That blind guy, some of the street people have known him for years – he's never fought with them, as far as I know. Have you seen that Darrell Gentile guy?" Ann rolled her eyes. "He started in on Quakers with me. I told him to go discuss it with The Professor – you know, the man with the signboards."

"Who can 'proof that God exists'? Yeah," Brett laughed. "But some of those people put me off. I've seen some of them bloodied up from fighting. And Ludi can get a mean look in his eye."

"He's all talk. He just needs people to accept him."

"Yeah, but if we accept him too well he won't improve."

"It's only been two months. Belmont tells me he thinks he's been getting even better since he started the new medication. As long as he takes it."

"But, you know, he still pretends to be deaf," Brett said. "Doesn't it creep you out that he talks in that distorted drone?"

"Being creeped-out isn't a luxury social workers are allowed," she answered, a little wryly. She turned to him. "Don't forget," she said, just remembering herself, "he really did damage his hearing with those spindles he stuck in his ears."

"He hears everything we say."

"We don't say anything he shouldn't hear. And the voice doesn't bother me. He told me an interesting story a week ago. Want to hear it?"

"Sure."

"It's what got Belmont onto him again. He gave a concert."

"Belmont did?"

"No, no. Our Ludi Vann."

"But… how?"

"It's a long story. Something about feeling his age, maybe a kind of street sufferer's late-life crisis. He said he felt he was being punished for the sins of his youth by the vicissitudes of old age."

"'Old age'– thanks. He's only a little older than we are, Ann."

"Don't be fooled. He's in his late forties. Whatever. It's what he felt was happening to him. So he devised a scheme to undo his early sins, as he called them." Brett rolled his eyes. "Yeah, I know," she said, smiling a little, "but he was serious."

"How do you undo your sins, except have them undone by divine grace?" Brett wondered aloud.

"He said what he did was to undo his early piano pieces."

Yes, yes – undo the sins of my youth…! The flight of my inner time took form in my Opus Two piano sonatas…

but undoing them, will that do it, can sin ever be reversed? In a universe where dark matter constitutes twenty-three percent? But to be sinless as before the first scream... Can Knowledge ever return the smile of Innocence? To be sinless before the last rattle... Can a gardenia transfer its darkening stains to the wings of a monarch?

"Undo?"

"Rewrite them. But backwards. And upside-down – you know, the melodies inverted. They can do that in music."

They both snickered.

"So, you mean, note-for-note, starting with the last note first?" he asked, incredulous.

"And also turned upside down. He told me he copied out 'his' first three sonatas onto manuscript paper, starting with the closing note and ending with the very first in the original."

"You saw the manuscripts?"

"No. But I saw the Beethoven piano sonata book he used. I heard him at our piano. What happened was that his sheets got away, and someone found them," she said.

"What do you mean, got away?"

"He told me when he was finished, the 'consecrating act' was to scatter them to the wind on the streets. But Salmaninski, you know him, the guy who does the music series for MUNY, came across some of them, found out it was Ludi Vann's doing, and got him to rewrite the missing pages. They made a deal to put on a concert, with some local pianist playing the three manuscripts..."

Salmaninski and I shook hands on it, I didn't want any signed document, I know the treacherous ink companies have a well that reaches right into the Styx, the water they leaven their fluids with. No, we just shook hands on it, his hand pressed into and enveloping my hand as my hand, held, also held in return. I saw the X-ray man in the shadows where he lives, where he has lived since the dawn of consciousness

– Christ, it was Cain who, glancing into the ram's horn holding the still water as he shaved the next day, recognized him, given the genes of his momma and dada – the X-ray man held up the negative of our handshake, I saw spiders making love, calcium shot into form and desire, the mutual wrap of bones as if in the grip of a suicide-pact rigor mortis. So I knew we had a deal.

"I guess even musical people wouldn't recognize backwards, upside-down Beethoven" Brett said.

"Salmaninski phoned the other day to let me know what happened. He said Ludi only told him later about how the manuscripts had been composed. And apparently, from what I gather, he'd not been that accurate in his notation. Nobody knew he was calling himself Beethoven until after the music was performed."

"My god," said Brett, "it must've sounded horrible."

"He told me Ludi was called to the stage after the performance, and…"

...They applauded mightily! But I bow to no one. I glowered at them, until Salmaninski led me to the front of the stage. I saw the auditorium go quiet, and I spoke to them:

"When my muse speaks to me she has no respect for the puny order of things, not even for Schuppanzigh's fiddle. She aims at my ears, and mine alone, which have made themselves easy targets, hearing no other sound. No, not even Beethoven's heartbeat thuds in his ears. How hard to be him! But I..."

I saw them laugh. Laugh! They turned and looked at each other unbelievingly, some rolling their eyes. "I am Beethoven!" I cried in my deaf-man's drone.

"Let me tell you something about my other works! My happiest moment came when I was first awakened to the abyss. The abyss yawns best in C-minor, sometimes F-minor – your D-minor, now, that's a chasm with dark, committed hues – the thing is, the minor modes will deliver you to the

rim of the canyon of darkness but it takes a certain tonal shading to mute all hope, all transcendence, to start your free-fall toward bottomlessness."

They stared at me, some snickering, probably embarrassed by my topic, those for whom the abyss has been hidden by wreaths of plastic flowers, warning their children, yes, you can play near the flowers, but you must never touch them, you must never seek their secret. Refrain from sniffing the Flowers of Knowledge that you not succumb to the scent of polymer despair. Those who swallow the metaphysical pill every Sunday, sip the serum of certain salvation. But I didn't care:

"The third of my children, my 'Eroica,' *look, talkin' E-flat major, the brightest mutation of the abyss – shining darkness, more shiny than dark – yet check out the measures in the development section, first movement, just before I bring in that new theme, screeching major sevenths and minor seconds after the promise of C-major, you think that's not face-to-face with depthless darkness?"*

I saw Salmaninski coming for me, his face contorted. I could tell there was noise in the crowd. I fairly shouted:

"Beauty has made me mad! But she likes it that way! My F-minor sonata, my Appassionata! *– point in case you want a case in point, those torrents, those… those cataracts of tones plunging and soaring. Gentlemen, ladies, don't you comprendo? I'd cut to the chase! She gets away, gets away always, but… SHUT UP OUT THERE! STOP LAUGHING! I HAVE MUCH TO TELL YOU! Shit-hooks! Cattle! Ass-faces! – yes, she gets away but… but she leaves certain… indications, vague traces, instant memory…"*

But I had lost them. The last thing I did was pull down and crumple up their banner announcing the concert as part of the Atonal Subscription Series – ASS is oh so right! I raised my mighty fist, shook it at a fleeing music lover.

I turned to Salmaninski, who was hanging onto me, and I landed the fist on his nose!

Then: divine laughter!

* * *

The Martian came to me again last night, emerging from the bulbless lamp in the dingy room my hosts have provided me. I explained the piano to him, an affair of little hammers whacking strings, a loom on which mysteries in secret patterns are woven into the fabric of time… an abacus on which the beads of beauty are calculated. It's different on Mars, he said. We do music differently.

Oh? I said. And it's still music?

It's music all right, he said. Only we don't have no hammers banging away at strings, nothing so crude… What we have is like stretched strings inside all of us, kinda a sinew of the finest fiber connected to bowel from brain. It expand, it contract, it emit vibrations, no one can hear Martian music but each Martian.

It ain't tones?

Shit no. It be pure-from-the-gut feelings, don't need to hear nothin'…

But ain't you got composers, somebody ordering the gut vibrations?

We does. But it be the same orderer of sunsets and Earthsets, even a Venusset from time to time since it be those that make the sinew jump in *aesthesis* extraordinaire; the music is always with us we can see it in the faces of each other we share the tonality of turbulent times as much as the peace of our underground reservoirs. We walkin' music, man, unlike you poor earthlings gotta have a damn Walkman strapped over your auditory organs.

That's far out, man, I allowed.

Look, as you enter the heavenly zones above the earth and your moon, things are more internal, he said. You take

Neptune, he said, a planet so subjectively involuted that each inhabitant there is a monad serving as a cell in the brain of God. The earth is the fallen-most planet because you suffer the damned objectivity of things. *'Course* you gotta hit strings with felt hammers controlled by elephant-tusk pressure-points, what else do you know but banging one object into another?

The sound saves us, I said. We dig it.

Sheeeit. If that's how you gotta get off I say the fuck with it. I'm glad I'm a damn Martian, Ludi. No slam-bang – "oh, dig them vibrations" – for us.

Well, I said, it's all we got we make the most of it.

Ain't no pianos for us to tune. The perception itself is music.

I aspire to that, I told him. I used to walk in woods to hear what I saw, Stephen Spender wrote a poem about me doing that.

Ain't no good if you gotta bang things to get it out.

I don't always do that, you know. Sometimes the notes glisten on my eyelids, birds take them over, I once farted a perfect E-flat…

Now you're getting closer, he said.

* * *

In some ways there have been further improvements with "Ludi Vann," although it is disturbing to note that in other ways his pathology is worse. Perhaps the former is owed to his living at the halfway house with the Quaker couple, who supervise the taking of his latest medication (Clorazil, 400-mg qd, in 100 mg capsules); indeed, as a result of this I was able to get him a job with

Bernie's Trophies, in which he helps in the construction of merchandise.

But, regarding the downturn that is certainly there, he seems to be even more unshakable in the notion that he is Beethoven. This shouldn't be the case. He is more evasive and creative in his answers to direct questions from me, and more abusive at times. At least he's stopped insisting he's deaf; in the past it got to the point of my pretending to write in his "conversation books" as I spoke, while he reciprocated by pretending to write his spoken words; the page was full of vague marks. He no longer points to the nearly blank page as our true communication. But still the Beethoven persona prevails.

My resolve was to stay with reality therapy - just throwing the facts in his face - to see if his Achillean denial of reality had a heel. But this therapy is contraindicated, as the transcript of the tape of our last session reveals:

Belmont:

Now, one of the things we need to work on, Ludi, is – is your authentic identity. You know Beethoven died in 1827. I'd like to probe your, well, your *contemporary* identity, who your mother brought into the world –

L.V.:

I was born to Johann Van Beethoven and Maria Magdalena Leym who were exiled nobility hiding their true identities in the devotion to drink and toil respectively. I was born on a cold December day though I remember my first light not; I remember only my first thought.

Belmont:

Really? That's quite remarkable. What was it?

L.V.:

It was some questions.

Belmont:

What were they?

L.V.:

When will the crystal bullet be shot into my brain?

Who will drive the colors of harmony into the tympanum of my inner ear, membrane stretched over a chasm to vibrate as the trembling of hope?

Who will push the golden spikes through my eardrums, my punishment for catching Beauty without her clothes?

What muse will have stripped herself bare, holding aloft the great spikes, blood bronzing gold?

Belmont:

Very poetic. But, now… were those the questions you really had, Ludi… or that, say, you might have had if you'd been some sort of prescient Beethoven?

L.V.:

They're questions I asked when I remembered being him.

Belmont:

Ludi, you've got to wake up from this charade. I'm telling you straight. Don't you ever find it a bit ridiculous? Say, just sometimes?

L.V.:

Who are you to tell me who I'm not?

Belmont:

But, Ludi, I'm a doctor, *your* doctor.

L.V.:

So – *who* are *you*?

Belmont:

Someone trying to help you. The one with truth on his side – a king of reality.

L.V.:

I too am a king!

Belmont:

Ludi, look, the therapy I'm doing with you is to… to look at the facts. And the facts are that I'm Belmont and you aren't Ludwig van Beethoven.

L.V.:

Fact? Facts be arbitrary, be da staples man put inna cosmic fabric.

Belmont:

Come on, Ludi, you're not a black man any more than you're an old, dead, composer.

L.V.:

Shia, we *ahll* be black, my frien', you don' think you' bleached skin, you' fuckin' *thin lips*, you' Jew-nose not a *disguise?*

Belmont:

Come on, Ludi. I'm not buying the persona or the dialect. We both know the truth.

L.V.:

Truth? Let me tell you about truth!

Truth is the moan the passage o' time make as it coalesce into the world, heaving into solidity, leaving everything over in the past while leaping out ahead in the promise o' meaning, o' redemption from the lostness o' the hours – time as it gravitate and fly into history and hope…

Belmont:

So time is the…

L.V.:

Time? Time be the sigh o' meaning that first created itself in order to exist… what damn truth can there be in a world with time as its substance, Belly-boy? The world can be redeemed only when its time be drawn into music. Shia, see Nietzsche: music proof da worldt ain' no *goof.*

That why trufe be beauty.

So you' damn trufe a convenience and a comfort, doctor. It get you by. I hang into the chasm that would surround and frame everything once and for all.

Belmont:

That would be… time?

L.V.:

Aye, time. I a technician o' time management, I make chords by stacking tones in mental colors, I calculate the mathematics o' mesmerization, make time dance on the headt o' a pin, use its flow in a ju-jitsu of cadences, 'n' like that…

Belmont:

Ludi, I didn't understand a word you said… [Here I saw him staring intently at me, and was surprised that he got up and came gently over, sincerity on his face. He dropped all the phony speech patterns.]

L.V.:

Doctor, I long ago learned it's fact that makes truth, not truth that makes fact. You want "Truth"? [Here he smiled almost magnanimously, a look reminding me of Brando's sabotaged sweet smile, then said a little condescendingly,] See "Interpretation." [And as suddenly as he had begun he reverted to his dodgy manner.] Look, Belly-boy, the bare fact is that you be Belmont, the shrink; the beautiful truth is that I be Beethoven, caster of sound. Which be better, I ax you?

O it's so strange to be a man
When our freedom's finality
Hides out in daily banality –
Making the most of it as Ludi Vann.

Belmont:

But better isn't best. Look, Ludi, if you really believe in "freedom's finality," find out who you really are! Shuck off this assumed shell of a historical persona. You're *not* free! Everything you pretend to be doing has already been decided; *it's all in the biographies of Beethoven.* What are you hiding from? [I was a little surprised at my sudden tirade. A long silence ensued in which he wouldn't look at me.]

Look, Ludi – you can admit it. Beethoven is long gone from this world. Only one man came back after death, if the story is straight, and that was…

L.V.:

Jewsus. He showdt da way. Everybody come back. [Oddly, he looked at me accusatorily, and another long silence followed. Presently, I said:]

Belmont:

I'll bet you could tell me your mother's maiden name. Pretend I'm a credit card application. [Unamused silence.] What was your mother's maiden name?

L.V.:

Leym, lame-headt. What your mother's maiden name, "Cum-dumpster"?

Belmont:

Look, I don't think remarks like that are…

L.V.:

'Nother thing, Belmont. *Who are you really?* Everybody be somebody from befo'. You on my case, you make me take drugs to silence da 'lectrical outlets wherefrom da Morse Master speak, leave me exhausted, a wretch before my deathless beloved…

Belmont:

Your who?

L.V.:

None of your business you'll get to her.

Belmont:

Your… "Immortal Beloved"?

L.V.:

She be here everybody somebody from befo'. Bline Boy lead me to her.

Belmont:

Where? Here in New York?

L.V.:

She very close to me I play piano for her in her illness she teaching me French. So leave her alone. I know you're somebody, somebody from before, Belmont. You look like some picture I saw – you're from before and I'll find out why you poisoning me.

Belmont:

Ludi, please. I'm only trying to help you. It's my job. You're suffering.

L.V.:

Shia, it a great privilege to suffer. Jewsus showdt us that.

O muse, O muse
How did you know it's pain
That stretches the string of the lyre?

* * *

"Oh, he's actually pretty good at it. He can speak in whole sentences. He can even conjugate some of the irregular verbs," Ann said to Brett.

"But without the accent, I'll bet," he said, and Ann thought she caught a note of peevishness in it.

"Well, of course not. That takes years, living with French speakers, trying to imitate those almost absent R's, you know. Hey, how long'd it take you to be able to speak German? You had to live in Vienna to get all those strangulated consonants, you know."

"Sending him off to France might be a good idea, then."

"Don't be jealous, Brett. Look, maybe one reason he takes his meds is so he can stay straight for the lessons."

"I don't think so," Brett said. "He takes his meds because if he doesn't he has to go back out on the street. Where you aren't."

Ann thought this over.

"Maybe. But so what?" she countered. "What are you worried about?"

"He's in love with you, Ann. And I'm not supposed to be concerned here?"

"I wouldn't go that far. I don't think he's in love with me. What's 'love' for the mentally deranged, Brett? Look, don't you think he's happy being off the streets, with a pair of good Quakers like us running the place?"

"You know what I saw? I was up in his room…"

"Was he there?"

"Yes, Ann. I wasn't snooping. I brought him his meds."

"What did you see?"

"He had a biography of Beethoven open to some photostats of Beethoven's letters. I saw sheets of paper where he was copying them out."

"So? You know he's still… doing the Beethoven thing."

"That's just it. Shouldn't he be getting over that? Belmont thought there'd been a breakthrough, but I don't see it," Brett said with some passion. "And let me tell you, Ann: the handwriting was a perfect imitation of the photostats."

"Didn't he notice you looking at them?"

"He was staring out the window saying something, repeating phrases to himself."

"What phrases?"

"I heard him mutter something like, *'Au contraire, mon frere,* I say other, my brother' over and over again. He didn't see me checking the writing out. He had it down cold. It was as if Beethoven had written the copy as well."

"But still, so what?" Ann said. "He still has a long way to go."

"Yeah, but I got a good look at one of the letters. It was a love letter he was copying out from a section of the book labeled 'The Immortal Beloved.'"

"And?"

"The one in the book begins *'Mein Engel'* – my angel. Ludi had copied it out in Beethoven's handwriting. But he'd crossed out *'Engel'* and written 'Annie' above it."

Ann looked away. Then she said, "Still, we've got to be good to him."

"I know. But let's both be careful, okay?"

She said okay.

* * *

The world be can be redeemed only when its time be drawn into music, I tole da bastit. How did I learn that? I learned that from the Martian, who had come to me weeks before. He'd buzzed and fizzled out of the lamp socket and said he would save us, save us all, but for a deficit of volts, said he would come into each one of us and do shock therapy, leaving us convulsed but cleansed. Told me I should get on the electric company about it.

Man, I said, they don' lissen me no mo'. Been complainin' fo' years 'bout what they be sendin' out at me via all them outlets, working wireless on us, too.

But music gets you through, right? ax he.

It pass da time, said I.

It passes the time, he echoed. Then: no

Uh… no?

No. Music don' pass no time, it create time. It be a temporary cure o' the madness you Earthlings got.

What you sayin''? I gets by, they ain' got da Involuntary Commitment Ack on me long time.

Case in point: take Tuesday, for example.

Lass Tuesday? When it was?

When. Exactly. Was it Tuesday when it was?

Jus' about.

So how come it ain't that Tuesday now?

'Cause it be lass Tuesday.

But if it *was* Tuesday how come it ain' Tuesday now? What happened to it?

They has a tendency to slide into da pass. They hides in the great mound of gatherin' oblivion.

But, Ludi, they's a Tuesday comin' – it be the same as the last one?

The lass one gone.

Then how it coming again?

It a different one.

But it *Tuesday*.

Well. It da same but different too.

Yeah, but it be more same or more different?

Shia. Never axed.

You're deranged, Earthling.

Looky-yeah, looky-yeah – it like a wheel o' Tuesdays, keep toinin', toinin'… One go out, 'nuthah come in. Like bullets inna chamber.

Shia. Then it never really *is* Tuesday.

Fine by me. Plenny other days.

See, you all fucked up, Ludi. You only gets by 'cause music bind all Tuesdays.

It do?

You're fucking aye it do. How many sonatas you write?

Uh… thutty-two.

Not just piano. Shia, you can't count 'em. Sonata form be the Return of Tuesday.

Wrote some damn rondos.

The Return of Tuesday.

Theme and variations.

The Return of Tuesday. *Tuesday only makes sense in music.* No music in a world of Tuesdays be madness; no music in a world of Tuesdays be a roar of silence that would provide converts and supplicants to all the various religions, a roar of silence that can only be muffled by the basses providing absolute conviction to the song of the strings and woodwinds… You do the noble work, Ludi Vann, you redeem Tuesday.

What about da other days?

Don' ax.

Well, I dint. Because da teaching been pass.

Chapter Three

Ludi's Cadence Cart

Darrell Jimmy the Gentiles' Gentleman came to visit me at my new job in the Museum of True Value. Looked around in awe at all the gold trophies signifying entrance into a Valhalla of Value for the recipient of same. He said:

"An amazing phenomenon, this arrival of eternal value into specific three-dimensional entities. Why, it's as if several hundred of the Platonic Forms had made their way to the temporal realm of dust and decay, themselves unsullied, calling young men and women to athletic and intellectual achievements as a way of negating the fallen flesh of body and brain, dedicated as it were to excellence and thus transcendence."

"Well, it a big job," I says, no false damn modesty. "I da keeper o' truth, servicin' da anchor o' value like some kine o' axiological skin diver postedt to da ship o' culture."

"Means fitted to ends," he allowed. "You answered an ad?"

"Saw inna paper dey neededt a keeper o' values, someone goodt widh da chemical make-up o' da glue o' da pass. So I presents myself, and have da presence o' mindt to recite da chemical composition o' da formaldehyte o' traditional truth."

"But the appearance of all this gold! Ludi, it shines and dazzles the senses, reducing the beholder to an acolyte of achievement. One would think the chemical make-up of *Au* would be some sort of covalent bonding between the gods of light and bronze."

"Mos' museums traffic in it. Goldt be da metallurgic stasis o' da mindt o' da *bes'* godts, godts who sacrificed deyselves fo' beauty onna cross o' factual truth, Dee-Jay, so dey be savin' us from it."

"From 'factual truth'?"

"Aye. From the littoral fact against the ocean o' heaving, unmanageable truth engulfin' us every moment, which we might see but although we swimmin' in it we got da lifesaver o' speech, dreams, desire, drunken acquiescence *(music!)*... Wouldt you like a tour?"

"But what's to see?"

"Got da Hall o' Dominant to Tonic right through dat door, if you please."

"That one? The office door, with 'E: Lic. U.S.A. Sport Champs' on it?"

"It don' say dat. You got it all scrambledt up. It say: 'Musical Cart's Shoppe.' It open onto my workroom."

Awkward silence.

Then Dee-Jay say, "Well, another time, Ludi. I'm off to see a mulatto about a Weimaraner." And he left.

It too bad old Darrell Jimmy got the antsies coulda shown him what I do here, in the back. I been constructin' a great polemical machine which should put a stop to all the destructivity in the arts, in music primarily since all the arts conspire to the addition of music, but a rolling polemic, that is it got wheels and illustrate the necessity of true value.

I work on it with tools, getting it ready to roll in the streets.

What this machine do it sound the right notes at the right time (you know it was said of me that I "always knew the next note," an oversimplification I assure you in that there are *so many* next ones and it often a process of not knowing which be best, ever wonder why I put *two* development sections in some of my symphonies and sonatas, the extra one disguised as a coda? 'Cause of the *plethora* of proper next ones. But the thing is there are only certain right ones, even if you end up with a screeching dissonance because you can always resolve it with – the next right notes!).

So it a kinda organ-grinder wagon be playing certain cadences like a damn ice-cream truck play little kiddie melodies entice little snot-faced urchins proffering pennies so I entice patrons of museums, concert-goers, radio stations pushing my cadence cart. What it do be to show the damn necessity of the fifth degree of the scale returning to the first, that divine Pythagorean truth that make a final cadence the cosmic okay. Shia, it be the way of modulatin' 'roun' the circle o' fifths, secondary dominants.

Dominant to tonic. Dominus, lead us home.

See, it hold us in, it give us ground.

In ending cadences, it be man outside Eden (the "five" chord, say, in the key of C-major, which be called "G") till the mathematics of truth snap him back (the "one" chord, "C") to where he belong (temporarily – 'cause he res'less by nature). That V to I: the cosmic okay.

See, I'll tell you what my cadence cart do. You push it, it travel around the circle o' fifths, it a kinda music box but it got a computer circuit and an audio system make it sound like my orchestras. All it do, go G to C, C to F, F to B-flat, B-flat to E-flat, E-flat to A-flat, A-flat to D-flat, D-flat to G-flat (disguised as F-sharp), F-sharp to B, B to E, E to A, A to D, D to G, and *da capo*. The fifth degree always heading home for the first, which itself then become the fifth of the next tone. Well, a little music theory, but it not far from the divine mindt of God.

God put the mathematics into the string Pythagoras divided, where the first two overtones be the octave and the fifth. That why dominant fifth go back to the tonic one. It

God's will. He made the number of steps aroun' the circle match the number of the tribes of Israel. Ain' no tone not seeking its groun', ain' no supplicant unanswered.

So my mission clear, I got to push this cart 'roun' the screets into the museums and concert halls, gotta pay a visit to radio stations rollin' my Dominant-Tonic blaster, who can resist the mathematics of ground, the allure of home?

Each wheel got twelve spokes, my frien'.

I seen people, I see they lost, ain' nobody home these days.

I heard the music they writin' for presentation like Salmaninski's ASS concert (why they wanted me a tonal mystery). What they writin' these days be music scattered outside the mathematical universe. No more gravitational attraction between any of the tones, just organized noise!

And I know who done it. I know the name of the Destroyer Arnold Schoenberg, a Jew shoulda known better than to scatter the number of tribes of Israel into secret mathematical patterns, defy the Lordt Godt who put the attraction between tones as proof of divine order of things, even redemption, for "it was not the fortuitous meeting of the chordal atoms that made the world; if order and beauty are reflected in the constitution of the universe, then there is a God," diary entry, 1816.

Schoenberg: you run the numerology on that name and you get the triple-six.

Lemme tell you 'bout his "Twelve-Tone System." It the breakdown of all attraction between tones, it be the scattered tribes of Israel widhout even the Diaspora, only arbitrary arrangement behindt it: each note soundin' on its own. He the angel of homogeneity, DC to Godt's AC.

Whereas, whereas, I exist in the galaxy of tonal attractivity.

Look, you know what I do? *I make constellations outta the Milky way of tones in alla octaves, I imbue the mathematics of attraction with beauty.* You got to be deaf to hear the stars, my frien', you got to know the sadness that configures the logic of infinite spaces to write the second movement of my "Napoleon" symphony widh its soaring violins and horns over a Euclidean obligato.

Look, what you think attraction *be?* It nothin' less than that somethin' *belong* where it *ain't.* Tell me that ain't mankind after Eden.

I got to show the path back home. Home is where the harmony be, anything else the mere house o' random tones. The five-chord, and make it a yearnin' five by throwing in a minor seventh, be homesick man living in the promise. Schoenberg the evil bastit broke the covenant. He undid harmony and left the harm. I come along after I diedt las' century to mendt it just like Jewsus come back again. For the same reason.

But I been wondering did Schoenberg come back too? Everybody's somebody from before. He'd be working his evil again, just as I bring my goodt for the truth of mankind – Godt's groun', the Almighty's perfect love for us. Five-one, harmonic mantra; five-one, mankind's hope.

Five-one – *triumph o'truth* (see closing measures of my Fifth, last movement).

Gonta roll, baby: get the machine of harmonic revelation outta the Museum of True Value and on da roadt!

Offin' da man, offin' da man,
Makin' da mos' of it
As Ludi Vann.

* * *

"Blind Boy," asked Darrell Jimmy, "could you possibly abet in the project of slaking the thirst of a fellow human, one whose respect of the grape and its power is inordinate?"

"Shia," Blind Boy answered, "da Nectah Espress be late today."

"Ah well," allowed the Gentiles' Gentleman, "I'll have to let anticipation recapitulate its law. I just saw Ludi, by the way."

"Where you see 'im?"

"He actually has a job. Down on West Thirty-fourth. A place called Bernie's Trophies."

"You know, I heardt he got a job. Whut he do?"

"I asked the manager. He works in the back room, filing sharp edges off the metal out of which the trophies are wrought."

* * *

I locked the doors to my workshop and went out into the street then, amongst the men sitting with their backs to the wall eyeing each other as the dove of God fluttered in their mouths. The dove flutter in all our mouths it the imitation of flight words would make on their way to bursting into meaning, Roman-candling the silence, but they don't move, the words, the sounds of words, they never make it out of the mouth into the surrounding silence. But that how it look, it look like all sorts of meaning-transactions be going on; the faces move and contort but it an optical illusion, not a single flutter of the dove has pushed any sound to anywhere.

You think I don't see this?

You don't think my Dominant-Tonic pushcart has something to do with this?

God send the doves to the mouths of men for his amusement. Oh, he has men dressed in stripes blowing whistles as two hordes wrestle for the plain, you see them with their mouths open and faces red, the dove just a-fluttering. God know the fluttering of his doves look like the human tongue in spasms of words but the dove only flutter; the dove don't speak. And God wouldn't care even if the words could tell the truth or not, for this I have come to live with, my brothers: God is uninterested in truth, he care only about the ballet of tongue-uvula-lip, about the shapes of sounds, the exact ululations of beauty. It was words that denuded God of His Nature, made him human, made him sink into the concrete and asphalt where the men sit with their backs to the wall. In the beginning was the word, and the word was with God; *and the word was mum*. God spake the word as the silence of the past 'gainst a mute future so the present would have nothing to say, but nothing was said in a faulty translation of the word, scattered into languages where certain sibilances and assonances became copulas that impregnated the future with the seed of the past; and instead of emptiness the word became the words of the worldt. So God rinsed words of meaning like he sent the rain to cleanse the worldt, it rainedt forty years and frothy nights and the dove he sent Noah now flutter, as I say, in the mouths of men.

I saw a man watching TV, some sort of contest between the hordes and every so often his mouth opened and the dove fluttered, or oiled it feathers, nit-picked it down but the effect was silence. He'll go to his grave probably thinking he said something, that a meaning hung in the air and temporarily saturated the brains of others, that they nodded and exercised their doves in reciprocal brain-actions along with him but already it was the silence of the sepulcher, my friend. Something's gone that was there when I was alive before, it deadt and gone and people suffer for it.

"Tell 'em, Ludi, tell 'em 'bout da 'chine."

Bline Boy, that you?

"I's da one widdout eyes."

But are you really there like on the streets or just in my headt?

"Shia, Ludi, da damn screets is you' headt. You got you' screet signs tells you where you be, got you' alleys where you' damn subjectivity blossom like the stink o' gahbage, da stop signs and lights tellin' you watch you' damn ass. Consciousness be screets, avenues 'n' lanes in da bustlin' city o' Godt, ax me."

People suffer Schoenberg, they veep at Webern, they shelter they ears at Stockhausen and Stravinsky, they balk at Berg and Boulez, they hearts cry out because *God's rinse didn't stop at words but washed over music as well,* but people can't live with meaninglessness, it put a iceberg like cancer in the heart, freeze the flow of blood.

"You tell 'em, Ludi. And you got da 'chine."

I *got* the machine. I can show them the way back. That why I deaf: I know the abyss and how to make it echo in sound. Sound that damn mean something.

"You gotta create circuses light up da damn sky, Ludi! You gotta have da trapeze girl landt safely on her perch after bein' caught first on da scrong wri'ts o' heroes, you gotta have da midgets and other freaks in da siteshow shown as Godt's own inscrutable will."

I say amen, my brothah.

I say: You have to make the necessary emerge without its debt to the contingent showing on the books. All the overdue books circulating out there from the lending-library of cosmic ledgers.

* * *

Affronting the muse in my illness, she to whom the faculty of hearing is the gift she gives herself like an echo, I walk the walk, read the graffiti, breathe deeply the stench of garbage, of vomit and piss – all the betrayals of the spirit she repudiates! But she forgives me, because it's not kindly that we're here. She calls me her darkened mirror, who holds her image beyond the fecklessness of light, the whoredom of perspective, to know her as a blind lover knows his beloved in the truth of touch. My hearing is a Braille written in the mathematics of harmony. I touch her body. I speak in trumpet tones.

* * *

So I composed a song, the verses come to me widdout even the slightest bidding, like rain producing dark flowers. They were:

O the folly of youth
Op-ti-mi-sm!
Op-ti-mi-sm!
Comes to an end in
A discovery uncouth:
The value of Evil!
The value of Evil!
O Youth: thy innocence consecrated in
every breath,
Ignorance that knows only the beginning,
Adhering to it as hope!
Adhering to it as hope!
O Age: knowledge of the end, slow
divestiture toward death.
O Regret: here is thy sting:
Hope in reverse!
Hope in reverse!
Wisdom of my seeing.

I've already got the music in my head to set them to. I thought I'd modulate down to the relative minor for the verse belonging to evil. O come, come: it's an easy three scalar steps down from the tonic of the major key – a particularly dramatic descent, like being drawn down the cellar stairs to confront the sheriffs glaring at you over their now idle shovels. Well maybe it's not as dramatic for you, A-minor from C-major, but that's only because you've tamed your guilt, you've normalized your break from the Absolute in emerging from your mother's cunt, maybe you damn draint it into the IV's nailed into the arteries of Jesus, the vessels wherein course his soteriological fluids. That right, you got Grace™, it done been laid upon you, you sucked it up.

But suckin' muvvahs, I say unto you: you've instituted civility over rapacious passion, you've not walked the walk but you've seen the movie, you could imitate the walk at a party maybe, if you thought it'd be entertaining. I… I… am Beethoven! I hold *out* for you, you who have chosen cheap suffering and exalted happiness. I reject cheap happiness for exalted suffering, I drive past your sedentary selves! See measure 374, the coda in the first movement of the Fifth of my children.

Maybe do the innocence-of-youth part in F-major, say, since it the key o' my *Pastorale.* For there's a kind of innocence to nature, to cataclysms and murder, so long as these remain a realm apart from what men do.

Now, your men. What they do.

"Whut dey do, Ludi Vann?"

Took a trip to Paris my biographers ain't hip to. Did a little stint with *Le Terreur* in '94, when I was twenty-three, my job to count da headts dumped outta da basket, some still alive though abbreviated in life-support, you dig. You couldt talk to 'em 'n' ax 'em questions, like. They couldn't talk, but they blink, one blink no, two blinks yes, 'course sometimes they die before whether it was one for no or one be da firs' half of yes. I would say that happened a lot. You couldn't tell which it was… Da damn single *augenblick* o' Judgment Day will be da hell of that not knowing . . !

Now one of da headts belong to Antoine Lavoisier, man who inventedt oxygen, 'n' whose own now be reduced to da bloodt in his brain, he… I don' know how to say it, it was kina… I'll jus' tell you what happen. Raisedt his headt to my face, saidt, Tony, baby! How pale da lips! How blank and all-seeing da eyes! Saidt to him, saidt, Yo, *Monsieur le Philosophe, you unnerstan' it all now?* He blink *three* times…

"How da riddle to be expounded, how?"

"I done axedt da guru, Beebee. He only smile widh a quick look-away."

"Whut da hardes' thing da goo-roo done tol' you, Ludi Vann?"

"To forgive 'em. To love 'em. To watch their game shows and soaps widh 'em. To die da spiritual death widh 'em. Not to be Beethoven for 'em."

"An' you…"

"Tol' 'im to fuck off."

"You damn right. He a junk-foo' goo-roo."

"Shia, he da goldten arches o' da Himalayas."

"He da plastic sain' ridin' on da dashboardt o' da hearse."

"He da styrofoam peanut protectin' a damn UPS package o' some plaster Bodhisattva."

"He, you know, boob jobs."

"He cryonics…"

"He da joy widdou' it misspelling as woe."

"He gimp in da gray matter."

"…an' gray at da temple o' da Lordt."

"Let they be only truth widdout doctrine," I pronounce.

"I hears ya, bruthah. Faith widdou' props."

"Boy gotta have a credo."

"Shia," say Bline Boy, "I believes in da final resurrection of da fish. I believes Jesus done diedt fo' our fins. I believes inna…"

"I have tried to live by three tenets," tells him I:

1. Godt is evil; man is goodt.
2. The abyss is a mountain; descending is ascending.

3. Jesus was perfect, but he warn't excellent.

"You know, Ludi Vann, sometime descendin' be descendin'."

"True dat. True dat. Ted Bundy."

"Sometimes ascendin' be descendin'."

"Tammy Faye," I allows.

"Sometimes I get a notion I kin see widdou' my eyes."

"Shia, I damn hear widdout no aural nerve." I adds. "And I onto da guru, yeah, tol' 'im fuck off, your Beethoven got da real deal up his sleeve."

* * *

We (if it was Bline Boy, mighta been his synaptical clone live in my cranium) walked along he ax me, *"Quo vadis,* Ludi?"

"Onna way to da *bodega,* Beebee, searchin' out da two mos' primordial human artifacts…"

"Breadt 'n' beer."

"Au contraire, mon frere. Toilet paper and prayer candles."

We pass a wall with graffiti, "Know thyself – Socrates," and under that in a thin, cursive hand, "No 'thyself' – Gautama Buddha," and under that in wide black spray-paint, "Blow thyself – Ron Jeremy," and I ax Beebee did he know why masturbation better than crucifixion, no foxkin' idea, saidt he, so I tells him:

"Shia, impossible to crucify youse'f widdou' somebody else, someone *not* you, lend a he'ppin' handt. Widh da thirdt nail."

"Shia," said he, "you forgot whut be da same widh both, Ludi Vann, make 'em equal."

"Whaddat?"

"You be invokin' da name of da deity at da endt."

We got to the *bodega* but the spics made me leave, checking my pockets (I saw the upside-down exclamation point before every angry word), so I walked on home, meditating on the verses of my song, and on how strange that value can be dark, the hue of evil. Gentleman Jimmy right all that gleaming goldt be light married to bronze, but the core of bronze be closed-up, blackes' matter… These the thoughts that accompany me to the house, and I realize they already singing the ballad of my beloved and me, my immortal angel-beloved be the Light break over my window into my crepuscular room, but she there widh her husband – where I seen him before? – and that be dark, *dark,* lightless as the core of bronze.

Chapter Four

French Lessons

I down in her living room, and she like my homework. Translated from the workbook all the exercises 'bout Monsieur Davis learning the language. I like Monsieur Davis, he intelligent he ain't got the deathless beloved as his teacher but he doing it, he learning, kin say widh some truth, *"J'apprends à parler, à lire et à écrire le francais."*

"Now, Ludi," she be saying, her voice a gardenia for the ear, "most of this is excellent. But your verbs are a little off here and there."

"May I see?" I ax, and sit more closely to her, her scent a tendril beginning to root inside me. I see I misspelled *serais* inna sentence, *"Je serais l'homme le plus heureux du monde,"* prolly 'cause I got to thinking I would be the happiest man in the damn world if she would remember who she be, but she done forgot as she be transported further and further into the present from the past.

"It's the present conditional you need to work on, especially the irregular."

Oh, Ann, how irregular it be you married to some creep, name of Lark or somethin'.

"You know the verbs having an irregular base for the future – remember them? – have the same irregular base for the conditional."

I says, *"C'est la même chose."*

"Not exactly the same, but close."

"Close *chose.*"

"Very good. Let's look at *être,* okay?"

"Okay."

"Être has the future, *je serai,* and the present conditional, *je serais.* You forgot the 's' in your homework."

O Ann, you not know I forgot to post my letter to you in *Julliet* 1812? The one they found?

"How about if we move to the next chapter in the workbook, Ludi, the one on expression and poetry?"

"Okay," I say. *How about if you leave your husband we go to Vienna?*

"Ah, good, here's where more irregular verbs come into play. Oh, yes," she said, "look at this poem by Sandor Brennan. He wrote in both French and English, so we can compare his translation of this one with yours."

"You want me to translate it?" I see the poem begin *"je voudrais mourir plusieurs fois"* and maybe she give me it as a hint she know I be back.

"Right. Notice that it begins with the present conditional. Don't look at his translation, and don't allow yourself to look at the *Larousse.*"

"All right," says I, and opens my notepad.

"You don't have to do it right now. We can have another lesson Thursday. When do you get off from the trophy shop that day?"

"A la même heure comme toujours. Four-thirty," I tells her.

"Okay. You know you're doing well." She looked at me, I think, warmly.

My spirit drafts me up the steep stairs, I take her light into the room.

* * *

Once inside I switch on and off the lamp widdout a bulb maybe the Martian cool widh French if a boy speak Martian that boy speak French maybe he got some kina spin on a Brennan poem.

Bonjour, Ludi, he say when he outside the socket. *Maintenant tu ne fais pas de musique, mais de la langue.*

Shia, I say, I knew you spoke French, you got verbs like damn *"voudrais"* in Martian?

Shia, he say, we know about *"voudrais"* but we don' use it. It not a Martian reality, *voudrais,* ain't no conditional of any sort in our language. Not no more.

Or double-negatives, I says.

Not no way, Ludi, he say, our language has advanced beyond the brute positivity of appearing things to bear out the absolute equality of positive widh negative.

That damn goodt, I allows, be Godt's nature, he the AC of himself, he the galvanization of time, alternating between history and destiny, you sing it, my Martian bruthah, I says.

Our grammar attuned accordingly, Ludi. Martian lack the "would" the way a machine insensitive to desire. "Would" would mean the negative dimension dominate over the to-be-altered dimension of a positively given situation.

So... Martians, they be like robots?

Not no way. But we move in lock-step with the future. We have a tense in our language that predict absolutely the psychological outcome of any occurring event. We call it the future-complete.

Shia, we got the future-perfect.

We got beyond that, Ludi, the perfection of the future in arrival always be carried to a completion beyond that.

Shia. You mean it ain' really perfect?

You got it. Looky-yeah, what the future *mean*? It mean getting there in an unfading present moment, you dig. But that never happen, a new future always arising. And all there was of the present moment now be pass.

Yeah.

They always be that little grain o' sandt in the smoothness o' slippin' into arrival, it be call "disappointment": you Earthlings always got an appointment widh the future, but when it come you be *dis*appointedt.

That why Tuesday circle but never landt.

That it. On Mars we figured that bullshit out long time ago. Another name for the future-complete be future-regretted.

Future-regretted?

Everything happen from both ends, Ludi, terminus of pass as reveal by regret, terminus of future as reveal by hope. But we don' play the game no more: we regret the future and hope for the pass. Result: a kina stabilized present.

What kine that be?

The kine that tread water never expecting to get to the shore.

Da kine that make no promises, I surmises.

The kine that know the finish line move widh the runner. The kine that locate your planet in an orbit near others without hope of reaching them because they already your planet in mirror reflection, concave and convex.

You know, I says, I been composin' a *lied* include a verse 'bout regret bein' hope in reverse.

Then you know that mean hope be regret in reverse – the future-complete of which I done spoke. You take you' cock, the Martian said, it a compass pointing to the north when not wilted southerly in the warmth o' you' loins, it pointin' home, you set off over the tundra – an' then what?

Whut?

Nex' day you back at the Tropic o' Desire: once again The Promise peteredt oudt.

Shia, a boy gotta populate da planet, it da life-force, the force o' Fuck, keep things rockin' along. Human race-wise.

Shia, you oughta be a Martian, Ludi. Ain' no damn Martian submit to no "life-force," we done beat it at it own game.

Shia, how?

Looky-yeah, looky-yeah, the Martian said, what the "life force" gotta have so as to force itself on life but a time-space continuum? We done outdone Einstein by discoverin' a way to move faster than the damn speed o' light. We kin return the day before we damn leave.

Shia, dat cool. How you do dat?

We done discoveredt that the speed o' light peak at darkness, which loom beyond it as it secret meaning and destiny. You enter the darkness by remembering you' future as already pass…

Like… bein' deadt?

Like, as I was sayin', being in the present widdout hope for the future. We wait for Godot even after we damn killt him. The contemplation o' that crime accelerate us into darkness, where we damn fly faster than the speed o' light.

Shia.

Now, here da thing. We *does* arrive before we damn leave, an' that make two o' us. It a hyper-space cloning; no messy biology for us. It how we reproduce.

Shia, you mean you don' reproduce by… you know, like coming?

Shia, we reproduce by *going* – fast. But you Earthlings, you be slowedt by da particulates of desire in you' general atmosphere, an' you breathe deeply, deeply, my Earthling frien'. 'Course you go bangin' into each other, it the only thing you know in da triumph o' the lust-trance.

What dis got to do widh French?

Why you think you learnin' it? For *her.*

Yeah. She my one trufe.

Be da life-force pollutin' you' atmosphere. Damn glad I a Martian.

Ethnicity aside, now, this poem it begin widh *"je voudrais,"* that outside you' area o' expertise?

Shia yeah it is. *Voudrais, serais, ferais* can kiss my damn red *ais*. Ain't gon' work widh *aient.* You on you' own.

And he disappear.

* * *

je voudrais mourir plusieurs fois
de sorte que l'éternité erre dans les rues
et les heures sans fin attendent au coin
la femme qui crut m'aimer

I look at the poem for the first time and my heart jump into my throat. What she telling me here? I write:

I would like to die many times
so that eternity *erre…?* the streets
and the hours without end wait on the corner
for the woman who *crut?* to love me

Man, promised her I not gonna consult no dictionary. Gonna guess *erre* be some sort of like going, maybe related to damn "errant" in English.

and the hours without end wait on the corner

Less make that "endless hours," run a little smoother –

…wait on the corner
for the woman who *crut?* to love me

But damn *crut*... Then suddenly I sees it all, the message in the poem. *Crut* be like *brut* – brute – so *crut* be crude. But that the Beethoven I be! Deaf, I not hear, go wrong way uppa street, dress badly, shout at my detractors! That me! *Crut.*

So it be

I would like to die many times

(so in one of them I can come back to find…)

…the woman who loved *crude me.*

O Ann, my beloved, how clever you find this poem to tell me you know, you know, deep down you know who we both be again! Here a bi-syllabic poem for us, baby: *Until.*

* * *

"There's something very wrong, Ann. I've watched him working with you."

"Oh, you are so suspicious. You're snooping, Brett. There's a very sophisticated mind under the psychological cloud you see."

"It's a storm cloud, Ann. Look, there he was with you, sounding like a conscientious student to you, but I saw the looks, I saw the eyes. I think I saw him murmur something."

"Saw him murmur something? What sense does that make, Brett? Did you hear what it was as well?"

"Ann, I don't want to argue. You have to admit he's spooky. One side of him is all studiousness and growing competence and the other is a deep well with murky water."

"Well, what of that? He's still… off a little. The thing is, his devotion to learning a language has got to be good for him."

"Ann, he's learning it for you. He's in love with you. He wants you to love him."

"Oh, Brett. How can you be jealous of a sick man? There's no danger even if that's true. His meds are keeping him under control."

"I'm not jealous of that… that…"

"That sufferer? That human being whom God loves as much as he does you and me? That man who is our charge?"

"Okay, let me tell you something. Salmaninski came by yesterday. There was something he didn't tell you about the aftermath of the concert of Ludi's piano pieces. It wasn't that Ludi just stormed out after making a scene. There's more."

"What?"

"He punched Salmaninski in the face and broke his nose. I saw it was crooked and asked him about it."

Ann was silent.

"Ludi was lucky that Salmaninski didn't tell the cops; you know they'd have pulled the Involuntary Commitment Act on him."

Ann thought about this. "But he's so gentle with me," she said presently. "He's perfectly well-behaved."

"So was Dr. Jekyll."

"Okay. We've had this conversation before, Brett. What am I supposed to do, stop the lessons?"

"Why don't you give lessons only when I'm in the next room?"

"You're sure it isn't jealousy?" she said, smiling a little.

"Just concern," he said. "You trust him too much."

"You don't trust him enough."

"I don't trust him at all, Ann. Something's getting darker in him. I wonder about the meds."

"But he takes them in your presence."

"He puts them in his mouth in my presence. I haven't wanted to go as far as inspecting under his tongue."

"But then how do you explain how well he's doing in French?"

"It's because he wants to please you."

"Maybe," she said. "But that means I'm not in any danger from him."

* * *

"It's almost right, Ludi," she say when I comes in from work that day. "Now let's look at Brennan's own translation. Of course it has to be different from yours because he's writing poetry in English as to what the French says – also poetically."

She get out another book, and we read his words:

I would like to die many times
so that eternity would wander the streets
and the endless hours wait on the corner
for the woman who loved me then and now

"You did okay with 'goes down the streets' for *erre dans les rues,* Ludi, but I think 'wander' is a little more poetic for the verb. And it should be 'would wander' as the present subjunctive."

"But," I says, "what happened to *crut?* How did he get 'then and now' after 'who loved me'?"

"I was about to say your last line, 'the one who loved crude me,' was a nice try, although you slipped the past tense in there. But *crut* is the simple past of the irregular verb *croire,* to believe. So he probably meant she believed in her love for him, maybe was committed to love him. I suppose you can get 'then and now' out of that."

So she believe in our love. Vienna and New York.

"I didn't recognize it as a tense of *croire*. *Crut* seemed to mean 'crude' the same way *brut* does with 'brute,'" I says, covering the joy in my heart.

"Yes," she replied. "And that's another thing, too – *faux amis*. The 'false friends' that let you think you have a bonafide cognate when you don't."

So you not think I crude, I almost says, but know it not the right time yet.

"A lot of them are helpful. And there're so many of them. *Plat,* plate; *jour,* journal; *lettre,* letter; *mont,* mountain. But it can breed false confidence. You don't want to order a *glace* of water, but water *avec glace."* And she laughed, it sounded like little chimes, little ice shards tinkling in a glass.

"But *glace* and glacier are related," I adds, but for some damn reason something don't seem all easy with me, some little disturbing thing you don't know what it be.

"That's very good."

But it gonna gnaw at me till I know what it be.

"Next time, why don't you write a poem and we'll translate it into French?" she say. But what if the poem be about her?

"Okay."

"Or a small composition. Maybe something like 'My Worst Moment.' Nothing big."

"All right." I thinks about da time I beat up a Steinway for all da wrong notes, and I'm off to my room again, in love but wondering why I not feel right.

"You're getting there, Ludi," she call after me. "That really wasn't a bad translation."

"Thanks," I say, but there a grain o' sandt somewhere in my brain.

I'd worry about it but I got my mission.

Chapter Five

The Improviser

REPORT OF OFFICER L. BOUCHER, UNIT 21, NYPD:

Responded to complaint by Metropolitan Opera re homeless man pushing a hot dog cart (Sabrett's) through the grand lobby. Apprehended "Ludi Vann" just outside. Patrons said suspect had been pushing cart through the lobby howling and pointing to the spokes of the wheels. Complained suspect shook his fist at them but harmed no one. Met declined to press charges.

Cart stolen from licensed vendor, H.J. Barrios, who had reported theft earlier (NYPD No. 96-165). Now returned.

Suspect has a long history of mental illness. His doctor, A. Belmont, was notified and took him into his custody. Barrios declined to press charges as hot dog cart was unharmed, and he said he could use the publicity.

* * *

PSYCHIATRIC TRANSCRIPT No. 25, A. de Belmont, MD:

Belmont:

Ludi, I wonder if you know how lucky you are that you're not I.C.-ed again.

L.V.:

I wonder you know how lucky they be got someone trine he'p 'em.

Belmont:

What? Help them to hot dogs?

L.V.:

It was the wheels. Wheels toinin', dominant to tonic.

Belmont:

I thought you were getting better, Ludi, but it's obvious you're having hallucinations. Does that couple at the house bring you your medication?

L.V.:

Yeah.

Belmont:

And do they stay while you take it? They make sure you swallow it?

L.V.:

Yes and no. *Sic et non.*

Belmont:

Sick… et…?

L.V.:

The sick et none of it. [Great laugh here]

Belmont:

Ludi, what possessed you to take that cart into the Met?

L.V.:

Belly, what possessed you to take a career in messing with minds that still submit to the splendiferous mystery?

Belmont:

Come on, Ludi. We're talking about you. Look, do you want me to put you back in the custody of Bellevue?

L.V.:

Bellevue. "Beautiful view." I've been learning French. [Here he looked away a moment and I saw his face soften; then he suddenly said:] No. No, I wouldn't want that.

Belmont:

Then you'd better tell me why you went into the Met lobby with that cart.

L.V.:

Okay, okay. I did it because… because, see, there was an opera about me. But the composer abused music to tell my story.

Belmont:

Just a minute. [From a stack of recent newspapers in my office I consulted the Arts section of the *Times* to see what the Met had been staging the day of Ludi's intrusion.] Let's see… Okay. Alban Berg's *Wozzeck.*

L.V.:

I pronounce it "Woe-zeck."

Belmont:

Whatever. Look, I confess I don't know what it's about. Will you tell me?

L.V.:

It's about me when I was in 'Nam.

Belmont:

You were in *'Nam?* I never knew you were in 'Nam. There was nothing to go on when Sisters of Mercy took you off the streets and treated your ears. Is that right? You were in 'Nam? Jesus, why didn't you say something? That could explain a lot. You must have heard of Posttraumatic Stress Disorder. My god, that could be the key…

L.V.:

I never told anyone. But Berg knew.

Belmont:

You mean he met you sometime?

L.V.:

Naw, da mofo croak befo' damn 'Nam. But he was, like, you know, prescient. Prescient. Got da damn story from a gook who could smell da future, caught da scent o' napalm and dog-read it like tea leaves at the bottom of the terrible cup that would not pass from me.

Belmont:

[Although I immediately discounted that he had any material connection to the opera, I thought it best to let him talk about it in his own terms.] So this composer wrote an opera about you.

L.V.:

It's my story all right, Belly-boy. A captain sent me to a medic who did experiments with my diet. Here, they said, you should be eating more rice, less meat. It will affect the enzyme structure in your stomach so that blood will rush to your penis more easily and you'll get a hard-on with every shot fired, you'll ejaculate to see little yellow people crumple, you won't notice so much that they die like humans just as they were only pretending to have been human all along… You'll see them saying good-bye to the villages and hooches and rice paddies with their eyes as the blood runs out from the sides of their mouths but you'll be concerned only with the mess in your pants.

Belmont:

Ludi…

L.V.:

There's a special mission for you, soldier, the Captain said. Yessir, I replied, saluting. Yeah, there's a little unworthy piece o' shit you got to terminate, Lieutenant, that's why we been feeding you different. You man enough? Yessir, at least

I think so. Good. Good, soldier; that's a first step, thinking so. An essential step.

Belmont:

They gave you a mission?

L.V.:

We got this gook cunt, they said. Gook cunt who ain't talkin'. We keep ringin' her up, but she ain't answerin'. Here they laughed and leered at each other.

Belmont:

Ringing her up?

L.V.:

They attached wires to her body, then cranked an electrical dynamo. We're tired o' payin' the phone company for ringin' her up, Lieutenant. Them bills come in once a month. That's a lot of silence to be handin' Ma Bell a pretty penny for, don't you think? Sure, I said. How 'bout you slit her throat with that damn bayonet you never used?

Belmont:

My god. Ludi, you should have been telling me about this in the early sessions!

L.V.:

So where is she? I asked. Why, Lieutenant, they said, you know her. You know her real good. She's the whore you been bangin'. Marie Tranh. Didn't you know she was betrayin' all the secrets you been tellin' her, troop movement, sapper raids, artillery location? That's why you get the job.

Belmont:

And did you have feelings for her?

L.V.:

What they didn't know is that we'd been together a while; we already had a little kid, we called him Hopp-hopp, who at the time was about three years old.

Belmont:

Ludi. Jesus. This is tragic.

L.V.:

I took her for a walk by a rice paddy. She showed me the electrical burns, the bruises. She denied she was V.C., but she had a pair of earrings with "VPA" engraved on them.

Belmont:

What's "VPA"?

L.V.:

Vietnamese People's Army. I pulled my bayonet from its sheath, held it to her throat. What about these? I said. She said she found them. You found a *pair* of earrings? Okay, okay, she said, I'm cong but don't kill me. Let's go away, you can desert. I was stunned. She loved me so much that she'd confess to me and want me to run away with her. I realized I wasn't the man the captain thought I was; look, she was responsible for hundreds, maybe thousands of deaths of our troops, and the man I was *couldn't slit her throat.* I waded into the rice paddy, dragging her, the knife at both our throats. Someone had to die that night. Some little piece of shit had to be gone from the society of men. The moon rose blood-red, casting its hue over Hue, into the water. I still had her in my grip. Someone had to die that night, to be dead to the ways of a world in a perpetual crisis of violence.

Belmont:

…And… did you…?

L.V.:

Someone had not to be as he was.

Belmont:

Yes… yes. That's right, Ludi. Someone had to be *someone else* forever and ever! Maybe someone exemplary, a great giver of beauty to mankind…?

L.V.:

But Berg told it with the wrong music. Ugly, ugly, atonal, dissonant. Schoenberg had corrupted him!

Belmont:

Yes, yes. But the important thing is that we're making real headway here. [Here he let out a great, roaring laugh.] Yes, it's a relief, isn't it? You might even feel like crying – just go ahead. [He kept laughing, with what seemed was an intentional hoarseness in his voice. And then he looked at me mockingly and said:]

L.V.:

Belly, you pathetic unriddler of the universe, I've never been outside the continental U.S.A. And I four-effed the draft. I shook my fist at them, told them that if I knew as much about warfare as I did about thoroughbass I'd show them a thing or two. They said I had mental problems.

Belmont:

What? You mean all that was . . ? [He laughed the great, hoarse laugh again.]

L.V.:

Beethoven was always a great improviser before my hearing started to go. I loved variations on a theme.

Belmont:

Ludi, I threatened to send you back to Bellevue if you didn't tell me about pushing that cart into the Met. You've just about improvised your way there.

L.V.:

Look, Belly-boy, I told you the truth about the music. Okay, so I… personalized the plot a little. Can't you take a joke?

Belmont:

I can take you out of the halfway house. What do you mean about the music?

L.V.:

I told you. The music was ugly, part of the lostness of the world now. No ground, no truth. I was trying to show the path back. The wheels had twelve spokes, the number of keys in the chromatic system.

Belmont:

You mean, you were… protesting the kind of music in that opera?

L.V.:

Protesting by teaching. Twelve in number he createth the tones, and each reacheth out to the others in the divine harmony of his universe. Dominant and tonic he createth them.

Belmont:

So… that's what you were doing with that cart? Why didn't you just tell me that? Why'd you have to go and put me on?

L.V.:

Because I don't trust you, Belly-boy. You're someone from before, and I've known that for a long time. I'll bust you like I did Blake, Blake's here now, and like I did Lark.

Belmont:

Who's "Lark"?

L.V.:

Someone who has the darkness of the core of bronze. The other one illumines light.

Belmont:

Ludi, look. You're not making any sense. It's obvious that you're suffering a relapse. You were making a lot of progress, but something's different now. It's obvious you're not taking your Clorazil. You've complained about it before.

L.V.:

You're poisoning me! And I'll find out why!

Belmont:

Ludi, the deal with the halfway house was that you had to stay with your medication. It was always up to the couple, the Quakers, to let you live there, but that was only on the condition you stay with the medication. They can evict you.

L.V.:

No!

Belmont:

I'll have to tell them. It'll be up to them.

L.V.:

You know I'm on to you. You'd blackmail me into taking poison.

Belmont:

Once you get back with your meds you won't think it's poison.

L.V.:

Because my mind'll be dead.

Belmont:

No. Because your illness will be under control.

Feeling a little foolish for having believed his story, I again exhorted him to take his Clorazil, then showed him out. I made a note to place a call to the couple at the halfway house.

Today's session was revealing, but disturbing. Despite the abuse he shows me, I suppose I'm actually a little fond of him; I really care that he improves. But how can I help him if he isn't reasonable? Of course, that's a rational question about an essentially irrational situation, though the temptation to ask it is ever-present, as if the very fabric of interpersonal relationships were woven with the tenuous thread of reason.

And embroidered with hope?

Chapter Six

Confrontations

Brett hung up the phone, a disturbed look on his face. And yet what Belmont had said to him had only confirmed his suspicion. His eyes went to the stairs that led to Ludi's room. Ann was out, and would be almost the whole day.

Of course it would be snooping; but wasn't that justified now?

But what if Ludi showed up while he was in there? He remembered the bulbless lamp in the room, and that Ann had bought some bulbs a day or so ago. He went to the kitchen, opened the pantry and removed a sixty-watt bulb. He slowly twirled it between his fingers, an absent-minded motion accompanying the question of whether he would really do it. That is, he knew he could get away with it – but to him, a man of infinite conscience, a man whose honesty was a spiritual matter, even the act of dissembling went against his grain.

Even so, he ruminated, it was a matter of Ann's safety. His too. And so, bulb in hand, he approached the stairs he had seen Ludi mount day after day in his weird frock coat, battered top hat in hand.

Although he was almost certain Ludi wasn't there – he had seen him leave that morning, presumably for the shop – even so, Brett knocked lightly at the door of Ludi's room and called, "Ludi?" He tried the door, found it locked, slipped his key in the slot. He opened the door and looked over to the disheveled bed. The window was open and the ragged muslin curtains undulated slightly.

His eyes roamed the room, lighted on the rickety desk where some books and papers lay. He was ashamed at having such cheap furnishings for the tenants, but there wasn't much budget behind the halfway house; everything had to be gotten in second-hand shops and by donations. He put the bulb down by the lamp and walked over to the desk, wondering what he had hoped to find. The letter that he had seen begin with *"Mein* Anna" wasn't out on the desk, but he noticed two books, one a German-English dictionary and the other the *Larousse*, and a piece of paper with Ludi/Beethoven's handwriting on it. He slid open the middle drawer of the desk, then a bottom drawer on the right side. A legal-sized piece of paper caught his attention. There was something immediately interesting about it.

My god, Brett thought, looking more closely at it, does he really try to write music? The paper had the grand staff drawn on it with the help of a ruler, but the notes looked a little funny. He opened the drawer and pulled out the sheet. That's it, he thought, the notes are… three dimensional…! What…? He almost chuckled. Then he saw the bulks of quarter-notes were little yellowish pills, with stems drawn tangential to them. They needn't have been glued on the paper; they were slightly melted, sticky.

Brett looked at them closely: Clorazil, 100 mg.

My god… so he's only been putting them under his tongue until I leave! And then he does… this with them.

He saw a key signature of two sharps. He read the words under the melody spelled out in soggy pills: *"Freu-de schö-ner Göt-ter-fun-ken, Toch-ter aus E-ly-si-um…"*

Fear formed in his stomach; night was falling in some way that couldn't be wholly washed in the light of dawn. A thought darted into his solar plexus: *and he's in love with my wife...*

He heard steps on the stairs and hurriedly put the paper back; he pushed in the drawer, then rushed over to the lamp and began screwing in the bulb. The door opened and Ludi Vann strode in, glaring at him.

As casually as he could Brett said, "Oh, hello, Ludi. I don't mean to intrude, but I thought it about time I took care of getting you that bulb." Ludi kept glaring at him, then slowly said:

"Hello, Lark."

"Hey, Brett, remember? A kindly Quaker. And part-time electrician, it looks like."

"I've known it was you a long time," Ludi said, with measured malevolence.

"What are you talking about, Ludi? You know me. We're friends."

"Everybody's somebody from before. I've dealt with you in the past."

"Come on, Ludi." Brett would have moved but Ludi was blocking the doorway.

"And I've made Belmont, too. I know who he is now. My angel helped me. My Annie."

"My wife? How'd she help you?"

Ludi walked over to the desk. He was still wearing the absurd frock coat, reaching down to mid-shin, he always wore regardless of the weather. He grasped the paper on the desk and held it up to Brett, pointing to the words *"belle"* and "beautiful." An equal sign joined them. Then, in the same arrangement, *"mont"* and "mountain." "She reminded me about cognates. About *mont,"* he said, "because she was warning me."

"Warning you – about what?" Brett asked as he angled himself towards the doorway. "About a beautiful mountain, *belle-mont?* Oh, I get it. Belmont, your doctor. A beautiful mountain?"

"She knows about him. Look." Ludi pointed a little further down the page, at the German word *"schön."* He had placed an equal sign between it and a word, another "beautiful." To the right of that was the German word *"Berg";* it was equaled by a word, another "mountain."

"I don't get it," Brett said.

"Belmont. *Schoenberg.* Two things equal to the same are equal to each other. It's geometrically certain," Ludi said with a serious look. "He died in 1951 but didn't take but a few years to show up again because he belongs to the world he helped create."

Brett didn't know what to say, was chilled to see the glint of conviction flash from the blade of Ludi's inner logic.

"Listen, I've got things to do. Why don't we talk about this later. That okay?"

"If it weren't for you she'd be mine."

Brett now stood in the doorway. He felt a surge of anger, an emotion long dormant, now strong. "Now look, Ludi. What's this 'my Annie' business? You know, she *is* my wife," he almost sputtered. "And we've been awfully good to you, wouldn't you say?" The two stared at each other. Brett then said, "You haven't been taking your medication, have you? Not swallowing it."

Ludi glanced down at the bottom drawer of the desk and saw that it wasn't quite closed.

"That's grounds for getting you out of here, you know that?"

"You'd take me from her? I wouldn't see *her?"*

"Won't see her. I just talked with Belmont on the phone. He said you weren't on your medication. He told me it was my choice whether we'd let you stay or not. And you've got to go."

* * *

Ludi gathered what things he wanted from his room, knowing he could never come back, his mind still dwelling on the violence of what had just taken place – his raised fist, his host's defiant face. The sight of Brett Yearly dead at the bottom of the stairs, head askew, horrified him as much as it shocked him into the knowledge: it was time to leave, to act.

He wasn't panic-stricken; no one had seen or heard. But his resolve was tempered by a deep angst; something would prey on his mind about this violent day, even though he would step over Brett and out onto the streets.

He moved with deliberation, putting folded clothing and toiletries in a decrepit satchel. He knew exactly what to take and exactly what, as he glanced a last time to the paper folded in four on the desk, to leave behind.

* * *

Moving as a man with a duty, Ludi strode into the stream of people on the sidewalk, taking vague note of the brown stain on his right index finger; the jar of ink from where it had come, and the rest of the special paper, rode in his satchel. What gripped his consciousness was to act on what he knew, now, of Belmont. Of Schoenberg.

It was all so clear. *Of course* Belmont/Schoenberg had been poisoning him, first with Lithium and then with Clorazil, *because he knew who I am.* What else would the great disorderer of the tonal universe do but try to destroy his archenemy, the bringer of order, sense, *beauty,* to the raw truth beneath it all? – a truth which is chaos, demons inhabiting the formless waters that beat away at the strand where marooned mankind tried to make meaning of it all, casting tones skyward to lock up into constellations. Into Arpeggiated Triad, with its belt of Thirds, Tetrachord, darkly gleaming C-Sharp Minor, Devil's Interval, Six-Four Chord, its azimuth extending into the star-glowing galaxy of Cadenza…

It pained Ludi that he could never return to the haven the halfway house had afforded him, especially once he had carried out his plan. But there was no choice; the only thing to do now was fulfill the knowledge that had been granted him as to who was who and what had to be done with him. Oh, Ann, he called in his anguished consciousness, will I ever see you after I've completed my mission?

He made his way to Belmont's office.

Along with the tattered satchel, Ludi carried two things under his frock coat: a can of black spray paint, and an old canteen, a totemic item for him in that it was from the nineteenth century. He had filled it with gasoline a few days ago, when he'd hit on his plan for Belmont/Schoenberg, at a gas station where someone had left unattended the nozzle in a car's filler port; no one saw him lift it out of the car for a moment and squirt in a pint of gas.

He walked into Belmont's building and entered the elevator, getting off on the fifth floor. One or two people saw him, perhaps recognizing him as that street-crazy coming in to his doctor again, but he didn't care. He rounded the corner of the corridor and strode to the door with the letters "A. Belmont, M.D." on the frosted surface.

"Belly. Belly-boy," Ludi said in a determined voice. "Schoenie. Schoenie-boy." No one answered; the door was locked.

He pulled the can of spray paint out and wrote "SCHOENBERG" in looping, broad letters on the surface just below Belmont's name, overlapping onto the wall to the right of the door. He uncapped the canteen and poured gasoline over the bottom part of the door, sprinkling the remainder around the baseboards, then pulled out a book of matches, not noticing that a few drops had landed on the back of his right hand. He stepped back quickly as he struck a match and flung it at the base of the door; the scene leapt into flames as at once fire blossomed on the back of his hand. For a moment it didn't hurt, and in that moment Ludi beheld his burning skin almost dispassionately. He thought: this is the part of me I gave to him in all those talks, let it burn. Then he howled in agony and pressed the hand into his left armpit, extinguishing the flame.

I've done it, I've done it! pounded in his head as he fled to the stairs and ran down them to the lobby, forgetting his satchel. His hand burned with a deepening ache, but he took that to be his sacrifice in the act of revealing to everyone where the destroyer of the world of tones had been hiding.

* * *

In point of fact, Ludi Vann had not taken any of his medication since getting the job at the trophy shop; the notes of the composition Brett had found in the bottom drawer comprised a goodly portion of the "Ode to Joy" melody. Ludi had thought it was his Ode to Freedom, and at a certain point had crossed out *"Freude"* and written *"Freiheit."* He made his way now down a busy avenue toward Broadway, swaggering just a little, a mad look on his face; people got out of his way.

In his head he heard the sustained dominant-to-tonic, tonic-to-dominant opening of the Ninth Symphony, a suspenseful prelude to a great event. The event had been accomplished, but he gloried in those tones: E's and A's outlining the dominant of D-minor. But this beginning became only the introduction for the last movement. Ludi faced his orchestra, saw his hands waving as he conducted. He raised his fist, closed his eyes, shook his great mane at the sudden shift in harmony on *"vor G o t t…!"* The music became bouncy, Turkish, with drums and cymbals, and he smiled at his orchestra, dancing a little. He cued instruments, pointing and then space-sculpting the tones he wanted; he turned toward the singers, raised his fist to the chorus, nodded at the baritone. He conducted mightily, his head vibrating as if the music had gone right to that part of consciousness that knew itself without the thrust of the world, the intrusion of others. The hand pained him wildly as he moved it through the air, but the music was everything.

Ludi knew what would happen next. He would be out of synch with the orchestra and the singers and chorus, because he was deaf. Not that he didn't know the music, but that tempo is made of time, which spends longer moments some places than others, and a conductor's ear had to catch these dalliances. No, he would be conducting furiously several measures past the actual last tones, stirring the silence as the audience watched, appalled. Then the contralto would gently approach him, an angel of mercy, turning him around to the aghast audience who recognized for the first time that – Beethoven was deaf! The outpouring of pathos and love for him had been overwhelming…!

And so she approached. "Ludi? Ludi? You know me. Ann. What are you doing here in the middle of the street? Look, the cops are here. They're going to book you but Brett and I will get you out."

Ludi turned. Anna! And the audience – though they were on the sidewalks, stared at him. The applause of horns and shouts of drivers Ludi had held up crushed the air. Anna! My beloved! She smiled. She hadn't been home since the morning.

A cop grabbed Ludi, pulling him onto the sidewalk. "What the hell made you think you could direct traffic?" he shouted. "How do you like the sound of that?" he added over the blaring horns.

"O friend," Ludi said to him, grinning joyously and squeezing Ann's hand, *"nicht diese Töne! Nicht* 'em."

BOOK TWO

Convalescence

Chapter One

Dreams

Now back in Bellevue, and with a new psychiatrist, Ludi Vann was put on a different antipsychotic drug and an enforced regimen for taking it. Luis Sepulveda, his doctor, was trying something the research had shown to be more effective in cases of bipolar disorder: Risperdal. Ludi complained, as before, that he was being poisoned; as the drug began to work he lost that notion. But there were side effects, different from the previous drugs.

He had a room to himself, brighter than the upstairs flat he'd inhabited at the halfway house, a room overlooking the lawn of the place. He had visitors. And he had dreams.

Schoenberg came to him in his first dream. "Ludi, Ludi, why dost thou persecute me? All men are brothers. We are brothers in tones."

Never!

"Ludi. Ludi. We have a mutual friend who wears a dark cloak. Come, let us philosophize together."

My music is a higher revelation…

"I know, I know. '… than all of philosophy.' But the same tar sticks to both our heels."

Evil tongues wag ill truths.

"Evil, no. But I speak of darkness."

That right! Ain' no light in your universe, Schoenie. Dense mathematical abstractions only da Rain Man know secret pattern to.

"Let's stick with darkness. With tar. You also weave out of dark strands, my colleague."

You insult me to flatter yourself.

"Yeah, yeah. But where do you begin? You begin out of nothing. Your tones emerge from *silence.* It's all *ex nihilo, nicht war?* But you hide the *nihilo,* you make a theme refer to itself, vary itself, develop, and return to itself – all the suppression of the void it emerged from. Why, your development sections are shops of self-manufacture. *You forge necessity out of contingency!* Look at your Fifth – the last measure is the first one driven into – forced into – self-arrival!"

My themes refer to themselves as Nature's own mirror sends her patterns forth! As is my Fifth so is the vein pattern of a leaf! I a organic logician, a mathematician of echoes, a searchlight on vanishing points…

"You make something out of nothing. You overcome the abyss of silence by making the thing found itself on its own sounding."

O, you so right, muvvah! That my triumph and transcendence. Even you can see that!

"All the wheeling around the circle of fifths, all those absorptions of dominant to tonic, V into I, all distinctions merging into a grand finality, like the arrival into C-major at the end of the Fifth…"

Apostates yet can hear the wordt o' Godt.

"Oh, hell, we apostates have perfect pitch for silence as well. Which is my point, Ludi. You think you've made a great gift to mankind, my friend. But it's a Trojan horse."

I a creator, not a destroyer!

"Is there any difference between what you do with all that self-reference which builds itself out of itself to establish itself in the grand tonic of forever-and-ever and, say, the paltry human ego?"

And what of that? Ego be Godt's doing too.

"Then why does he beat it down with age and death? He cherisheth it *not!* Pride is the source of all sin. The apple that corrupted Adam and Eve was polished to the degree it gave back their reflections to preen in."

Jew-boys never get ego. No tonic forever and ever redeem anything, you a Jew. No final transformation o' da las' dus'. Oh no! Twelve-tone technique, serial technique – when have you ever transformed the darkness!

"That's our honesty, Ludi. It's our acquiescence to the dawn of destitution. No one could possibly compose like you after the Great War. Except Rachmaninoff."

Here we agree. Wretch-maninoff. Da saccharin Scriabin.

"He's the secret emptiness inside sentimentality. And that's what I oppose."

Shia, he da sweetness o' da smell o' rottin' flesh.

"I would certainly say he's the perishable past exposed to the heat of the present."

Da enemy o' my enemy ain' necessarily my frien'.

"But, you see, Ludi, I and my disciples… *we honor the present you would cover up."*

Enough, Schoenberg! No more tonight! Why do I let you say these things…?!

"God made you deaf and you missed the lesson."

* * *

Some brain chemistry must have resulted from his new drug, for even though Ludi was becoming more lucid, the dreams were odder and odder. And he would have them for a long time. For years.

In the next dream he was able to remember, an angel in dirty raiment came to him.

You, like, a fallen angel? he asked.

"All living beings are fallen angels, divine intelligences who grew concrescences of bodies as they plummeted to earth," he answered. "Pestilent vapors irritating ectoplasm produced the pearl of body. Now you move around in a husk of flesh remembering your angelic natures in glimpses of beauty, in pleasure, in the anguish of decision."

What about the unfallen? Ludi asked.

"To the unfallen, any world is merely ideal. Any angel who runs afoul of any other angel is immediately thanked by the fouled angel for the opportunity of forgiveness, which is cheap: given the unreality of our world, compassion, forgiveness itself, spring from a fathomless pit, as the fallen know it, whose bottom keeps undercutting itself as God's self-consciousness of doubt becomes temporal and tragic. Fallen, we be Buddhas o' da breakaway floor, broken girders in da constructed universe. We inhabit a hole da totality of which add a 'w' up front – for 'wonderment,' for 'whut-up,' for *why.*"

You not from a Christian heaven?

"This a new regime. It *was* a Christian heaven until the nether aspect of His nature kicked in for its period of dominance, period of duration, P.O.D., whatever – the directives were never quite clear on nomenclature and acronyms."

Da Cat like variable – shia, don' I know, he AC electric all da way! Ludi cried in the dream, noticing he had no will to say anything, or to say it in any certain way.

"Dat right. True dat. True dat. Ludi, I sat on your left shoulder when you toldt Belmont dat Godt be Alternating Current, it was I who whisperedt it in you' inner ear. Hey, you wanna know why they's life they's death they's truth they's lies… look to Godt's AC, the alternation of opposites necessary to *causa sui* between himself as cause of himself and effeck of himself, as I told you to tell Belmont.

Yeah, you tol' me.

"You take a lady, say, pushing fifty, the press of time has written edicts on her face, her eyebrows roam acrost her forehead, a woman who has suffered the blues of too many 8:32's in the crepuscular onset of night – say she sittin' at a concert o' Chinee harp music, she drawn into a universe of tallow-tree tones, oblivious of her past; what separate her from the terrible scenes of her history, what be the great divide between former bouts of anguished terror and this tranquil moment?"

You axin' me?

"I tellin' you, the holy anguish o' Godt's self-separation into divine Cause and divine Effeck. It give only times infinitely outta touch widh each other."

You preachin' to you' disciple.

"Pain. You take pain, for example. All suffering is undergoing. But it all Godt undergoing the struggle o' self-foundation. Every ringing tendon, every burning woundt be Godt's own *agon* in da contes' o' Himself, for the agony of a second aspires to an eternity of suffering, the temporal moment magnifies itself by a power of infinity. Time, a worldt, a worldt in time, be his own blood spattered into nebulae, into soil and water, mud and sky, into cells in parthenogenesis and *parousia*, into the head that emerge from the mud and go: 'mud?'"

Shia, true dat, true dat. The suffering o' da innocen' be da holy mystery o' Godt's own pain. Jewsus done rescuedt Godt by casting His pain into apotheosis.

"You ain' lyin'. It no less for Jewsus splayed on his model-T than you see a cage of freezing parakeets outside the door of a house where you're serving a summons. It thirty-six degrees on the damn Fahrenheit scale, two birds are shivering, one be deadt. The water trough a residue o' yellow-green slime. The two living parakeets dying of hunger."

Mud?

"Dum."

Umd?

"Oh, *because,* Ludi: it Godt's own suffering the fact his I-am-that-I-am come from Himself – that he got to, you know, jump over the abyss between 'I am' and 'that I am' – and the gap be like, impassable Nothing. *Nothing really does separate Godt from himself.* It the scandal of divine masturbation, the forgery of positivity – only to be discoveredt in the solitary night o' da negative chasm. 'It *back,'* say Godt, 'this cancer of my failure to *be* widdout going outside myself for the adoring consciousnesses of the death-bound, for whom I appear in self-foundedness as the catastrophic *causa sui.'"*

And my suffering holy too.

"Your suffering most sacred. You coulda' bagged it in 1802 – we have the testament of that possibility on your part – but you embraced it; you aspired to eternity. That your Godt-like nature."

It da right thing. My art a higher calling than the banality o' bagging it.

"But where was I?"

So it change, the former Heaven?

"Godt change. You gotta understand, the periodicity of divine AC appear to mere mortals like you as eons, upheavals in culture, time frames. He change into the negative aspect o' Himself by what you reckon as the early twentieth century. You take a idle chair, say, it riddled widh da 'not' o' no-one-sitting. Only Godt's subsumption o' his own contingency, his own nothingness, couldt allow da lack o' buttocks and back pressin' 'gainst fabric and foam to figure into dat piece o' furniture's passive objectivity 'n' taciturn truth… da new negativity swep' positivity into da pass. It come home in your century when groundt disappear, when your anchor in the eternal sea floor slipped into the

silt of temporal truth. Angels smoked ethereal cigarettes, some got metaphysical emphysema; several of us wrote in cafés, about cafés. A few of us learned the blues scales on our harps. Some of us went out and scored hits of Anguish; another few flirted with despair, for we fell into adoring ourselves in the mirror of consciousness; later some of us submitted the silver-nitrate backing of the mirror to a kind of acid, to destroy the reflection and give us a clear view of Godt, but got stuck in the transparent glass. We fornicated more, in those days, 'nothingness' became a great wordt in the literary arts. We sat on the shoulders of Paul Bowles in Tangier, Jack Kerouac and Bill Burroughs, too. We blew kisses to Allen Ginsberg and vouchsafed the cosmic wink to J.-P. Sartre. *We created Heidegger*. We used the wordt 'man' a lot, in those days."

I read Beckett before I find out who I am. Who Beckett now?

"He a Buddhist monk in da Tibetan undergroundt, confounding da Chinee widh true lies."

Dat be right. Las' time he be da Despondent Buddha.

"And music too."

Umd?

"Music change. It change to be in accordt widh Godt's nature. His new Nature."

No, now, wait, wait. I ain' havin' you sayin' this shit.

"Schoenberg sit at the lef' handt o' Godt."

No! You mustn't say things like that! The Beethoven I was originally, he sittin' at da *righ'* handt o' Godt!

"So what? Godt be *lef'*-handedt. Now. Less jus' say his Ambidexterity has broken to da lef'. By way o' renewin' da Mystery."

Godt spoke to him – me – in brass and strings. I took the nothingness in my heart where the worldt juts in and transformed it in concluding cadences. I did Godt's work!

"Ludi, Ludi, de-luded Ludi." Ludi saw that the angel's patched and torn robe had become a shabby business suit.

Get away from me, false angel! Your breath stinks, your raiment is rent and filthy!

Chapter Two

Psychiatric Sessions

"I ain't havin' you say this shit" recurred to Ludi from time to time after he awoke from the last dream. He recalled that he had said something like that in the previous one, too. As he got better he realized who it was he was arguing with; that is, he came to think that the conversations held in his dreams were aspects of himself, that what he heard differed only in content but not in voice. This bothered him (though Sepulveda considered it a breakthrough), and when Ann Yearly came after a few weeks he told her he heard voices in his head, but that they were his own.

"I should have bagged it," he told her, "when my hearing failed, I wake up and wash my face, the water in the basin goes down the drain pulled to the center of the spinning earth where there is only the tiniest particle of matter, only an atom. What could be more absurd than that? Where does the pull of mass come from, then? What else could it be but the heaviness of God's heart?" Ann left that time but returned a few weeks later.

* * *

As for Belmont, the office was repaired soon after the fire. Not much had been destroyed beyond the door – the sprinkler system had come on and an alarm sent, with a quick response. The door had had to be replaced and some of the carpet nearest it had been scorched. "Occupational hazard," Belmont commented to those who asked.

The truth was that he was sad to have lost Ludi. He recalled the crude scribbling of the first "conversation books," the strange fact of Ludi's having been able to repair the office computer with little else than his touch, the fact that in the last two years his conversation had become more articulate – though Ludi had still insisted he was deaf. The Clorazil had had effect enough to allow Ludi the job at the trophy shop – really, the mockery of a job, filing burrs off metal edges – but Belmont had hoped that a normal routine might help transform Ludi into a functioning person; that had been the idea. But then this "Immortal Beloved" development Ann Yearly had told him about. Jesus, a well-read mental case, a researcher, no less, on the life he had crawled into, like a hermit crab into the abandoned shell Beethoven's death had left on the shore of Western culture… Belmont smiled a bent smile to himself. Yet it had had deadly consequences; he suddenly was sorry that he had put Ludi in that particular halfway house, with those gentle Quakers. But that house had been Ludi's choice.

Yes, it was the "Immortal Beloved" episode where Ludi had stopped taking his medication, Belmont surmised; he had seen the "Ode to Joy" melody made of Clorazil notes. Well, it was out of his hands now. It was in Sepulveda's hands. No way he – Belmont/Schoenberg, an accident of name (a musician friend of his had explained to him who Schoenberg was in the history of music), evil nemesis of a contemporary Beethoven – could resume with his patient. It was in Sepulveda's hands.

Sepulveda's hands were skilled, so to say, in that he had a warmth to his manner that encouraged his patients to talk, to consider, to mull over their psychiatric problems with a view towards getting over them. Of course, chemical therapy like Risperdal had to come into play: brain structures were recalcitrant, oblivious of conversational revelations. He had noted the increasing lucidity in Ludi Vann; Ludi himself noticed that the dream of Schoenberg, that of the angel of God's negative phase, had not repeated themselves. The other bizarre dreams didn't stop, though.

Sepulveda got him to wonder how he had become Beethoven. "After more than one-hundred-fifty years, Ludi."

Ludi looked about the office. It seemed to him that Sepulveda had an attraction to stainless steel. His desk bore stainless moldings in which Ludi caught the distorted image of his own face, and the thought came to him: as the face, so the mind. The carpet was much richer and deeper than Belmont's had been, and the walls seemed somehow warmer, in hues of pinks, than those of his former doctor. A huge window overlooked the grounds, where the less afflicted patients wandered, the walking wounded. "And you're not somebody from before," Ludi said. "They all were, a lot of them, anyway. I told you about that."

"No, Ludi. I'm as contemporary with myself as anyone else," Sepulveda said. "If I've lived before I have no inkling of it. The question is, who are you now? Who was it who became Beethoven?"

"Dave Letterman once asked me that. I seem to remember."

"You know, of course, Belmont sent over your case history. He said you knew your way around computers. Can you tell me anything about that?"

"But why should I think about all that? You say I'm better, so maybe I can just get along. The electrical outlets and lamp sockets have been silent a while. That's all I know. Maybe I could work with electronics again. Without them calling my name. Without the drama."

"Ah," said Sepulveda, "so you have worked with computers. Does anything about that come back to you?"

"Just that they talked. Circuits closed in an order that held some strange pattern of my own brain electronics. The color code of wires spoke in hues of knowledge – of me. I made a lanyard of them, once, wove them together into a mandala with the story of my life portrayed in the warp and woof."

"Warp and woof."

"Woof. Like a dog. Da houndt o' faith dat heardt *not* da dog whistle."

"Yes," the doctor said, "this 'hound of faith' thing – and always in street English – Ludi, could we talk about that?"

"Deaf. Deaf! He wasn't Karl, but God welsh it! How could he have heard?"

"Who is Carl?"

"Karl is…" Ludi stopped. "Karl… was…"

Sepulveda got up and went to a file cabinet, pulled out a folder, then returned to Ludi, who sat, legs crossed, in a rather large leather chair. The doctor read a while, then looked up at his patient. "This woman who came to see you – Ann Yearly – she told me that your 'Beethoven' had a crush on her while you were staying at the halfway house. The Quaker."

"Bline Boy tol' me she do da dance. Location o' da spiritual honey."

"Is that how you feel now? Today?"

"No. The memory triggers the words. I've lost faith in the phrases… and the dialect. But they come back. I can't control them."

"But that's progress," Sepulveda said, "that you recognized both those as old bad mental habits. There've been great reports about your medication. Maybe you can remember who Carl was to you when you were…"

Ludi looked out the window. Lush green, the sky its azure foil, rushed into his consciousness. Sepulveda saw Ludi's eyes grow wide, then shut tight. "No," his patient said, "nothing comes. The Beethoven I was was in love with her. But after that, blank."

Sepulveda returned to the folder. About to say something, he thought better of it and had Ludi returned to his room.

* * *

Ann knocked as Ludi was again contemplating the green outside his window. She poked her head in to his "Come in."

"Your doctor says you're doing a lot better. Can we visit a while?"

Ludi nodded, and she sat. The room was small, she noted, sparely furnished, but not uncomfortable.

"Your friends have been asking about you. Gentleman Jimmy wants to come visit, if that's okay with you," she said.

"How about Bline Boy? Has he been around?"

"I found him on Forty-second. I told him what happened… with Belmont's office. Where you were."

"Ah, I don't know. Gentleman Jimmy still has his LS-Demons. Sepulveda seems to be doing some sort of chemical exorcism on mine."

"That's good."

"No more Beethoven's nemesis or conversations with angels. Only a certain drabness. I'm going gray in the soul. I remember the shining darkness, its black-hole allure, and it's all leavened with light now, getting brighter and brighter. And bland. I'd bail into that darkness given half the chance…"

Ann said, "Ludi, I still want to ask you about… about Brett. He thought you were in love with me."

"Beethoven was in love with you. I remember writing your name as if you were the Immortal Beloved. When I was him."

"Did you argue about me? He was jealous of you, Ludi. I thought you two might have… had it out over me."

"Well, his demon-rival is being anesthetized into a dimension of nonexistence, thanks to the wonders of chemical science. Beethoven is being returned to history. So tell him not to worry."

"You didn't know? Oh, Ludi! He's dead. He was found at the bottom of the stairs outside your room," Ann said, with trepidation in her voice. "Were you there then? Did you see him?"

Ludi's face went blank, then his brow furrowed. "No," he said presently, "I didn't know." He rocked a little in his chair, and slowly a troubled look came to his eyes. It grew, and became a kind of violence. "'Were you there *then?* Did you see *him?*'" he said mockingly. "That's the rhythm of the Fifth's opening! Did you come to taunt me? Wring out my humiliation?" He stared out the window, face working in the shiftings of disturbed thought.

Ann got up and walked to the door. "I need to know what happened to Brett, Ludi. We treated you well. God won't let you repay our kindness with contempt," she said softly. "Or with madness. It's not God's way." Ludi spoke not, heard the door close. He sat in silence for a long while. "God's way. God's way," he began saying to himself, absently. "God-sway. The trajectory of mystery as history." In a while he muttered, "Don' know nuffin, muffin. Dat da truth, Ruth."

* * *

On the way out, Ann stopped at Sepulveda's office. She knocked gently. "I don't have an appointment," she said to his receptionist, "but is there any way I might talk with the doctor? I've seen him before about one of his patients." She gave her name. The woman pushed a button and said the right words into the phone. "You're in luck," she said. "You can go in."

When Ann was seated she spoke to the man in white about Ludi, about seeing him just then, and his sudden refuge into anger.

"Of course, I'm not allowed to discuss case specifics," Sepulveda said to her, "but since you can illuminate certain aspects of his pathology, let's talk. Our last discussion was a little brief, though the notes I have from it have already been useful." He asked her more about Ludi's stay at the halfway house, his habits, what they found in his room.

"We brought him his things after the court turned him over to the hospital," she said. "Not much. A few articles of clothing, mainly. We gave Dr. Belmont his music made of antipsychotic pills – he laughed at how his hopes for Ludi had come to such a bizarre end. A man named Salmaninski, a music promoter who had come to like some music Ludi wrote, came by."

Sepulveda was surprised. "He actually wrote music like his alter ego? I wasn't aware of that."

"Well," said Ann, "it was more like recomposing music. He told me once about writing some piano sonatas of his – of Beethoven's – backwards and upside down."

"Really?" Sepulveda said. "Well, he does have a very mathematical mind. I've noticed a fixation with anagrams."

"Salmaninski put on a recital of them – kind of an ugly scene at the end – and we knew him from that. He hadn't known until the recital that the composer of the music he'd liked – he's very avant garde – considered himself Beethoven. At least, that's what he told me. I'm not sure I trust him, God forgive me for judging. Anyway, it got him a broken nose, I remember."

"Oh, we're well aware of his propensity for violence. He was in a straitjacket for some time," Sepulveda said.

"But that's what I want to talk to you about, doctor. You know that Ludi thought I was Beethoven's 'Immortal Beloved.' I think he must have been jealous of Brett, my husband."

"We were just talking about that in the last session. He – whoever he is who thought he was Beethoven, and we still have no hint of his real identity – admits to the crush on you. Or to Beethoven's crush on you. He's waking up from his delusions. He does have relapses, but in the sessions so far he hasn't mentioned your husband."

"Of course, you know that Brett was found dead at the bottom of the stairs outside the room Ludi had – and on the same day of the fire at Belmont's office."

"It's in the report, though there's no proof it wasn't anything other than an accident. Coincidence. I've been angling to get at that with him. He does talk about a certain 'Carl' in a violent context, but he can't seem to tell me who that is. My deep sympathies, by the way," he said, meeting her eyes.

"Thank you," she said. "Would it be a breach of ethics for you to tell me if he… if he… tells you what happened? If he did it?"

"The best ethics include compassion."

"Thank you, doctor." She rose to go. "Please press that with him."

"I will," he said. He closed the door behind her.

Chapter Three

Toward Recovery

Ludi's progress was due in large part to the "depot" technique of long term injection of Risperdal, rather than its administration in continuous oral doses; it made faking it, as he had before, impossible. The prospects were promising, despite the lapses into nonsense and black English. Sepulveda had shown Ludi the progress he was making by comparing the "conversation books" from the early Belmont sessions to what Ludi was saying these days.

Sepulveda sat across from Ludi, this time in the latter's room. The reason he was there, instead of vice-versa, involved the vague notion that being on Ludi's ground, so to speak, rather than Ludi having been summoned to "the office," might help in getting him to open up more. A strategy was necessary, he'd thought, because what he wanted him to open up about was the strange "Karl" business (he now knew it was spelled that way), and the concerns Ann Yearly had raised. Not that he didn't know who Karl was in the real Beethoven's life – the man's nephew, nearly driven to suicide (according to the literature he'd recently consulted), probably by his overbearing uncle – but that he suspected a key to this strange man lay in his violent language about Karl.

"Tell me about Karl."

"Isaakarl."

"You're Karl?"

"Not me. Karl. Beethoven was Abrathoven."

"Who are you, then?"

"Just the aftermath of a divine calculation from the Old Testament, my dear medico, best I can tell."

It flitted through Sepulveda's mind for a millisecond that the Spanish word might have been a gibe at his Hispanic heritage, his slight Puerto Rican accent. But what he said was, "Well, fine. But it doesn't help to be speaking in code here, Ludi."

"The brain strains, the mind minds. The future promises, the past binds."

"Yes, you used to rhyme with Dr. Belmont. It's there in the 'conversation books.' Were you referring to Isaac and Abraham – the near-sacrifice in the Bible? Because, you know, Karl was almost 'sacrificed' – at his own doing – by Beethoven, according to some accounts. Is this the 'Abrathoven'?"

"I dunno. I'm only saying what comes into my head."

"That's good, Ludi. We might get somewhere that way."

"It be cool."

"Yes, it be cool. So what about Isaac and Abraham?"

Ludi thought a moment, and his mind flew away. His look had been lingering on the white of the doctor's smock; it seemed to suggest to him something so pure that it would need to be stained to enter the real world. White was an abstraction, all colors run riot together, canceling everything out, making everything equal – like Schoenberg's system, a Marxism of music, where G in the key of C held no privileged status – the keyless society; like atheism, where the lord of the dominant no longer could be expected to return the world to the perfection of the tonic. Didn't it symbolize the homogeneity of all things in the twentieth century, the ruin of hierarchy, where Good and Evil lay together and in their passion knew not who was who was who – only each other? That was God-sway. The trajectory of mystery as history; a decline – and it was white.

Sepulveda asked, “What are you thinking about, Ludi?”

“The final snow obscuring every shape. God’s own dandruff. The mountain and the valley in bed together. Why I lapse into black English. From time to time.”

“Look,” said Sepulveda, “if you’re more comfortable with it talking to me, I be down with that” – and immediately blushed at the lame patronization. Getting over it, he added, “There’s something you want to tell me. Want to. But won’t. Why do you bring in Isaac and Abraham?”

“Abraham. He called it off. Or God called it off. Isaac lived.”

“Yes, but… what has this to do with ‘Karl’?”

Ludi stared blankly. After a long while he said, “Abraham heard. That’s why he stopped.”

“…And?”

“Beethoven was deaf. He couldn’t hear God calling off his dogs.”

Sepulveda considered this. Presently he said, “But Karl lived too.”

“I know,” said Ludi. “That’s what I don’t understand either.”

* * *

After a long night begun with strange thoughts that developed into stranger dreams, Ludi Vann awoke. His eyes were glazed. He saw all the things in his line of sight, but they remained chimerical, and, once materialized, were drained of meaning, dull presences. Sometime in the night, though timelessly in his dreaming, he’d remembered something.

It was Isaakarl and Abrathoven, with Karl dead, his eyes gone white. And then Beethoven was holding him; Karl smiled into his eyes. Some great major chord was sounding in resolution of the dissonance of a fourth, and a very white light was all around.

Ludi started from the pillow. It was more than a dream. It was a memory of a vision. The vision had ended when the pain had begun in his ears.

Ludi sat up in the bed and was still for a while. It bothered him. He knew the memory was real, coming from when his madness had been like a storm where the wind and the rain were all there was, even though for everyone else it was a sunny, balmy, day. But something more was bothering him, too. It was the fact that in his memory the events were clear but the features of the faces remained indistinct. He puzzled over that as he arose and began the routines that rhyme with the arrival of morning light, night driven into the dissolution of its own darkness, routines that once again stirred meaning into things around him.

As he moved about – bathroom, the coffeemaker the staff had brought him, the hunt for his right slipper – he noticed that an old Hank Williams song was wandering the recesses of his mind, with the words:

> *Heeeyyyy, not-lookin'...*
> *Whaaatcha got cookin'...*

and when it became annoying Ludi began concentrating on the second theme in the first movement of Beethoven's Fifth, struggling occasionally not to let the gentle logic of that E-flat melody become misshapen into the sentiment of the Country tune; as the two melodies merged in the distorted harmony of the twentieth century, Ludi clutched his head and moaned.

At the session when Ludi told Sepulveda about the dream, the psychiatrist took a new interest; though given to chemical therapy, he was also a student of Freud, and took dreams seriously.

"When you held your head," he asked, "did the music stop?"

"It subsided after a while," Ludi said.

"Let's get back to the dream itself. You're distinguishing a simple dream from a dream of a memory? Is that really possible?"

"The memory of a vision from long ago."

"It really was a… vision, Ludi? As in some mystical sense?"

"It goes back. Quite a ways. Back before Belmont, when I injured myself."

"Your ears. So as to be deaf."

"So as to be him."

"Let's discuss your not being able to make out the faces in the dream, Ludi. Can we work on that?"

"'How 'bout cookin' something up with me?'" Ludi quoted.

"I don't get… oh, oh, right. The song."

"You have it already, doc; it's like I said: I remember everything from the vision, which I know was clear at the time – I saw faces then – but it was all blurred in the dream."

"Yes, that's interesting. That's what we need to get into."

"All I can tell you is, it was like I was on the verge of seeing. I could feel a tingle, more like a tension…"

"Of wanting to see but needing to look away, maybe?"

Ludi paused, considering this. "Yes. That's true."

"Now, that's good. That's very good. That tells me where the blur was coming from."

"Yes. Sure. But the question is *why*. Why didn't I want to see… who was killed and who killed him?"

"But it was Beethoven. And Karl."

"Right. But without faces I could make out."

"But, Ludi, you were Beethoven; no one can see his own face – without a mirror."

Ludi thought for a moment. "But who was Karl?" he said presently.

Sepulveda thought for a moment, wondering if he should go for broke. Then he said, "Was he… was he Brett Yearly?"

"No!" said Ludi. "No. Ann told me about the accident. No, Beethoven wouldn't go after a married woman. I think there's proof of that…"

"Do you remember what Brett looked like, his face?"

"No," Ludi said. "just a kind of vague memory of a gentle guy."

"You should try to remember him, Ludi," Sepulveda said. "It would mean a lot to Mrs. Yearly if you could remember anything. Will you try to remember… for her?"

Ludi sat quietly. It occurred to him that she really meant nothing to him now – just a player in a charade his strange mind had invented. "I'll tell you if anything comes up. I tell you everything anyway."

"You do, Ludi. I know it's hard. But it's to help with your recovery. And if you can help her…"

"I know. She said I owed it to her. To them."

They talked a little while more, then the doctor left. Back in his office, he made extensive notes on their conversation.

Chapter Four

A Bald Man's Epiphany

One day, after about three months from the time the depot injection technique had been started, Dr. Sepulveda heard an amazing remark from his patient.

"Okay, it's over – *comoedia finita est.*"

"What is?" he asked.

"No more relapses. The other day I was shaving, doc. Up by the sideburns. I saw my hair is almost gone. I'm nearly bald. I saw it for the first time."

"It happens to a lot of men, Ludi. It's a genetic thing."

"It didn't happen to him. To Beethoven. A full mane to the end."

"And so you're saying…?"

"I could never be him. The hair thing is unmistakable."

Sepulveda engaged in a long reflection that in real time took only a few seconds. How strange the human psyche! The man could not speak German, could not compose, was taller than the historical Beethoven, was born after World War II, but *not having hair* snapped it for him? Of course, the Risperdal had prepared the way for such a revelation, but it took something that ordinary to bring it about. We figure out what to do, how to approach a sick mind, what to prescribe – and then one fine day male-pattern baldness completes the therapy, banishes a delusion… Anyway, hallelujah!

"Well, this is our breakthrough, Ludi," Sepulveda said in a well-composed way. "Only I'll feel a little odd still calling you 'Ludi.' Maybe you can remember another name."

"Maybe. But I keep thinking I was in jail once. So…"

"Bingo," said Sepulveda. "The Sisters of Mercy, Belmont, our entrance staff – did they ever take your fingerprints? Of course you may not know. But do you remember if anyone did?"

"No," said Ludi. "But I have vague memories of a cell, jackin' the shit with other cons. Nothing much."

"We'll get you fingerprinted as soon as possible."

"Not yet. Let's consider it an avenue. But I got stuff I want to think over first. The 'Karl' thing."

"I want to think it over with you. But let's do the fingerprints soon. Knowing your background could help close out your treatment here. Medicaid sure would be happy to have us finish it up. It's a pretty sure route to your real identity if you were in jail. Was it Rikers?"

"I dunno. I think it was a state prison. Maybe in the South. There was a piano in the rec room. A guy played violin with me one time. Do they have a piano in Rikers?"

"I doubt it. But we'll figure out your real name, then where you've been."

* * *

The final dream Ludi Vann had before he left Bellevue seemed to him to have been an appeal to a public at large. He found himself saying:

Would you like to spy on my mind, *be* my consciousness without being my… being? – *his* ego, *his* suffering? Go ahead. Since mind isn't located anywhere, it doesn't matter where you are. Mind arises like a harmonic off the clang of world against senses, with its own inner overtone series playing up and down into words, into thoughts, knowledge;

it can be had by anyone, it can be yours if you let it. Go ahead. There'll be a price, but take a peek:

"What I was thinking when I started off the Ninth with all those A's and E's come to hum like the wings-of-doom into D-minor: to contrast it with D-major in the *Ode to Joy* theme, didt da same damn thing widh da outer movements o' da Fifth, da A's and E's like da orchestra tunin' up.

"Yeah, you look at da worl' da fuckah goin' *down*. Commode to Joy. Joy *who?* She da ho do da little trick widh, you know, widh, like her ass? No, dat be Lazara da Living Endt, raised from da deadt by Idiot Boy widh da Jesuspecker. Seen her in N'awleans. No, Joy be 'Joy Bejesus,' da Christian porn star, do them 'Secondt Coming' fuckflix.

"But, now, Lazara, she console herself that she a witch.

"I say, Lazara, you into broom-stick travel? You a frequent flyer? She say, shia, Ludi, you ain't 'nitiated inta da mysteries. They's ways o' travelin' and they's ways o' standin' still. Shia, Lazara, name a mystery or two, say I. Or twenny-two.

"'Ludi, I got my man comin' by, my daddy-man.'

"Wordt on da screet somebody damn croak him.

"'Naw,' she say, 'he still death-worthy.'

"Sonata form allows doubt to be the core of faith, if you take the Development section in its true depth; for here the pristine beginning, the Exposition, with its careful arrangement of themes, is abandoned as all hell breaks loose. All is *in question*. All is *tested*. But such belongs with the essence of faith… holey Beckett bucket…

"Lazara a frequent sweeper. She had her way she be raptured up at the Secondt Coming. In the post-Armageddton future she move aroundt by rapturing from place to place. 'Course they be speed limits, no ectoplasmic excesses in the time/space o' da Rapture, since, you know, all acceleration be an attemp' on the mindt o' Godt, Einsteinian assault at the speed of light on original commodiousness.

"But why did I change the coda that for Mozart and Haydn were mere turns of tumblers in the final lock, why did I make it into *another development section* in so many of my works? Because faith is facilely affirmed in the Recapitulation…

"Shia, ain' even 'spose a be a change o' key, once you reach da Valhalla o' Return, the recap.

"He said his mule developed a kind of Buddhistic quietude. How fortunate for you, I said.

"'Yes,' he said, 'we are all fortunate. That God is good is shown in the three proofs of His benevolence: 1) provision of a paschal victim, 2) fermentation of grapes, 3) nymphomania. But He calls us gently to salvation with the vicissitudes of age. God sees but He waits – for us to grow old. Then He strikes. He weakens your wick after forty just to remind you who's in charge. His wisdom is subtle. He has given us openings at both ends and the task of having to distinguish, often failingly, the gaseous content issuing from one from that of the other, a burden having bent men to the confession of creeds. O, you have negative knowledge of Him, sinners, in the temporal futility go by da brandt Anguish™.'

"But that completes faith as well, the Recapitulation. And *falsifies* it as simple return. So I, I who have seen these things, I…

"'Say your name.'

"Ludwig van Beethoven.

"'I restored the essence of faith back into faith…'

"I restored the denseness of fate back into face…

"'By creating a new development section…'

"By negating a new vanilla confection…

"'In the coda.'

"In the soda.

"'State your name for the court, please.'

"Ludwig van Beasthaven.

"'Employment?'

"I'm sort of a free-lancer.

"'Occupation?'

"Technician of time management.

"'Job description?'

"Tone-thunderer.

"'Title?'

"Ear-warrior.

"'Duties?'

"I cage fleeing frequencies by way of bringing Godt's silence to Man.

"'Would that be, then, FM-modulator?'

"I am an adept in the trochees of triple rhythms. I have cracked the Euphonic Code.

"'Very well, Mr. Beasthaven. May the court then take you as the orderer of tonal universes by which the spirit of mankind is revealed in the highest?'

"Yeah.

"'Objection. My esteemed colleague is leading the witness.'

"'Overruled. You may proceed, Mr. Torquey.'

"'Thank you, your horror. Now, Mr. Beasthaven, are you married?'

"I'm sort of a free-lancer there, too. No pun intended, ho ho.

"'None taken. Address?'

"At large.

"'At Large? Is Large the halfway house?'

"Is small the halfway house. 'Large' is short for 'largesse.'

"'Method of transportation?'

"I tried astral projection for a while but found my ethereal body was tethered to a peg between my legs, a kind of kinetic prayer-stick that would sometimes itself arise as a projection, shriveling my astral body into it and releasing it in some unspoken but urgent hope that it would spatter into a pattern of itself…

"'Objection. The statement aspires to Barthelmeism.'

"'Overruled.'

"…sort of an Other to itself between which the relations of love and hate might obtain, tears variously salted with joy and frustration.

"'But instead you drove your nephew Karl to suicide, isn't that so, Mr. Hoven?'

"Negative. To near suicide, Mr. Mada. I wasn't through with him.

"'But astral projection failed? As a means of transportation?'

"Mostly I walk, I do the ankle-amble, the shoeful shuffle. It was cruel of God to give us feet and knowledge of feet. I leave an invisible spoor. I walk my shadow like a dog.

"'You are aware of the leash laws, Mr. Haven? The crap-scooping codicils?'

"Oh, the leash is most reliable, counselor, woven of the refused luminosity of solid shapes. Only the traffic lights track me, they stop me and release me in the pattern Fate has decreed for my bipedal progress. Locomotionally. Transportationally. Walkin' the walkily.

"'Very well. Do you swear to tell the opinion, the whole opinion and nothing but opinion?'

"That's the way I see it.

"'Has a dog a Buddha-nature?'

"A mule does, apparently.

"'Well, now, Mr. van Beethoven, I don't believe we're discussing mules.'

"What kind of dog?

"'What kind of dog do you know best, sir?'

"Da houndt o' faith. That heardt *not* the whistle o' Godt. Dat da kine o' dog.

"'What kind of god?'

"Da godt in DOGWHISTLE dat come out GOD WELSH IT when you run it through da descrambler. When you know da cote.

"Of course, the coda comes to an end and there is faith. But I supplied the final test of faith by making it *a second* development section, carrying cadence into credence. That's my motto. Praise the Lord and pass the admonition. Leave 'em devastated and ennobled. But be sure they pay you.

"'Witness has evaded the question, your onerousness.'

"Oh ho ho, *au contraire, mon frere;* it a damn geometric certainty, got Euclid writ all over it ass: if you say yes or no you lose your Buddhahoodt.

"So what are the mysteries?"

* * *

Had enough? O voyeurs, take note: I am not an inhospitable man, I crave the society of men, I who am *the tissue of their stares* – except for what belongs to gracious God, which is shadow in the darkness and thus inapparent, unclutchable by the claws of ego that instead close only on mind, steadily squeezing it into the vacuous light of self-knowledge.

But *nicht diese Töne!*

I've had enough of displaying my wound to you. You owe me! O, you rode my strange brain waves, you… you… *tourists* of the emotions, visiting where you would not live.

Could not live.

You, superior to street-crazies like I was, you who ride in the gondola of Reason tethered under the balloon heated and sent aloft by your passion for something to guarantee the dailiness of your world –

It a hot air balloon, my frien'.

You sinners of rectitude, of the straight and the ordinary, whom Beethoven redeemed in his suffering: *of course I am not he* – even he was not he until the world exalted him! – but I *consecrated his suffering* to you.

Tell me something back in return.

Wander the whorls of my fingertips, find the center of the maze I left long ago.

Tell me who's there now.

BOOK THREE

The Letter

Chapter One

In Vienna – August 2006

Martin Spratt sat in an open-air café on *Der Ring* in the late summer evening, not far from the *Nationalbibliothek* in Vienna. He had been waiting to have dinner with his colleague, Roger McKane, who was so late that Marty had not only ordered, but had eaten, dinner. His waiter had just left, and now he drank white wine. He knew the tardiness of his fellow musicologist would be worth the wait: Roger had stayed late at the hotel waiting for lab results to arrive on the complimentary fax machine. Wonderful hotel, thought Marty; wonderful people at the *Bibliothek*. In fact, it had been a wonderful time in Vienna, and he allowed himself the quite conscious vanity of feeling like a cosmopolitan player in an important drama – for he was a man on a mission, something like (he blushed at the silliness) a musicological James Bond, minus the Aston Martin, of course, and the homicidal license, the sultry beauties. At any rate, his research on *Der Freishűtz* was long over (what plodding *that* had been, he recalled a little ruefully) – small potatoes to tracking down the authenticity of a Beethoven letter.

Putative Beethoven letter. Actually, he mused over a mouthful of Riesling, not even putative; he had decided it was a fake.

He recalled Roger's recruitment of him for the project, musing over the conversation they'd first had about it, and that his colleague's incipient skepticism had been warranted.

"It's Eastwind's wishes," Marty remembered Roger had said, answering him. "He says he would like a very thorough investigation." They'd sat in the former's office at the Eastman School of Music.

"But what could we give him that Brixton's hasn't?"

"I've wondered about that, too. Something on the order of corroborating data. He wants to be sure."

"That may be impossible," said Marty. "I hope you told him that."

"I did. But he said he wants everything from watermark research to accounts of contemporaries if possible."

"But why us, Roger? The Rossini table thing?"

"He mentioned that. He said if he gets any fatter himself he'll have to have a table like that. Said he also was fascinated with historical detective work, dabbled as an amateur."

"But published nothing, I take it."

"His interest is more that of a collector. He has a number of autograph originals. Showed me a Reicha manuscript – well, a partial one – a quintet. A Chopin mazurka the various archives and museums have been hounding him about."

"The Chopin is interesting. Is that all?"

"You know," Roger said, "the man is odd, enigmatic. Drops hints. But unflinching eye-contact. Striking features. Moves from one thought to the next, absolutely dominating a conversation. He expects you to connect all the dots instantly."

"Hmm. Well, one thing's certain. He's offering us enough. As authentications go."

"And, too, don't forget the articles we can get out of it."

"Not to rest on our laurels. You have tenure, but there's still me," Marty allowed; an Englishman, he felt a slight grammatical ambivalence in the last phrase.

"You know," Roger went on, "the travel allowance he's giving us doesn't restrict us – you – just to Beethoven. You could visit the Vienna *Nationalbibliothek* for your von Weber piece."

"I think the *Freischűtz* project has fired its last round," Marty replied. "But, you know, looking into this letter could open up all sorts of projects. A veritable wealth. And not just academically; who among music lovers isn't interested in the 'Immortal Beloved' thing?"

"You're right. And even just ordinary people, after the movie about Beethoven's love life."

"You've seen the actual letter?" Marty asked.

"Held it in my hands. He made me wash them first."

"Understandable. Give me something of an exact translation."

"Well, as I said, a note to Count Lichnowsky. Like, 'I have returned from the waters' – you know, the Karlsbad springs – 'but can barely think of composing so strong are visions of my Immortal Beloved, who met me there, and who is ready to end her maiden years in marriage to me.' Something like, 'Though you must hold it in the strictest of confidences, our betrothal lights my way almost as my muse in the B-major work…' Then a few details about having some of the count's men help move him to his new place. That's about it. The handwriting seems to be perfectly Beethoven's. Especially the signature."

"Hmm," Marty hummed again, "and Eastwind doubts the thing?"

"I doubt the thing. How many instances are there of Beethoven actually using the phrase 'Immortal Beloved' except in the original letter to her, the one in the archives?"

"Probably none."

"And then there's Solomon's research. About the Immortal Beloved's identity," Roger added. "You know about that, of course."

"I certainly do," Marty replied. "In fact I'm teaching it in the Romantic Transition course next term. That's right – 'maiden years' raises some questions if Solomon is right. Is that why Eastwind is having us investigate it?"

"Eastwind…" Roger began, trying to be accurate, "Eastwind is a very thorough man. He showed me the architectural plans for a house he's just had built. He helped design it, and it lacks nothing; everything was figured out, down to the depth of the pool where he can still reach up to the bottom shelf of the veranda bar. An exacting man. And, don't forget," Roger added, "he paid seventy-five thousand dollars for it."

"A scrap of paper with Beethoven's signature on it."

"With Beethoven's childlike scrawl, laboring for open 'E's', the little serif flourishes."

"So much scratched ink – seventy-five thousand dollars," Marty marveled.

"Ink scratched by the hand that placed all those little blots and squiggles harboring the sounds of angels. Or at least the best of humanity."

"You held it in your hands, Roger?"

"Ever so lightly."

"So when do we get it for the tests?"

"He required that we have adequate security," Roger said. "A wall safe, mainly."

"Then we get it?"

"For a while."

"May I hold it, just one time?" Marty asked.

"Remember, it might not be the real thing."

* * *

And now, sitting at his table waiting for Roger, Marty thought it was not the real thing. Not that the trip hadn't been worth it. He glanced up and out at the busy sidewalk, with its river of businessmen, students, the random parade in which, he noted, there were some striking *fräulein*. He noticed a shape that seemed not to hear the drummer of the moving ensemble of *Volk*, a man walking only as Americans do. A face came into view, almost following the heavy, framed glasses that seemed to float out ahead of it, much as a bumper goes before the moving vehicle. Behind the thick frames someone recognizable materialized. Marty waved from his sidewalk table, and the man, holding a briefcase in a way that suggested important contents, came over.

"Have you ordered, Marty?" Roger asked. "Sorry to be late. The faxes didn't get in from the Zurich lab until a little while ago."

"I have. I've even eaten. But the service is excellent here. Our waiter should be round shortly."

"Good. Great service and better Schnitzel, I hear." Roger took a seat to the left of his colleague.

"I had the Schnitzel," Marty said. "A well-deserved reputation." After Roger had made himself comfortable, he casually asked, "And the faxes?"

"Interesting. Very much so." Roger opened the briefcase.

"Well?"

"Well, it's not a yes-or-no thing on the surface. The watermark is one-hundred percent. The paper is authentic. It's the ink, according to the lab boys."

"In what way?"

"Well, take a look." Roger reached into his briefcase and handed him some documents. "It has to do with certain… impurities. Twentieth century molecules mixed in with nineteenth, you see. A certain ferrous coefficient that raises red flags."

Marty looked up from the papers. "Ferrous? As in metal?"

"As in a tool that might have been used to scrape dried ink off a nineteenth-century manuscript – from which to make a reconstituted ink. For that matter, there are molecules pointing to a recombinant fluid – a light oil base – that probably wasn't around in Beethoven's day," Roger said.

The waiter approached with a menu, and Roger ordered a glass of Riesling.

"But this is not conclusive evidence the letter is a forgery?" Marty asked.

"According to them, suspicions are in order. But they said the judgment was up to us."

"Oh, that's helpful," Marty allowed.

"And of course the *Bibliotheken* gave us absolutely nothing that we didn't already know. But that's not the main thing, now. The main thing now is your research on Solomon's theory."

"Here, their not giving us something we didn't already know is far more conclusive, as I am ready to argue – though also trivial, I've been thinking," Marty said. "But as a matter of fact, if there's some question as to the physical properties of the thing there's a greater one about the content."

"There's simply no squaring of the 'Immortal Beloved' with our letter, is there, if we take Solomon seriously."

"After everything I've been through in the archives, I back Solomon's detective work a hundred percent, for whatever that's worth. The 'Immortal Beloved' was Antonie Brentano. The 'Immortal Beloved' letter is to her. No question in my mind," Marty said.

"So here's what we're going to have to tell Eastwind," Roger said, after a moment's reflection. "Beethoven never sent the original 'Immortal Beloved' letter, though it was meant to go to her at the Karlsbad springs. And our letter – Eastwind's letter – expressly mentions them as 'the waters,' from which he is returning, after seeing his inamorata there. So whoever wrote it knew about that."

"Right."

"So we tell Eastwind, but, look, whoever wrote this letter tips his hand with a very crude mistake: Antonie Brentano was married, and the writer speaks of her as 'ready to end her maiden years,'" Roger added. The waiter brought him his wine.

"Of course," said Marty, sipping from his glass thoughtfully. "But, you know, Roger," he added with a frown, "what I've been thinking is that that in itself is hardly proof that the letter is a fake. Why would Beethoven reveal to anyone that the love of his life was a married woman? He tells Lichnowsky he's in love, but covers up the distasteful truth of who it is with this little subterfuge. Simply invoking Solomon is ludicrous as a proof of the letter's phoniness."

"I had thought of that," Roger said. "That occurred to me as I was walking here, after the faxes suggested we take another route on the authenticity of it."

The waiter showed up and Roger ordered the Schnitzel. The two researchers drank a bit in silence. Then Roger said:

"Well, you know, Marty, our work is over, here. Both of us think the letter's a fake. We'll inform Eastwind that, in our considered, professional assessment, he got taken."

"That's true," Marty said. "A shame, though. It's letdown enough that it's not the real thing; worse, we end our great wanderings on expense account."

"Too bad for Eastwind. As far as we're concerned, the greater pain is having to go home. Well, at least we have articles to write. You're sure to get tenure."

"Oh, probably," Marty answered, a little absently. "But will Eastwind accept our conclusions? We really don't have a prima facie case that our professional opinion is valid."

"Good point. But we've been very thorough. Everywhere from the Frankfurt *Stadtarchiv* to the *Deutsche Staatsbibliothek* in Berlin. Münster and Mainz, the *Beethovenhaus* in Bonn. That should grant us some credibility, I would hope."

Marty thought for a moment. "Say, Roger," he said, "have you ever considered how Eastwind got the letter? I mean, if it is a forgery, there should be a trail, shouldn't there?"

"You mean, how Brixton's got it? From whom?"

"Precisely."

"Well," Roger said, after a reflection of a few seconds, "finding that out might constitute even more thorough research on the part of two academics, one of whom might be in an even better position for tenure." He looked at Marty with the beginnings of a sly smile, a face bordering on wryness. "And we certainly could present a conclusive case to Eastwind if we traced and identified the forger."

"I presume Brixton's has all the documentation. They certainly considered it authentic," Marty allowed, noting the look from Roger.

"Of course," said the other, "but the documentation must have been forged as well. And the lab they used mistaken."

"Just so." Marty smiled back at Roger. "Why, I think we have a responsibility to pursue every avenue of the investigation."

"We certainly do," Roger said, slightly exaggerating for effect. "We're obliged to pay a visit to Brixton's, examine their records."

"Leaving Vienna for London is a hard proposition," Marty said with intended irony.

"Then I'm going to enjoy this meal just a bit more. Why don't you order some dessert – something Viennese, sumptuous, celebratory?" He signaled the waiter.

"Heigh ho," Marty replied, raising his wine glass and feeling more like a player in an international drama. In his mind he floated the line, "The name is Spratt. Martin Spratt," and felt foolish again; not much of a Bondish ring to that, was there? To Roger he said, "I'm British, but I haven't been to London in over a decade. To London it is."

"In the service of a rich patron, to boot," added Roger.

"Yes," said Marty, "we're giving him his money's worth. He wants the truth, and he's paying for it. But where does he get his money?"

Chapter Two

Brixton's

Corey Harrison was not pleased when his secretary told him of the inquiry by the two musicologists. As he finished reading their fax at his desk, he looked away with vague concern, hearing the first strains of dismay. He reviewed in his mind the various past assaults on the reputation of the auction house, with his experts called to give courtroom testimony in the inevitable lawsuits. Actually, he'd always felt the press had done Brixton's more good than harm in that the reported testimony portrayed the honesty behind the errors, showing the house in its best light, despite the scandals. And now he wondered: what went wrong? Perhaps the conclusions of McKane and Spratt about Eastwind's letter were at fault here; the documentation he'd received three years ago had been impeccable. And yet they indicated they had been more thorough than what had convinced Brixton's. Brixton's? Who was kidding whom? He knew full well that he alone had authorized the sale of the letter. But certainly the two men were professionals, with professional reputations – indeed, their names were familiar to him – so they were probably on to something. Maybe not, but probably so.

At any rate, he reflected, we have to let them see everything we have. He pushed a button on his phone and spoke to his secretary. "Patricia, would you reply to the researchers on the Beethoven letter? Yes, please tell them you've spoken with me and that they are welcome to review our documents." He listened a moment, then replied, "No, no, dear. I don't need to do anything now; this will be your response. Yes. Thank you." He put down the phone and thought a moment, then ambled across the room toward the files of past transactions. West Indian by birth, he had become fascinated with historical artifacts while finishing a degree in history at Yale, and had moved to the United Kingdom, where he knew people of color were treated better, generally, than in the United States, to pursue his affair with the past; postgraduate work at Oxford had afforded him the credentials eventually to head up Brixton's.

The two filing cabinets, sturdy, gray pillars, had once struck him as twin monoliths to antiquity, the great keepers of the past, as stolid and uninteresting as gray could make them lest they draw attention to themselves and not their precious holdings; for what they contained was the chronicle of items manufactured in a past from out of which the present had emerged – as dependent as a child on its parents, though equally as rebellious. What Brixton's did, he'd ruminated on that occasion, was a kind of practical genealogy of the present, ancillary in character to the work of historians. He opened the top drawer; the folder tabs jutted up, announcing the paperwork behind the icons and secular relics of that past, totems which, with perhaps the magic of fetishism, could draw history into the present by the draft of their mere physical existence. Then he realized he wasn't in the music drawer, and pushed the file back.

The proper drawer included composers' names in alphabetical order. "Berlioz" – ah, yes; the manuscript of the *Messe*, a youthful indiscretion. But it had brought a high price, though more a mess than Mass when performed. He overshot the nearest tabs, his eyes landing on "Rossini"; that had been a funny item: the table with a half-moon cut out of it for the composer's great girth, so he could at least reach the food he had apparently loved so. A distant chime in his mind brought forth a name connected with that one; no, a pair of names. Exactly, he recalled now: Spratt and McKane. He certainly had trusted their research then.

His eyes went to "Reicha" – not a big seller, though the manuscripts had not, comparatively, been that high-priced; indeed, wasn't it Eastwind who had bought so many of them a few decades ago? He glanced back up the tabs. "Mozart": a couple of quills supposedly used on the *Requiem*, collected by those present at his death. On to "Janácek," up to "Hummel," then to "Haydn" (it really was his wig, he thought to himself – well, probably; authentication had been one-hundred percent, which, he mused, most likely meant no more than about a fifty-percent certitude); "Gounod," "Franck" – a lot of stuff there – then a skip to "Delius"; ah, "Chopin," a thick folder detailing the sales of everything from original manuscripts to articles of his clothing. The spittoon thing had been an obvious fake, the item manufactured after 1849, as its fluting revealed.

And then, past "Berlioz," "Beethoven." Recently the score of the *Ninth*, though in a copyist's hand; regardless, it had been enough that the great man had appended comments in the margins, sometimes some very nasty ones about the copyist's ability. And then, lo, the letter to Lichnowsky about "the B-major work," with him commenting on his lovesickness for the Immortal Beloved. Yes, yes.

Harrison pulled the file, and returned to his desk.

* * *

Spratt and McKane wired Eastwind that their researches in Vienna were ended, and that they needed further funding for a stay in London; he hated telephones, Eastwind, and so the relatively primitive methods, by comparison, of Western

Union had to suffice. A telegram came back to the hotel with a money order of £5,000, and a single word: "Persevere."

"Interesting," said Roger, on their plane into Heathrow, "that he didn't even ask what we had found in Vienna."

"Or even where we had looked," rejoined Marty.

"His strange ways aren't new to us. At least we have more time – and luxury," Roger said. "I've always adored London."

After settling in at the Regency, and waiting a day, Marty called Brixton's.

"And what is it specifically you're looking for, if I may ask? It might be helpful to know ahead of time for our meeting," Corey Harrison said on the phone. "I'm afraid there isn't much of a trail beyond Metropolitan University of New York. In fact, I was thinking your researches might be more profitable simply by your going to their music department."

Marty considered this, but flashed on his nostalgia for London and, too, Roger's love of the city. "I do appreciate your forwardness, Mr. Harrison…"

"Oh, please. Just Corey. You might remember me from your researches on the Rossini table."

"I do indeed. But I do think it would serve Mr. Eastwind best if we were uh, as thorough as possible."

"I understand," he said. "So you'll be round about eleven? Would you care to have lunch?"

"That's an excellent suggestion. I've been away a long time; I don't even know what fare is offered these days. But let me ask Roger."

"Very well," Harrison replied. "Perhaps my files do have something for you – and our cuisine as well."

"That's good of you," Marty said in a kind of closing cadence. "See you at eleven."

He hung up the phone and reported the conversation to Roger.

* * *

In Harrison's office the next day the two musicologists, seated at a low table with the man hovering behind, scrutinized the contents of the folder. There was a facsimile of the letter, and a statement by the Municipal University of New York Department of Music testifying to the authenticity of it as established by an American team of researchers.

"Hmph," allowed Roger, "not a very good choice for confirmation, that group."

"Oh," said Harrison, "you know something about them?"

"They're not the sharpest pencils in the drawer," he said. "They've let some things slip by that better labs have caught. They did Haydn's wig, which in my opinion could never have been authenticated without a DNA analysis on his hair. There's a lock of it out there."

"I see," Harrison said. "Of course."

"It's one of the reasons we didn't use them. The Zurich lab was much more thorough than they ever would have been. I even doubt they use spectrographic analysis."

"Well, of course, it's Swiss versus American. I thank you for the copies of that report," Harrison said. "If there's a lawsuit from Eastwind, we can claim American incompetence. No offense."

"None taken."

"Say, Roger," Marty chimed in, "what's this about the concert promoter? The chairman of the department seems to want to take credit for finding the letter, but if you read between the lines this man, Salmaninski, seems to be the real discoverer here."

"Yes, as a matter of fact I had noticed that," Roger said. "But it's not clear he's the one making the claim of finding it among the surviving artifacts of the fire."

"Yes, the house; that's a weak point," Marty went on, "the house, supposedly belonging to a German émigré, burned down because it was a wooden hovel. A man with a treasure like that could have bought a house with something like real property value."

"I suppose the New York Fire Department could verify the fire," Roger allowed.

"Well," Harrison added, "is that really a weak point? There are eccentrics out there living in reduced circumstances, with perhaps a Rembrandt in the cellar. They might not even know it. Or perhaps he cherished it beyond monetary value."

"I see your point," Marty said. "It just strikes me as a little too convenient – a *German* émigré, not named, by the way; a letter discovered in the smoldering ruins, somehow untouched by smoke – and smoke was notably not mentioned in both the lab reports. And on top of it all – oh, wild happenstance – it's a letter Beethoven wrote in 1812, if the research is correct on the date of the Immortal Beloved affair. Why would someone of the chairman's standing pretend not to notice things like that? Red flags abound."

Roger said, "It might be that he hints at the involvement of this Salmaninski as a way out of responsibility. You know, something like, 'He said, and I believed.'"

"And you have nothing more, Corey? There are no further documents?" Marty asked.

"All you have is all I've ever had," he responded, with a little shrug and a smile that were meant to convey exoneration.

"Then I think our business here is concluded. You've been very kind," Marty, rising, said to the man.

"Yes," added Roger, standing with him, "very good to us."

"Thank you, gentlemen. But let's not forget lunch," Harrison said. "My expense, please."

"Good of you," Marty said, "but thanks to your directness and the paucity of the material here, it looks like our stay will be shortened – which means our expense account allows a bit of lavishness, wouldn't you say, Roger?"

"Eastwind's being very generous," Roger said. "Won't you let us treat you?"

Chapter Three

New York

Spratt and McKane left London a few days after their interview with Corey Harrison and flew to New York. Roger had an apartment there, and insisted that Marty stay with him. Once they had settled in they set up an interview with Leonard Salmaninski, who, they discovered, was not full-time faculty at MUNY, though he did teach a course in Modern Music there. The chairman of the music department was on sabbatical, but the acting department head gave them Salmaninski's phone number.

After contacting Salmaninski, the musicologists did some more detective work. City records confirmed that there had been a fire destroying an old house, one of the few turn-of-the-century wooden frames, in the late nineteen-nineties. The records had indeed stated it belonged to one Augustus Heidemann, who had died in the fire. An interview with the fire department in that borough also confirmed that many objects, mainly from the attic, had been damaged by neither fire, smoke, nor water.

The day after the researchers had confirmed the account of events given to Brixton's the three met on the MUNY campus and went to an office Salmaninski used; actually, it was little more than a cubicle in a large room for adjunct faculty. They found that Marty had been right that Salmaninski was the sole discoverer of the letter. Supposed discoverer.

Marty noted that the man was tall and just a bit stocky, with hair that was long enough to be a kind of belated socio-political statement. His manner struck him as someone who was aware of a certain moral taint that he had resolved to forget, Marty reflected, then chastised himself for being so judgmental.

"It really was just sheer luck," Salmaninski was saying, "just sheer luck – I've always been lucky, Polish, but with the luck of the Irish, maybe we had an Irish milkman, ha ha – but, yeah, I just happened to see the fire department there, at this blaze that'd destroyed most of the old house. And let me ask you, if you saw a group of nineteenth-century artifacts lying on the ground, untouched by the calamity…"

"But how did you know the century?" Marty asked.

"Oh, come on. You know you'd recognize the kind of ornamentation on a snuff box, say, or even the kind of thing – like, say, a snuff box itself – as belonging to a previous century."

"I suppose so."

"Sure you would. And that's when I saw the box – just an ordinary box that, say, a watch would come in, and about the same size. I still have it by the way – well, of course, I suppose it could be construed as looting, but it was just curiosity at that point.

"I opened the box to find a piece of thick paper, folded in four. I don't read German, and besides, the handwriting looked indecipherable, but the signature was unmistakable."

"Ludwig van Beethoven," said Roger.

"Ludwig van Beethoven," said Salmaninski. "Your lab work is just wrong. What can I say?" He was holding his arms up and out in a gesture of bafflement.

"Actually, we consider it inconclusive, cautionary," Marty said.

"Man, it blew me away. Of course, at first I was skeptical too," Salmaninski added.

"Then what did you do?" asked Roger. "After all, the letter wasn't yours to keep. It still belonged to the Heidemann estate."

"Right you are. And because I knew you'd ask, I brought the newspaper with my ad asking for relatives of Herr Heidemann, or anyone knowing any of them, to contact me. 'Course I didn't say why." He presented them with the pages from the *Times* classified ads, dating back a year and a half after the fire. "It ran for a whole month."

Roger and Marty perused the ad.

"Of course I got a lot of responses from nuts and cranks, but I did actually hear from a Heidemann or two; as it turned out, they had no idea of Augustus, of the house fire, or any possible location for any relatives. And look," Salmaninski went on, "because I'm above board on this – I know you don't, but I trust the lab work the university had done on the letter – I'm still willing to give any real heir or relative of any sort a good portion of the proceeds from the sale, what's left of it – less my commission as finder, so to speak – if anyone turns up and can prove a direct relation to Heidemann. I'm an honorable man."

"And after waiting, you contacted Brixton's," Roger said.

"Not right away. The college dawdled over it for a few years, then sent it to the lab, which kept it longer than it should have. Then it came back, and I got in touch with Brixton's. Their estimate of what it would go for on the auction block kind of made me agree to put it up."

"And that's when you made a contract with Brixton's," Marty said.

"I did," Salmaninski said, "but I felt I should go through my home base – the university."

The two musicologists looked at each other. Roger said, "I guess that's all."

Marty said, "Thank you, uh… is it Dr. Salmaninski?"

"Ahh, just call me Lenny. You know, like Bernstein. I explain music too, like he did."

"Well, we do thank you," Roger said. "You understand, we had to interview you, given the doubts… uh, the hesitations, of the Zurich lab."

"Aah, forget it. The Swiss can't help being anal," he said, a quantum more casual in his manner now, almost brash Brooklyn. "I know, it's a great find, and we're talkin' a lotta money heah (Roger noted shift in pronunciation). You gotta be sure."

"That's our commission," Roger replied.

"By the way, you guys into modern music? My Atonal Subscription Series meets tonight. It's always under-attended, even though it's like top-flight. Maybe that's some kinda comment on the tastes of New Yorkers, huh? You dig Stockhausen?"

"Alas," said Marty, "I'm afraid, that is …we have a conference call scheduled tonight."

"With the guy who wanted the letter checked out, right? Tell him he's got a treasure all his own there." Marty and Roger thanked him for meeting with them as they shook hands, then left the room and began walking down the corridor. Salmaninski leaned against the door jamb and watched them, watched until the door at the end of the long hall opened, and then shut.

* * *

That night, over dinner in a downtown restaurant, Roger said to Marty: "He's lying through his teeth."

"Was it that obvious?" Marty asked, a little taken aback at this assessment.

"No. The mark of a good liar is the absolute appearance of veracity in what he's saying."

"The same could be said of someone who's telling the truth."

"Well, sure. That's why lying is possible, I suppose. No, it wasn't obvious. But deep down in that man there's nothing but sleaze. Did you notice how his manner, his voice, his way of speaking changed after we appeared to believe him?"

"Well, yes," said Marty. "It struck me as curious."

"It struck me as revealing. You *were* only appearing to believe him, I'm sure."

"Actually," Marty began after a moment's consideration, "it's not that I believed him. It's just that he made me wonder if we can be so sure that the letter *is* a fake. After all, Solomon's theory is only a theory. There's no way to prove absolutely that it's true."

"That's right," Roger said.

"Solomon wasn't *there*. And we weren't there either."

"That's right," Roger said again. "But there might be a way of proving that Salmaninski is a bunko artist."

"Like what?"

"The thing is," he said, cutting into the steak on his plate, "I still think his story is bogus as hell. As you said to Harrison, it's oh-so-convenient, all the facts just happening to cohere into the picture he'd have us accept."

"Yes," replied the other, "but look. Here's what plunges us into the Valley of Decision: the facts might be convenient, as I said, but be so because Salmaninski's story is *true*. Because if it were true, these things *would* appear as they do – even down to the émigré being German. And we've certainly had confirmation on the fire, and the house's unfortunate owner. All we can ever have here is appearance."

"Surely you're not saying appearance is reality."

"No. Of course not," Marty said, reaching for the bread plate, and adding slyly, "I'm not a postmodernist. You heard my lie to get out of the Stockhausen. We're both of us philistines."

"But you doubt your own acceptance of Solomon?"

"Deep down I don't. But the surest road to self-delusion is a lack of self-doubt," Marty said, somewhat mournfully. "Let's just say I'm on a camping trip in the Valley. I hope it's only an over-nighter."

There was a silence between the two men as they ate. Maybe the thing, Eastwind's quest, was getting old, if not already having clattered into a cul-de-sac. For that matter, Marty missed his wife. Roger, a little older and married longer, missed his Newfoundland. And they both had to be back for the fall semester at Eastman.

At length, Roger said, "Well, here's the deal, as I see it: we tell Eastwind that we consider the letter a fake, as we decided in Vienna, but that our attempts at finding out its origins, including, as we hoped, who the forger was, have come to naught. But before we do, there're two things I want to do. I want to see if Salmaninski has any kind of record of flim-flam…"

"A criminal record."

"Right. Because there was no reason for him to hand over to MUNY what would have been a coup for himself alone. I mean, if you found something like that, would you run to Eastman? No, I think he knew he couldn't try to go it alone if he had a record; he needed a cover of respectability."

"I see."

"Probably, if I'm right, that would explain the tentative character of, what's-his-name, the chairman's, statement."

"Right."

"And, two, I want to visit the site of the fire."

"The fire that burned away the present," said Marty, "to make a gift of the past. According to Salmaninski."

"That's how it appears."

"Just so," said Marty. "And lest we forget: persevere."

"Perseverance," said Roger, with not a little mockery, raising his glass, "is my middle name, as difficult as that is for the Driver's License people."

* * *

"I suppose we could have predicted it would have been built over," Roger said when they arrived at the site of the fire, according to fire department records. They asked their cabbie to wait, then took in the Bowery, less bleak than in former times, but still showing some kinship to those days. They spent a little time walking around.

"Certainly the right part of town to have been the location of a dilapidated building," Marty allowed, after a while. "I've already turned away two panhandlers. Putting up a homeless shelter makes a lot of sense. But how were they able to build on the property?"

"Perfectly legal, if abandoned for so many years. And no one had a lead on Heidemann's heirs. So the city got it."

"So Salmaninski's story checks out again."

A black man with a white cane was tapping by them, but slowed a bit. "Well," said Roger, "there's still Salmaninski himself to check out." The man suddenly said, "Whoa," and stopped. "Less try re-verse." He jerked the cane around as if it were a gearshift; the tip behind him, he stepped confidently back a few paces while making the "beep… beep… beep" of a truck backing up.

Roger turned to him. "Sorry, my man, " he said, "I'm about out of money."

"Not axin' fo' no money. You lookin' fo' da music man?"

"We don't need any street musicians right now," Roger said, rolling his eyes at Marty. "But look, have a nice day."

"Shia, you tellin' a bline man a look? Don' need a look, I kin hear-see ya. Ear-Braille ya."

"Excuse me," Marty said, "did you mention a music man?"

"Dint you say Samminski da Polecat?"

Roger and Marty looked at each other. Roger said to the man, "Have you eaten? Would you like some lunch?"

"Ah, man," he said, "your finances bein' what they is 'n' all…"

Soon the three were in the taxi, headed uptown. As they rode, Roger and Marty introduced themselves. "Bline Boy Eddy," said their guest, "I's da one widdout eyes."

At the restaurant – nothing expensive, and open-air – and after they were about halfway into the meal, Roger said, "No free lunches. You've got to tell us everything you know. About Salmaninski."

"You not cops?"

"No. It's just that we're checking out a very important letter he sold to an auction house. A lot of money was involved."

"He da one foundt dat letter. A pretty goodt take on dat one. You know da cat?"

"We've made his acquaintance," Marty said. "We know about the scam."

"Don' know 'bout no scam."

"Did he find the letter where we ran into you? Where the old house that burned down used to be? You know, the shelter now?" Roger asked.

"I mean, now lunch be one thing. But a boy gotta think aheadt, you know. Into da future. But I knows a damn lunch be 'bout all you can affordt."

Roger remembered the technique detectives in movies used with street informers. He got out a twenty. "Oh, my wife has a job," he said nonchalantly as he put the twenty in Bline Boy's hand. "That's a twenty."

"No shia. Not only it be a twenny, it one o' dem new twennies."

Marty said, "So you have partial vision?"

Bline Boy leaned back in his chair, snickering. A woman behind him looked back disapprovingly, and scooted her chair forward. "Yeah," he said, "yeah, I got vision partial to money," and laughed a chortling chuckle.

"So what can you tell us? Did Salmaninski ever talk to you?" Roger asked.

"Many a time, my man, he be a frien' of a frien'."

"Did he tell you where he found the letter? Was it where I asked you about?"

"Yep."

Roger looked disappointedly at Marty, who shrugged and looked away. They all took a bite of their food; fish sandwiches for the musicologists, a Reuben sandwich with coleslaw for Bline Boy, who was finishing his lunch.

"Yeah, but dey don' call it no shelter, it a, whut-do-dey-call-it – a halfway house fo' screet people. Been dere fo'ever. Still dere, righ'?"

"Right," said Roger, almost skipping a heartbeat. "That's where he found the letter?"

"Yeah, man. In Ludi Vann's room after he done relapsed an' dey foundt 'im direckin' traffic."

"'Ludi Vann'? And who would that be?" Roger asked, with a look to Marty.

"He a frien' o' mine. He be on da screets a long time. Knew 'im in 'Lanna befo' dat. Got to know da Polecat widh him. He was Ludi's frien', done got his nose bustedt for tryin' to he'p 'im."

Roger shot a puzzled look to Marty, who said, "How was he trying to help him – this 'Vann' individual?"

"Shia, you a Brit, ain' you? Dass okay. We all foreigners here," he said chortling to himself. "But you know, man," he said, turning to Roger, "I couldt be mistaken 'bout dat twenny. It a fifty, ain' it? Good oldt Grant, a boy fondt o' da Nectah Espress too." Roger peeled off a ten and another twenty and handed the bills to Bline Boy.

"Well, as I was sayin'," he went on, "da Polecat he do music fo' da collich, 'n' he put on some o' Ludi Vann's stuff."

"So this guy, Ludi Vann, was a composer? A musician?" Roger asked.

"You know, he be dee composer, in his damn sadt headt."

"*The* composer?"

"Shia, don' know no white guy not heardt o' Beethoven."

Marty and Roger stared at the man, then at each other. Marty said, "Beethoven? He was… Beethoven? How could that be?"

"It be in his mindt, man. Da cat was crazy but brillian'. It be true, you know, fo' him. He lived it. I like humoredt 'im, cause dey ain' no talkin' 'im oudt it."

"And that's where Salman… the Polecat got the letter? Found it in this Beethoven guy's room at the halfway house?" Roger asked.

"You dint hear it fum me, man. See, he tol' me 'bout it befo' he got da dollah signs in his eyes, den tells me don' say nothin'." After a moment, he said, "Man, dey got desser' here, whatcha wanna bet?"

Roger signaled the waitress. "Why are you telling us about it now?" he asked.

"See, Ludi Vann be a frien' o' mine. We pals. I got to thinkin' he couldta soldt it hisse'f. But da Polecat got da letter firs', when Ludi not home. Done rip off his frien'."

"So where is he now," Marty asked, "this Beethoven brought to life? You said he got sick? He relapsed?"

"Dey take 'im to, you know, Bellevue. But, man, he be gone fum dere a long time ago. Usta visit 'im. But he outta dere. Never saw 'im again." He paused. "Dey maidt 'im better."

After a moment, Roger asked, "A white guy?"

"He white but he think he black. He saidt all men be bruthahs."

After lunch they returned Bline Boy to where they'd picked him up. He got out of the cab, and touched Roger's arm and face.

"Ain' tol' you nuthin', now. 'Member."

"Don't worry," Roger said. "But don't tell me one more thing: how did this Ludi Vann get the letter?"

Bline Boy chuckled. They heard the tap of his cane. "Shia," he said, "I tol' you da cat was brillian'."

* * *

The two musicological detectives knew where to go next: the property records for the borough where the halfway house stood. They found it was owned by the Society of Friends of New York; contacting them, they got the names of Brett and Ann Yearly. Ann Yearly was still doing social work as a Quaker, they learned from the director, but was now located in Nyack. Bellevue could tell them nothing about the man who'd gone by "Ludi Vann."

The men spoke to a secretary for the Society of Friends in Nyack and got Ann Yearly's phone number. She said she would meet with them.

They sat at her kitchen table in her modest house, drinking coffee. She told them about the strange charge at the halfway house who had suffered the delusion of being Beethoven. But it was long ago, she said, and told them what Sepulveda had told her at their last meeting: whoever Ludi Vann was was out in the world, with crucial parts of his memory never recovered. He was better, and she'd heard he'd completed a Ph.D. and done well in computer technology somewhere. She'd lost contact with Sepulveda, and, once, she said, when she'd tried to find out where "Ludi Vann" was working, she was told there was no record of that in the files the psychiatrist had left behind. If anyone ever learned his true name, it was kept from her.

"You wanted to find him? Why?" asked Marty.

Ann looked away. "Oh," she said, taking a breath, "it was just something that never got cleared up."

"Ah," said Marty.

"My husband fell down the stairs and died of a broken neck, and I always wondered if Ludi had any… any knowledge of it. But I never found out."

"How dreadful. I'm so sorry," Marty said.

"Terrible. I'm sorry," Roger said.

"I think I'm over it. Though sometimes I think I'm not. But I'm a strong woman." She turned to them. "Why are you looking for him?"

Roger said, "We're on a commission from a man who bought a letter reputed to be that of Beethoven. It was found by a man named Salmaninski…"

"I knew that man," Ann interjected. "He knew Ludi, came to see him at the house."

"Yes," said Roger, "we know. We talked to a blind black man…"

"Blind Boy. So he's still around."

"…who told us that Salmaninski told him he'd found it in Ludi Vann's room."

Ann was shocked. "Well, I mean," she said with a little laugh, "he was a kind of expert on Beethoven, in a crazy way. But having a real letter…"

"The letter is a forgery," Marty said. "At least, we think so."

Ann's eyes went to the side. She looked out the window, her face bearing the traces of mind searching memory. "And I know who forged it," she said.

"Really," Roger said, with a note of excitement to his voice, "someone working with Ludi Vann?"

"No. Ludi worked alone. My husband told me that he was copying out Beethoven's handwriting, and that the copy was indistinguishable from the original."

The researchers contemplated this. "So," said Roger to Marty, "we have our forger."

"Only we don't," said the other.

"He was planning the scam all along," Roger said, a man having a revelation, "with Salmaninski."

"You're wrong there," Ann said. "Ludi was incapable of dishonesty. Everything was true for him, including himself. He was copying out Beethoven's 'Immortal Beloved' letter – yes, I know about that – because he was, the Beethoven he was, was in love with me. My husband told me about it. He was rewriting it to me, with my name instead of the name Beethoven wrote in the original. That's how he learned Beethoven's hand."

"And what he applied to the letter we have," Roger said. "That's why we never questioned the handwriting. Or signature."

"My god, Brett warned me." She stopped, short of breath; this was not a new thought, but the logic of it hit her as if it had been forged in the shop of the solar plexus. "And I didn't listen."

Roger and Marty felt awkward, could think of nothing to say.

"I'm okay," she said. "But look, if you find him, please, please let me know. You promise?"

"Certainly," said Marty. "But it looks pretty hopeless. Is there anything you can think of that might help us find him? You never heard the name of the computer business he's in? No brand names? Anything like that?"

Ann shook her head.

"Any scrap of information, anything at all that you might have saved from his room – relatives, phone numbers, any stray jottings of addresses?" asked Roger.

"I never knew of any relatives. And no."

"Any idea where he finished his doctorate?" Marty asked.

"No. I just heard he had, from one of his street friends. A guy they called 'Gentleman Jimmy,' or something like that. But I'm pretty sure he left the city."

"Anything else that you might have heard?" Roger asked.

Ann thought for a moment. "Well, nothing specific. I did hear about him some time after I stopped visiting him at the asylum – I mean, it had to be him – no, it was something I saw in the *Times*. Or maybe it was some magazine. *Newsday*. It was in *Newsday.*"

"*Newsday* wrote about him?" Roger asked.

"No. Not about him. Well, not directly, with his name and all. Just a minute," she said, leaving the room. "I still have it. It was an article about a movie that had a schizophrenic character in it."

She returned with an old article about a made-for-TV movie with James Garner and James Woods. "I thought of Ludi when this actor said he'd researched a role where he was a schizophrenic – yeah, look – James Woods. See, he hung out with the street schizophrenics for a while." She pointed to a circled paragraph. "This was probably Ludi – don't you think?"

The two read:

> "They're highly intelligent, most of them," Woods related. "I spent some time with a man who is working on his Ph.D. Before his illness was brought under control he thought he was Beethoven. He said he looks back on that period as the happiest in his life."

Chapter Four

Los Angeles

Aboard the plane, aloft and heading west, the two men speculated between themselves on what James Woods might be able to tell them. The truth was that they felt a little guilty about the trip; both knew they probably could have simply called the actor's agent, gotten his number, and talked with him by phone. But Roger, who had assumed the head role in the investigation with Marty's tacit consent, didn't like Eastwind; he had found his mien, as the terms of the investigation were being worked out, to be that of inflated self-importance, with the accompanying manners of bullying and arrogance – a man, he reflected, whose main project in life was to keep the eye of his ego focused approvingly on himself, giving his existence the validity of a tautology. Roger, who had taken a logic course in college, considered tautologies vacuous ("It's either raining or it isn't" – always tautologously true – was of no use for deciding whether to carry an umbrella, was it?) and was happy to spend the man's money. But he also had a conscience, as did his colleague, and his dislike of Eastwind did not quite pacify his uneasiness about it, slight though it was. But, after all, Marty had never been to Los Angeles.

"The City of Angels. I rather hope they aren't low flyers, these feathery intelligences. I'm allergic to down," Marty said.

"Don't worry about that," Roger rejoined. "Most of them are porn stars these days." Marty spilled his drink on that one.

"I suppose," the latter said, attempting to dry his lap with a napkin clearly not up to the task, "the main thing should be to pump his memory of the man he called attention to in the article. It might even be possible that he stayed in touch with him."

"Possible, but not likely," Roger said. "We're still grasping at straws, you know."

"Yes, I know." And in this knowledge the two rode the giant metal intelligence as it pushed the horizon farther and farther westward, that the sun might sink into the Pacific.

* * *

With the help of the hotel internet connection, locating James Woods had not been difficult. The man's agent got back to them in a few days, and told them the actor would meet with them the next day. Did they know how to get to La Cienega Boulevard? Roger bought a map, and rented a car.

James Woods received them in his living room. They had explained earlier over the phone why they were looking for a "Ludi Vann," and now they chatted a while about New York and the homeless. The street-crazies.

"Yeah, I remember him," he said, "but I'd be awfully surprised if he'd been involved in some scam."

"It's just a theory, at this point," Marty said.

"It's been a while, but I probably would recognize a photo of him," Woods said.

"We don't have any photos," Roger said. "Maybe you could tell us what he looked like, say. Or just what he was like; obviously he was very intelligent."

"He was smart in a poetic kind of way. I know it's odd to put it like that. I mean, he understood things, but his mind put a kind of fast-breaking curve on them. See, when I met him he was getting better. He still had problems but it was like he understood them. Give you an example: I once told him what I just said about his mind – I mean, I could talk to him like that. He said that was because the things that came our way always had a spin on them, that… oh, something like… that the earth turning on its axis put a Coriolis Effect on them." Woods laughed a little. "It kept things turning so that we never saw their true natures. He said his twisted mind turned them back. He called himself the Anti-Coriolis, the A.C. He said it was God's nature in him. He was really off, but when I knew him he could talk about it."

"Interesting," said Roger.

"And you knew he was working on his doctorate," Marty allowed.

"Had been. His illness had interrupted it – something in computer science at a university in the South. I mean, he was still strange, off somewhere in his mind. He was fairly articulate, though he tried to sound like he was a black guy on the streets when we talked – that was weird for me. The thing is the other street people respected him. I mean, they knew he was crazy, but they were crazy too, so we all got along, mostly."

"Can you tell us what he looked like? Did he resemble the historical Beethoven in any way?" Marty asked.

"Just the way he dressed. His hair, though it was thinning a lot. As an actor I did notice mannerisms he was affecting – he shook his fist, sometimes walked with his head a little to the side, murmuring melodies in a kind of tone-deaf way. He'd say things you thought probably the real Beethoven had said."

"And you don't have any photos from when you were on the streets with those people?" Roger asked.

"Oh, no," said the actor. "That would have blown my act a little. It would've been hard to explain. But…

heeeyyy, wait a minute. I just remembered something. I saw a documentary about some New York street people – crazies – some filmmaker made a while before I'd done my thing there and knew Ludi. The thing is, I recognized him from that film, and was fascinated. That's why we kind of buddied-up. I kidded him that we were both movie stars."

"He's on film somewhere?" interjected Marty. "How good…!"

"Yeah, if it's still around. It was Ludi Vann, all right, but only for less than a minute, if I recall. Yeah, that's right. Jesus, he was really nutsy-looking, like he was putting it on. Oh, what the hell was the name of that?"

"Do you think you could find out?" Marty asked.

"At this point it's essential that we have a photo, any visual image, of him," Roger added. "It'd be all we have left to find him."

Woods thought a moment. "Yeah," he said. "Yeah. Let me make some phone calls. Where are you staying?"

* * *

Marty and Roger were staying at the Los Angeles Sheraton, which was, for their tastes, sumptuous and boring. Neither of them thought much of American television, and though it was still warm enough – fall was on the way – the great sprawling swimming pool held no allure for them ("water, but no allure," Marty had commented mischievously). They were obliged to wait; they knew it would take a while for Woods to get the information about the documentary. And then Roger thought it would be fun for Marty to experience the kitsch of Hollywood, hear what he would say of it; Marty had a way with arch expressions – dry humor that could wet one's pants. Once, when they had first met, Roger had mentioned that he'd just gotten back from a musicological convention in Indiana; Marty, new to the faculty, new to America, had asked where it had been held.

"Ball State," Roger had replied.

"How singular."

Like most Americans, Roger loved the British diction. Properly employed, he'd mused, the British should record all answering machine messages – well, upper-class British ("I'm rather unable to come to the phone just now; would you be so good as to leave a message?" – with the intonation for a question falling on the last syllable, instead of rising to hang in the air, as it does in the former colonies), make all public announcements, read the phone book on a special TV channel set up for that purpose alone. With Marty, he reflected, you could almost hear the extra "u" in words that Americans spelled with the economical (and, he thought, bland) "o": "colour," "favour," "parlour," which, it seemed, gave them the "flavour" of the old world, of being nearer origin. Wasn't that what we all wanted, he ruminated, closeness to the source? As a palliative for death?

They had a rental car brought around, and made their way to the monumental place.

"My god," Marty said, looking up from the freeway, "there really is a gigantic sign spelling out 'Hollywood.' It's hard to believe the thing's really there, with all the images establishing it in the domain of the media. Might we visit it? I think I should have to touch at least one of the letters to believe it."

"I don't know how to get there," Roger said. "But sit tight – you won't believe the place itself."

"One imagines an earthquake, with those enormous letters hurtling down the hillside, plowing into cars, invading homes, chasing fleeing pedestrians," Marty said drolly. "Cause of death: captured by a rolling 'O' from the 'Hollywood' sign, somersaulted into a stupor…"

"...released into the path of a gigantic 'Y', which straddled the victim," Roger continued the thought.

"Indeed. Given the *coup de grâce* by a rampaging 'W'. An alphabetical fatality."

"The tragicomic thing about it, Marty, is that I'm sure there are people here who would say of the deceased, 'Well, that's how he or she would've wanted to go...'"

They were inventing the final details of the catastrophe ("The letters come to rest in words like 'wholly,' 'lowly,' 'dolly,'" imagined Marty. "And finally," added Roger, 'why.'" "So it ends on a philosophical note, then," concluded the other. "I suppose that *is* the natural order with disasters") as they arrived at Hollywood Boulevard. Luckily, Roger found a parking space on Las Palmas, and the pair made their way to Grauman's.

Marty thoroughly enjoyed inspecting the handprints, kneeling, like other tourists, to fit his rather large hands into the hollows of the hands of various stars. Roger watched, amused at his colleague's willingness to be just a part of the crowd. They made their way on the Walk of Fame, and, reading each star, found James Woods's. They visited film museums, they visited Madame Tussaud's, the gift shops. They returned to Grauman's and found a seat in an open-air fast-food restaurant.

"Well," said Marty at long last, stretching his arms out to indicate all of Hollywood, "this is all that's left after the death of the gods, isn't it? Mortals cast into the firmament of film."

"Right. Where they live forever," Roger added. "Did you know there's a movement in film technology to computerize the images of bygone stars, resurrect them technologically, with their characteristic moves, facial expressions, voices – and have them star in movies again?"

"Well, really, how could immortality not belong to the gods?"

"That's what Hollywood is really about, in a way." Roger paused with that thought. "Perhaps it was what 'Ludi Vann' was about, though with the dimension of pathology."

"And this *isn't* pathology?" Marty asked facetiously, then said, "You mean, to *be* someone who had already suffered and triumphed over all of life's pitfalls, and who had survived death – in fame?"

"Something like that."

Marty said, "You know, it's odd: here we are at one of the most bizarre outcroppings of the human psychological apparatus, and we're involved in something much the same with our search; think what the mind of this 'Ludi Vann' must have been like to have simply shucked his own being for that of a famous figure. So much so," he continued, "that he mastered all the personal aspects of the man, made them his own, including his handwriting, and especially his signature."

"It makes you think the human psyche is formed around an abyss. An occasionally inviting one," Roger said. "But this 'Vann' man didn't research his character enough. He should have read Solomon; the 'maiden years' bit blew it."

"Assuming Solomon is right, and also that the *'Mädchen Jahre'* phrase wasn't Beethoven's own cover story."

"Neither of us think it was," Roger said. "But you know, it's probably true that this 'Vann' was intelligent. If it wasn't the true Beethoven who wrote it, the 'maiden' thing would be almost too crude a blunder. Why would he even have thought of throwing in that phrase?"

* * *

When they got back to their room they saw the "message" light was flashing on the phone. Roger called the main desk and was given a number to call.

"It's a piece called *What Rain? What Sun?* by a guy named Carlo Taglia, lives in Santa Monica," Woods said. "I talked to him and he says he'll show it to you if you come to his studio, in L.A. On Melrose."

"Yes. Certainly," Roger said. "What's the address?"

Woods gave him an address, with some directions for finding it. Roger thanked him and hung up.

"You see," he said, addressing the pang of his conscience more than he was Marty, "it turns out we had to come here."

Taglia was a hawk-faced man of about five-eight with bushy, though graying, eyebrows; although he was close to seventy, his manner was energetic.

"Yeah," he was saying to the two men, "I'm still pretty proud of this. Did Jimmy tell ya it won two awards?"

"No. He didn't mention that," Roger said.

"Yeah. Some of my best work. I was trying to get inside these guys' minds, but do it with, ya know, a lot of symbolism. I conceived of it as art more than just a series of interviews with street-crazies. But you'll see."

They talked a while about Taglia's being in New York in the early nineties. He told them about his other films. They drank wine and Roger told him about their quest.

After a while, Taglia put in a video and turned off the lights. Marty took out a notepad, but, noticing that there wasn't enough light to use it, put it away again. The big-screen TV grew to whiteness.

Before any captions, while in the real-time of a hand-held camera, a distant figure with a piercing gleam coming from his head made his way toward the viewer. The gleam was a mystery.

"Yeah, it took a lot to get that shot, which I wanted to sort of define the whole thing. This guy, we had to wait to when the sun was just at the right angle, otherwise no gleam," Taglia said. It became clear to Roger and Marty that they were in for a running commentary from the man, but their curiosity about actually seeing this strange "Ludi Vann" was so piqued that they would have put up with just about anything.

As the man – a white man – on the screen got bigger, and his clothes showed in their forlorn raggedness, the gleam on his head began to look like a kind of shell; as he came to stand in front of the camera, the viewer saw that it was a helmet, something like a motorcyclist would wear, perfectly chromed. A voice off-camera asked, "Why the headgear? What does it do for you?"

Eyeing the camera with some suspicion, answering in a kind of rasp, the man said, "Protects me from the rays they send to get into my mind. What's in the camera?"

"Just film."

"Just film? Nothing else?"

"We're not with them," another off-camera voice said. "Where do the rays come from?"

"The spaceship."

"What spaceship is out there?"

The man gave a little chortling laugh, made a kind of amazed half-turn away from the camera, then turned back. "Man, there's spaceships everywhere. Didn't you read the *Book of Urantia?* We don't run our lives, the supergovernment runs our lives. But you can keep them from running your thoughts if you block the rays."

"What thoughts do you have if you don't have the helmet?"

"I don't know."

"You don't know."

"I don't know 'cause they turn off your observing mind when they're putting in their thoughts. They have free rein without you ever knowing it. But you find out they've been in there later."

"How do you find that out?"

"'Cause you want to do things you usually wouldn't do, buy things you won't ever need."

"Like what? Can you give us an example?"

"Sure. They made me buy an umbrella once."

"But you might need an umbrella. For the rain, for the sun, maybe."

The man stared incredulously into the camera. *"What* rain? *What* sun?" He turned and walked away.

The opening title faded in over the image of him getting smaller down the street. The credits came next. Taglia hit the "pause" button on the remote. "The funny thing is, I gotta tell ya, the funny thing is we had to do that take five fucking times – mainly because of getting the gleam right." (Marty found the man's manner of speech vulgar, but knew publicly copulating nouns – what might be grammatically parsed as the "coital intensive" in which a good ravishing inseminated the word with semantic truth, endowing it with an afterglow of arrived meaning – had brought an accepted immodesty to language.) "And would ya believe, each later time the guy seemed not to notice we'd just been through the same thing? Each take he said something different. One time he said the spaceships operated through radio and TV."

Marty said, "You mean they don't? I thought he was talking about commercials." Roger laughed. "Hey, I've made a commercial or two in my day," Taglia said, not really taking offense. He hit the "play" button.

The screen showed a middle-aged black man with signboards into which he was sandwiched. The front board of the sign read, "I CAN PROOF GOD EXISTS AND THAT ANGELS SURVEILL US HOURLY." The camera traveled around to find a different message on the back board: "GOD IS SUBTLE BUT CAN THE CAT BLOW?" "Oh, this guy," Taglia said, hitting "pause" again, "oh man, this guy was some sort of philosophy professor who just burned out. We talked with them before we put them on film. This guy was teaching at some technical school down in central Florida, I think he told me. Christ, he must've lost his mind to move to New York. I guess there're more atheists in New York. That was his thing – proving the existence of God. Something about a saint named Anselm… But – wait'll ya hear how he does it."

"There are several proofs," said Marty. "Thomas Aquinas adduced a number that Catholic catechists used to have to learn. Don't ask me how I know."

"I thought you were Church of England," said Roger.

"No. I'm a bead-rattler from way back, but I've lapsed to the point of de facto excommunication by now, probably. Anyway, the most famous is St. Anselm's," Marty went on, "which is that the very idea of God's perfection is more than just an idea in that it necessarily implies his existence; or, as perfect, he wouldn't have the character flaw of not bothering to exist, so to say."

"Yeah," said Taglia. "I grew up Roman Catholic. That's the proof we had to learn too, come to think of it. I watched the whole thing last night; it's probably what this guy is raving about. Watch." He pressed "play."

The man on the screen had emerged from the signs and was standing behind a garbage pail, using it as a kind of lectern, where across it lay the signboards. He spoke to an invisible class.

"*I am that I am* almost a perfect palindrome-proof of his existence," the man began. "Final proof: that he can't be proven. But they's proofs and they's proofs like the time St. Anselm be talkin' to his own Idiot Boy – maybe the same one as ours, just handed down in reincarceration."

Again the "pause" button. "Holy shit," said Taglia, "wait'll ya meet this 'Idiot Boy.' He's on next." ("Play.")

"Saidt, 'Aight, Fool, who hath said in your heart ain't no Godt, I ax you, how you define Godt?' Replyeth Fool: 'Ain' none greater, the supremest of all bein's.' Anselm: 'That is essentially correct.' Fool: 'But it be only an idea in my headt; don' mean he like exiss.' Anselm: 'But what could be greater than a mere idea?' Fool: 'A ham sammich.' Anselm: 'Precisely, my good man: a really existing thing. Ever try to eat an idea?' Fool: 'Tried fucking one. Still do.' Anselm: 'But wouldn't it be greater to have the *real thing?'* Fool: 'Whut she be like?' Anselm: 'That jus' it. 'Cause she really exiss, you gotta fin' out, get to know the bitch, you know.' Suddenly Fool see the light since he think with his dick – a common mark of the whole army of fools, rather a huge strike force – an' say: 'I been a fool!' Anselm: 'The least of your imperfections.' Or something. An' then: 'Thanky Jesus, thanky, thanky.'"

Here the man sang:

"It the mondo-logical goof,
It the condo-logical spoof,
Be the ontological proof
    Yeah, yeah
    In my soul
    Yeah, yeah.
The Ontological Proof.

"BUT. Gaunilon, a monk at another monastery, attacks! 'I'm thinking of perfect pussy, *pudenda pulchrissima*, vulva of velvet you stick your stiff monk's dick innit, feel like damn stardust poured down a rainbow, you come, it be like the light of a thousand stars bursting into the visible yet Platonic Idea of the damn Fourth of *Ju*-ly, know what I'm sayin? Now that got to be, you know, perfect pussy, an' like your mental retardate be sayin', what else kin it be but IDEAL only? Like, by your lights you couldt give me da ho's phone number, you know, now, whussup widdat? I mean, how it be dat da bitch not necessarily slide down da chute o' da Potential onto da plane o' da Actual? 'Cause it perfect pussy. It *oughta* exiss, dammit.'

"Anselm responds: 'Even perfect poon remains, of course, on the plane of the possible; the proof only works for God.'

"Gaunilon, he go: 'Shia.'"

Taglia pressed the "pause" button again. "This guy was so far out, we just let him talk. I'd thought about editing out this next part, but ended up saying what the hell." He hit "play" again. The image on the screen raised its arms as if in benediction.

"But gentlemen, gentlemen, this is mysticism.

"Then St. Anselm undertook to prove to Godt that The Fool exiss: 'O Thou who hath said in His divine heart there is no fool but the fool-for-Christ, how wouldst Thou define The Fool?'

"Godt answer: 'He who hath denied me.'

"St. A. say: 'Right, sir. Art Thou then saying, sir, that a man who truly denies Thee does not exist?'

"Godt: 'No man liveth except he liveth in me; even to deny me is to affirm me.'

"St. A.: 'But then Thou admitteth the idea of such a man?'

"Godt: 'He is, in a sense, a Divine Idea, under the species of such Ideas called Dumbfux. But because he cannot exist he remains only the most supreme of the Dumbfux ideas.'

"St. A.: 'But, beggin' thy pardon, beggin' yer Grace's indulgence here, he bein' the most supreme, shouldn't he have the added perfection of existence (may it please Thee that these words are uttered!)?'

"Godt say: 'Nice try, O saint-to-be, but I rely on one of my subtler minds, several centuries after such fine mentation faded from your skull, name of Immanuel Tank, said that existence itself not be any kind of real predicate, can't be an addled perfection. But granting, for the sake of argument, that it were a real predicate, why yes (and why does the Granger Collection woodcut of you have you with a five-o'-clock shadow? A disgrace to the profession of faith, ax me) – yes, should such a fool exiss he a mark' man.'

"St. A.: 'A mark man?'

"Godt: 'I'd have my divine "I" on him day and night, that sniveling, sinning and grinning bastit. I got torments for that fucker conceived as if the mind of de Sade were the Idea of Pain turned inside-out: I'd cut his five limbs off, just a damn torso widh a headt, an' I'd have him waited on by a naked, nubile bearer o' da brandt o' eroticism marriedt beauty to obedience.'

"St. A. spring his trap, expecting the Godt of the Hebrews, the Godt of Augustine, Spinoza and Kant, the Godt who suffered a hormone change when his son was born, no longer 'Smite them, hip and thigh,' but now 'Oh, let my boy rescue you before the eschatological dawn of doom,' he expect him to wriggle into the net: *'But he would still exiss,'* say the boy.

"Godt: 'You're missing the point, my dear Anselm: *he'll wish he dint.'*

"St. A.: 'I'm not sure I… Could you go over that again?'"

Here the man on the screen began shouting, waving his arms.

"Godt say: 'No! *Cogito ergo mum.*
Subito ergo bum.
Bogito ergo Bacall.
Even divine grace will pall!'

"St. A. answer back: 'Precisely, my dear God' – an' here the saint transform himself into a divine hobo, hitching a ride to nowhere on [singing] 'this train, this train don' carry no gamblers' – [speaking] 'The Fool knows of your death, of the divine *mum*, of the mumskull who, dazed behind

His mirror shades, watches the arising and the chastising, the sweep of history etching its rune on the pristine plane of time… Let me tell you something, O doubtful Godt, O solipsistic Cartesian Certainty: The Fool exiss because he *suffer your absence.*'

"'Succinctly put, my dear St. A.,' Godt allow.

"Thus, brethren, my children," the man on the screen said, with a magnanimous gesture, "both God and the Fool exist. They are accommodated to each other in the relation, Unknown and Question…" The sound began to fade as the man started to cite St. Bernard's proof of the existence of Dog. Taglia offered to fast-forward to the scene Woods had said contained their man, but both protested that he keep going.

"Okay. Now that I recall it, your guy Ludi Vann is off-camera on this next one, talking to the guy they called 'Idiot Boy.'"

"I wonder why they called him that," Marty said.

"Idiot Boy is on camera," Roger said. "But we don't see Ludi Vann?"

"Right. We just had this Idiot Boy guy look into the lens and say his thing. He thought he was Jesus, I think. Heard voices. Claimed to be clairaudient. You'll see. Ludi Vann is just a shot in the next sequence." He hit "play" again.

The screen presented a black man in his late thirties, a man whose eyes were deep and whose face bespoke tragedy as the truth of the world. If the blues were both despair and reconciliation to despair, Idiot Boy was indigo. When he spoke it was slowly, with an intense gaze. Off-camera, the voice of Ludi Vann was telling the crew about their subject:

"Idiot Boy loss his mindt fum an episote o' necrophilia widh a beautiful corpse, she not really deadt jus', you know, like froze but I.B. here think she snuff, take her to the warm room where they you know bring the deadt up to room temperature for funerals and viewin's an' suchlike, he work up a hardt-on ram it inner SHE WOKE UP, now a screet-ho in the French Quarter N'awlins go by the name Lazara – Lazara the Living Endt, little trick she do widh her, you know, like, her ass. I.B. say when he done it she be the Virgin Mary only thirteen, he himself turn into the Imitation of Christ.

"Idiot Boy, you tell Ludi Vann 'n' these nice people who gon' make your soul shine oudt the TV screams how did it feel to be Jesus, you know, raisin' the deadt, you who have the Jesuspecker, the wand of life, it's true my symphonies confer life but it a little different – waving my dick at the players showing them the beat and beatitudinousness of every measure – fum wielding the Holy Roodt…!"

"So that's the voice of our elusive Vann," said Marty, as Roger sat absorbed by the scene. "Notice the street-black diction?"

"My god," commented Roger, "notice the insane *rant. This* is our forger?"

"That's your boy," said Taglia, who had turned down the volume. "He's really far gone." He turned it back up.

The camera focused more closely on the face before it; Idiot Boy spoke:

"I the big eyepools they swim in, they surf my tears, they necessary accidents waiting to happen, I wash they feet widh my tears they the explorin' I the implorin'. They: every gesture an' wordt a mockery o' truth. Me: I hear in every wordt angelic hosannas, I transform every gesture into acts o' grace an' cosmic utility, they greates' crime my own site pierced…"

"And Lazara the Living Endt?"

"She take each wafer o' cum the sacrament o' my sufferin', she swallow an' look into John's eyes an' say, 'this is his body…'"

"Well, Idiot Boy," [and Marty caught a hint of sarcasm in Ludi Vann's voice] "you got a big gig widdat, being Jesus, 'n' don' you worry now an' again 'bout like *nails* and beams that are *crossed* as in city power poles?"

"Nails kin be jolts, kin be lethal injection, be the knotted rope mercifully breakin' the neck, you know, you know. I listen in on they last wordts, I die widdem, man, it like telepathic, I'm in their presence when they talk they las'."

"You hear 'em?"

"Somehow they be voices in my headt, they confess, they say goo-bye like to family, you know. Las' time, man 'bout to be 'lectrocuted say to his weeping ma in the visitation room, saidt:

'Aw, Ma, it's time for me to go away
To ride the longboat into the sea
I hear the trumpets in Time's knell
Sounding three notes for me.

The first tone, it be a vibration
    in the air, a baby's crine;
The second, the lingering of sorrow and elation
    left over in an empty sign.
But the third, this moment be the
    endt o' da l i n e –
Be that lingering's cessation.

Let me sing you the *code*, old mudder,
Let me show you the *mode,* used udder:
    The first is the third as hidden,
    The third the first fully bidden.
    That I should account for my sinning,
        a lingering in a no-loitering zone,
Is a tallying to the sum of my beginning;
        first and third are the same tone.'

"Now, she say, she say, heardt what she saidt [falsetto voice]:

'O son of mine, when you were inside me
I was inside myself
That is what it is to be a mother
They cannot take you away
Without taking my nature from me.
I am your mother.'

"'N' he saidt:

'Aw Ma, I gotta go
In nothing hence;
I was only a moment's passion
In lingering consequence.'

"She: 'Mother!'
"He: 'Other.'
"She: 'Son!'
"He: 'None.'

"Then they pull the switch, man, sent 'im out on a megahertz wavelength, his mama go home read a damn book to get her mind offa it."

"What book, Idiot Boy, can you see as well as you hear these things?"

"I see when I hear, Ludi Vann, jus' like you hear when you see."

"Right. Fieldts o' lush foliage risin' up in F-major, like. What book, then? *The Tibetan Book of the Dead?"*

"Shia, man, no *Bettin' Book O' Da Debt."*

"Like the Bible, you tellin' me?"

"Naw, naw, man. Not the Babble. It be, you know, like John Grisham or somethin'."

The man's face got smaller as the camera began pulling back. Taglia hit "pause."

"Fascinating," said Roger.

"Not the best poetry, but their muses are demons," Marty observed. "What did you think of Ludi Vann's voice?"

"Distinctive," Roger replied. "Thankfully, he didn't try to sound like a deaf man – unable to hear himself."

"Well, no shit." said Taglia, "He was about as deaf as I am. He got my words without even looking at me, to like read my lips." He rose and brought the wine decanter over, refilling his glass and Roger's; Marty hadn't really drunk any of his.

"Why didn't you interview him?" Roger asked. "He certainly sounds ripe enough."

"I tried," Taglia said, "but he wouldn't talk with us. It's this next one's got him in it. Let me tell ya what I had in mind. I wanted the street-schizos sitting in a line with their backs to a wall – maybe a little symbolism there, but not as much as what I did with the Walkmans. I gave each of them a Sony Walkman and had them put the headphones on; then the camera travels down the row, showing that each radio is tuned to a different station."

"I get it," Roger said.

"Right. Not brilliant, but a nice touch, I thought. Your Ludi Vann will be pretty obvious 'cause he's taken his off – the only one who wouldn't go along with it – he's just glaring at the camera. Which was okay with me; he was *really* tuned to a different station." Taglia picked up the remote. "Here we go."

The men and their Walkmans came to the screen, with the camera beginning to pan slowly down the line, left to right. They were about ten in number, and among them were the chrome-helmeted man and the burned-out philosopher

– his sandwich-board signs behind him with "GOD IS SUBTLE" just visible. The fourth one in, after three who had not spoken to the camera, was Idiot Boy, silently mouthing some lyrics, eyes closed.

The camera moved to his right, bringing forth a man whose eyes were jumping with fire, whose whole face moved as if to a bold inner rhythm, a face craggy and handsome, but with the eyes dominating: jet black, wide apart, wide open – and fairly driving into the camera with a surge that suggested the process had been reversed: he wasn't being filmed; no, he was bringing film into its truth, creating it for the first time. His determined visage, strong and ironic, had reached into the camera and was turning it inside out. And then one noticed that the soundtrack had become the first movement of Beethoven's Fifth as the camera lingered on this mad, bony, face.

"He told me he was Beethoven, and that he heard his music in his head all the time," Taglia said, "so I…" He stopped. Roger had risen and was pointing at the screen. And though not a believer, he was shouting the name of the savior over and over. Marty was up and trying to calm him. "Get a grip, Roger! Here, take a seat. Calm down. What is it?!"

Roger looked up, incredulous, into Marty's eyes. A realization broke over his face. "Of course," he said. "Of course. You wouldn't know."

BOOK FOUR

Eastwind

Chapter One

Eastwind

Louis B. Eastwind – "Beastwind" to many – sat in the great chair he reserved for business matters, the padded leather yielding to his considerable weight. Other great chairs around the huge house had other functions, most notably in the dining room, but this morning he sat in the great chair of the study, opening mail. Usually Roy, his manservant and secretary, sorted and stacked it, but he had left suddenly to hide out from a warrant charging him with spouse abuse. Eastwind had met and despised at first sight his factotum's wife, a slender shrew whose sole function, thought Eastwind, had been to be the receiver of the blows women like her provoked in men like Roy; there was something artful in that, a rare economy of means and ends, it seemed to him, though it made for the occasional hiatus in the man's otherwise faithful service.

Eastwind puffed on his nearly omnipresent cigar, riffling the day's mail, tossing away envelopes, crumpling advertisements and lazily aiming them at a nearby wastebasket. A request from a religious society landed on the heap at the basket's base, slightly displacing the postal detritus there. "Missionaries," he muttered contemptuously, the cigar waggling, "these days there're more missionaries than spies. A fine state of affairs." A political advertisement beginning "Honesty is the best policy" was crumpled with equal contempt and sent toward the basket's rim. "'Honesty is the best policy' is already dishonest, isn't it?" he said under his breath, an oft-entered realm of rhetorical questioning.

A few bills, which he put on his desktop near the clock radio, a postcard from a vacationing girlfriend ("Glad your not hear," she'd written facetiously, though Eastwind knew the spelling was sincere, bringing him to the instantaneous reflection that being literate was, thankfully, unrelated to a young – well, a youngish – woman's erotic capacities), a trade magazine that had an article about his great product and the bountiful success he was having with it; the morning's take. Ah, and the letter he'd put aside, with the Los Angeles postmark. The letter he'd saved for last.

He slit the envelope with a silver letter opener and removed the single folded sheet. Opening it, he read:

> Dear Mr. Eastwind,
>
> Our researches on Auction Lot No. 765 are now concluded. We regret to inform you that in our professional opinion the letter is a forgery, as we indicated in our wire from Vienna; confirmation has now been made.
>
> Per the terms of our agreement, we are to return the letter to you and collect the remainder of our fee. We therefore ask you to make an appointment for us to discuss our findings and conclude this business.
>
> Sincerely yours,

The signatures of Roger McKane and Martin Spratt followed. At the top of the letter was a phone number.

Eastwind put the letter down; actually, after the Vienna wire, he'd been prepared for that news. Well, all was not lost. Brixton's was about to get the most devastating lawsuit in their long existence, and he could probably make out better were he to throw in mental suffering, professional embarrassment in the music community, etc. At any rate, finding out that the letter was a fake needn't be taken too hard – except that it would've been nice to own the authentic article. Eastwind had a collection, acquired in the last three years, of letters of famous people.

He rang for his housekeeper Polly to instruct her as to the finalization of the plans for the evening: a victory party, which also included his playing a little piano piece, was to be a celebration of his successful defense in the lawsuit Custom Craftware had brought against him, and required both some further polishing and as well the setting up, on the patio adjoining the pool (where the piano had already been moved), of chairs and tables for the occasion. The caterers would be delivering this afternoon, he reminded her, and the extra staff – among them bartenders – would need her coordination, at least at the beginning. Oh, and a little brunch, if she could rouse the cook. A cheerful beauty, she nodded and left the room, humming Bette Midler's *Wind Beneath My Wings*. "Lousy lyrics and worse aerodynamics," Eastwind muttered to no one in particular as he placed the musicologists' letter near the telephone on his desk.

The rest of the day would include practicing the piano, a grand Yamaha Disklavier nine feet in length. But not a lot of practice, he thought to himself. He recalled that Glenn Gould's ideal pianist was one who could sit down and play just about anything without even warming up; that's why the great eccentric wouldn't shake hands with most people. Well, Eastwind congratulated himself, I've certainly shaken the right hands to be able to live up to that perhaps neurotic notion, and as well another of Gould's: not having to practice really at all, past a certain point of mastery – which, he reflected, would be the point of his little piano performance.

After brunch, Eastwind reëntered the study and reluctantly picked up the phone receiver. He'd developed an aversion to telephones some time ago for reasons he couldn't remember, but probably having to do with his not wanting his voice to be reduced to an electronically vibrating diaphragm that took from him the advantage of physical presence to his listeners – intimidating presence. But he pressed in the number at the top of the musicologists' letter, noting that the area code was not for the west coast, but actually the 212 of New York City.

Roger answered. As was Eastwind's style, there was no "hello," only some curt expression of what was on his mind. "You're in New York," he said, almost menacingly.

"Oh, Mr. Eastwind. How are you?"

"Disappointed. But not devastated. I'm thinking lawsuit."

There was a silence. Then Roger said, "So you got our note."

"Obviously. Your phone number didn't just pop out of the air."

"Oh, right. Of course. Well, then you know we should redeliver the letter and uh, finish up with our arrangement."

"If you're in the city you're not too far from my place. Do you know how to get to the Hamptons?"

"Assuredly. When did you have in mind?"

"I'm having a little party tonight. Perhaps the details of your research will go down a little more palatably if I'm in a good mood."

"Tonight? I'd have to ask Martin."

"Whatever," Eastwind said, with a little more edge to his voice. "I'm sure he'd like to get paid as well. And I would like the letter back. I suppose I could make a placemat of it – if you can convince me your research is one-hundred percent."

"What time?"

"Eight is about right," Eastwind said; he gave him the address and some rudimentary directions, then summarily hung up. In an exaggeratedly academic voice, but one that mimicked Roger's perfectly, he said aloud to himself, "'I'd have to ask Martin,'" adding, "twit"; at the same time, in the New York apartment he was sharing with his colleague, Roger was saying in an exaggerated curtness that had Eastwind's driving tenor to it, "'Your phone number didn't just pop out of the air, did it?' – prick."

Eastwind went out to the patio and sat at the Yamaha. What he played was almost embarrassingly simple. It was the theme from *La Folia* of Corelli, from his Violin Sonata No. 12, with its very simple chord changes. Originally written in D-minor, the theme had been transposed by Eastwind a whole-step down to C-minor, a key he was more comfortable with. So simple: C-minor to G-major, C-minor to B-flat major, which led immediately to E-flat (the relative major of C-minor), then back to B-flat, which suddenly gained the tension of a fully-diminished seventh chord that impinged on C-minor – and so the harmony of C-minor arrived, but a bit unstably; this was remedied by the usual dominant-to-tonic ending cadence. And then the variations were to begin – six of them; he considered that sufficient to make his point.

All Eastwind did at the keyboard was make sure that the changing harmonies in the original Corelli, with their veneer of melody, were under his fingers – that the voice-leading was well structured and excluded the sneaking parallel fifths and octaves that identified an amateur, a forger of the Baroque style. But no variations followed; instead, at the end of each run-through of the harmony/melody of the original, he reached, a little jokingly, down with his left hand toward the bottom notes the keyboard offered. After half an hour of this he noticed how bored he was, and retired to the chair in the study; wasn't boredom the silent knell of mastery? He lit an old cigar and opened a bank statement from a day or so ago.

He had waited to examine the statement because he knew there were no surprises – except possibly pleasant ones. His product, once freed to manufacture by the first court ruling four years ago, had been more successful than even his backers had expected. Deposits from Yamaha and other piano companies that had incorporated the features of a disk player abounded. That is, were continuing to abound; his success had been a steady affair for the last four years. He had invested with the cunning of a savant of the market, and had become immensely wealthy in that time.

The house alone, finished less than three months ago, bore this out. "Lavish" would have been something of an understatement; and when someone in his sparse inner circle had used that term, Eastwind had turned on him and said, "I prefer 'magnificent.'" Was he sensitive about the correct words for the place? It would be easy to say he was as sensitive as any *nouveau riche,* who, having come into the fate that old Dame Fortuna had granted him, needs to believe in the cosmic necessity of his luck. Or that Eastwind considered his great (though new) wealth – manifest in every pillar, the vaulted ceilings, the columns and arches that surrounded the immense swimming pool, the tapestries, the chandeliers, the great artworks (though, strangely, none of them originals), the classical molding, the burnished bronzes, the best wood for every piece of furniture, the gold and even the brass – as portending his great *human* worth; what else are such objects for but to drain off the contingency of one's existence to leave over the firm footing of necessity? But against Shakespeare's "tide in the affairs of men, which taken at the flood, leads on to fortune," it was rather that Eastwind's own pedestal had emerged from the recession of troubled waters. Should geometry marry its austerity to metaphor, it might be said that the three points defining the plane of its bottom didn't quite line up; a surface was produced but it was warped by the weight of his past, and he felt the accompanying wobble.

In the service of precision, the terms of classical mechanics might also be employed in the accounting of the orbit of his inner life: rich in thought, it was defined by an attraction of forces that were the direct product of the pull towards the darkness germane to the human beast and the thrust of the ever-dawning light of self-knowledge, a relation, he'd written with a flourish of erudition in his journal, "that varies inversely as the square of the distance these two are kept, lately with the help of my psychiatrist, from each other." At the perigee was a despair that was the souring of the promise of the hours, at the apogee the self-congratulation of the promise renewed. For Eastwind was a complex man, an educated man, a cultured man who knew not only great works of the music and literature of bygone centuries well, but also the writings of the existential philosophers, the Beat Generation, various twentieth-century poets and playwrights. For that matter, when he had entered his finished house for the first time and let its magnificence – for that really was the true harmonic that came to pitch over its fundamental extravagance – dawn on his consciousness, he had smiled a smile of self-knowledge and uttered a fragment from T.S. Eliot's "The Hollow Men." It was the least likely poem his acquaintances, who knew him through his curtness of manner, his arrogance, would have imagined him knowing; and too, he'd once said he didn't like poetry, a remark they understood in the context of a hurricane not abating for the sake of wind chimes.

And yet the eye of the man's blustery winds – his eye, the self-eye of inner knowledge, the "I" he was conversant with as part stranger – was anything but calm.

It was in this uneasy peace that his universe of self rotated around a sun that had come into existence through the cataclysm of his life, with its recent cooling and contractions, and that now bathed his ambition in the rays of success.

For him, after everything, this great mansion of a house, its depth of beauty, emanating in the silent constancy of white noise having homogenized the harmony of the spheres, was equal to the arrival of the tonic key after embattled and tenuous outer harmonies had collapsed onto their foundation. Beside the fact that he enjoyed the aroma, it was one of the reasons he smoked cigars.

Chapter Two

Revelry and Revelation

At seven-thirty his lawyers arrived, with other members of the firm, their wives and husbands, girlfriends and boyfriends. Other guests – notably a few journalists – showed up, including the music critic Thomas Antonioni. Eastwind was pleased to see him make it. Antonioni was a recent acquaintance, and surely what he wrote about this evening could bear on the further success of his product; even if he hated the music, he *would* write about it. The extra staff seated the arrivals out on the veranda by the pool, leading them to the extra tables, bringing them ordered drinks. Precarious trays delivered and collected while the bartenders kept busy behind the pool's small bar. Roger, briefcase in hand, and Marty, impeccably dressed, made it just at eight-o-clock. A mild din had arisen as the guests talked among themselves, most of them not Eastwind's professional acquaintances but friends of friends; because he had few friends, the growing density of people in the patio area was testimony to the word that had spread about this eccentric, even flamboyant, man.

Indeed, he had a flair for drama, and had planned out how to inaugurate the evening. When the number of guests reached about forty, Eastwind, in a tuxedo, suddenly appeared from behind a curtain that had been placed over the door to the pool cabana, and bowed to scattered, perhaps bewildered, applause. He strode to the front of the impromptu cabaret as an automatic silence fell.

He appeared to be supremely self-confident. But it should be observed that those who dealt with the man on something of a daily basis had recognized a certain defensiveness to his demeanor, subtly betraying insecurity; for instance, he was fond of taking some unfortunate physical characteristic of people he'd meet and turning it into a nickname, reducing them to harmlessness for having, in essence, become their ridiculous feature. There was "Bug-eyes" for an intimate's girlfriend, a woman who had a mild thyroid condition; there had been "No-neck" for a man who, insulted to learn his name, had threatened him and ended their association. But this defensiveness was also the case with language, in that he hid out in the equivocality of puns and double entendres, where the speaker couldn't be pinned down because such words, rent with their own ambiguity, fled away in two or more directions at once; for that matter, there were people who thought his philosophy of language included the dubious proposition that any pun was better than no pun. Once, recognizing Isaac Stern in the city, he'd said, "I suppose it could be said that you leave no tone un-Sterned"; the great violinist had chuckled a little and made his way down the street. And so Eastwind began:

"Friends, humans," and with a glance toward the bar, "countermen, lend me your ears." A little laughter from the mostly literate crowd. "I thought I'd kick off tonight's celebration with a little tune and a set of variations." With a little self-mockery he added, "It's the world premiere of this composition, and the social premiere of my compositional method. I know, I know, whatever *that* means." More laughter. Eastwind could facilely adopt the collusive manner of self-parody to counter his usual boorishness; he could be charming, a fact that disturbed those who knew him well, and that those who assumed he was only a boor –

spoke boorishly, ate boorishly, boorishly sat at stool in the morning – found disconcerting.

"Of course, some of you know of my work. But all please relax. Please drink. But do listen," he said, walking away and around the piano, which didn't exhibit its keyboard to them; rather, the great concert grand dominated its space, its great wing arching off to the left, its nose closest to them, as if, seated behind it, Eastwind could drive it like a truck through the audience. He placed his weight onto the plush leather piano bench, his right foot feeling around for the damper pedal. No music rack (as he really was no sight-reader anyway) was in the way of their view of his face.

Eastwind's flair for drama showed itself again in the way he brought his hands up just above the fallboard, and then let them descend as if two great spiders were about to contend with each other in the unseen arena below. The hands landed in a solid, almost dense C-minor chord, and he began ringing the over-rehearsed changes. The tune was one a few in the audience recognized, among them Antonioni, who wondered what it took for an amateur to think he could compete with the great composers, among them Liszt and Brahms, who had contributed variations on it. Probably an ego – as it seemed to him – like his host's.

Eastwind finished the theme – it really wasn't very long, under twenty seconds, actually – and smiled at his audience in the little silence that followed. His left hand reached down and sounded, *mezzo-forte,* the lowest C-sharp on the piano in a transition to the variations. The first variation began by picking up on the notes of the closing cadence, making them dance into the treble while a left-hand passage descended in an elongated meditation on the opening of the theme. Toward the middle of it Antonioni noticed that, because the Corelli was so short, Eastwind had fashioned a bridge theme that took on its own aesthetic tension against what it bridged – a little development section, the critic noticed, germane to classical variation form. Then the first part of it returned, with a small coda – clever, if not ingenious – that locked the music neatly into the immediate past. Eastwind looked up wryly at his guests.

Again, his left hand reached to the lowest part of the keyboard, and sounded the lowest D-natural there. Immediately, in the key of D-minor, the audience heard the theme cascading gently down in a variation that was all *legato,* with patterns in the right hand ending up in the correct harmony to keep the original structure intact; the left hand seemed to swim in limpid waters. And again, a bridge section, then a return to the cascading tones. No coda.

The lowest E-flat sounded a bit louder than the other low notes that had come between variations – almost as if Eastwind were slowly climbing up the chromatic scale by way of transition to each new variation. Now the most violent one began to rush at the audience, a torrent of triplets driven against an insistent dotted rhythm, *fortissimo*, in the left hand. Eastwind bobbed and weaved behind the body of the massive instrument, his face, though with a trace of mirth – was it mockery? – contorted into the passions the music evoked. Antonioni picked up on something he hadn't expected from an amateur: Eastwind had wrought changes *in the harmonies* as part of the variation – very sophisticated; this was something Bach had pulled in the *Goldberg Variations,* he remembered his piano teacher, one Edward Kilenyi, pointing out. And the way this worked with the implied melody the triplets were giving out suddenly piqued Antonioni's interest further; he had heard something like this before. But where?

The next variation slowed the triplets down, providing a somber *pianissimo* accompaniment to a repeated melodic note that almost reluctantly moved to its nearest neighbors. Something shimmered, came to golden appearance, then slunk into the night of E-minor; something undulated in fully-diminished seventh harmonies, Antonioni noticed, then fell into gentle patterns that bore out a newly arrived harmony. And then he knew where he had heard something similar to it – how obvious: the opening *Adagio sostenuto* of the "Moonlight" Sonata. Beethoven.

The F-minor variation returned to torrents of sound, great cataracts of rushing notes, with sudden pauses. And Antonioni knew from where this came: Beethoven's "*Appassionata*" sonata. Not that it *was* any particular section of the sonata, but that its compositional aesthetic had much in common with it. Now that he thought about it, *all* the variations so far could easily be called Beethovenish. What an oddity, he thought: a man who presents variations on an Italian folk tune in the manner of Beethoven – a tune that the great master of variation form would himself have surely disdained. Well, probably.

The low note that introduced the next, and final, variation was G-natural; Eastwind had chosen to end the variations in that key because it was the dominant of C-minor, and he could finish as he had begun, in that key: the simple reiteration of harmonic changes. This variation was fugal in character, with a bold subject and piquant answering harmonies.

Antonioni realized that he knew Eastwind's secret. In his later sonatas Beethoven had thrown in powerful fugues, calling them "musical skeletons." Or maybe the great man had meant it derogatorily, but couldn't wean himself of the tradition. Either way, Antonioni knew the truth: Eastwind's stuff was re-fried Beethoven. As his mind roamed over the implications of that, the final chord in Corelli's theme sounded, and the applause that followed drowned out the critic's thoughts.

Eastwind rose from the piano with a modest smile on his face, and came out from behind the instrument. He bowed slightly again and again as the applause lasted, looking genuinely humble. The accolade began to fade, and someone said for all to hear, "Amazing."

"I'm just the vessel, my friends," he said. "It's really not anything conscious that I do." Smiling.

Roger and Marty sat in awe. Roger said in low tones to his colleague, "I think I understand this."

"Really, you're too kind," Eastwind was saying, "as indeed most of you are about to see," he added in a kind of open aside. "But first," he continued, turning to Antonioni, "let the critic give us his opinion. Not to put you on the spot, Tommy, but though we artists love praise," he said, quoting an old witticism and smiling broadly at his guests, "we love truth more." Everyone laughed.

Antonioni said wryly, "Louie, I won't give away your secret if you won't put me on the spot." More laughter. But Eastwind's smile faded.

"*Right you are* that there's a secret to it. In fact, while it would be wonderful to let those of you who don't know my secret go on thinking that I'm a gifted composer – and pianist, too – I'd rather you marvel at what has created that illusion, since I'm really the composer of *that.*" The audience had grown silent.

In a spontaneous notion that he could demonstrate what he was talking about by taking someone out of the audience, he suddenly said, "Roger – Roger McKane, an associate of mine in musicological research – is here with us tonight. Roger, didn't you tell me your instrument was piano?"

Roger was aghast. "Yes, but I haven't played in public in…" he protested. He suddenly resented that the curt man on the phone only hours earlier was now his friend and colleague.

"That's the point, that's the point," Eastwind countered. And then, to the audience: "What if I told you anyone who knows a piano keyboard – or actually, just a part of it – can do what I just did? Come on up, Roger."

"Really, you see, I haven't..." Roger said, though he rose.

"All the better," Eastwind said, and indicated to the serving staff that they were to swivel the piano around so that the keyboard was visible. A dark, oblong attachment protruded from the lower end of it. Roger walked to the instrument. "Yes, take a seat, Roger. You can surely play three or four notes for us."

"Yes, but which ones?" Roger said with mock despair as he sat on the plush seat the staff had moved with the piano, "there're so many of them." His wit was not lost on the crowd.

"That's the beauty part," Eastwind went on, moving to the device at the bass end of the disklavier, not visible before, where he pushed a series of buttons. "*Any* notes you choose. *Three Blind Mice. Chopsticks,* if you like."

"Aha," Roger said, looking at the strange protuberance, "a little technological help. So that's your secret." Eastwind smiled at the audience. "My colleague has put his metaphorical finger on it while his physical counterparts are still hesitant. The secret is that I've provided a software program that picks up on anything played, then develops that music – in the sense that composers create out of something given – according to its own artificial intelligence. This is the end of the exquisite anguish that human beings have had to go through to create music. This is Tchaikovsky without tears, Wagner without veeping. It's Beethoven without the brow-furrowing. What you heard from me was the computer recomposing a theme from a Corelli violin sonata in six different ways," he said. And then, "Roger? Go ahead. Anything."

Roger said, "Since you mentioned Wagner..." and began the opening of the composer's *Tristan und Isolde* prelude, with the special chord that was a watershed in the history of music, and that he had lectured on at the classroom piano many times. He stopped at the resolution of that harmony, radical for its day.

"Sehr gute," Eastwind said. "An excellent choice. *Tristan und Isolde* – a uniquely erotic opera. After we're through with it," he said, throwing a wry grin to the audience, "there won't be a dry seat in the house." Some people laughed. "Now, Roger, how about a variation on that? Try the lowest 'A' on the keyboard." Roger struck the bottom-most key lightly; while everyone, Roger too, watched, the keys moved up and down, the pedals moved on their own, including the soft pedal that shifted the keyboard slightly to the right from time to time, as out flowed a kind of extemporization on Wagner's melody, harmony at first faithful to the original, then straying, somewhat oddly, into less daring chords.

Antonioni grimaced. The music might have been an essay on the implication of the opening of Wagner's opera, he thought, something like Godowsky's musical commentary on the Chopin etudes; perhaps there could have been eloquently wrought musical enlightenment. But what was happening was jarringly anachronistic. The computer was having *Beethoven* develop Wagner's music – Beethoven, who, though radical in his day, would have eschewed such "modern" harmonies *Tristan,* composed over thirty years after his death, contained. Well, probably. But it was the most execrable pastiche of styles Antonioni had ever heard.

When it finished, Eastwind said to the gathering, "There you have it: my own computer software that develops any melody even the rankest amateur – no, not you, Roger – just anyone who wants to make music at the piano, can come up with, no matter how minimalist, how banal. Given the story of Tristan and his sister, I'm tempted to throw in the notes to *Dueling Banjos* – you know, from the film *Deliverance* – right now." Some laughter at that; a woman squealed with delight. "So you've seen the movie," Eastwind said to her in wit gainsaid that brought more laughter. That was Eastwind all over, Antonioni reflected: sophisticated intellect and crude comedian. Did he know they called him "Beastwind"?

Roger had retreated and resumed his seat next to Marty. "So what did you think?" he asked in a quiet voice.

"Eastwind is a horror story on several fronts," Marty replied. "The variation on *Tristan* took years off my life."

But their host was going on, "So tonight is a kind of celebration of my invention and victory in the fight we had over it." As the audience grew quieter, he said, "The firm of Gittels and Peres successfully defended me several days ago against the lawsuit brought by the company I was working for when I came up with the device, and this party is really a thank-you to them. Barry, David, take a bow, guys." The two attorneys stood, one tall and somber, the other shorter and bald, smiling, as the others applauded. Eastwind brought his hands together again and again, and then said, "We got the rights to go into manufacture four years ago, though the evil bastards I used to work for would have gotten all the profits – or just about all of them – if we'd lost. But this ruling seals it. Gentlemen, a marvelous job." More applause, with Eastwind joining in again. "And now, let's get to the food. Enjoy it, folks, and thanks for coming." There was a further smattering of applause from his guests, and then they made their way to the buffet tables, some toward the piano to inspect it, many to congratulate Eastwind. Above it all, a crystal chandelier sent its opulent blessing of light.

One of the guests who had joined those surrounding Eastwind was Antonioni, whose presence he acknowledged so strongly during the little bits of conversation with the others that they soon yielded to the music critic.

"I thought your secret was that you were using Beethoven as a model," he said when they were alone. "I hadn't realized you'd even computerized his style."

Eastwind looked nonplussed. Then, after only the skip of a heartbeat, he replied, "So you knew it was Beethoven."

"That became clear after the fourth variation. Jesus, how did you get a computer program to be able to develop a melody so convincingly in Beethoven's style? You even mixed in his different periods."

"It has to do with putting together an artificial intelligence program that has a store – a memory – of Beethovenic devices, which I got from analyzing his piano sonatas, especially bridge themes and development sections, as I was just saying to the last guy I was talking to. You know, the sort of thing Beethoven did, pulling themes apart, building on fragments. The way he handled rhythmic changes in the *Diabelli Variations,* say. By the way, that's the name of the program – 'Diabelli.' I kind of distilled his musical moves, you might say."

"Yes, but…" Antonioni began, as the word "diabolical" snuck into his mind, "how can it all relate to whatever someone happens to play?"

"Well, you'd have to have a background in computer programming to understand it. It's sort of like sampling – you've heard of that."

"Sure," said Antonioni, "some contemporary music uses that. Things I've heard in Carnegie Hall."

"I sort of arranged what I call a 'roamer' program within it all, something that arranges a kind of… a kind of elaborate echo, or series of them, if you will, in the way it hits on what's in the memory of developmental gambits. If you will. The 'roamer' roams at random, but it will 'recognize' what to roam to only if that turns out to reflect – even in very abstract ways – what notes were fed in from the keyboard. All this at the speed of domesticated lightning, you understand."

"Yes, but..."

"That's the best I can do to put it in layman's terms. It's really much more sophisticated than that. What I did was a real breakthrough, because nobody has ever done something like that with disk-player technology."

"Yes, but... this 'roaming' circuit..."

"Program."

"Program. It doesn't choose and judge. It doesn't recognize aesthetic merit."

"Sometimes I think you don't either, reading your reviews."

"Yeah, yeah. Look, whatever your computer program is, it isn't spontaneity. Randomness is only ersatz spontaneity. It isn't the spontaneity of creativity."

"Of course not. Creativity is suffering – the 'exquisite anguish' I mentioned. Did you know Beethoven's notebooks for the first movement of the Fifth Symphony have page after page *after page* of crossed-out measures – just to keep an intensity consistent with the opening notes? That would be child's play for my program. Why should anyone have to undergo that? There are at least two hundred thousand permutations of short-short-short-long for even just a little bridge passage, say, that my 'roamer' could come up with. Why should that matter?"

"Because it's only... codified creativity. And that degrades music-making. It isn't authentic."

"Music-making is wherever and however you get it. Tommy, Tommy, Tommy, what a romantic you are! What's authentic anymore? Everything is leveled off these days into image. *The days of greatness are over*. All we're left with is imitation. Think of politics and movie stars. Think how much we live in the media. And think of all the happy amateurs at their disklaviers, pretending they're Beethoven. Or in his presence."

"It's forgery, Louie. Pure and simple."

Eastwind smiled – a smile Antonioni later thought of as condescending. "May I remind you, dear critic, of the old saw, 'Talent borrows, genius steals'?"

Antonioni knew getting to hate Eastwind could be a great joy in his life. "Genius doesn't cover its larcenous tracks very well if it hands us a Frankensteinian monster like the *Tristan* variation we just heard," he said.

"I thought it was brilliant. For an artificially intelligent piano."

"Louie, it was a head of historically conditioned compositional devices – things that were uniquely Beethoven's – grafted onto the body of Wagner's music. The bolt through the neck stuck out five feet on a side, for god's sake."

That stopped Eastwind.

"You could have at least gotten past Beethoven," Antonioni went on. "He's not the model for *all* music. In fact, he's more of a transition, not that what he wrote isn't great. Why did you stop at *him?"*

Eastwind looked as if some new thought, something too radical to be allowed speech, had come to him. "I don't know," he said. "I just did."

"Christ, what if someone keyed in…say Debussy? Or a twelve-tone row, a la Schoenberg, for that matter? Imagine what would come out. It would be insane."

But Eastwind had stopped focusing on the man. "What did you say?" he said, almost as from a distance.

"It'd be nuts. Insane," Antonioni said. "The thing works as a kind of technological parlor trick, Louie. It's stunted in its very conception. Even if it is selling well."

"This is the end of the discussion," Eastwind said, suddenly collected, impassive. "Please leave. Write anything you want, but please leave."

"Goodnight, Louie. I have to write what I know."

"Goodnight." The two walked in opposite directions, Eastwind toward the table where Roger and Marty were having hors d'oeuvres. He sat, seeming to the two somehow soberer than the success-intoxicated man he had been minutes before. A middle-aged woman approached the table and put her hands on his shoulders. "Oh, Mr. Eastwind, I'm sorry. I need to leave early," she said. "I just wanted to thank you for a brilliant evening. From the bottom of my heart." She was actually very good looking, and Eastwind had noticed her perfect derrière earlier; the touch of her lips on his cheek aroused an echo of male excitement. When she left, he shot a rakish look to the musicologists, and muttered, "Or from her heart to her bottom."

The rest of his guests were at their tables with food and the company around them, and Eastwind could now retire a little from the scene. He nodded to Marty at Roger's introduction, then looked over at Roger and said, "I not only want the letter, I want to know why I shouldn't want it."

Roger opened his briefcase and handed Eastwind the box in which lay the rough paper folded in four. Eastwind took it, opened it, and unfolded the letter. "There's a translation inside the box," Roger added.

"I know what it says. But I would like to see what you have," Eastwind said, putting on his reading glasses. The translation read:

> Most Honored Count,
>
> I have returned from the waters, refreshed in my health, but can barely think of composing so strong are visions of my Immortal Beloved, who met me

> there and who is ready to end her maiden years in marriage to me. I ask you to hold it in confidence that our betrothal has been decided, lighting my way almost as the muse herself in the B-major work I have begun this summer.
>
> I will again need your men in the moving of my lodgings from the wretched place where you last visited me. Were you to send them in the morning tomorrow or the next day I can ride with them.
>
> yr. ever faithful
> L. van Beethoven

Eastwind held the original up before his face as if it were a napkin. "So give me a good reason I shouldn't blow my nose in it. Convince me that I have a new task for my lawyers."

Roger was a little surprised to find he was no longer intimidated by Eastwind. In fact, he had suddenly realized with what contempt he held the man when Eastwind had so easily admitted his "secret." For Roger, anyone who wasn't a fatuous devourer of his own hype would have wanted *to keep* a secret like that. Roger loved music, loved the sensuousness of sound, the curving shapes of melodies that orbited their harmonic suns with the force of tonal gravity that gave them the configurations of beauty – an attraction something like love itself, he had once added as a poetic flourish to a class of jaded-looking undergraduates. In short, he was horrified at Eastwind's invention, exactly because what music was for him *was* human, created in a way that was uniquely human, for humans who had a capacity for the unique. Had he been less polite as a matter of his upbringing, he would have grimaced at the *Tristan* variation even more demonstrably than Antonioni. For that matter, *of course* he was a philistine, as he'd admitted to Marty, looking to the past as the glory days of music. He'd always considered twelve-tone music, in its atonality and abstract method, especially when it came to serialism, where all the variables were, in effect, pre-programmed to function mechanically, to be only at core an early acquiescence to the technical mindset that had come to its latest – and hideous – fruition in the composing machine Eastwind had invented. Although he would admit to himself (were the dark, cold torture called self-doubt to come to him in the night) that such music surely had its own validity: the secret shapes of beauty had as many modes as minds to accommodate them; for that reason Roger considered Beauty to be essentially feminine, incomplete without the penetration of the beholder. All the manner of beauty could do was ever to encode itself – as artifice first for the ultimate sake of art, in method, in technique – lest it give its mystery away, rather than, by preserving it, draw the listeners beyond themselves. Well, he knew that; it was just that taste had a way of becoming truth.

By his lights, from everything he knew about the history of music, and more than that, the *way* of music, a compositional computer program was simply sonic despair, the oblivion of human value as lived and suffered. Why are we in such a hurry to obviate our humanity, he wondered; was it a way of preëmpting the inevitable failure of the sun?

And yet, in the leeway of these reflections, Roger pulled back about the shallowness of Eastwind's endeavors; there were secrets and there were secrets.

"I'm sure you will recall," he said to the man coolly, "what doubts the Zurich lab had that we reported in our Vienna wire. The ferrous factor concerning the ink. The questionable element in the ink itself, something that might have indicated a reconstitution. These are certainly not to be taken lightly."

An unlit cigar in his mouth, Eastwind puzzled over these words. "So, what we have is something not based on certainties, but only on doubts – and maybe doubts that can be allayed. For instance, did they comment on how the ferrous particles differed from those of a writing instrument in the early nineteenth century? Could they be the originals left over from Beethoven's pen? We all know we're not talking about quills here. Metal writing nibs were out there." He lit the cigar.

"They commented that measurements of difference were inconclusive."

"Inconclusive?" Eastwind spat out smoke. "Seems to me a whole lot of 'inconclusives' are supposedly telling me I got took."

Marty leveled his gaze at him. "Were those the only reasons, you would be right to say that. As it turns out, the matter of content intervenes here. What our supposed Beethoven wrote."

"Oh? Something that doesn't jibe historically?"

"Right," Marty continued. "Are you familiar with Solomon's research on the 'Immortal Beloved'? That she was a married woman, wife of a friend of Beethoven's?"

"No," said Eastwind. "No. I think I either heard about it or read about it a long time ago. What does that have to do with anything?"

"Quite a bit," Marty said. "I made it my particular task in the fulfillment of your charge to investigate all contraindications to the validity of Solomon's research."

"And? So?"

"I found none. The 'Immortal Beloved' had to be Antonie Brentano, married to Franz Brentano. And so look to your letter, where it says she's ending *'ihre Mädchen Jahre'* – her maiden years."

"*That's* what you're going on?" Eastwind said agitatedly. People at nearby tables looked over. "Christ, has it occurred to you that Beethoven might have wanted to hide the fact that he was carrying on with his friend's *wife?* What does that prove?"

"It doesn't *prove,*" Roger said, entering the fray a little testily, "it suggests. Look, here's Beethoven, supposedly writing Lichnowsky about having the count send his men to help him move – and it's true Beethoven moved a lot – but he begins, first of all, by carrying on about his 'Immortal Beloved' – which he never did to anyone, since it was a private term of endearment – in a way that is patently false…"

"Hardly 'patently.' Theoretically false," Eastwind interjected.

"And then, he refers to a 'B-major work' – not *'your* B-major work,' something Lichnowsky might have commissioned, or at least have known about, but just out of the blue."

"These are minor cavils," Eastwind said exasperatedly.

"But there's something more – something very strange. Look at the original, where he writes 'B-major.'" Eastwind put on his reading glasses again. "Just to the upper right of the 'B'," Roger said.

"What about it?"

"If you look hard you see the outlines of a little 'flat' symbol, not quite obliterated. Our forger first wrote 'B-flat major,' then stupidly put an inkblot to hide the flat."

"Stupidly? Why would that be stupid?"

"Because Beethoven *almost never* wrote in the key of B-major – or, for that matter, B-minor. Except for one piece where he goes through all twelve major keys, and some inner movements, say the slow movement of the 'Emperor' piano concerto. 'B' meant for him always B-flat. Look through his compositional bibliography. No key of B-natural ever appears."

"I don't see anything beneath the blot," Eastwind said. "It looks like a smudge."

"The lab did. We have the fax of the enlarged X-ray photograph. The flat sign is there. I can show you it if you want."

"I'll take your word for it," Eastwind said, removing his glasses.

"Oddly," Roger went on, "B-flat would have been perfect for something Beethoven *did* write about the time the Immortal Beloved and he were involved – a piano trio with the keyboard part expressly composed for Antonie Brentano's ten-year-old daughter, Maximiliane, with even some fingerings written out. It's very strange that a forger who was so skilled in everything about Beethoven wouldn't have used something like that to make his work credible."

Eastwind seemed to be listening away from Roger's words, pondering a distant landscape. He returned to Roger. "Did you tell me about this, sometime earlier?"

"No," said Roger. "Marty and I considered it a kind of collateral matter. We hadn't noticed it until rather late in our investigation. But it certainly contributes to its being a forgery." He added, "All in all, why would anyone think this was the true Beethoven?"

Eastwind glared at Roger. "Why would anyone take an inkblot to be necessarily deliberate? For that matter, the letter is more than just a comment on the 'B-major' thing and his love life as well; it was primarily a request for help from the count's men," Eastwind countered.

"Meaning?"

"Meaning it had a purpose, and so as not just to ask for help, he made it into a kind of 'newsy' memo, where he was writing whatever came into his head."

"There's no record of of him starting any B-major piece in the summer of 1812," Roger said. "No scholarly work on the Beethoven oeuvre ever mentions anything remotely suggesting that."

"There's no record of my shtupping my thirty-one-year-old on the balcony of the Hotel Mutiny in Coconut Grove two years ago, but she still recalls it, I can assure you."

"Well, then," Roger said, registering in his unconscious that Viagra might work for him too, should he ever have the occasion, "we're at an impasse. All we can do is give you our reasoned opinion. That's all you asked of us."

"What I asked – no, make that *required* – of you was definite proof of the letter's authenticity. Or inauthenticity. All I've gotten is a series of paltry hesitations, just like you at the piano tonight."

"We've done our job, Mr. Eastwind," Roger said with a little edge to his voice.

"I don't think so," Eastwind said evenly. "The rest of your commission is still pending."

Roger hesitated, not wanting to cinch the case in the way he knew would be a quantum leap; he and Marty had hoped their musicological spade-work would suffice; neither of them wanted to level the site. And yet, Eastwind had to be answered; there would be no new evidence, no further investigation, and so he said:

"Actually, we've done more than our job, Mr. Eastwind. We've found the forger."

Eastwind looked at Roger coldly. "What?" he said, then shifted his eyes to Marty, who looked away. "Why didn't you tell me this at the beginning?"

"You didn't ask," Roger said lamely; he knew the real reason was to avoid turning down avenues that ended in wilderness. "As it came about, we traced the forgery to its origin, even to where it took place."

After a moment, and gravely, Eastwind said, "You're absolutely, one-hundred-percent sure of this."

"As sure as the sun rises in the east."

"Could you get him to confess, be brought before the law?"

Roger said, "That might take some doing. But his identity is certain. We spent a long time with his police and prison records. This letter wasn't his first fraud."

"You're certain, then."

"Absolutely," Marty said.

"A long history of scams," Roger added. "We even have corroborating witnesses. Well, one, anyway."

"I still don't understand why you didn't tell me this before, at the outset. What was all that lab business, the historical inconsistencies, about, then? Christ, if you've got an admitted forger, or potentially admitted one, then the matter's closed. I'll call Dave Peres tomorrow. We'll get a lawsuit going, and you two'll be my star witnesses, unless you can get the scam artist himself. Was he working with Brixton's? Oh, that'd be great. That's guaranteed millions."

"No," said Roger. "No. Brixton's was duped too."

"I don't care. They're liable and I'm suing."

"That's not a good idea, Mr. Eastwind," Roger said evenly. "Best to let it drop."

"Let it drop? Of course not. Look, this is the sort of thing that should happen least of all *to someone like me!* Nobody should scam Louis Eastwind and get away with it."

"It's not advisable, Mr. Eastwind," Marty said.

"Look, who are you? Do I go to my attorneys for musical advice? You expect me to take… *musical academics* giving legal advice seriously?"

"If I were you…" Roger began.

"If you were me, you wouldn't survive it," Eastwind snapped, his voice severe. He glared an ugly glare at Roger for a few seconds. "Look," he said, with studied coolness,

"Barry Gittels is standing over there at the bar. I think I need to talk to him." He started to get up.

"I wouldn't pursue it," Roger said, "Mr. Vann."

Eastwind stopped, taken aback. "What did you call me?"

"Ludi Vann," Roger said deliberately. "We have a video of you when you were… different. When it was a different time for you."

Eastwind sat again, then looked down. He put out his cigar; slowly he brought his eyes up to Roger, and then to Marty. "So you know about my… my period of… illness."

"Our researches were most thorough," Marty said.

"All right, all right!" he fulminated after a futile moment. A number of his guests looked over. "It wasn't my choosing to lose my mind! Fate chose that. It came on me all of a sudden. I didn't know who I was, everything fell apart. But I take my medication now – or rather, it's injected monthly, with tests and everything – I visit a psychiatrist regularly. Because those days are over. I can barely remember them, any of the people I knew, what I did. There're some huge gaps. Occasional flashbacks, strange dreams. That's all. But I'm not ashamed of it; madness and genius are often the alternating current bringing greatness to glow."

Inwardly, Roger noted his disgust with that self-assessment. To him, Eastwind might have been best ironically characterized as a Richard Wagner without the talent: nasty, arrogant, temperamental, but not with these things being based on the creativity that meant "genius"; from the outset, he had thought there was something clownishly imitative in Eastwind of what the popular consciousness took to be the characteristics of genius. No, what Eastwind possessed was a category of cleverness merely.

What Roger said was, "It's not that you don't have our sympathies."

"It's not that I want them!" The crowd began to hush. "What I want is to recoup my loss on this fake letter. So what if I… had a bad period in my life? What's that got to do with anything? You didn't need to research *me!* You don't understand. It has great… personal meaning for me to get even with someone who would put something over on *me,* of all people. On Beastwind."

"Because you were a scam artist yourself? You had a bad period before your illness, as your police record shows," Roger said. Eastwind went white.

"We know you served prison time for a number of forgeries," Marty added, as the man grew paler.

"We know it was you, Mr. Eastwind," Roger said with a level gaze, "who, when you were 'Ludi Vann,' wrote this letter."

The man stared at them, stricken.

"The question is *why* you wrote it – wrote it in ways that defeat its purpose as a forgery. Unless that was part of the illness. Or maybe," Roger said, a little surprised at the thought and drawing back a bit, "you were testing your skills on us."

Eastwind's eyes roamed the room. Suddenly he clasped his hands to his ears and pitched forward a little. "Can't they be *quiet!?"* he nearly shouted at them. Roger and Marty were mystified; the crowd had been silent since his last outburst. "The din… tinnitus roar! Go away. Everyone go away!"

"We still need our check, Mr. Eastwind," Roger said, rising.

"Don't mumble! What? Leave. Leave me!" He jumped up, knocking over a chair and tipping the table; a wine glass shattered on the floor, catching the further attention of the guests. The ashtray he had placed his cigar in fell to the patio tile too, and circled tightly around and around on its rim as it made its way to resting unshattered; the insistently rising vibrations held everyone hypnotically. Eastwind shook his fist at them all and shouted, *"Nicht diese Töne! Nicht* 'em!"

No one spoke. Horrified, they saw Eastwind take a stance before them and almost recite:

"Compelled to contemplate a lasting malady, born with an ardent and lively temperament, susceptible to the diversions of society, I was obliged at an early date to isolate myself and live a life of solitude. How great was the humiliation when one who stood beside me heard the… knell of *reason,* and I heard nothing! For ten years I avoided all social gatherings because it was impossible for me to say Bay… Beastwind was… was… *mad.*

"Now you know *another* of my secrets. So get out! Get out! Leave! Go home!" The crowd, stunned, stood as still as deer in headlights. After a moment his attorneys moved toward him, but he waved them away. Roger and Marty saw they would have to pursue the remainder of their fee later, perhaps even through legal means; as they left Roger made the dry remark that, apparently, "those days" weren't over.

The serving staff beat a retreat into the kitchen. Baffled, and not a little fearful, the guests moved into the main house; they hurriedly collected their belongings and then got into their cars. Driving off, they threaded their way through the congestion created by everyone leaving at the same time. Many were nearly speechless about the very strange man who'd been so charming before the evening had come to its sudden, inexplicable, end.

* * *

The veranda on the pool was empty. Eastwind surveyed the tables and chairs, the food left uneaten, the drink glasses, some still with liquor or wine in them, the overturned chair, the shattered glass, the upside-down ashtray on the floor and his dead cigar a few feet away. Slowly he turned around, then fixed his gaze on the Yamaha concert grand next to the pool; his eyes narrowed into malevolence and in a moment he was pressing his great bulk into the curve of the piano, grunting, yelling out as he pushed and it began to yield, rolling it slowly, until it suddenly lurched into the pool. The plume of water from its plunge, silent for him, reached up as high from the formerly placid basin (Eastwind oddly observed) as the chandelier reached down from the ceiling into auspicious space.

The piano stool, looking like a plush leather Ottoman, stood slightly askew, with one leg over the lip of the pool. The man edged over to it, then sat with deliberation, feeling it shift a little. He put his face in his hands and sat there a long time.

Chapter Three

Dreams Again

The roaring in Eastwind's ears kept him awake most of that night, though he did fall into fitful bouts of oblivion – or, not quite oblivion; he dreamed.

In his dreams old faces came to him, along with strange things they spoke. Idiot Boy ("Shia, Ludi Vann, one o' them mofo guardts saidt to the boy they gonna shoot, saidt, 'Die for me. Utter my name as the bullets enter you' chess, let 'em be exitin' you' back suck oudt my sins.' Boy done saidt, 'Looky-yeah, looky-yeah, I couldt do that they wouldtn' be my bullets, you dig? Face you' own damn lead'"); Darrell Jimmy the Gentiles' Gentleman ("Even science occasionally reveals the symbolic truth of the feminine. I refer you to the 'XX' chromosome, gentlemen. For instance, when two X's are combined by joining the ends of any two of their legs to any two ends of the other's legs, they present a square. A square. Let me apprise you of the properties of a square, gentlemen, a line segment gone Swiss-kaleidoscopic, the main relation within which being the diagonal. Now, given the equality of the sides – so that the lengths are essentially *one* – the diagonal will always be expressed by the square root of two. The square root of two, gentlemen: an irrational number. This was the discovery of the Pythagoreans that precipitated their demise as a cult of rational mathematics. I emphasize irrational, gentlemen. For what else could pertain to the eternal feminine, to what is essentially a hole through which the universe is granted its innumerable openings as human life? I refer you to my publication in the *Solipsist's Newsletter,* Volume Twenty-three…"); Bline Boy Eddy ("You seen da junk foo' goo-roo, Ludi Vann? Goldten arches inna damn Himalayas. Dey supersize you' ass, give you a ego-muffin twice as damn big, get through wichyou. It be da Deli Lama now").

And the Preaching Professor came to him, carefully shucking his sign-boards and placing them in a stack. He spoke in his professorial voice. "This is the rest of the story, Ludi, as ontological proofs go. This is just for you. Ahem:

"Then St. Bernard undertook to prove to Aloof, Mr. Zoological Insouciance, that Dog exists. St.B.: Now, Aloof, who hath said in his heart there is no dog, a word with thee. Aloof: Ain' no such a thing as 'dog.' St. B.: You a cat man. Aloof: Cat man be as cat man do. St. B.: You believe in cats. Aloof: I a cat man of inverted scope and subjective range. St. B.: But if you had to define 'dog' how would you do it? Aloof: 'Dog' would be whelped of a canine mother, the Mother of Dog. But that is only a conception, immaculate or not, that doesn't imply… St. B. bites Aloof's right calf, tears a huge hole in his leg, munches the bloody flesh. Aloof: You son of a bitch! St. B.: *Quod erat demonstrandum,* I do believe. Aloof, often given to jabbering in Latin, gets it in a big way. And so the saint say, thanky Jesus, thanky, thanky.

"But then you see it was the hound of faith, this St. B., the faith-hound, heard *not* the dog whistle kept Abrathoven from slaying Isaakarl – DOG WHISTLE = GOD WELSH IT – deaf to the sound, tone deaf to God's infinite mercy, that dog damn aurally impaired and keeps eating his hearing aids. Thinks they're dog treats."

Eastwind awoke with a start and lay panting, this last dream clear in his mind. It was disturbing, though distant chimes resonated slightly in his memory. After a while he connected it with another dream, one he remembered from his Bellevue days, the funny dream that had gone crazy like this one, ending with the prosecutorial voice at him: "What kind of dog are you familiar with, sir?" And he answering: "Da houndt o' faith heard NOT da dog whistle, 'God welsh it' you know da cote."

He wondered if his dreams were speaking to him some way.

Rising onto an elbow, he looked at the digital clock near his bed, noting the date as well as the time: four in the morning, September 26th, 2006. It struck him that he had missed his appointment with the psychiatrist, who gave him the Risperdal injections, by almost a week. So. That was it. Looked like the shrinks knew their dosages and timetables.

He thought of the piano at the bottom of the pool. He thought of his reputation at the bottom of the pool. All he knew now was that he would see Dr. Wilmot tomorrow, and that knowledge let him sleep again.

* * *

Dr. Wilmot, a petite woman with a confident air, had Eastwind sit in the wide chair almost touching hers, so that their conversation – their exploration – seemed more of a chat between old friends, a convention he didn't particularly like but that he went along with; he had been making some progress with the psychiatrist, though the dreams were still tormenting him.

Besides, the visit was necessary, overdue as the injection of mind-straightening chemicals was. It was worth the discomfort of his dampness. Outside the rain was driving against the window; he had gotten pretty wet getting in from the Mercedes, Roy having apparently taken the umbrella with him. But his discomfort owed more to his jumpy psyche, which he knew he'd have to keep under control for the session.

The doctor got out her legal pad and number-two pencil; now it was the routine, though she knew that sometimes breakthroughs weren't always the result of the meticulous analysis of notes. Sometimes spontaneity, even outlandish leaps, took one further. Oddly. But the format, the routine, was useful; it allowed her to fish in troubled waters.

"You were telling me about the dreams just now, a kind of recurring theme. Why don't we get into that, Louie?" she said, as disarmingly as she naturally was for him. Indeed, with her, Eastwind's manner was entirely different from his usual dealings with people; despite his simmering psyche, he made himself passive, open. He wanted answers. She added, "You said there seems to be something that comes up over and over again."

"The hound of faith," he replied.

"That 'heard not the dog whistle,' right?"

"Right. Hearing impaired."

"Ate his hearing aids."

"Well, as I said, the dream last night had the Professor in it, and he said that."

"How often does the Professor come to you?"

"Almost never. He's only a vague memory… from those days. But I dreamt him last night, along with some of the other old cronies. From then."

"Okay," she said. "But what of the 'God-welsh-it'?"

"Well, you know, that's an anagram."

"Right. For 'dog whistle.'"

"It's a phrase that has… haunted me – I almost said 'hounded me' – ever since the arrest and Bellevue."

"How are you doing with anagrams these days?" she asked. "You told me they used to torment you."

"They're coming back. Probably because I'm late for the injection."

"Well, we'll take care of that in a moment," she said, with a glance to the cabinet across the room. "But could we talk about what you take to be the meaning of 'God welsh it'? I think if we look at the implications of 'welsh' we might get somewhere. Or at least be put on some kind of path. Do you think it might mean that God let you down, or someone down?"

"Julie, I've thought about little else since last night. Last night I had a party, tried to be a star, but burned out and fell apart…"

"You want to talk about that?"

"No. Except that two of the guests, professionals I hired to do some… research for me, knew about my… the Beethoven years. They nailed me. Then the dreams, no, first the tinnitus. But the dreams took me back to those days on the streets."

"Well, that's another part of your being overdue on your injection. It's not uncommon for effects of a psychosis to reëmerge if your meds have run out and there are triggers of some sort," she said. "Tell me something, Louie. Is faith a big thing in your life? Are dogs?"

"Not dogs. Faith… faith, I don't know. It's a darkness that vanishes in the light of my rational mind. And when I wasn't rational, there was only darkness, only the sepia gleam of the lie that made me him. I don't know how it relates to dogs."

"Then it's a symbol, isn't it, that we're attempting to interpret, this 'hound of faith'?"

"It's something I think has some weird connection to a vision I remembered – no, it was a dream of something that happened before – when I was in Bellevue."

"Oh, yes. It's in Sepulveda's notes. 'Isaakarl' and 'Abrathoven.' The murdered and the murderer in a final reconciliation. Then the pain in your ears."

"That's it."

"Then this is what we need to explore, Louie. This is what I want you to think about, meditate on, question over and over until you're sick of it. Because few people who suffer as you do get a clue like this. You understand?"

Eastwind shifted uneasily in his chair. He noticed his thoughts were racing, that he was hearing her words in different combinations in the background of his mind. But he studiously ignored that for the sake of keeping the exploration going. "I've thought about it a lot," he said. "I talked it over with Sepulveda, but it always came up a dead end. And yet, there were times when I thought I was right on the verge. Of seeing."

"Look," the psychiatrist said, leaning forward into his face, "here're some strategies. Take the fact that Abraham was to sacrifice Isaac, you know, but God had an angel call it off. Think about what 'welshing it' would mean in that context. Ask what it means that the 'hound of faith' couldn't hear a dog whistle, and relate it to Beethoven's deafness. But tie it all in with how the 'Beethoven' you were relates to Beethoven's nephew, Karl…"

"I've done that," he replied a little edgily. "I remember doing that."

"… and what killing anyone has to do with Beethoven and Karl. You know he didn't kill his nephew."

"Right. He might have driven him to try suicide, but Karl survived."

"And also," she said after a pause, "ask if you've ever killed anybody."

"I know," said Eastwind, who heard her words reassembled as "kill anybody if you've ever asked," but ignored this, "the Brett Yearly thing. Sepulveda asked me about that."

The doctor reviewed for a few moments what she had written on the pad, then turned to Eastwind.

"Well, you have your homework, Louie. See if you can dredge anything up with those questions." On the word "questions" Eastwind's mind returned to the previous night, to his being found out by McKane and Spratt; it was McKane who had posed the question of why "Ludi Vann" had written the letter with such red flags. His eyes darted about momentarily, and the psychiatrist noticed.

"What's wrong, Louie? You suddenly look haunted."

He said, "For some strange reason I thought of last night, at the party. Perhaps a spurious association. My mind... you know... it's doing its thing." He smiled wanly.

"Ah, yes," she said. "You said some people doing computer research confronted you with your past – something like that? How did you handle that?"

"It wasn't computer research. It was something more like... forensic musicological research. Oh, yeah. I should tell you about that. See, I'd bought this letter at an auction a few years ago, supposedly a letter of Beethoven's. I'd had these musicologists – they teach at Eastman, they're reputable, kind of twits, though – I had them check it out for authenticity."

"What's this have to do with their knowing about your... bad old days?"

"Look, Julie. You know of my... criminal record from back in the eighties. My prison time for scams, forgery."

"Yeah... I do," she said, looking at him in the eyes. "Have to factor it all in. Frankly," she added with mild relief that he had brought it up, because she thought it could be a disruptive point, "I've occasionally wondered if you were scamming me with some of the stuff you told me. But it always came back to your having gone straight. Your doctorate. And your suffering."

"The letter was one of my own forgeries."

"What?! You're kidding!"

"Done while I was a sick man. I vaguely remember working with some early nineteenth-century parchment and special ink while I was at the Yearly's halfway house. I'd learned Beethoven's hand. I'd worked on it for a while."

“And what was the letter?”

“Crafted nonsense, really. I certainly didn’t recognize it when I read it. Later.”

“You wrote it in German, of course. Can you speak it?”

“I can read it. I almost minored in it at Emory. And I knew how early nineteenth-century German – even certain expressions – would be used in a letter.”

“Well, they say karma is a kind of boomerang. I hope you’re not beating yourself up too much over this, Louie. It must have been devastating.”

“I lost a lot of face. My piano is at the bottom of my pool. I pushed it there in anger.”

“Some boomerangs hit hard, I guess.”

“But you know, something one of the musicologists said has stuck with me, something with the knell of truth to it. He said the real question about the fake letter was *why* ‘Ludi Vann’ had written the things he did in it.”

“If you can unravel that, it might help. Or maybe not. But you think it’s important,” she said with an earnest look at him. “Why *did* ‘Ludi Vann’ write what he wrote?”

“I don’t know. I don’t know. I’ve forgotten so much from those days. The present is a merciful curtain over the past, though there are rips and holes in it.”

“More homework, Louie: peek into those holes. And remember, next session we talk about the strategies. You’ll try them?”

“I’ll try them. My dreams might help me,” he said, again a little edgily. “But I don’t like getting back into those days.”

“They won’t ever be over for you, Louie, until you make the past… well, *past.* More past.”

“I know. I’ll do it.”

"And, Louie," she said, getting up and moving toward the cabinet where the syringes and the vials of antipsychotic drugs were kept, "don't let it go over a month again."

"But, you know," he said with an urgency to his voice, "it occurred to me just now that the more I stay straight, the less I can get back into what I did in those days. I'll never remember – from the outside."

The doctor stopped and considered this. "That's a pretty radical thought, Louie. But my professional advice – not to say my ethics – can't go with you there." Eastwind was looking out her window, face contorted.

He said, "I'd hate doing it. Already I'm falling back into some of the strangeness of those days, Julie. Look how hard it's raining out there, look at those branches whipping around – it's already started something."

She peered at the chaos outside the window. Their conversation had been punctuated throughout by what sounded to be pebbles thrown against the glass. "What," she said. "Tell me."

"Do you know Beethoven's Sixth Symphony, the movement with the peasant party interrupted by a rain storm?"

"I played clarinet in a symphony orchestra before I got into medical school," she said. "Yeah, we did that piece. Big clarinet part in that movement."

"The lightning bolts! The thunder! It's with me."

"But that's just it, Louie. You're tormented enough as it is. Let me shoot you up…"

"Not now. Not yet."

"I'm against it. Say no to that."

"See, that's the Fifth: 'I'm-a-gainst-it; say-no-to-that.'"

"I can't let you…"

"'I-can't-let-you'!"

He gave her a distressed and forbidding look, and there was silence between them. In a moment he opened the door and made his way into the driving water.

* * *

More dreams. And in them more of the bizarre notions and happenings that Eastwind had lived as Ludi Vann.

He could feel the pull of his madness especially in these dreams. It was as if he were caught up in a current that bumped and slammed him into the rocks and crags of the irrational as he saw the shore of reason receding in the onrush. And yet, something in him hung on; he rode a small raft of hope that, once he'd tumbled over the falls, he would face his demon, the hidden past; the hound of faith might be chased down and chained up. Or maybe it would return to being a simple phrase that no longer held mystery – and misery – for him. He occasionally yelled in the night, and sometimes Polly looked in on him.

He turned the daily doings of his household over to Roy, who had returned when his wife had refused to press charges for the latest round of brutality. Her bruises were gone, and her rancor, though never to leave, had abated; she loved him and somehow his violence toward her was part of that. At any rate, Roy was an excellent manager of the household. Though a violent and seemingly seedy man, he was completely honest with Eastwind; he had all the account numbers and never practiced to deceive. He was paid well.

Roy had arranged to get the Yamaha concert grand with its soggy computer out of the pool. This involved hiring a huge crane that would lower its great cable through sections of the pool cage that Roy had removed, including a beam and a strut. Before all the proceedings began, though, he had a friend of his come over who would help with getting the piano on the solid patio. The friend, a guy they called

"Smokey" for his devotion to marijuana, had brought a little grass with him, and he and Roy and the now less-rancorous Susan, the wife who had come over for the evening, smoked the slender joints out in the pool area of Eastwind's grand house. Long-time friends, they'd been doing this together for years. Eastwind didn't approve of dope. Once when Roy had asked him if Smokey could pay a little visit, he had refused with the line: "No. Our cultures might clash." He found the exaggerated perceptions and hilarity of a marijuana high pointless, even disgusting. But now that the man was *hors de combat*, the trio simply made sure the door to his bedroom was shut and went ahead.

Smokey expelled the smoke after holding it down; a slender stream shot toward a screen panel above him. He beheld the piano resting in the pool, toward the shallow end, in about three feet of water. It had landed on its three legs, even though the pedal assembly was bent hideously sideways, having caught on the edge of the pool as the instrument had toppled into the water; its wing seemed to float on the surface. The image captivated him.

"Hey, Roy."

"Hey, Smokes."

"Ever heard a piece by Debussy called *The Sunken Cathedral?"*

"Man, just because I work for Eastwind don't mean I get into the classical songs."

Susan allowed that the Fat Man ruled; she and Roy broke into spasms of laughter. Smokey liked The Grateful Dead, but had musical tastes far beyond pop and rock. "No, seriously, it's a great piece. It's about this old legend where this old cathedral has sunk beneath the sea, but every so often it rises."

"Cool," said Roy.

"Shit," said Susan.

"Yeah, and its bells toll. Then it sinks below the surface again."

"A hazard to navigation. For ghost ships," Roy said, and chuckled at his witticism. His wife giggled along with him.

"Yeah," said Smokey, "I thought of it looking at the piano there. What a shame. Looks like a new concert grand. One of the nine-foot suckers."

"Yeah, a Yamaha Disklavier," said Roy.

"I thought it was a Kawasaki," Susan sputtered in laughter.

"Damn," said Smokey, "I would've loved to play it." He had taken piano lessons up through his truncated college career, and still played – simple things like the first movement of the "Moonlight" Sonata and the Debussy. "Why did he push it in the pool?"

"He has demons," Roy answered. "You know, he was crazy a while back."

"Hey, you know what would be really cool?" Smokey continued.

"What?" Susan answered.

"Shit," he said, "I wonder if you could get any sound from it playing it under water."

The trio broke up on that.

"But, you know," Smokey went on, "I'm serious. I still remember most of *The Sunken Cathedral.* I learned it when I was taking lessons. Wouldn't it be cool to hear it from under the water?"

"No, man," Roy said. "That would be un-cool. Eastwind wouldn't like that. Besides, not all of it is under water. Just the keyboard."

"But you said he was down for the night," Susan said. "Why are you such a wimp for that blow-hard?" Roy glared at her menacingly. "Isn't his bedroom door shut? Let's ask Polly." She walked away toward the kitchen.

"Well," Roy said, a little uneasily, "it might be okay if the door is shut and he's like, really out."

Susan returned shortly, not having found Polly. "She says it's okay. He's out of it for the night," she announced.

They all giggled some more as Smokey stripped to his underwear and climbed into the pool. "Man," he said with a little shudder, "I thought it'd be warmer than this."

"You got to suffer for your art, man," Roy allowed as Susan buckled.

"I'll really need to bang it out," he said, turning to them, "'cause those felt hammers are a little water-logged." He lifted the lid and affixed it to its strut, then moved to the keyboard. He arranged his fingers for the opening of the piece and slammed them down at the keyboard. As it happened, Roy had been draining the pool as part of the removal procedure, and the strings of the instrument just crested the water, creating a kind of hydrostatic harp. A strange, drowned clang made its way eerily off the surface.

"Far out!" Roy said.

"Shit!" said Susan.

Smokey teased some soggy, descending parallel seventh chords out of the engulfed instrument; they blurred horribly, but not without a weird enchantment to them.

"Wow," Susan said, "that's the *Phantom of the Opera,* right?"

"No, you dumb twat," Roy said. "Didn't you hear him say it's a sunken cathedral?"

As was the case, Eastwind's bedroom door had been left open by Polly a few minutes earlier and the strangulated sounds permeated his unconscious mind. Something in him recognized the music, and a reverie of being underwater began to emerge in his sleep-slain consciousness, deprived as it was of the world of his bed and bedroom. He began to see his thoughts as bubbles from someone pacing the bottom of a turbulent ocean, and found it was himself. He spied an anchor of brass refuting the restlessness of the sea, and saw the words, "that the line might hold." The bright object fascinated him, showering off gleaming shimmers, and he thought of the depth-invaded ocean, disturbed dream of itself, having turned it into gold. The bubbles streamed with the current of this Morpheatic Sea, fled in an orderly drift towards something.

Eastwind followed the bubbles. He saw a great cathedral, barnacle-encrusted, green as if the depths had loved it so much as to transfer their hue to the corroding granite blocks. And the great rotten wooden door with its inscription, "*Ubi Johannes?*" in misshapen letters. As he pulled at the crumbling mass, he translated: Where you been, Jack? He answered in his mind: oh, you know, chasing the ends of emptiness, moving the horizon from here to there to witness more things troubling time-space. He entered the church and the water was gone.

A priest stood with his back to him, raising a host the size of a pizza above his head. He lowered the great wafer, a white man becoming black; he turned to Eastwind, and casually took a bite. "Shia," he said, "ain' the damn Wrigley people improvedt this thing yet. Godt be subtle but the cat sure ain' delicious." It was The Professor in priestly garb.

Eastwind approached the altar. He crossed himself and knelt. "Bless me, Professor, for I have…"

"Yup," said the other, "it all a big deal widh the angels and widh the musicologists…"

"For I have… have…" Eastwind stammered.

"Shia, we all make mistakes, Ludi," he replied, "unless I got it wrong."

"I wrote a letter," he began.

"Yup. Rome done circulate your manuscri't, you got pontiffs pontificating on the damn pointlessness of it. The patheticalness."

"You know. You know about the error with the flat sign."

"Ain' worth even one 'Hail Mary,' Ludi. No damn 'Our Father.' 'Cause it ain' no big deal."

Eastwind was taken in a dream-aback. "But I wrote B-natural instead of B-flat. That changes everything up a half-step."

"Yup."

"It's an affront – in mathematical harmony. It accelerates every cosmological relation."

"Shia," said the professor-priest, "even Jesus warn't too goodt in math. He was perfect in general, but he warn't excellent. He thought excellence be triumph in the temporal worldt. You hadda check his addition and subtraction."

Jesus wasn't good in math. Eastwind stopped to consider this. He looked around, noticing the cruciform floor plan, the equilateral arches granting the transept its width, the geometrical assurances of the vaulted ceiling that it would expand the perfect octaves and fifths and fourths of medieval music into into the harmony of the spheres, revoiced to convey divine love redeeming rebellious pride.

"That be the tru'," the professor went on, "he thought *two* could exiss widdout *three.* Thought two would groundt itsel'f on one, ain' no further business, you know, widh three. It a limited base-system. One, two; one, two… Less jus' say it offend 'gainst the Trinity."

"That's odd," the dream-Eastwind allowed.

"Well, you know," the dream-priest went on in a lowered, almost conspiratorial, voice, "he take the pair o' nail-points of his handts on the beam of the cross to be the Two: reunification between Man and Godt, you know, somethin' like Elvis drivin' a 'fifty-eight Chevy, the young Brando on a Triumph motorcycle. Custer and Sitting Bull. Mountain and valley and damn vice-versa, not to say versa-vice. Murdered and murderer in final reconciliation. Like. But ain' no escapin' the thirdt."

"There's not?"

"Shia, what of the damn vertical shaft in the architectonic here? I ax you! Whut it be that press it unforgiving woodt 'gainst his heels, calves, thighs, balls, ass, spine and the damn medulla wherefrom his autonomic functions issue into divine existence? It be that draws us beyon' ourse'fs, drains us into the pass, holds out the damn future. He thought Two be the self-embrace o' the eternal One. Shia, poor math make for poor posture, Ludi, *pietà* posture. You miscalculate and you Michelangelo it. Forget about you' B-natural."

"You mean, it's not a mistake?"

The man looked at him with Sepulveda's dark eyes in Julie Wilmot's kind face. "Not for what you were intendin'."

"What was I intending?"

Suddenly the sanctuary began filling with water. "Take a deep breath, Louie," the professor-priest said, alb beginning to float up. "We can puffer-fish it to the surface."

The dream-Eastwind took a deep breath. "You're sure that'll work?"

"Just keep that little bubble, Louie. It'll save you."

Eastwind awoke to a heated fray between Roy and Susan, with Smokey shouting at them to cool it.

Chapter Four

A Visit to the Streets

Mountain and valley and damn vice-versa, not to say versa-vice. Murdered and murderer in final reconciliation. These words of the priest-professor struck Eastwind a day or so after his cathedral dream; the latter phrase jogged his memory of the vision he'd had just before taking his own hearing over a decade ago. Dr. Wilmot's advice, "Ask yourself if you've ever killed anybody," came to him. I know, he'd replied to her, the Brett Yearly thing. And now the Brett Yearly thing was beginning to claim his waking consciousness more and more, and he realized he needed to know what had happened. But he despaired of ever finding that out.

A strange plan came to his troubled mind. Despite its implausibility he found his thoughts returning to it, and eventually it came to take the shape of a vague hope.

Eastwind began visiting the Bowery, a much transformed one from his early days there. Dressed as someone with little means and less luck, he approached various men, most of whom had nothing to say except to ask for money. One offered him a drink from a bottle in a bag, another a hit of crack. After a day of wandering he would go to where his Mercedes was parked (far away) and return home. But he returned day after day, three days in a row. On the third day he talked to a man who said he had known Bline Boy Eddy. Eastwind almost asked him if Beebee, his nickname for his old friend, was still alive or still dead. Still alive, came to him, or stillborn. Variations began caroming and ricocheting in his mind: still blind or still sighted except when he sighted a still… then blind drunk, drunk blind. Still cited, quite still. Quiet still. Quiet. *Quiet!* Still… still.

"He still here?"

The man said he'd seen him a few days ago. Eastwind sat where over a decade ago he had sat, back to the wall, the whiff of urine both repulsive and reassuring. Hours passed, and when he eventually heard a tapping he looked up. "Bline Boy," he said.

The man stopped. "Ludi Vann. Shia."

Eastwind fell into the persona and the dialect. "Be me."

"Where you been, man? I heardt all sorta things."

"I been… away."

"Where you go?"

"To… to Canada. A Canada o' da mindt."

"Where?"

"Da frozen north," he said, and saw the letters of those words do-si-do. "Da Zen for thorn."

"You back for goodt? You got a place?"

"Nah. Visitin'."

"Mahn, who wanta visit here? *Livin'* here be a different thing," Bline Boy said. He wore a heavy coat and an obvious bowler.

"I be lookin' for, you know, we callt him 'Idiot Boy.' He still aroun'?"

"Shia," said Bline Boy. "'Idiot Boy.'"

"You remember… he listened in on da about-to-die."

"A bruthah?"

"Yeah. He be, like, present in his mindt at executions. Lass wordts."

"Da necrophilia Jesus! Usta be Lazara da Living Endt's daddy-man," Bline Boy said, jabbing a little with his cane.

"Dat da cat. Where he be a'?"

"Shia, he still be workin' at da funeral home. Bugg's. Dat righ', dey call him 'Bug Man' now."

"Shia, he always a little buggy."

"Heardt he bent, Ludi. Guess time done weigh heavy on dat boy."

"It goin' aroun'."

"Yeah, he at Bugg. Heardt he practically run da damn place now."

"Where Bugg a'?"

"Shia, Ludi, you buys me lunch I takes you there."

And as in so many times eons ago, Bline Boy placed his hand on Eastwind's upper arm, and they walked. But unlike anything that could ever have happened before, he walked him to the distant parking lot where his car gleamed dully under a half-hearted sun.

As it happened, Eastwind took Bline Boy to the same open-air restaurant the two musicologists had.

"Shia, you hardtly Ludi I knew," Bline Boy said.

"Somethin' damn change in my brain, Beebee. Lotta gimpy gray matter done met da master sergeant."

"Whut his name?"

"Sgt. Risperdal. Norwegian fella."

"Da mindt dottors, dey done curedt you. What I heardt."

Eastwind thought: or can. Or know what chemicals can keep my madness at bay. But it had been almost six weeks since the last injection, and he knew his old illness, while far from being in full force, was dogging his consciousness; he hung onto his rationality like a lifesaver, consciously trying not to drown in the old perceptions and urges. But Beethoven's melodies were playing like aural shadows off the illuminations of reason, and on the drive to the Bowery he had noticed a four-note motif from the coda of the first movement of the Fifth starting to develop – as if by the master, but quite differently from the symphony; the retrograde of the notes sounded at a level a sixth above the original, harmonized against its inversion. Surprised to discover this, he winced mentally; Beethoven was never that Mozartian-mathematical. Then it struck him: Christ! It's all anagrams, in a way, with note letter-names – my own genius. It's happening, it's happening, he admitted in anguish, Ludi Vann is in the wings! He thought of Lear: "O, let me not be mad, not mad, sweet heaven! Keep me in temper, I would not be mad!"

Sweet heaven? What was that?

"I dreamt 'bout you, Beebee, jus' a few weeks ago," Eastwind said, once they'd sat at a table. "You 'n', shia, 'member da Professor? Oh, yeah, 'n' – you 'member Darrell Jimmy?"

"Da Gentile' Gen'leman. Yup. What we doin'?"

"Talkin'. Oldt times onna screets together."

"Da screets done change a lot you be gone." Bline Boy sniffed the air. "You know, Ludi, I got a feel fo' dis place. Was here a few weeks ago. Some white guys axin' 'bout da Polecat, dey bring me here."

"Da Polecat," Eastwind said, trying to remember.

"Samminski or somethin' his real name."

Eastwind recalled a big man with a façade of a face, and felt a dull violence. "Shia, he get his nose fix? I done bustedt it inna oldt days."

"Man, he kin affordt to fix it, got a lot o' money now."

"Shia," said Eastwind, monitoring how he spoke, "I got money too dese days. Gonna lay some of it on you later, Beebee – my frien' from da pass. Fuckin' rollin' in it."

"Thass cool."

A waiter approached suspiciously. "You guys been waited on?"

"Yeah, we eatin' da air, promise-crammed. My compliments to da meteorologis'," Eastwind replied.

"You…uh, you got money?"

Eastwind said with a glare, "Shia, jus' tellin' da man here 'bout my stock options," and pulled out his gold Mastercard. The waiter took their order.

After a silence, Bline Boy spoke. "Ludi, gotta tell ya how da Polecat got his loot."

"So how?"

"He scammed some place 'bout a letter he saidt you write, dat he foundt at da Quaker house when you got bustedt. Da white guys be axin' me did he fin' it in you' room."

Eastwind sat immobile in the sudden understanding of how the letter got out, how it made its way to the market; McKane and Spratt hadn't mentioned how the letter got to Brixton's, nor had the auction house, at the request of their source. Salmaninski, thought Eastwind. The Polecat. The Skunk. A number of vague associations occurred to him, one troubling in particular. He leaned into Bline Boy. "Beebee," he said, "somethin' I gotta know. When did da Polecat fin' da letter?"

Bline Boy said, "You know, it be when dey sent you away, widchou settin' fires, direckin' traffic 'n' all."

"No, no," Eastwind said, and almost started to speak in his usual English; he said, "Does you know da day, anythin' like dat?"

"Shia, he fin' it when he foundt dat body, dat Quaker fella, deadt at da bottom o' da stairs."

"Tell me: he da one discoverdt da body?"

"Thass whut he tol' me. Den look fo' you in you' room. But da cops done got you."

Eastwind pondered this. He felt some clarity of order was about to dawn, poised to bring light to certain caverns of the past.

"You gotta show me Bugg, we through," he said as they ate.

"Shia," said Bline Boy, "I got dis righ', you jus' gotta crane you' neck 'roun', look 'cross da screet." Eastwind looked over and saw the red-brick building with "Bugg's Funeral Home" in stainless steel letters.

"Man," he said to Bline Boy, "behindt me all da time."

* * *

When Idiot Boy beheld him it was as if Eastwind was drunk in by eyes that pulled all things into them to assess their tragedy; the aged dark man seemed to wash the world in his gaze, engulfing it in a strange twilight where glinted the hues of sadness and compassion. "My man widh da Jesus-pecker," Eastwind said in empty bonhomie.

Idiot Boy said slowly, "My man, Ludi Vann. You come back. You enlightened now?"

"I got da nugatory nirvana," Eastwind said. "My thirdt eye still suffer from night blin'ness."

"You be back 'cause you ain' diedt the death," Idiot Boy said. "Whut happen you' hair, Ludi? It mos'ly gone."

"Da sweet bird o' youth done finally molted. You 'Idiot Boy' or you 'Bug Man' now?"

"Call me 'Idiot Boy' like you usta," he said as they moved into the building. "Still don' know shit from Shinola in the worl' o' the livin'. My clients comfort me widh a kine o' certainty. They's predictable-like, you dig? You still 'Ludi Vann'?"

Eastwind considered how to answer. The smell of formaldehyde overwhelmed him a moment. "Yes and no," he said, speaking in white English. "There's been more of me added to the man you knew. Or restored to me." Neither of them cared about the change in his speaking style.

"That why you come?"

"You still hear 'em, Idiot Boy? Jus' before they deaths?" He naturally reverted to the dialect.

Idiot Boy looked away, toward a gurney where lay the corpse of a young black man, fluids draining. He turned back to Eastwind. "Yeah, I still gets they lass wordts. Sometimes in every sentence the livin' speak. Periodts at the endt like punctuation at military funerals. Like."

"Man, you still thanato-audient."

"Shia, don' know no fancy wordts. I the receptacle o' they lass wills. I listens in place o' Godt. I listens fo' Godt."

In Eastwind's afflicted consciousness the "fo' Godt" became "forgot," then a series of phrases began to chase each other around – "Got four because he forgot; he forgot because he got four…" They came into phase and fell into the key of D-major; in a moment he heard the thunderous *"vor Gott!"* from the Ninth Symphony. He was clutching his head as he noticed that Idiot Boy was telling a story.

"… a boy once in his death row cell, the assistant wardten show up jus' befo' they's gone shave his headt, not on official business, you know, the boy a dark man I seen in my mind as I heardt they conversation." Idiot Boy took on the voices:

"'Sometimes at the end the answers to secret questions can save you,' the wardten fella say. 'Interested?'

"'Shee-it,' say the boy. 'Don' do religion. Toldt da chaplain to fuck off.'

"'A way out. Not so much out as… back.'

"'No goin' back now.'

"'Look at your hands,' say the wardten fella. 'Start there. You see those scars? You have many scars.'

"'I been a busy boy. Got more scahs 'n' you.'

"'If you can tell me how you got each scar – you must remember perfectly – you will be taken back before this moment.'

"'Whut da fuck you talkin' 'bout? Who you think you are? Shee-it, you mus' be crazy, man.'

"'You will be beyond your present peril.'

"'Whudafuck…? Whut you mean, "beyon'"? You mean you let me go?'

"'You're out of here. But each and every scar. You must not miss one.'

"'Shee-it… for real?'

"'For super-real. That one there, top of your thumb, for instance. Let's start with that. How'd you get it?'

"'Dat wahn… got it wukin' on muh cah. Scrape it on a headter bolt.'

"'The '86 Camaro.'

"'How you know?'

"'I know. I'll know if you're jiving me.'

"'No fuckin' jive, man. Dis wahn, dude cut me in high schoo'. Bassetball dude.'

"'That is correct. One Jevon McArthur.'

"'Jumpin' Jevon. I fix his ass f'dat.'

"The wardten guy point to da boy's shouldter, like, say, 'And this bad one – stitches for that.'

"'Triedt to get away from a house I was robbin' – sunumbitch come home, seen me in da kitchen – I slidt down da drain pipe, fuckuh broke and d'edges slash me up.'

"'The cops took you to the emergency room.'

"'Yeh.'

"'Go on.'

"'Dis one, you know.'

"'That's where she stabbed you.' The boy looks at 'im right in da eyes, saidt,

"'Dat da wahn.'

"'But you fixed her ass – you finished killing her.'

"'Se'f defense, man.'

"'The electric chair, man.'

"'Hey, I'm getting' 'em right, ain't I?'

"'You've got more to go. Take off your clothes.'

"'Shee-it, man, all a dem?'

"'That's the deal.'"

Idiot Boy turned to Eastwind. "Some o' the scahs, they be like real funny shit, you know, Ludi. Hadt one scah on his dick from gettin' it caught in a piece o' damn PVC pipe. Hadt to have it sawt off."

"His dick?" Eastwind had been drawn into the story.

"The pipe. I saidt scah, not no *stump.*"

"I dig. So…"

"So he got on down to a kine o' dimple on his right thigh where some boardt he be jumpin' on when he a young 'un broke an' a splinteredt edge done ram his leg… Got on down to a scah on his right foot little toe and couldtn't 'member.

"The wardten-man: 'I said you must account for every one.'

"The boy: 'Mahn, How I 'member shit like dat? I couldta been a little kiuh.'

"'All of them. You know every mark on your body. This is the next to last one.'

"'Shee-it,' say the boy, 'dis be *da las'* wuh.'

"'There's one more after this one. A crucial scar. As for this one, does a pair of sandals you wore to metal shop one day help at all?'

"'Sandals…'

"'You were bucking the regulation footwear.'

"'In metal shop…'

"'Did you drop something?'

"'… Oh, shit, at da ban' saw…'

"'At the band saw. That bar you were cutting.'

"'Fell right on muh foot, jus' about loss muh toe. Mahn, bloodt *ever*where. Dey use me as a 'sample. Hurt like hell.'

"'Very good. And now the last scar.' He lock eyes widh the boy. 'Actually earlier than any of the others.'

"'Shee-it, mahn! I done tol' 'em all!'

"The wardten fella, he holdt his glare. 'There is one more. Or no deal.'

"'Whut da fuck! Look at me! You wanna look up muh ass, check muh nuts? Dis be it, man. I got no mo'.'

"Wardten saidt, saidt, 'There is one more.'

"'*Where?* You show me.'

"'To show it is to tell it. It's you who must tell me.'

"Man," said Idiot Boy, fixing Eastwind with a look, "like, that boy, he couldtn't fin' it, calledt that assistant wardten a faggot, saidt they never was no deal. The assistant wardten, he say to the boy:

"'Had you found it the mystery would have gripped you in release. You would have been free. But whatever…'

"He like lef' 'im screechin' and coisin'. I later heardt the boy at the 'lectrocution, man, hadt that nigger in the chair, you know, he sudden-like began to yell beneath that hoodt they slip over his headt, shoutin', 'My belly-button! My belly-button!!' you know, but real muffledt-like. That wardten fella, he mutter somethin' like, 'Dumb shit,' shakin' his headt, face o' disgus' as they sent that boy off."

"So you still hear *and* see," Eastwind said presently.

"Sometimes see."

"Can you… can you go back to things, to last moments, in the past?" he asked with concern, dropping the black English for good.

"Man, Ludi, I don' know when they happen. The soundt o' voices, the scene, it jus', you know, like come to me. Don' know no when. Couldt be pass, couldt be future even. All I know it jus' happen fo' me."

Eastwind contemplated this. "But is it… is it *real?* I mean, like did you ever read in newspapers about any executions you heard?"

Idiot Boy looked over to the gurney. "Don' readt no newspapers. Don' watch no news. Damn things turn lies into truth."

"But, I mean…"

"Man, you know I got work to do. I 'bout the only embalmer Bugg got. Why you come see me?" He got up and ambulated a bent-over shuffle toward the brightly lit room. Eastwind walked along with him, the glare of the lights cutting deeply into him, seeming to scour in their antiseptic whiteness.

"Look, Idiot Boy," he said with a note of desperation. "Look… what's your real name? I feel silly calling you that."

"Ain' got no real name."

"What were you called when you were a little boy?"

"Never calledt. Spoke to."

"Look, the thing is, see, I'm not Ludi Vann anymore. Never was Beethoven. My name is Eastwind. I might've killed a man when I was Ludi Vann. I've got to know."

Idiot Boy turned to him. "You came to me 'cause you want me to hear. Fo' you."

"Yes. I need you to hear, see – if you can – what happened back when I was at the halfway house. You remember, when I had that job at the trophy shop. When this man… he was a good man, a Quaker… got killed."

"Man, don' know if you can, like, order up anythin'. I don' control it, like."

Eastwind was agitated. "But, what if I told you what I know about… what happened there? All I remember?"

"Don' know. Ludi, I got a family comin' for a viewin' in two damn hours, dig? You come back tomorrow night."

Eastwind's face broke into hope. "That's good, Idiot Boy."

"We kin try," the man said. "Maybe we kin get you to remember you' navel base." He looked at him with compassion.

Eastwind smiled. "'Dumb shit.' Sometimes it's too late to get it."

"Yeah," said Idiot Boy, "but you gotta die the death in any case."

Chapter Five

Home Again

Eastwind hadn't wanted to drive back to the Hamptons that night and decided to find a hotel. His mind had been juggling letters that seemed to have appeared at random, and that he had first assembled as AIM PLOY; he had assumed this wacky mental scramble was something referring to his intentions with Idiot Boy. The letters wandered around each other, then formed the world OLYMPIA. A very distant jangle of chimes sounded.

Eventually he found the Olympia Hotel. It was much as it had been when he'd first arrived in the city, though a lot more run down. On the way there "Olympia" had faded from his troubled mind as other letters from billboards and street signs began rearranging themselves ("Rayban Sunglasses" advised, NAY, BAR SNUG LASSES, then shifted into BAR GUNSELS ANY ASS; POTS shouted the octagonal signs at the end of streets, sometimes POST and OPTS, an occasional TOPS that ran itself backward as SPOT); as well he heard music and words, sometimes little phrases – though he could listen and not be absorbed; one of them was "Room 567."

The desk clerk said there was no fifth floor.

Eastwind knew it was the place. "Is Sabina still here?" he asked tentatively, and visualized the letters of that name rearranging themselves; or is she at a baSin? In Saab?

"Tell me the words," the clerk said with a pointed look.

Eastwind's strained consciousness took the phrase as "Tell me, the words." He blurted out, "Let Mel, the sword."

"You know Mel?" said the clerk. "Samurai Mel? Okay. But Sabina died five years ago."

"What of?"

"I think it was, of death. Yeah, coroner said it was death. She'd had it a long time. It was congenital. Nobody knew."

"Then you did have a fifth floor at one time?" Eastwind said cautiously.

"We had a fifth but it became the sixth out of a sense of architectural ambition. That meant the former fourth was affected with a kind of passive structural transcendence to become the fifth. But we call it the fourth."

"Why?"

"Because the lobby was threatened with becoming the first, and the cellar with being the lobby. We thought it bad for business. So it's the fourth. Sabina's twin sister works that floor."

"She's here tonight?"

"Unless it was she who died and Sabina is working. Sometimes Death's hood falls over his eyes and the scythe goes a little awry."

"Twins can confuse anybody," Eastwind said, deciding he would drive home after all.

"Sometimes Death wheels around mindless of the scythe, like the old sight-gag of a man turning with a beam on his shoulder. Levels somebody without meaning to."

"Would that be… Fate?" Eastwind asked, urged by a distant echo.

"That would be Chance."

But Eastwind had already turned away.

"Why don't you ask her if it was she who died or if it was her sister?" the man called after him as Eastwind crossed the heavily frayed carpet, making his way to the car.

After the drive, at home, he collapsed into the great chair in his study and looked through the mail Roy had neatly stacked for him. It was late, and everyone had either left or was in bed. He weeded out uninteresting items, this time with no waggling cigar, no sarcastic mutterings under his breath; a kind of searching despair colored the passing of time now – as it had been ever since the revelation of his own forgery. He fingered through more mail, then saw the return address of Roger McKane on the last envelope of the pile. He ripped it open.

> Dear Mr. Eastwind,
>
> Though Dr. Spratt and I are filing in civil court for our fee (which we are sure to gain, since our agreement was contractual), there is yet a matter that we can't in good conscience postpone until the litigation has concluded.
>
> Ms. Ann Yearly, whom we contacted in our search for the authentication of your letter,

(Eastwind noted a little wryly that "your letter" was probably a calculated double entendre, and was slightly buoyed that, despite the annoyingly different meanings of words scrambled into place by his brain, there were still significant meanings, ironic, darkly funny, that occurred to him)

> had us promise that should we find "Ludi Vann" we would let her know who and where he is. We are about to do that, though it might be better if you contacted her. She was very urgent in her need to see you.

An address and phone number in Nyack followed, and then Roger's signature. Eastwind put the letter down slowly. He knew that Ann Yearly's concern was also his. He reflected that he might be able to give her an answer about Brett's death if Idiot Boy could… oh, but how mad, how tenuous a notion that was – even though he knew he would be at the funeral home the next night. "I be workin' on it, gal," sounded in his mind, and he noticed that the black English was still with him. He saw again that he was falling more and more into his past.

And yet, now that both dimensions of his mind were in play – a tenuous sanity that watched alternately in anxiety and amusement the rantings of the other part of his mind, that part which had gripped him in a forged identity, compelled him to wear a frock coat (Jesus, did it stink in summer!) – he could observe some of how the old mind worked. He wondered if he had just been at the Olympia Hotel. "Dat really happen, or jus' in my damn headt?"

He wondered about the street-black English, and lit a cigar. It had been part of his whacked-out persona. But surely: the distortion of the canon of structure and pronunciation of English – was it not Beethoven's stretching of sonata form, his crescendos into *pianissimo* softness? – this gentle anarchy that had its own eloquence, poetry even, was it not a rebellion against classical pronunciation and syntax in the same way Beethoven rebelled against the careful structures of the Age of Reason? Wasn't "Ludi Vann's" Romantic persona all of a piece? He really didn't know if that was any kind of explanation, and dropped his speculating.

He walked out onto the veranda by the pool, took in the dark, grinning, hulk of the concert grand that had been lifted out of the water; Roy had handled the job well. He peered into the instrument, at the sounding board, beheld the warped and cracked wood. Well, no matter; it could be repaired. Or replaced. The disklavier feature had of course been ruined; he wondered if he even cared. Glancing up, he studied the great hole in the pool cage where screen and beams had been removed for the crane's sling, then glanced over at the bar. He moved to it, found some sloe gin, and made himself a drink, spilling a little on his pants. "Shia," he said, then "shit." He would be through forever with that way of speaking sometime soon. But for now he had to let himself regress to more of Ludi Vann; it was the only way to engage Idiot Boy tomorrow night. He would have to let Ludi on stage to strut his stuff: only Ludi would remember what happened. He would have to reverse Lear's prayer.

He took a pull on his drink, ambled over to a chaise longue and made himself horizontal. He drank slowly, and after a while put down the glass; and then the night glided in through the broken structure above and settled over his conscious mind.

* * *

When the moon arose to shoot its cold light onto the veranda, the back of his eyes sent a phantasmic glow to the brain; a diaphanous scene unfolded in his mind as he dreamt he was Ludi Vann, back in those days, delusional and homeless. He was watching a football game through the window of a bar he was no longer allowed in. He asked a cherub sitting on a branch of an iron-girded tree outside the building to have God explain ball games to him, and then God was there – a grizzled old man in a trench coat with a Gabriel-horn pin on the left lapel – and he'd asked him why he let men dressed in uniforms direct their passion to the mobility and resilience of balls.

"It's easy, Ludi," God said, in the dream. "The explanation is a model of possibility and necessity in a poise only the most accomplished of dancers and seducers approach."

Why, then, O God? he cried, the sound of his voice drowned out by a great cheer in the bar that reverberated against the cold glass. Test the elegance of my comprehension against the holy design of thy purpose!

"Well, Ludi," he said, "it's like this. What is my nature but perfection? What is the most perfect geometric shape? Oh, don't say the circle, yes, yes, halos and all that – I'm talkin' *solid* geometry, given my truly existent nature, three dimensions if you please. The sphere. The sphere, Ludi. How else could I have created the universe, projecting the image of my perfection into planets, stars, moons? I am sphericality *par excellence;* indeed, before I became a Judeo-Christian I was the great sphere of Parmenidean Being.

"Now, to the first part of your question. The uniforms these men wear unite them in the joint venture of playing with the godhead. You want a simple answer to the second part, to wit, *why?* They devote themselves to the various balls in an attempt to attain to My Nature. They play with Me, Ludi, with the divine; you take tennis, for example: a conversation between angels; ping-pong the chatter of cherubim.

"My creation is a hymn of balls in motion, my dear Vann, from the greatest sun to the particles that worry the core of the atom; if each were a note such a harmony of the spheres and spheroids would sing out as to make your paltry symphonies kazoo-fodder. Therefore, is it surprising that there should be a universe of balls in the gentle mock of my creation, what makes sport of my creation, sports?

"The golf ball: you send it forth so that you might catch up to it, like an ambition, a hope, the future you've made present in dread. And the point is to fill a hole that lacks it, to cast completion as the goal of every stroke, the project of sexual intercourse (different balls, different holes, yass, yass, of course) – to arrive as a sphere filling its uniquely designated space – what is this but Divine Me, My Nature manifest?

"And too with the balls that honor my Plenary Essence in the fullness of their momentary placement within hoops. Little steel balls that arc and arabesque along the edge of the laws of motion, journeying toward the ultimate gutter, drawn by the scourge of gravity like a man to his death, as they wrack up pinball points on my divine scoreboard.

"Balls that put my universe in play.

"Balls, once hurled, that are then submitted to the indignity of body-English, which, prayer-like, would undo the sins of the past, when – O my silly creatures – it's the weight of the past that gives heft to the arc of the future; hence the balance of the rules governing all games played with balls…

"Balls that duck wickets, that know the knots of the weave of nets like a lover knows every scar, every mole of the beloved's body; balls that suffer the bat, the glove, the fullback's midriff, balls that lie outside, inside, sent above, beneath, beyond, balls foul and fair: ubiquitous balls! That I be manifest in my Truth!"

Ludi saw God's face maniacally and divinely contorted, saw the words vibrate off him and shimmer in the air.

"They hurt themselves for Me, strive against rival tribes in My Name. Divine play, cosmogony as cosmic agony. They want to 'win,' the pathetic losers (because they are human and destined only to add to the soil they churn up); they would attain to Me, thus they must bounce spherical Me around to their favor.

"A lemma, Ludi: human endeavor is in essence only *conical* in shape. The circle of the base represents my creatures' original unity with Me, but they make it merely *once*, thrusting past in hope – their very breath – towards a *next*, a future vanishing point, which is the center of the circle raised to the vertex crowning a cone. *They wear the dunce cap of their daily desires*. So I cut their conical existences at an angle to the base, slice them with the plane of the possible – the broken condom, the phone call in the night, even the dead battery in the morning – thus producing pathetic ellipses to the perfect circularity belonging to my spherical Nature.

"Ellipses. Think what that means vis-à-vis my single-centered circumference-of-self, Ludi – they live in the distortion of my image by having *two* centers, two foci: themselves as knower and known, self and other, word and thing, the twin seeds of their ovate world."

"Our failings are epic," Ludi allowed in the dream.

"The stuff of pulpit and polemic, my dear Vann. But never the simple geometric proof, demonstrable with a string loop guiding a piece of chalk as it rotates around the two pins of the foci, that an ellipse provides."

Ludi found himself asking, "And what is the string here, in thy divine parable, O God?"

"The tenuous thread of your miserable strung-together moments."

"What is the chalk here, O Plane Geometer?"

"Your own flaky excrescence of ego, crumbling to dust."

"And what is the meaning of the circumference thus produced, O Euclidean Expounder?"

"To the Godhead, an immensely humorous circuit of doings lived in the illusion which the shape provides: that you have 'been somewhere' and 'done something,' traversed an eccentric topography, arrived at a 'new' place. A *new* old place!"

Here, in the dream, God laughed.

"My mother, the Mother of God, thanks you for the hilarity, my angels thank you for the hilarity, St. Hilarius thanks you for the hilarity, I thank you for the hilarity; for let me remind you, my dear Vann, that the very word 'ellipse' implies lack, insufficiency, and in the moral realm, depravity. So of course you lopsided creatures want to play with balls. Get it?"

"Lopsided?" Ludi asked.

"Bent over backwards, past-heavy; falling forward, deathward. At the same time."

"Seems a painful posture," Ludi ventured.

"It is. And absurd. You endure it in the hope that its contradiction might attain to the apotheosis of paradox, to make it, finally, to the very manna of mystery. In the interim, why not 'Play ball!'? Get it?"

"Isn't there some sort of, say, brace a body could wear?"

"Used to be. But these are modern times. Now we give them various painkillers. Televisin® mostly, designed to eliminate the physical presence of the world with its coefficient ache-of-self, the I of the beholder. But also we provide them distraction that games afford. *Ball* games, Ludi. Get it?"

Ludi thought he got it, but raised what seemed to his dream-self a polite objection. "Beggin' you divinehoodt's pardon," he began, slipping into black English as he often had in his days of madness, "lemme ax you: they's football, ain' no sphere there."

"Ah, yes. A flattened sphere, as it were, as if a titan of old were resting his massive ass on it, pushing the equations of sphericality into the calculus of eggs; elongated, a three-dimensional ellipse. Another ovate modification of the godhead. But notice, Ludi Vann, the American game of football is more violent than any game played with spherical balls in America, with the one exception of soccer, an aberration. The violence of football exists in direct proportion to the deviation from the sphericality of the ball, and inversely as the square of the ratio between its mean and major axes."

"You mean, a rounder football would produce a more… *mannered* encounter between offense and defense?"

"Shia, a perfect sphere in the handts o' da NFL produce a pre-Mozartian minuet. Stamitz, mayhaps, or one o' da Bach brats, say."

"Well, I dunno, Godt," Ludi said, "I allus thought the damn scherzo, widh its, you know, widh its jocose violence, shia, it be an aural gut-jabber, don' want too much ceremony, like."

God said, "Well, Ludi, I loved you because you *defied* me as Pattern; adding an 'i' – my own 'I' to your 'thou' – you *deified* me as Passion, which, you know, a God of a certain Bent could dig, like when I used to be Zeus with a closet full of costumes I wore to get into the pants of various – and here's the important part, *many* – maidens."

He was gone then, and in the dream Ludi was left with snickering cherubim in the tree whose visages were maps of the godhead run into Knowledge, the faces of sexual children. O, where are your brothers, he asked, do you really have a class of angels called "Masters of Howlers"?

"'Deed we do, Ludi Vann, we sent one of 'em, a novice howler, to listen to you wail out the parts when you were composing your *Missa solemnis* – a most instructive racket; he's one of our finest now."

They were gone then. Ludi turned back to the bar's TV, thinking he could catch the score, but the glass had frosted up.

As he was waking Eastwind heard a voice he strained to recognize, saying something about "…distortions of the godhead that betray the failure of self-grasp, like the embarrassing track our elliptical orbits make where we've tried to come close to ourselves, only to stretch the curve into distant bulges: irredeemable pasts and their reflections as unattainable futures."

Then he awoke. He found the journal of dreams he kept for Dr. Wilmot and added this latest. Let her sort that one out, he thought as he closed the notebook.

Chapter Six

A Visit to Heaven

Later the next day he drove to Bugg's, found a parking lot nearby, and walked the rest of the way. It was evening, and the lowering sun gleamed dully off the brushed-steel letters naming the place; the preternatural glow at once claimed his consciousness, sending it into the closing chords of the Sixth Symphony, and the sign itself began playing with phrases coming out of "Bugg's Funeral Home" – one suggesting he NAG GULF RUBES, another providing the tawdry imperative to REAM FUN HOLE – but part of him knew that was what he wanted. On the drive he had rehearsed in his mind what he would say to Idiot Boy, that is, what he actually remembered from that day, in the hope that – as insane as it seemed – the other part, the missing part, would come from Idiot Boy's weird raptus with endgames.

Idiot Boy's mournful face appeared behind the isinglass upper half of the door, radiating cubist atomizations on its quasi-opaque surface. The spasmodic splinterings and regatherings played on Eastwind's troubled mind; he saw the bursts of shifting shapes on the pebbly glass as visual music, as sections of the orchestra playing against each other, heard them bristling with sound.

Good, he thought to himself, goodt.

The door opened. "Ludi Vann, my man."

"Idiot Boy, bearer o' da holy roodt." He stomped his feet the way he'd seen old black men do to the blues, though he knew it to be a kind of down-and-out dance white people could never understand. He never concerned himself about being a white man with black ways; Idiot Boy could never have conceived of him as a racist mocking black culture, because his friend from the past knew his heart, and, too, had absolutely no sense of solidarity with anything – except, perhaps, his duty to the dead.

The man said, "Come on in."

He walked inside, and Idiot Boy in his crimped gait led him to the embalming chamber. "Ready to contemplate you' navel?"

"I been thinkin' o' ways to go after this, Idiot Boy. Thinkin' of everything I knew 'bout what happenedt that day."

"You know," his host said, "migh' be bes' you make you'se'f comfortable, you know, like lie down and die." He indicated a plain pine casket, unlined, resting on two folding chairs. "Here you' psychiatri' couch." He smiled so warmly that Eastwind was disabused of any inclination to protest. "I gotta take off my shoes?" he asked.

"Everything. Naked as you come from you' mama's womb." This too struck Eastwind as cohering with the weird logic of the moment. He took off his clothes and left them in a pile over his shoes, then, a little self-consciously, climbed carefully into the coffin. "Man," he said, supine in the box, "it col' in here."

"Thass whut they all say."

"You hear that too?"

"Nah. Jus' jivin' you." He pulled up a chair and sat nearby. Eastwind saw him put on a pair of sunglasses.

"You jus' tell me the scene, Ludi. Who be there, whut, you know, be goin' down, like that." He added, "Jus' take you' time."

Eastwind found he was staring up into the inside of a light fixture that was a polished metal cone with a single bulb glaring down at the coffin. Before he could begin recounting anything to his host, the light began to hurt his eyes, and he said, “Man, Idiot Boy, can you get that light out of my eyes?” Idiot Boy reached over to the switch on the wall and the light went out.

In the after-image Eastwind beheld a fusion of light and his reflection in the metal of the fixture; his image seemed to glow. And suddenly he wasn’t there. He was flying away, soaring above all the world, following an angel.

* * *

The next thing he knew was that he was in a tree with a host of them. On the branches to his left they were weeping; their tears struck the ground and peonies and asphodel, periwinkles and nasturtiums sprung up instantly. Angels to the right of him were smiling in high humor; some were laughing. He had never seen such beautiful faces. In the background he seemed to hear a hoarse voice shouting, almost trumpet-like; a great silvery sound, the most beautiful music he had ever heard, held the air. An angel – a cherub – from the happy group fluttered down and picked a gardenia off a bush, flew back and brought it to his nose. “This is the scent of heaven,” she said. “We put them on earth so people would remember.” Ludi – or whoever he was, or had been – burst into tears. “Oh, me,” he said. “Oh, me.” The angels grew bleary to his vision, and when he blinked the angels on his right were weeping, those on his left laughing and smiling. The voice behind them spoke:

Right is lef’
’N’ lef’ be right
Both equal in eternal sight;

But back-and-forth
Throw out another dimension
Cast the first two into dissension.

Bring it on home – (clap!… clap!)
Bring it on home – (clap!… clap!)
Back to me.

Ludi beheld the old news seller who had held up the headlines, back in the days of madness – a kindly Jewish man, now with wings. He was bearing a newspaper with a banner headline: "LUDI VANN TURNS SELF IN." A subhead stated, "God Yawns as Sins Recounted."

"Still God's herald, on my corner with the headlines," he said. "Chanter first-class. I take my Howler's in an eon."

Ludi broke down again, but this time in laughter. He laughed and laughed and felt himself expanding as he drew in great breaths to mollify his heaving diaphragm. Soon he was huge; the branch he was sitting on broke, spilling him onto a lush meadow. Abel, the Jewish angel, swept down beside him.

"Is heaven a meadow?" Ludi asked.

"Indeed. The space of the plane you came from is a meadow in dismemory, an eternal lea swamped with time. The world you left is only heaven submitted to the clock."

Ludi suddenly blurted: "God explained ball games to me last night."

"You should return the favor with your confession," Abel said. "But you must forgive your trespassers first."

"Am I dead?"

"Do you thirst for return?" the angel asked. "Are you still a feeling sponge that has soaked up the soda water of earthly desire?"

"Indeed I tingle and burn. I seek."

"The tang is bubbles, my friend," Abel said. "Inside them is the substance of your yearning. Let's just say the question of your return to the earthly plane is moot. But you owe the headsman the reconciling speech, in any case."

Ludi said, "I forgive them all. My mother for expelling me into the world, my father for the constant reminder of my passage through his territory. I forgive the cops, the creeps, the bums who beat me, the whores who faked it, the thieves, the pimps, the posses of good citizens; the ones who lied, the ones who told the truth. I forgive Salmaninski. I forgive all the snitches, the mayors, the priests, the bishops, the archbishops, I forgive Cardinal Sin, I forgive the Pope. I forgive God."

"Repeat after me."

"Repent after me."

"I forgive all, for they were merely playing the roles decreed by piety."

"I give for all, for they were dearly praying their holes accede to satiety," Ludi said.

"I've never heard it so eloquently repeated," Abel allowed. "And now for your confession."

"But am I dead?" Ludi asked. "Has Idiot Boy killed me? Did I die?"

"The life you knew was waking death. Walking, sometimes scrounging, death."

"But everything seemed real," Ludi said. "Everything supplied its own absent answer."

"All that was real was the seeming. Come, come, Ludi – it was the very net you yourself wove. But the absence was the key. The presence you felt was the agreement of question and answer; but it was always the mutual reflection making up two, Christ's hand-wounds, left and right. We sent you the teaching of Father Professor on this. Didn't you get the dreams we sent?"

"An interpretation eluded me."

"Where a vertical shaft provides the cross-beam its support?"

"Something like that."

"Pressed against buttocks, balls and back?"

"A kind of hat rack on which crowns of thorns are hung."

"Right. The agreement inherent in your former reality was always empty, Ludi; it collapsed as the present onto the spike of the past, fled towards the future. A back-and-forth."

"The engine of desire, calibrated in onans."

"The empty maw. Consciousness-in-ego. The vacuous suck of temporality. Condemned to be hole, those who chased their future as the shadow of their past, and in their panting added the 'w" to make 'whole,' found only a cruel pun. But you might make your confession now."

Ludi contemplated this. "I was false to people," he said.

"Rather a common sin. The others require it, in most cases," Abel said, nodding understandingly.

"I took their money without giving the goods."

"You cheated yourself, since they were you. Your cheated self came to be cheated of sanity. So you've sort of paid for that one."

"And I…" Ludi stopped.

"Go on," said Abel. "You must remember every sin. We have an eternity, you know."

"I think I… I think I killed a man."

Abel looked at him sternly. "Don't make anything up. No drama here. Just the facts."

"No, really," Ludi said. "That's kind of how I got here. Trying to find out what happened."

Abel flattened out the newspaper that had drooped in his hand and perused the front page. "Ah, here it is, list of sins, A-6." He turned to the section. "Let's see: lies, fraud, scams. Hmm – a number of pecker peccati… After that the print is smudged."

"But I think I might've pushed a man down a stairs," Ludi said. "When I was mad."

"I can't read any more of it."

"But he was dead… was it an accident?"

"Sometimes Death wheels around mindless of his scythe, like the old sight-gag of a man turning with a beam on his shoulder – and levels someone without meaning to. Sometimes planeloads."

"That would be Chance," Ludi said.

"Well, it should be here on A-6. This is the newspaper of record, the *New York Times*, Heavenly Edition. Oh, wait. The crossword is on the same page."

"But… how…?"

"One-across: 'Twisted strip.' Six letters."

Ludi was silent. "'Twisted strip,' Ludi," repeated Abel.

"Uh… what's one-down?"

"'Famous sonata.' Nine letters."

"Okay, 'Moonlight.' What's two-down?"

"'Oratorio *Mount of* ______.' Six letters."

"That would be, uh, *Mount of Olives,"* Ludi said.

"Right," said Abel. "And that works with fourteen-across: 'Spanish cheer.' Three-down is 'Composer of one and two down.'"

"'Beethoven.' Ah!," Ludi suddenly said, "of course. One-across is 'Möbius.'"

Abel nodded solemnly. He began turning the paper over and over until it was a belt of newsprint, running in a loop over his arms; the inside became the outside as the outside became inside. Soon all Ludi saw was a nauseating, twisted blur. He looked away.

The angels had descended and formed a circle around him; Abel fixed him with a look as he crumpled the newspaper, then rose on the beating of his wings. The angels in the circle alternated in mood between happy and mourning, with the smiling ones changing their faces to sadness as the grieving angels transformed theirs to joy, and this change was accelerating: faster and faster became the shifting between grimace and happy beam. Soon it became a machine of alternating current, a generator sending electricity into infinite space, drawing, as Ludi suddenly took it, the earth from west to east, pulling the three dimensions of time and space into the allowance of events, things, distance to be traveled; into the origin of hope, the promise of arrival, the strength to endure the perpetual against the despair of once.

"That's why I was in love with electricity," he said, as he began to turn at the center of the dynamo. "That's why electronics made me create Beethoven." But he was spinning with greater and greater velocity, rotating as if grasping at something circling just out of reach; he spun and spun, finally whirling into a harmonic of stillness, and lost consciousness.

* * *

"Man," said Idiot Boy, "ain' never seen nobody jump oudt a coffin." He was wiping Eastwind's forehead with a damp handkerchief. "'Course, ain't seen nobody jump in, neither. Shia, Ludi, you the livelies' corpse ever been." The casket lay on its side; the chairs on which it had rested were upturned.

Eastwind moaned, and slowly sat up from the floor.

Idiot Boy said, "Shia, man, you fall asleep an' dream?"

Eastwind held his head.

"Where you been, man?"

Eastwind looked around, then murmured, "Time drenchery…"

"Say whut? Where you go?"

Eastwind blinked up at him, speechless. Then he asked, "Did you do something to me?"

"I jus' coveredt you' face widh this ol' handkerchief." Eastwind sniffed it, caught the scent of formaldehyde.

"I flew away somewhere. But not to anything in the past," he said. "You listened for me?"

"I didt."

"What'd you hear?"

"Shia, Ludi, jus' heardt you say over 'n' over somethin' like, 'Oh heavenly scen', oh me. Oh heavenly scen', oh me.' But dint hear no las' wordts." Idiot Boy handed him his clothes.

As he dressed, Eastwind contemplated briefly the desperation of trying to use Idiot Boy's strange savantry to find out what had happened that day with Brett Yearly. What kind of despair had brought him to that?

"Ain' no guarantee, Ludi. Tol' you I don' control it."

It's my madness, Eastwind went on to himself. I'm almost him again; the visit to heaven – wasn't that really only my unmedicated brain marinated in its own foul juices? "It's okay, man," he said. "It's just me. I'm still crazy." He buckled his belt, set a chair aright, and sat.

Idiot Boy rose, pulled a flask from his pocket and poured some bourbon into two glasses he took off a nearby shelf; he added a little water from the faucet of the sink below, then turned a mournful gaze to his guest. "Befo' I figure some things ou', I be crazy too," he said. "I seen whut lies they be in the day-to-day grine."

Eastwind looked over to the freezer locker, with its numbered drawers. "And your clients here don't have a lot to say," he added.

"They keeps the volume down."

"And speak volumes."

"You damn straight."

He took Idiot Boy's drink and had a swallow, said, "Yeah, well."

Idiot Boy smiled. "You know, don' feel badt 'bout bein' crazy, Ludi. It Godt do it. It go widh the kink in the braidt o' hisse'f. You jus' be one o' the wrinkles in the mask he hol' up to the worl'."

"Idiot Boy," Eastwind said, after another pull on his drink, and starting to feel it, "you always suffered the most, always were the most far-out of us all, in those days. I'm just telling you."

"Dint choose nothin', jus' a nature infeck me."

"You gave the most." Eastwind paused, then looked up slyly at his host. "I've gotta tell you something. I happen to be very, very rich. And I think it's too much money for one man. Know what I'm saying?"

Idiot Boy looked down into his drink, then at Eastwind with an open face. He said, "Nice o' you, Ludi. But don' wan' no money. Mo' than I needt jus' sendin' bodies back to they origin."

"But you must have hopes, some kind of dream that money can help bring about…"

Idiot Boy shook his head. "I dream a dream of emptiness. You look 'roundt you what you see? Stuff that there not longer than time itse'f, shit that be no bulkier than the space it take up. I done undone lastin'ness, Ludi. It the lesson of m'job."

"I know. You hung out with Fat Face, that guy from Japan."

"A man buildt a great house, a damn pine box greater. Fancy car, shia, it a damn hot dog cart to that beat-up hearse outsite."

"The guy they called Denny Zen. Wore the robe."

"Beautiful woman jus' a promise."

Eastwind sipped his drink. The second movement of the Seventh Symphony was playing over his mind; the music brought him to the reflection that Idiot Boy hadn't even a tragic view of life, as mournful as he appeared to be. He stood, a little dizzy. "I got to go, Idiot Boy. The demons are humming."

"You kin stay here you don' feel like it."

"Nah, man, I'd be afraid to sleep here. Might wake up dead again." He finished his drink, then moved toward the door that opened out into the lobby. Idiot Boy walked behind him, more slowly.

"It was a whacked-out idea, my old friend, my fellow street sufferer," Eastwind said, a little drunk. "But I thank you. Always were good to me, back in the day."

Idiot Boy shook his head. "Nothin'," he said. "Nothin' special."

It was around eight, then, and outside the air was cool; it stimulated Eastwind to greater vivacity, sharper perceptions. Lighted letters cut through the night, pairs of headlights swam down the streets; buildings in glowing checkered patterns crowded into the sky, blinding the stars. He made his way to the car, fleeing HUGE ANT IS STORY BOND as announced by the Greyhound Bus Station sign, drove up Broadway, wondering at FORTY TELL NUN hanging above the left-turn-only lane.

And on his way toward the Hamptons the music in his head faded into a harmonic setting of a single mantra: oh, heav'nly scent, mmmh; oh, heav'nly scent, yeah.

Chapter Seven

Return Visit

Home again, Eastwind found he was strangely energized, even though it was late enough that, as with the previous night, his house-staff members were either gone or asleep in their quarters. He sat at his desk again, and his eye caught the letter from the musicologists. He wondered, am I even able to read, with the letters doing their strange scrambles? But he had noticed that the anagrams came only in phrases on signs, as if their secret meanings might guide those of the public who, searching a way, could descramble them. "You gotta know da cote," he heard an old voice – his own, from the past – saying. He picked up the letter again, and noticed that he could read it without difficulty. He returned to the request that he contact Ann Yearly.

No, he thought. No, never; not without knowing what happened – and that last hope was gone now. He crumpled the paper and let it fall into the wastebasket next to the great chair.

Despite the weird happenings in his mind, there was yet reason left (he noticed). And so he thought it best to send payment to McKane and Spratt; a lawsuit was pointless, he knew. They certainly had answered the question of the letter, though they hadn't solved its mystery; would he let them sue him – and win – because they couldn't tell him *why* Ludi Vann had written it with all the inconsistencies they'd pointed out?

That question – why – piqued his consciousness as he sat at his desk. Maybe, he ruminated (recalling his original plan in refusing his medication), maybe the lack of brain-straightening chemicals might still let him reënter the pathetic character – close now, though soon to be exorcized again with Risperdal – he'd been those years ago, so violent, so deluded, so exalted in his own mind: all a chimera he gave his blind assent to as a self-consciousness, a truth for him as certain most of the time as awareness itself – though, he recalled as well, there were moments when he felt he was only playing at being… him. He wondered if that made him responsible for what he did, and then found himself enmeshed in the hopeless conundrum that he was genuinely mad to have ignored at those times that he wasn't really mad.

His tinnitus had been getting louder, and to get that logical twist out of his mind he listened more closely to it. Let it be a shrill, wordless mantra, he thought to himself, let it engulf me, encircle me like a barrier to this scene, this situation, this moment; let me be taken back to that day at the halfway house.

He concentrated on the ringing, almost scrutinizing it for some shape, pulse, even an origin. Slowly he began to hear something familiar, a kind of tuning-up of an orchestra before a performance. His mind flashed to Schumann; poor man, he thought, driven to attempt suicide by the concert "A" sounding in his afflicted mind. God, no! Was there a punishment for true genius – like Beethoven's deafness? But, but… The name 'Beethoven' at once clarified what he was hearing: the opening orchestral hum, its jabbing A's and E's that suddenly strode into D-minor – the opening of the Ninth.

He let the symphony crowd over his awareness of the room, the view of the pool, his sitting in the chair of his study, and these receded from his mind.

The first thing he was aware of was the wood of the stairs of the halfway house as he – Ludi Vann – made his way toward a dingy door. He opened it and strode in, glaring at Brett Yearly, who raised himself from the lamp he was tending. Things grew a little hazy, then Eastwind focused on something Brett was saying. "…We've been awfully good to you…" The two stared at each other. Brett then said, "You haven't been taking your medication, have you? Not swallowing it."

Ludi glanced down at the bottom drawer of the desk and saw that it wasn't quite closed.

"That's grounds for getting you out of here, you know that?"

Eastwind couldn't make out what Ludi had replied, only what had followed from Brett:

"I just talked with Belmont on the phone. He said you weren't on your medication. He told me it was my choice whether we'd let you stay or not. And you've got to go."

Ludi looked away a moment, then came back with a raised fist. But something was churning within him, something seemed to be moving the room around him. Eastwind vaguely heard Brett say, "Yeah, yeah, I know. Rage against your fate somewhere else," as the room whirled faster and faster; Ludi seemed to be listening for something, a voice, knowledge, a guiding direction. The fist was poised in the air, air that now seemed to rush about his head in glissando whispers as he tried to make out words. Eastwind knew that this was the crisis of his madness, for one side of Ludi knew himself mad and pulled against the willful delusion of the other side; but the other side in its very willfulness pulled just as strongly in the other direction. It was this furious tension that broke over him as his fist shook and strained forward. He heard only silence, then there was a moment of darkness.

And Eastwind saw that when Ludi collected himself Brett lay at the bottom of the stairs, his head at an odd angle, mouth open, pupils gone into his lids.

He saw, too, then that Ludi slammed the door, sat down at his ramshackle desk, breathing heavily. He looked off toward the slow motion of the drapes, eyes to the side. He reflected on himself in this pose: Beethoven listening to a musical phrase, maybe the driven undulation of the beginning of the *Appassionata*'s third movement, about to snap to Ries that there could be no lesson today because he must hurry to the manuscript paper…

He reached down and opened the bottom left-side drawer and got out a sheet of paper from a very special box hidden toward the back. From the drawer above it he retrieved an ancient pen and a jar of brown ink.

He dipped the tip of the pen into the viscous fluid and began: "*Sehr geehrter Herr Graf...*"

Eastwind awoke, eyes starting. He was both elated and disturbed to have had the scene – the one he'd wanted Idiot Boy to tell him of. But as to what Ludi'd had to do with Brett's resting at the bottom of the stairs… He reflected that the hand that had been a fist had been in shape enough for Ludi to have penned the letter. But what did he *know?* He'd listened for the truth as a harmonic of his tinnitus, for a voice emerging into overtones that might hum the missing answer, and had heard only the fundamental monotone of his mystification.

Eastwind sagged in the chair. He recalled the strange events of the night – a visit to heaven! Rather, he thought, as he had before at Bugg's, a rancid distillation of brain chemicals, producing their own bogus elixir. But the gardenia had smelled so real, so profoundly full of something more metaphysical than the matter of the brain. He recalled his exclamation "Oh me," uttered over and over again, so slain had he been by that engulfing, entrancing aroma.

"Oh heavenly scent," Idiot Boy had told him he'd heard him say, "Oh me." Strange, he reflected, that that was the upshot of such a weird and yet – engaging – experience. "Oh heavenly scent, oh me." Why should that have come to Idiot Boy? He'd wanted the last words from that scene. Maybe there weren't any, but if there were he knew now they were engraved on a granite boulder that was rolling further and further down the slope of the past.

"Oh heavenly scent, oh me."

He wrote the words down on a pad on his desk, unconsciously spelling "oh" with the archaic "o".

Deciding to look for an anagram, he found several combinations of the letters that produced random words: "COME THE SLAVE… HOME ON LEAVE…" He noticed that he was using the outdated form of "oh" and threw in an *H,* but that was no help. Again, he wrote out

OHEAVENLYSCENTOME

and then he saw something he'd not seen before:

"COME… SEE ANN…"

But the rest of the letters stayed a jumble, all random consonants, with only two vowels. He stared at the remainder for a while, trying all the possibilities that came to him, but all he saw was HOLYVET. And "holy vet" juxtaposed with the first part made no sense. He thought, when I don't want anagrams to come they do, and when I want them to they don't.

But there was still "COME, SEE ANN…"

Eastwind pondered this, thought it unlikely – indeed, thought it was still his strange mind playing with him. Then he thought of Ann Yearly, how good she had been to him in his days of madness – he recalled that she had taught him French – and that she had told his researchers how much she wanted to see him. Maybe "COME, SEE ANN" was the message from the trip at Bugg's. But, no – ridiculous. We'll forge anything, he mused to himself, and then gazed momentarily into an abyss that had been opening up just outside the periphery of his consciousness ever since his social shaming; we make meanings, it occurred to him, as if they made themselves, while all the while it's only our own doing – an arrangement he grasped darkly to imply the mathematics of zero.

No, he thought; no, it would be a kind of message only if I wanted it to be.

Still... He retrieved the crumpled letter that had Ann Yearly's phone number.

* * *

The next day Eastwind got to Dr. Wilmot's office early in the morning, ready for the injection that would, he hoped, banish his demons to hell, leaving over an ordered world. He reflected that he was past ready for it; the dreams the last two nights had been exceedingly weird – surely owing to his being off his medication. In the one last night, coming to him in exhausted sleep after his struggle with the Ann Yearly anagram (if it was an anagram), he'd been Ludi Vann again. He was in a public library at a computer terminal, and he was typing.

"...created tones in order to save all the people who dream of heralding angels stricken mute, who search the heavens for a sign, a hint, a nod or a wink, but find only the vast indifference of cloud banks, who want the impossible, who yearn for the future they know will be only a lie whispered in pre-coital passion to the present to cuckold the past…

"All those who hope the meanings of words will get them by, in the meantime…"

He heard, as if a voice-over: "I myself have searched the heavens for da face o' Godt, I too looked for a sign (SIGN=SING). Where my damn *"In hoc signo vinces,"* I ax you? Goodt enough fo' damn Constantine. I search da cloudt banks fo' da letters, scrambledt outta antiquity by da currents o' history, I looks fo' some wordts…"

And then in the dream another conversation with God began.

GOD: Thass right, Ludi, my supreme nature protect me from full appearance, I speak backwards to the non-dyslexic and forwards to the dyslexic, I anonymous in *euonymus*, your genus of burning bush, loquacious in low cumuluses, you kin peg me in anagrams you clever enough.

L.V.: Well, now, Godt, I got the anagrammatical affliction, but it might be hardt to get anything outta *"In hoc signo vinces"* except "In this sign shall you conquer," you go widh da English. Widh da cross o' Jesus da sign.

GOD: A point of disputation, my dear Vann. You mispronouncing it. Not "conquer" but "concur." "In this sign shall you concur." If you ignore the Latin.

L.V.: And you… you kin?

GOD: A deceased language. "Drive your plough over the bones o' da deadt," say my boy Billy Blake. So I authorized that translation by way of promoting religious tyranny. It insured red and rheum would sink into the earth; it co-legitimized the rack and the stake. Scourge and fire to purify the flesh. Cathedrals and catharsis, the cup and the cross, crusades and crafted cruelty. They could reach towards me only in catechism and cataclysm.

L.V.: All that alliteration…

GOD: Sorry. I was accessing the "C-words" section of my website.

L.V.: Shia, you got a *website?*

GOD: It be at http://divine.org. You got computer access?

L.V.: Here at the library, they lets da homeless get on-line.

GOD: Well, boot on up, dear Vann, O made-in-my-image.

L.V.: 'Course you got a website! You all electricity. How I not think Your Nature not be guided through all the circuits and bands and diodes-to-joy? Shia. Okay, aitch-tee-tee-pee colon, double forward slash… Enter. Man, there it be, pearly gates 'n' all.

GOD: Click on "Options."

L.V.: That a right-click or lef'-click?

GOD: Left-click. Ludi, you ain' too cool widh these things, is you?

L.V.: Sorry, boss. Been malingering in the hope of finding croutons to go widh my dumpster salads.

GOD: What do you do for dessert?

L.V.: The occasional mint-flavored dental floss.

GOD: Now scroll down to "Hidden Effulgence," and left-click it.

L.V.: Okay… got it. Single click?

GOD: Come on, Ludi. It ain' as hardt as the fingering in some o' you' damn piano sonatas.

L.V.: Okay. Now what?

GOD: See where it say "Anagrams"? Hit "Open."

L.V.: Don' see it.

GOD: You don't see "Open document"?

L.V.: Oh, yeah, yeah. Okay. It open.

GOD: Okay, click on "Latin".

L.V.: Right… Okay, there it be. *"In hoc signo vinces."*

GOD: Right. Well?

L.V. Well… what?

GOD: "Well what"!? Well, *what is my meaning?* It's an anagram.

L.V.: Oh, man… gimme some he'p.

GOD: Go to "Help," left-click.

L.V.: Oh, right. Okay… Okay, says here they be sixteen letters, one aitch, two oh's, two seas, two esses, three eyes, one gee, three enns, one vee and one ee.

GOD: That is correct. Now get busy.

L.V.: Uh… Uh… Okay: "GOOSE SIGH IN SIN…"

GOD: Nope. You've repeated the gee.

L.V.: Shia. Okay, wait, wait… Okay, "GIVEN VICE…"

GOD: Now you done repeated da damn ee. You 'bout as competent as my prophets, Ludi, who almost never got it right. Did I ever tell you what really happened with that Mary virgin?

L.V.: Uh… "CHOSEN VISION…"

GOD: You'll see that goes nowhere. It leaves over "CHIG." No, my evangelists never quite got it the way it happened. It was *she* who approached *me.* She had a secret, she said.

L.V.: Man, I ain' getting' *no*where widdis. Kin I go to "He'p" again?

GOD: But how could she have had a secret from Me, Omniscience personified? It probably had to do with my having to create them free – always was the damn rub.

L.V.: It say check out "False Friends."

GOD: I beheld her from behind my mirror-shade glasses, the ones I wear for the destined-to-dust; the past-heavy deathwards see only their own supplicating image, never me, my eyes.

L.V.: Right, right, right. Okay, it say, it say, "'IN HOC SIGNO' might suggest 'IN CHOOSING,'" but it a damn deadt endt.

GOD: Well, be edified then, Ludi. As I was saying, she said she knew a secret about Me, something hidden to the Divine Nature she wouldn't reveal.

L.V.: "CHIC VISIONS GONE." Shia, leave a damn enn over.

GOD: N-n-not reveal in words, but there was another way, I surmised. An alternative route.

L.V.: "CHOOSING NICE SIN…" Damn! Leave over da damn vee.

GOD: She had a hidden vee, I knew, a cleft deepening to where I might read the Braille of her secret with the touch of my foreskin.

L.V.: "SINNING CHOSE… VOIC…"

GOD: I deciphered the secret with my Holy Rood, Ludi. I became aware of Myself as *need.*

L.V.: Wait a minnit, wait a minnit…

GOD: I confess I used my lust to fill up my Nature. By entering a mortal, other to me, and in whom I discovered I am most Myself.

L.V.: "VOICING CHOSEN SIN." Got it.

GOD: O, thou art my faithful servant, Ludi. Have I not blessed thee with deafness that your tone-casting might know more fleet arcs? Are you not among my elect, mine very own? I took your hearing that you might know My silence. Given the chattering of men. The commercials! The obscene panting of the fine print. The cacophony of the daily clang. The utterances of fools. The true lies that escape the throats of men to lodge in the ears of the hearing, that make their way into the inner ear and put their feet in the stirrups and hammer their forgeries on the anvil therein, imprinting the brain, which in turn directs that the true lies be repeated as often as possible. I saved you from all that, Ludi.

L.V.: Thanky, Lordt, thanky, thanky.

GOD: Have I not blessed you with music of the inner hearing? Music beloved the world over, testament to your genius?

L.V.: Shia, Godt, I jus' make it soun' like it is. Or was… see, I got this archenemy, guy name of Schoenberg…

GOD: I think of her often, of her fortunes in theology. The Assumption. Mariology. I note the many statues that miss her likeness entirely, for I alone knew her face and form.

L.V.: Shia, looky-yeah, looky-yeah, Boss: "CINCH GONE VISIONS."

GOD: Her revirginization, the hymns to hymenization…

L.V.: Hey, know what? I bet they a damn computer program you couldt use like to unravel all anagrams. Shia, we couldt come up widh a whole damn bunch o' IN HOC's. Lemme hit "Search."

GOD: NO!

L.V.: Shia. Damn "Error Message."

GOD: Click "Okay."

L.V.: Okay?

GOD: Goddamnit, Ludi, error damn okay! "To be an Error & to be cast out is a part of Gods Design." Same Billy-boy Blake.

L.V.: Shia. And was it your plan that the spawn of your lust shouldt die onna cross? Why you let him suffer so?

GOD: He ignored an error message. *The* error message.

L.V.: You know, you a serious sort.

GOD: If man is not in error, *what am I?*

L.V.: But you been goodt to me.

GOD: I punished you no less than I torment those in Dante's Hell, my dear Vann, where the punishment fit da damn crime. *I took away what you loved more than me.* I made my Absence manifest in the silence of your ears, thereby making you create out of nothing, in the image of my own Creation. I made you da damn Ex Nihilo Kidt.

L.V.: Thanky, Lordt. Thanks. Thank yuh. The critics have been kind to me over the centuries. They ignored some crap I wrote.

GOD: *"Wellington's Victory."* I know. Here the Godhead blanched. Here the Heavenly Host molted not a few light-polished feathers.

L.V.: Shia, da library closin'?

GOD: But know what happened? The glint of their falling feathers seared the eyes of those proclaiming your greatness. Homer-like, they sang the song of you.

L.V.: I hate you, Godt.

GOD: Fine. I love a rebellion. Satan is mine own. We still have those bimonthly department head meetings that began with the Job question.

L.V.: I love you, Godt.

GOD: Good. Praise me with dominant into tonic. Preferably in brasses.

L.V.: Your humble servant.

GOD: No, no, Ludi: my *noble* servant.

* * *

Dr. Wilmot was horrified at the specter Eastwind presented. "My god, Louie, you shouldn't have done it. I never should have let you try going it without your med. You look like you've been to hell and back."

"Wrong direction," he said, loosening his belt for the injection, "but I know what you mean."

"Wrong direction?"

"Long story," he said. "I included some of it in my dreams book. I think it was a dream. Of heaven."

"I still need time to go over the dreams book," she said. "But was it worth it – your quest? Did you learn anything?"

Eastwind thought about this. "No," he said. "Maybe some hints. But nothing I really trust."

"Okay," she said, preparing the syringe. "It's about time for this. Almost two months. Did you do any of the homework I asked you to?"

"It seems to me now that I was always metal to the magnet of the moment, always sort of preoccupied. I was still rational enough, though," he added. "It was just weird perceptions and aural hallucinations."

"Well," she countered, "maybe we can get into those things now. But let's get the injection going." She had him lie prone on the padded table in the middle of the room, and he slid his trousers down. "This is a pain in the butt," he said in an attempt to keep his dignity with a little joke, however lame. The last time he'd played on the word "embarrassed" and she'd snickered appreciatively. This time she replied, "Literality is a sign of recovery," and he laughed a little, at ease with her. "Okay," she said, "last time it was the right buttock, so here we go." She swabbed a patch of skin on his left buttock, then deftly pushed in the needle; checking the instrument for blood, she pressed the plunger and watched the liquid slowly vanish. In a moment she dumped the syringe into a special container and put away the chemical vial.

Eastwind pulled his pants up, buckled his belt, and returned to the chair next to hers. Outside the day was a little gray, though no rain was likely. He looked out to his Mercedes parked across the lot, beheld the dull asphalt with its oil stains, saw the hibiscus bushes that ringed the area, thought of gardenias. What does a perception like this mean? he wondered to himself. Is there any redeeming value to having this ordinariness sink in day after day? Was it only the perpetual ellipse, life fatted with false meaning? Again it was the question of meaning that had held him for some time now, often as lightly as the clothes he wore, but occasionally weighing heavily – like the previous night when, encountering the possibly exhorting anagram from Bugg's, he had thumped his perception only to hear a hollow.

Dr. Wilmot said, "Let me know if there're any complications. There shouldn't be, what with my trophy in darts." That broke his mood, and she asked, "What were you thinking about, Louie?" She sat next to him. "You looked pretty pensive just now."

"Nothing," he replied. "Just the question of – why we suffer the everyday glaze over things. Whether anything means anything at all."

She smiled. "Well, let's suppose so for now. Temporary meanings. It's all we can muster at the moment, but they sometimes supply an answer or two, Louie. Let's get into the letter again. Last time you raised the 'why' of it. Is there anything in your dreams diary about that?"

Eastwind reflected a moment. "Yeah, come to think of it," he said, "a whacked-out dream with the Professor again. This time he was a priest. We were underwater."

"And how did you breathe?"

"We were in a sunken church, a kind of medieval cathedral. I remember confessing that Ludi had named the wrong key in the letter."

"The wrong key."

"Sorry," he said, realizing that he hadn't told her what the letter said. "There was a reference to a composition, supposedly Beethoven's, but in the letter I put down a key for it that Beethoven almost never used. I – Ludi – was troubled by that. It was my sin."

"And did the professor, the priest, give you a penalty for that?"

"No. He said to forget it." But here Eastwind began recalling more of the dream. His eyes moved to the side and downward.

"And?"

"He did say something else," he said. "He told me I'd made the mistake on purpose."

"Did he tell you what your purpose was?"

"No. The dream ended there. You'll see in my journal."

She got out her notepad. "You said you dreamt about heaven? Care to talk about that?"

A little embarrassed about the project of trying to use Idiot Boy's clairaudience, he hesitated before answering. Then he said, "Come to think of it, I did follow one of the suggestions you made. I asked myself if I'd ever killed anybody. So I tried to find out about what happened at the Yearly's halfway house with Brett, wanted a… friend to sort of help me concentrate. But it turned into a kind of strange dream – of heaven. I think I just needed my shot."

"I'll look at your journal. Any other dreams? Visions?"

"Well, yeah," he said, "a real crazy dream last night with me as Ludi again – God confessed to me. It's there too."

Dr. Wilmot raised an eyebrow. "I look forward to reading that one."

"And, as for visions, just before I fell asleep I was trying to remember what Ludi might have known about Brett lying at the bottom of the stairs. Kind of a whacked out way to do it, Julie, but I concentrated on my tinnitus – you know it's been worse since I let the injections lapse. And I saw Ludi writing the Beethoven letter. I'd hadn't remembered that; I was just going on what the musicologists had found out. But what I didn't get was anything about Brett's death – whether he fell or… or was pushed."

"You really are concerned about finding out about that. What do you think the reason is?" she said, with an earnest look.

"It's been bothering me. And I found out Ann Yearly wants to know what I might know about what happened that day. The musicologists told me. So I'm kind of doing it for her, too. She was awfully good to me."

"That's interesting. But is your concern for Ann Yearly only that?"

Eastwind looked out the window again. He had discovered over the last weeks that he could launch into the most abstract thought against the most concrete of perceptions; his mind flew away from what she'd just asked and contemplated again the question of meaning. And what if, he speculated, what if indeed there was absolutely no ultimate meaning to anything? Wouldn't that be the most profoundly intriguing thing, something that would itself lean toward meaning? And what freedom! Another thought came to him: and what nihilism. But no, he countered, meaning is nihilism's most attractive garb. God got tired of the empty suits walking around, stripped us naked again.

Dr. Wilmot didn't notice his having entered this realm of speculation because she was reaching back over her desk for the heavy Manila folder containing all the papers about his case. She pulled it onto her lap and began looking through it. "Seems I remember Sepulveda's notes had something…" she said a bit absently. She leafed through several more pages. "Ah, here it is. Yeah, probably significant, Louie. Sepulveda wrote in his notes that both you and Ann Yearly told him that you were – that Beethoven was – in love with her. Had you forgotten?"

Eastwind was startled. "Yes," he said, "I had. I'd put all that out of my mind." He marveled over that a moment. But in the back of his thoughts something was beginning to stir, to move letters around; they came to consciousness with the "HOLY VET" that had followed "COME, SEE ANN" falling into another order: THY LOVE. He was surprised, but immediately skeptical, wary of forged meanings. And yet, there was something intriguing about his insane persona having loved Ann Yearly. Had he really loved her, or was he only doing as he was supposed to, being Beethoven, in his delusion?

"Well, we might be making progress here," the psychiatrist said.

They talked some more, with her advising him on what to look for in the changes he would experience with the new shot of Risperdal. She urged him to try the other "homework" ideas she had recommended before. Finally, she warned him against missing his next injection, then sent him to the outer office where her receptionist made out an appointment card for him.

As he got into his car he heard himself thinking that he really should see Ann Yearly.

Chapter Eight

Ann Yearly

Eastwind dialed the number, musing with a little anguish that each touch of his finger on the keypad might be the prodding of his fate. The sudden "brrrr" of the metallic ring at the other end struck him as a dark musical trill portending a close in the minor mode. Three rings; and he found himself saying, thank god, she isn't there. Then a voice he had loved in his madness said, "Hello?"

His first instinct was to hang up, and the index finger of his right hand hovered over the button the receiver would depress. But something in him was an anchor having found its necessity in the resistance of the sea floor; the vessel of his intention held. "Hello," he said. "It's Ludi Vann."

"My god," Ann Yearly said. "I've wanted to talk to you for a long time. How are you?"

"Under control," he answered. "I don't really go by 'Ludi Vann' anymore. Things have worked out for me some."

"I'd heard you were better and that you'd finished the degree you'd been working on."

"Yeah. And more."

"I suppose the two professors found you, and gave you my message."

"That's right," he said. "How are you?"

They talked a while about some of the things they had known before. She asked him some simple questions in French to see if he remembered anything from his lessons, but he answered most of them with a stock *"mais oui"* and an *"un peu."* He told her his old new name. And then Ann said, "There's something important I want to talk with you about."

"I know. Brett. I know."

"Yes. Brett."

"I'd rather come see you and talk then. I'm actually not much of a drive from Nyack."

"Good," she said. "When did you have in mind?"

"I'm thinking soon, Ann. Are you home tomorrow?"

They arranged to meet the following day, Ann giving him specific directions to her house. He could tell from them it wasn't in an upscale neighborhood, and thought she probably was still working with the homeless.

* * *

The shot of Risperdal seemed to be doing its work. Less and less now did the letters of billboards leap out in revealed messages as he drove up Interstate 87 toward Nyack, and only a little did the thrum of the Mercedes's motor suggest a harmonic obligato against which melodies might arise and be defined. But still the thoughts, the moods translated into words, the conversations, came to him.

He actually wondered if he was anyone at all anymore. As he drove, a dialogue in his head with Ann that began with a kind of impromptu poem was going on:

Anna,
I don't know who it is who sings this song,
Presses these lungs, galvanizes this tongue.
Don't know who utters these sounds,
Directs these eyes, makes his rounds.

It's not as if I don't care –
It's that my substance is air.

And she replying: You can't grab at a soul, Ludi? Weave together your moments into a flimsy thing waving at a certain frequency in the transmission of the present?

I come in and out, snap in the winds of the world, droop in timeless sleep. I… suppose myself to be, I guess, a sort of… present guy.

How?

I achieve a kind of dynamic stasis – a confident present – when I accelerate the mega-hearts into a temporal vibration I call Hope.

It resonates.

It resonates at a close harmonic to itself, it has the pristine ring of identity to it, though bifurcated with an infinitely slender crack…

So who are you now? Do you own a house?

I've always rented.

Didn't they do a piece on your digs in *Ostentatious?* Wasn't there an account of some party where you debased yourself before the guests and had to crawl under the weight of their half-lidded gaze?

Yeah, yeah.

But you say you rent. Not own.

I've been a tenant who's changed his location without moving. Once or twice. But I don't know where I live.

You don't? No way of finding out?

I have an approximation, there's a map printed in dotted lines with an "X" somewhere. But the writing at the bottom says the "X" doesn't mark the spot so much as crosses it out.

Printed, or cursive?

The hand is obscure…

An oncoming car was honking insistently, focusing Eastwind on the road. He jerked the wheel to get back in his lane, but overcompensated and couldn't bring the Mercedes into the sharp turn of the highway which cut to the left; the car veered down the embankment, seeming to hang on two wheels while he tried to steer through the low foliage. He was going about seventy and heading for a chain-link fence he was trying to avoid with all his strength; the car bounced and rumbled over the scrub brush and then plowed into the fence, almost rolling through it. The Mercedes came to a stop with the chain-link screeching over its hood and half the roof. Ahead of the hood, its ornament ripped off, a post with fence attached dangled obscenely a few feet off the ground.

Eastwind let the pounding of his heart soften, then unbuckled his seatbelt. He got out, saw that he seemed to be functioning adequately, and ambled around the Mercedes. The car had some minor dents, the right headlight was smashed, and the paint job was gone, but, he thought, he might still be able to get back on the highway. Then he saw the collapsed right front wheel, the fender crushed into its tire. This baby's officially immobile, he thought to himself, the price of reverie at high speed.

He looked around. No one from the highway had seen his mad descent. He looked behind the wrecked fence and saw wrecked cars, piles of auto parts – and a man making his way toward him.

"Afternoon," the man called out, a look of sly amusement on his face. "Most people come in the front way, but I guess you're in a hurry." He was of medium height and wore a sleeveless white shirt, even though the temperature bordered on chilly; his hair approximated a feathery helmet. He dodged through the piles of metal, then ducked under the elevated fence-bottom and approached Eastwind, who asked,

"That a junkyard?"

"It sure is." The man looked at the Mercedes. "You've come to the right place. Nice car," he said. "Or was. You okay?"

"I think so. Just a little faint."

"You were lucky. You did better than my fence."

"I'll take care of that."

"I know. But let's get the cops out here," he said, pulling a cellphone from a case on his belt. "Ought to have an official report. Medics too. Just so I don't get sued."

"Wait," Eastwind said.

"Wait?"

"Yeah, hang on a minute." Eastwind looked around again, saw that it was only the two of them and that the scene wasn't visible from the highway, which curved urgently away behind a thickening arbor. "I'd rather not… look, none of that is necessary. I've got a lot of money. I'll make good on the damage."

The man smiled his wry smile again. "I've had other people not want to involve the, uh, official agencies. Show up with cars all dented up, once or twice one with bullet holes, and wanted to get rid of them without… complications. You got a problem with the law?"

Eastwind was actually thinking that his having been off his medication, his allowance back into society on the basis of staying on it, could be a problem if there was an investigation. But he didn't want to talk about that. He said, "Let's just say I hate paperwork."

The man put away the cellphone, his smile fading a bit. "Not fond of it myself. Tell you what. This car isn't going anywhere without a wrecker in front of it. Let's say you leave it here, I'll work up an estimate on the fence, and you can have it back when I get the money."

Eastwind thought of Ann. "The thing is," he said, "I've got to be somewhere."

"Well, then, you've got a situation, I'd say."

"Look, could you drive me to a rental car place?"

"Nope. I've got to be here all day." He paused, then added disingenuously, "People got to have their junk."

"But wouldn't you have some… old junker I could drive?"

"Well, I do, come to think of it," the man said. "But this is getting more complicated. You'd have a car of mine."

"Yeah, and you'd have a car of mine."

"But yours is wrecked. Like my fence."

"What is your junker?" Eastwind asked. "What make and year?"

"It's a 'ninety-two Hyundai Sonata. New brakes."

Eastwind glanced at the sky above; dull sunshine overlit the afternoon.

"Look," he suddenly said, "why not you just take the Mercedes – for junk parts if you want, or to fix up and own – and I'll take the Hyundai? Let that cover the expense of your fence, too. Call it even."

The man said, "Mister, if you have a lot of money you must have inherited it. That's an awful deal for you." He stared at Eastwind, and a frown crossed his face. "This car hot or something?"

Eastwind reached into the Mercedes through its still-open door and pulled out his registration from the glove box. He handed it to the man with his driver's license. "If it's a match, is it a deal?"

The man scrutinized both documents, walked to the rear of the car and checked the license plate number. Then he walked back to Eastwind and handed him his license; he tucked the registration in his shirt pocket and shook his head. "Man," he said, "you sure drive a hard bargain."

Eastwind laughed. "I sure can't drive a hard car. Take me to your junker," he said, slamming the wrecked car's door. They both bowed under the fence and then threaded through the piles of automotive detritus, with the man introducing himself as they passed a stack of old tires.

"Don't worry," he said as they neared an A-frame just off a blacktop road, "there's no junkyard dog. Had one, but he went deaf and I couldn't call him."

* * *

Eastwind inspected the Hyundai Sonata, dented, white, with half-worn tires and an interior to match, but found it decent. He knew his impromptu host, whose first name was Alvin, was getting the much better end of the deal by far; he didn't care, and it astonished him a little that he didn't. Alvin had him come into the A-frame shack that served as both office and home; he found the paperwork for the Sonata and made a note on it that a trade had been effected. Eastwind looked around and noticed several old reel-to-reel tape recorders, stacks of tapes.

"Now, you've got to sign your title over to me," Alvin was saying, "and mail it to me. My address is right there. If you don't you're facing big problems, you know."

"I know," Eastwind said. "Don't worry. I'm a hundred percent" – *these days,* he thought to himself.

"Well, good," said Alvin. "I used to think I was a hundred percent but found a little vacuum in my math."

"A vacuum?"

"Kind of a moral vacuum. Cost me my wife. Not that I miss her. I have my birds."

Eastwind looked around the cramped space of the house again, noticed a lack of cages – a lack of almost anything, besides the tape recorders; there was only the dank ordinariness of collected tokens of the everyday. "Your birds?" he said.

"Yeah… I record their songs. Fascinating, especially if you slow the tape down and listen to what they're saying."

He handed Eastwind the registration for the Hyundai. "Happy miles," he muttered, without irony.

"So what are they saying?"

"Well, you know," Alvin allowed, "it's not like they have a real language or anything. But we ornithologists – well, I'm an amateur – we make up phrases to categorize them."

"Phrases?"

"You know. It's for classification. We need something to go on to identify their songs."

"Oh, right," Eastwind said, glancing out to the Hyundai.

"So we make up phrases. Guy down in Florida has identified thirty different songs belonging to one species of wood thrush. Calls their songs, one of them, like, 'Hey, sweetie, sweetie.' A gentle man."

"I would say so," Eastwind allowed. "It's a gentle calling. Odd to find someone in your business who would have that interest."

"Well, it's a kind of balance I've struck between the nearly used-up and the completely useless, I guess. I've recorded a hundred and thirty-one songs that include not only the wood thrush but the scarlet tanager and the common barn owl. I've started on woodpeckers lately."

"Right." Eastwind was inspecting the registration slip.

"I slow them down and come up with phrases of my own. I hear differently from the usual researchers."

"You do?" Eastwind felt the urgency of wanting to be on the road.

"Yeah. I'm an amateur, published nothing, but I'm avid."

"Okay."

"I put their songs down in my own lingo, according to what I hear."

"I see," Eastwind said absently.

"Don't patronize me," Alvin said, looking up irritably.

"Didn't mean to," Eastwind said.

"But I'm different. I don't hear like that nice man in Florida."

"All right."

"Ask me what they're saying. Go ahead." He pulled out several pictures of different birds from his desk drawer. He pointed to one of them. "Tell me what you think this guy might say."

Eastwind hesitated. He felt he was still not quite right in his mind, and that, like the anagrams, various spooky meanings might obsess his thoughts. But Alvin went ahead.

"This little guy – he's real pretty. He says, 'Hey, mo-fuckah, mo-fuckah.' This guy," he went on, pointing at another bird, spangled in a raiment of feathers, "I have him saying 'Cheated on my wife last night. Cheated on my wife last night, goodie, goodie.'"

Eastwind turned away, mildly disgusted; he found Alvin's chatter beneath dignity. "You know," he said with a glance to the door, "I'm late already." He extended his hand for the keys that lay on Alvin's desk.

"Now this one," Alvin said, oblivious, "his song is 'nigger-chick, nigger-chick.'"

"I'll send you my title as soon as I get home," Eastwind said, and took the keys off the desk.

"Kind of goes with this little beauty. Says, "chink-a-wink, chink-a-wink, slanty, slanty.' Racist birds – who'd have thought it?"

Eastwind went down the steps toward the yard as he heard Alvin muttering, "Fuck-it-up, fuck-it-up, it's okay, it's okay." He walked over to the car and climbed in. He turned the key and the engine caught immediately.

"I'll hear from you, Eastwind," Alvin called from the doorway of the rearing structure as the Hyundai crept out of the yard. "Right?"

Eastwind nodded solemnly to him and muttered to himself, "You will, you will, surely, surely. You will, you will," and then snickered as he stopped at the road that ran past the junkyard. In a flash lasting only an instant he recalled a T'ai Chi mate – during his convalescence an open-minded therapist had recommended the discipline, and the state had paid for it – a co-participant who also was under the supervision of a mental institution, and who had made up moves with T'ai Chi-sounding names: "Absent-minded Intellectual Drops Glasses in Punchbowl," accompanied by certain slow-motion moves that recalled Mr. Magoo feeling about in an imagined piece of crockery; "Surreptitious Glance at Cleavage," with "Wife's Striking Slap" following as a kind of companion set of moves, involving what appeared to be the punch known as Chow Choi swimming through molasses. They'd all laughed, and even their Sifu, their teacher, had joined in. Alvin couldn't begin to match that zaniness, Eastwind thought – that hack, with his studied weirdness, his banal obsession.

He steered onto the blacktop, floored the accelerator, and let the abysmal asphalt suck the Sonata forth.

* * *

When her door opened Eastwind realized they were both old people, though it was true that the beauty he had known was remembered in her face. He took her hand and they embraced. "Come in, come in," she said.

The house was a modest wood-frame structure with a kitchen and no more than two rooms; he had been right about the neighborhood. "I take it you're still ministering to the disenfranchised," he said, letting it be a question.

"Oh, yes," she answered. "Same old me."

He looked above the faux marble mantle and was pained to see a photograph, blown up and framed, of Brett and Ann from their wedding, Brett looking exaltedly happy but dignified; Ann looked somehow strangely serious, though deeply at peace. Eastwind meditated briefly that the last time he had seen Brett's face it had been at the bottom of the stairs at the halfway house, eyes turned into their lids. He felt a pang of anguish at their happiness; he turned away and looked toward the kitchen. That moment in time, he reflected: is photo paper the only guarantee of the propagation of the second when human hope makes its promise? We neither know who we are or what fate will make of us, he thought a little uneasily; who knew, as the camera's shutter severed the past and future of that present moment when light had burst off the couple, that Brett would die an early death and Ann would mourn him in an austere wooden chapel?

"Would you like some coffee?"

"Yes. Black, please."

He sat at the low table in front of the couch. Ann brought him a heavy cup with the Shaker motto "'Tis a gift to be simple, 'tis a gift to be free" inscribed in the style of Old English, and he added a few cubes of sugar from a little jar on the table. He stirred the dark brew with a plain spoon she handed him. A silence ensued.

Ann finally said, "So what do you remember of those days when you were Ludi Vann?"

"Ann, it's mostly dreams, little flashes now and then. Reminders from people who knew me."

"I must be one of them. Remember how you played the piano for me when I was ill?"

Eastwind fidgeted. "Well, see," he began, with a little discomfort, "actually, that was from a biography of Beethoven. He did that for his 'Immortal Beloved.'"

"So it was a knock-off."

"Like everything."

"Well, that explains why it was so painful."

"Painful? It was painful?"

"Ludi – forgive me if I still call you that…"

"It's okay. But call me Louie."

"You could barely play the piano. There were more wrong notes than right."

"My god. I never knew. I can play the piano again these days," he said, and then reflected, *with a little help.*

"Well, you were deaf, at least sometimes. I got better anyway." She laughed a little. "It was okay," she said. "We were caring for you. We knew you couldn't help it."

"My god. I didn't hear what was there, and I heard what wasn't. Like my dominant-to-tonic pushcart."

"What was that?"

"It was all in my head. I thought – Ludi Vann thought – he'd invented something that sounded all the key-changes in an orderly way, around the circle of fifths in music. He wheeled it into the Met to protest… oh, I guess, some modern opera, a dissonant opera."

"So it was a real thing?"

"It was a hot dog vendor's cart that I… that Ludi Vann stole." They both laughed.

"Have you gone back to the city and run into anyone from… from before?" she asked.

"Oh, yeah. I went looking for Blind Boy. He's still there. He told me where I could find Idiot Boy. I spent some time with him. Ann," he said, looking into her eyes, "I've been trying to find out what happened that day. With Brett. But I'm still in the dark."

"What do you remember?"

"Only that we argued. He wanted to evict Ludi for not taking his medication. And he knew you were Ludi's 'Immortal Beloved.'"

"Brett warned me about that. He told me Ludi Vann was in love with me."

"Yeah. I had suppressed that until just the other day."

Presently Ann asked, "Do you remember anything else?"

"Only Brett standing in the doorway. I shook my fist at him. That's all. The next thing was seeing him… at the bottom of the stairs. But I don't know what really happened. It's tormented me, Ann." He took a sip of his coffee. "I've struggled to remember that day but always seemed only on the verge of it. You won't believe what I've done to try to find out. I hunted up the street people I knew then. I saw the Professor in a dream – you probably never ran into him…"

"Are you kidding? With his sandwich-board signs?" She laughed.

"Right. I've had dreams about him. I wonder if he's still out there." He sighed, leaned into the sofa back; faces from the past, like planets around a sun – no, not a sun, but the lunar Ludi – came to him.

"Salmaninski is still around," Ann said, a little hesitantly. "He's still doing concerts."

The image of the promoter came to him. There was something about that man's jaw, he reflected, something that dignified conspiracy and betrayal, as if these, too, were the faces of lesser gods belonging to some pantheon on which only the reflected light of the moon shone. He said, "He's not been my friend." He thought a moment. "You know, I could probably get him a prison term over something…"

Ann said to him, "The letter." Eastwind had surmised some time ago that she knew about that, even that he – that Ludi Vann – was its author. "The two professors came to see me about it. I mean, they knew it was a fake, but I think I put them on to where Salmaninski got it," she said.

"They were working for me," he said, but decided not to tell her why.

She got up and went into the kitchen, inspected her refrigerator. "Would you stay to dinner, Louie?"

They had a dinner of salad and a highly seasoned Manhattan chowder, on which Eastwind complimented her. He asked about her work.

"Always the same. Never enough help, never enough money. Downtown Nyack has a lot of homeless. And I still work in the city – New York City. We've moved from where you stayed, but we're understaffed and underfunded there too. Sometimes it seems so futile to me I almost just want to quit. But I feel for them – the homeless. Always have."

"I'm thankful for that."

"Sometimes I wonder if the sane ones have chosen that or if God made them that way like the… afflicted."

Eastwind thought of Idiot Boy's remark about Ludi's madness: *a tangle in the braid of himself.* "I'm still afflicted," he said. "God comes to me in dreams. We talk."

"What does he say?"

"Ahh… it's only me, my weird mind. He explains himself. A few nights ago he explained ball games."

Ann smiled an incredulous smile. Then a little sadly she said, "Brett used to say God made us choose our own fates. He used to say he believed all things were right – even our chafing at them. Louie, if you did push him that day he would have forgiven you."

"Ann," Eastwind said, "I've done very well with something I really did invent after I got better. I have a lot of money now. I can help you – the homeless program."

"I'd certainly accept it."

"Good. I may not have it for long. I'm losing my business sense. I practically gave away my Mercedes."

"I saw you drive up in an old car. Pretty dented."

"Runs okay. Great gas mileage. But no left-turn signal."

"How did you get it?"

"I traded it. I wrecked the Mercedes on the way here. I'm okay, and the car wasn't all that damaged, but somehow… I just didn't want it anymore."

"How did you wreck it?"

Eastwind hesitated. "Well, actually," he said, "I was

imagining a… a kind of conversation with you, wasn't paying attention to the road. I didn't know who I was anymore."

"Do you feel like that now?"

"I'm sort of back at square one," he said. *Or am square one*, he thought. *Without the theorems of plane geometry.*

"But wouldn't that be normal for someone getting over the kind of problem you had?"

"I was over it some time ago, with the chemical therapy," he said in a moody thoughtfulness. "But since then I've become someone… someone whose Mercedes-self is getting more and more dented and wrecked." *My life is the pull of curved space where the angles of square one don't add up.*

"Maybe it's best just to let that be, Louie. Just endure it for now."

"I really don't have a choice, to tell the truth, Ann," he said. He was pensive a moment. *If space is curved maybe the diagonal of the square is warped in the slender arc of promise…*

"What are you thinking about, Louie?"

"Swiss rainbows."

She thought his answer odd, but said nothing as she began clearing the table. Eastwind got up. "Let me help you with those, *s'il vous plaît,*" he said, and she laughed a little, answering *"Très bien, monsieur, si vous voulez."* He dried as she washed, and they kept a silence. After the kitchen was in order, he said, "I really should get back," and added, "I'm serious about getting some money to you, Ann. I'll send you a check."

"That would be good of you. Listen, Louie, whatever happened that day at the stairs, I want you to know that I hold you blameless."

Eastwind held her hands. "That means everything to me," he said. He thought he caught the scent of gardenias in her hair. "That's all I can say."

"There's nothing more to say," she added. "But Louie, if you ever find out – somehow – I'd still like to know."

"I would too," he said.

He went out the door into the twilight, then turned and waved at her as he got in his new junker.

"Don't make any left turns, Louie," Ann called out with a laugh. He backed out and then headed down the road as the streetlights came on. Looking in the mirror, he caught a last wave from her.

Chapter Nine

A Musical Lecture, and Coda

He drove back on the highway he had so immediately departed from on the way there, reflecting on having seen Ann; he felt a surge of happiness, a kind of liberation. He knew now what he had to do.

The strange impulses of his mind seemed under control, though his thoughts still refracted in various dimensions. He began imagining how things might have worked out otherwise. For instance, he thought, what if, once inside her house, she'd begun crying and accusing him of Brett's death, beating at his chest, raking her nails down his cheek to brand him with a set of parallel welts? What if she had only wanted that confrontation, not for forgiveness, but to drive home guilt? But that hadn't happened, thank god. He concentrated on his driving.

Another thought came to him, worse than the first: that after her cheerful good-bye, she'd shut the door and loathed herself… for lying about her feelings; perhaps she *couldn't* forgive him. Eastwind knew this was the old doubt, the old nothingness at the core of his acquired self, nagging out of its daily suppression. But it was only that. ("Only that"; he reflected on the poignancy of those two words, words that were the key and tumblers of the latch on the pantry wherefrom the manna of the Everyday made its way into the open mouths of humanity everywhere.) He had made an uneasy peace with this doubt, which, he mused, Cartesianly and continuously proved his existence. And yet he rested in his belief that Ann had been sincere; it's her nature, he thought. Does one break bread with the unforgiven? Does one *do the dishes* the bread was broken on with the unforgiven? His sense of absolution returned.

Eastwind headed into Manhattan, and in the glow of good feeling decided to see if he could find Bline Boy. Left turns were unavoidable, and this evening he found driving in the city more exasperating than usual with his not being able to signal a lane change; hand signals would have let in chilly air. It seemed he was caught in a rushing mass of rolling metal as he was swept down Broadway. Eventually he saw an opening in the left lane and shifted over, then pulled onto West Fifty-seventh street. He got out, thinking he could find Beebee another time; maybe he could reconnoiter a way to the Hamptons without this traffic.

Carnegie Hall glimmered in the lighting of its façade, and he saw that something was going on there this night. He looked over and saw the lighted glass-box marquee with its illuminated playbill. Without being able to tell himself why, Eastwind began a slow walk toward it. The glow seemed almost to draw him, and he wondered at that; there was always something happening at the hall.

He came to stand before the lighted box. His own image stared back at him; for an infinitesimal moment he took it to be a reflection from the glass, then saw it was deeper than surface; it was a photo of his face, juxtaposed with a picture of a Yamaha Disklavier; prominently in it was the little keypad attached to the lower end of the keyboard. A publicity poster Yamaha had made a few years ago.

Eastwind stared into his image. "That's me?" he murmured, a little incredulous. It seemed to him that he was looking at someone who was he, but who, in return, he was not; oddly, reciprocity had ceased. He felt a vague embarrassment about the man in the photo, someone he had known from the inside, someone who now was only outside, a husk. He locked eyes with his image, saw them staring dumbly back at him, nothing to be read.

Eastwind noticed the dark lettering above the portrait of himself and his invention:

SCHOENBERG BY BEETHOVEN
A Musical Lecture

and in smaller print, beneath the photo, he read, "Yamaha Disklavier is proud to exhibit its magnificent concert grand piano using the computer stylings of Louis B. Eastwind, inventor of 'Diabelli,' the software program that creates music for our enjoyment and edification." And then he read:

Leonard Salmaninski, MM
Eminent Musicologist with
Metropolitan University of New York
"Against the Aesthetics of Aggression"

Something churned in his stomach. He was both stunned and furious, though none of it was to be unexpected, he knew, given his contract with Yamaha. But… *Salmaninski?!* And *Schoenberg!* He recalled what Antonioni had said. In a moment his solar plexus began to ease up, and he made his way toward the concert hall's doors.

He entered the lobby and crossed to an auditorium door. An usher looked alarmed but Eastwind said, "Look at me. I'm Eastwind," and pulled open the door violently; he saw that the place was about a third full, with the audience taking up seats closest to the orchestra pit, which had been left open. He caught the great black wing of a concert grand, raised as if a darkly gleaming benediction over the gathered.

To the right of the piano was a blackboard with staff lines on it, and in between stood the tall and slightly stooped figure of Salmaninski.

Eastwind noticed that his mind was shifting to another mode as he took in the scene; he felt a sudden surge as a… a creator, and as he strode down the aisle he felt a further surge of righteous anger at the distortion of his creation; he realized with some anguish that he was hearing something from the first movement of Beethoven's last piano sonata – a passage that was particularly bold and forceful in character. He recalled what Julie had said about old triggers, and he thought that the Risperdal might be failing him. In a moment he realized that the music was coming from the piano, with no one at the keyboard. Still, his gait was all assertiveness; he was in the mood for violence.

As he was making his way toward the front of the auditorium, Salmaninski was reaching over to the little control panel at the left end of the keyboard. He touched a button and the music suddenly stopped.

"Now, of course, many of you know the piano music of Beethoven," Salmaninski said into a lapel microphone, "but I thought I'd just give you a taste of what we may call the 'aggressive aesthetic' of it. Because tonight we're going to get into a system of composition that consciously avoids all that – the twelve-tone technique of Arnold Schoenberg." Eastwind felt his stomach tighten again as he stood, holding the back of a seat; he did not want to sit.

"Maybe some of you saw Thomas Antonioni's piece in the *Times* about the Eastwind program – that it develops anything put into the keyboard pretty much along the lines of Beethoven's compositional devices. This is the chief feature of 'Diabelli,' the software he invented for this great piano." Eastwind saw the old smarminess of Salmaninski emerge as he plugged the Yamaha. "Ain't this a great sound, folks? Hey?" he asked, looking over to the looming instrument and bringing his hands together with sudden enthusiasm. A few members of the audience applauded. Salmaninski hadn't calculated, thought Eastwind, that they wouldn't want to be sold something; they were probably all music lovers, intellectuals, musicians themselves.

"How can a way of composing music overcome this 'aggressive aesthetic'? Well, we gotta start at the beginning, folks. Things like the fundamental tone and its overtones, and all that jazz, as jazz musicians used to say, which is the basis for – let's call it traditional harmony."

Salmaninski illustrated the overtone series at the piano, explaining how any note five steps up in a scale – he called it the dominant – leans back to its fundamental, which he called the tonic. He labored over a closing cadence, pounding out a dominant G chord that landed in a final C harmony. "Look, he said, "ever notice how Beethoven works that baby over at the end of the Fifth Symphony? But, see, the thing is, every composer up until Schoenberg is operating with the same deal, though in a more stretched-out way.

"Folks," he went on, "there's only one story in music up until the early twentieth century: the journey that returns home: the fall redeemed, if you like. In traditional music it's all the rise of the tonic into the dominant and the return to that ground. All of the places that composers visit harmonically on their way home are landmarks erected by the fundamental harmony; their travels, well, in a lotta cases, move according to dominant-to-tonic, what we in the biz call 'secondary dominants.' Wanna see how Mozart is gonna end up in a new place harmonically for his second theme in the first movement of Symphony Number Forty, which needs to be B-flat? Look five steps up – that's the roadmap to any dominant – from B-flat and you find F. And sure enough, here's Wolfie, he's got his violins sawing away in F-major – then he lands in B-flat. Because, you see, that was the way of Western music right up to World War One. But things changed."

Despite himself, and despite Salmaninski's vulgarity of expression, Eastwind found he was being drawn into the lecture. He slipped into the seat he had been standing in front of.

"So. Schoenberg. Now, in his early days, he also played the dominant-to-tonic game. But he came to feel it was worn out. I suspect too that the aggressive move of harmony was the same triumph of gaining ground a few feet beyond the trenches of the Great War, at the expense of thousands of lives." Eastwind was still glaring at the man, and yet what he was saying had an allure to it. Someone in the audience raised his hand and Salmaninski said, "Question? Yeah, speak up."

"I don't buy it," a man with a Brooklyn accent akin to Salmaninski's said. "What about Beethoven's gentle music? What about the first movement of the 'Moonlight' Sonata – you think that's aggressive?"

Salmaninski moved closer to the audience and addressed the man, who had stood. "It's the 'aggressive aesthetic' in the sense that almost every harmonic change there is pushed into place by the old dominant-to-tonic style. Listen." He went to the piano and played that piece to its arrival in the key of E-major. "Look at this," he said, starting it over, "let me call out all the dominants that indicate the coming tonics. Look at this. G-sharp major to C-sharp minor. C-sharp to F-sharp. F-sharp to B-major. B-major to E-major. Dominant to tonic, then the tonic becomes a dominant of the next harmony, and so on. See what I mean?"

The man said, "Yeah, but it's only a theoretical violence. It still isn't aggressive to our ears."

"Yeah, I'll give you that," Salmaninski said, getting up from the piano, "but if you doubt the meaning of what you call a 'theoretical violence,' listen to the last movement of the 'Moonlight'; it's a willful frenzy to get from tonic to dominant and back home again, victoriously. Get my meaning?"

The man had sat down, and didn't answer; he muttered to the man next to him. In his stead a middle-aged woman stood and said, "Professor, *you* sure don't get it. It's not about music theory, okay? It's about the human heart."

"I can go with that," Salmaninski replied, unfazed. "But who knows what evil lurks in the hearts of men, if I may quote. Nah," he suddenly said, as if overtaken by the negativity he was espousing, "it's human nature to be aggressive, destructive, dominant – yeah, to tonic; that's what needs to be destroyed. For that matter, my friend Pierre Boulez would like to destroy all the music of the past. Sure it's music theory; it's math, too. But how it sounds is unaffordable after World War One."

"I disagree," the woman said. "Call me a philistine. For me Beethoven is timeless."

"'So our virtues/ Lie in the interpretation of the time,' if I may move from The Shadow to Shakespeare, lady." He started to say more, but the woman turned and made her way out, passing sideways through the aisle; it was the same aisle Eastwind was sitting in, and she brushed by him; his eyes followed her to an exit. It occurred to him that she was Salmaninski's wife, with the scenario a staple of his lectures. His rancor still burned like a dull pain, but Salmaninski's ideas seemed to have a certain logic to them.

A very young woman stood and raised her hand. "What was the name of the Beethoven song we were listening to at the beginning?" Salmaninski turned away, wiping his face in his hands as his eyes rolled; an academic, he had long deplored the reduction of all music to the category of "song." He resisted answering something like "the Fuck-a-Duck Polka."

"Look, we can do more questions later, okay? I'd like to illustrate the method Schoenberg came up with that undoes all the violence of the former system. He wasn't the only one to have thought of it, by the way. But he made the biggest splash. Now everybody look under your seat; some of you will find a marble taped just near the front of it."

Shoulders sagged en masse as audience members felt the lower edge of their seats, Eastwind among them. One or two found only a wad of hardened chewing gum, and wiped their hands on their clothes.

"Now, twelve of you will have found a marble. Hold on to it for now. Notice that it has the name of one of the twelve different notes in the Western chromatic system inscribed on it," Salmaninski announced. Eastwind was one who found a marble, and saw it was marked "B-natural." "So, you're wondering, some of you, why twelve? Let me help you with that." Once again he crossed to the keyboard, sat, and slowly played a scale of all the notes, black and white alike, up to where it began an octave higher. "See," he said, "when you count 'em, there're only twelve different notes; then you start over again in the next octave." He snaked his way up through the higher register. "Just twelve. Like the disciples," he added, apropos of nothing.

"So," Salmaninski went on, rising from the piano and addressing the audience, "this is the basis for Schoenberg's new system. Except the notes aren't all in a line like I played there. Instead the composer makes a row out of 'em, where they're not consecutive like that, something with contours but no limitation as to pitch range. And he can initiate the row at any of the twelve pitches. In other words, the row can be all over the place – as long as the order of the row is preserved. Now, that can happen in four main ways. A composer can run the row forwards, backwards, upside-down, and both upside-down and backwards. The harmony – you know, the vertical blocs of sound under a melody, usually – is also some version of the row, with the top note of the chord part of the row, and the next note down in the chord the next note of the row, and so on." He played a dissonant chord and pronounced the names of notes, from top to bottom, that made up the sound. "These would be a fragment of the row, see."

The man who had first spoken to Salmaninski stood up again. "But that means the harmony is effectively random," he said, emphasizing the last word.

"Yeah. Exactly. That's how we leave old dominant-to-tonic-ville. The ego-triumph of conquering the next harmony in the old aesthetics of aggression is opted out."

"But… randomness?" the man asked with a kind of theatricality.

"Hey, welcome to twentieth-century physics, my friend," Salmaninski went on. "Ever hear of quantum theory? Some composers around the middle of the century even chose the make-up of the original row by random means. Which brings me to your marbles and this athletic mat, kindly loaned to us tonight by the Ninety-second Street Y's May Center, lying here on the stage." He walked over to it, bent down and dragged it to the front, bringing it to the right of the piano and before the blackboard; it was about ten-by-ten feet, and heavy. "I know you were wondering if I was going to wrestle with the subject tonight," he said to a few groans.

When it was in place, he said, "The real reason is that I want all you who found note names under your seat to lose your marbles…" A few giggles from the audience. "I want you to throw your notes at the mat, please. Try not to overshoot it. It's okay if you do. But I'm getting out of the way," he added as he edged toward the piano, "and you note-holders are going to create a twelve-tone row – a random one. Ready? Now remember, at least try to aim for the mat. Okay… throw!"

The marbles sailed over the orchestra pit in moderate arcs, mostly landing on the mat, as most of the audience laughed. Eastwind refused to throw his. One marble hit the blackboard, with Salmaninski cracking, "Ah, a pitcher from the Mets, I see," a remark that brought more laughter, as the team had been doing abysmally. Several marbles landed behind the mat, and he had to chase them with a broom and dustpan, all to the high amusement of the audience. He ceremoniously dumped all the errant ones on the mat, then lined all the marbles up roughly with the toe of his right shoe.

"All right, all right. We got our row," he announced. "Let me put it on the blackboard, along with its permutations." There was applause from the crowd, all except Eastwind. Salmaninski stared at the rough line of marbles and suddenly said, "Oh, wait." He counted, wagging a finger at the mat, and said, "We only got eleven." He looked around behind the mat again, then inspected its edges. "Crap," he said. "I know the marbles were under the nearest seats. Oh, yeah," he added, "check under the seat Madam Philistine had." A man reached over and felt around, then shook his head.

"All right," Salmaninski said, mocking the tone of a scolding schoolmaster, "who's holding out on us?" He searched their faces, letting his gaze range over the crowd. In a moment he found himself staring at Eastwind, who was glaring back at him, eyes glittering in anger, and who was holding the missing marble before his face.

Salmaninski grew pale – because he recognized not Louis Eastwind, whose image he had been familiar with for some time, but saw instead the mad eyes of Ludi Vann; the marble shone like a miniature moon, full in the light of its holder's ire. Speech failed Salmaninski for a moment, then something made him go on, even though his recognition of Ludi – older and almost bald – was tinged by a sudden knowledge of danger – possibly even violence; he remembered his broken nose from a decade ago.

"Not much of a pitcher, eh?" he said to him evenly – to a man, he thought, who had pushed another man down a stairs. "A rebel with a taws, I guess," and laughed a little emptily at his forced pun. People craned their heads around toward Eastwind. "Well, that's okay, sir." He went on, turning toward the mat, "don't play the game with us tonight. Let me figure out what note you have – " for a few seconds Salmaninski pored over the marbles lined up on the mat. "Aha. B-natural. Well, as it turns out," he said, more to the general audience and less to Eastwind, "I just happen to have another marble in my pocket here." He pulled one out. "And since we need to put it in the row," he added, "let me toss this fake B-natural onto the mat and let it serve as the real thing."

He boosted the marble into the air and saw it land about five notes into the row, clacking as it ricocheted a little against the one to the right of it.

"All right," he said with finality, "now we got our row, despite our romantic resistance fighter." The crowd applauded again, and though pleased, Salmaninski still felt a deep unease at finding Ludi there. *At my Beethoven lecture.*

"Let me get this on the blackboard, with its different versions," he said. Eyes trained on the mat, Salmaninski chalked the notes of the row, including his substitute, on the top set of staff lines, labeling each one. This took a little over a minute. Then he announced:

"Okay, folks, let's see what we got. Here's the row you – " he shot a look toward Eastwind – "we created." He called out the names of the notes as they had landed. "Like I said, those are the only notes in our system. Now what do you get when you run it backwards? Pretty easy."

He began chalking up the notes and labels on the next set of staff lines down, starting with the last, and moving in retrograde to the first. It took a few minutes for him to write out the inversion, and as he did he explained how an interval between notes can be turned upside-down. Then he wrote out that last row on the bottom set of staff lines, except starting with the last note first. Presently he said, "And this is the retrograde of the inversion. Remember, I said there are four main things you can do with any row, and here they are. Wanna hear what the original row sounds like?"

He went to the piano, touched a button on the protruding console, and played the row, giving each note about a second; its sounds cohered in fleeting shapes no more engaged than glances in a subway car. "Whataya think of that?"

The same man who had challenged him before said, "Sounds aimless. Floating. It doesn't finish."

"Exactly," said Salmaninski. "Exactly what Schoenberg wanted. It just stops, as opposed to finishing. Finishes are the residue of violence. The closing cadence says to the opening measures, 'You started it, I finished it.' Now," he said, glancing at the little box at the left end of the Yamaha's keyboard, "let's see what this magnificent Disklavier can do. You might have seen me touch the keypad just now; the Eastwind computer was recording the original row as I played it. Let's do the other three." He played them, then stood; he reached toward the keypad, touched a switch, and stepped back.

Before he had moved past it, the instrument erupted in sounds precise and thunderous. But it veered into a quagmire of ambiguity, a quest that had forgotten its goal. What followed was heroic gesture, a kind of developing babble in an unintelligible lingo. Every time the drive toward some seeming point got started the project was abandoned, left out on a dissonant limb. It was as if someone had cut out randomly chosen words from a Shakespearean sonnet and assembled them in iambic pentameter; all syntax, no semantics: a blind surge into a labyrinth of disconnected shafts, light darting and refracting unevenly as openings winked and disappeared.

Occasionally people in the audience laughed. Salmaninski was using a pointer to jab at the various versions of the row whenever he thought he heard a snatch of notes that were on the board in a particular order. But he was faking it hugely; he thought to himself that the only people besides the composer who would really know what the row was doing at any time would be idiot savants, pegging every version of the row, but with a rope for a belt and shoes with laces they simply couldn't figure out how to tie.

As a pianissimo passage began, Salmaninski grabbed the opportunity to speak. "See, you gotta put away the ears we inherited from cultural history. Look for the…" He was about to say "beauty of it," but his voice died before the first syllable of the rest: Ludi Vann had made his way to the stage, and was climbing onto it. *And here comes Beethoven*, he thought grimly.

The audience was surprised to see Eastwind on the stage; some who recognized him thought it was an appearance of the mastermind at the exposition of his invention; some, though, recognized him only as the lone hold-out, and didn't know what to think. He strode to the piano as Salmaninski stared at him, immobile. Eastwind raised his fist above the computer panel at the end of the instrument, then slammed it vehemently onto the narrow box, bending it down at a weird angle. He kicked it and it fell off, dangling by thin colored wires. The piano stopped as if stricken, and all that filled the sonic void was a roar from the audience.

Above it, and bringing it to silence, Eastwind shouted, "I am Eastwind. I have made this thing. And I renounce it!"

There was a great hubbub in the audience. “Yeah,” thought Salmaninski as he strode to the intruder, “last time you were Beethoven.” But suddenly he saw it *was* Eastwind, and stood thunderstruck; he had never associated Ludi Vann with the image of the inventor, and the one was transmuted into the other for him in a cataclysmic alchemy of recognition.

“I will not be Frankenstein!” shouted Eastwind. He wanted to say that Beethoven had his place and Schoenberg his, but before he could speak this piece of conventional wisdom Salmaninski’s fist crashed into his face; blood spurted from his nose. There was pandemonium in the audience, with the Brooklynite thinking, Jesus Christ, what is this – professional wrestling? Eastwind punched his attacker in the stomach, and Salmaninski crumpled, pulling Eastwind down as he fell. The two wrestled on the floor for what seemed a long time as the loudspeakers in the hall, still fed from Salmaninski’s lapel mike, shouted out thuds and grunts. Salmaninski broke free and stood shakily, then kicked Eastwind in the upper chest, driving him to the edge of the stage. Eastwind was grabbing at Salmaninski’s ankles when he suddenly rolled off the stage into the orchestra pit, landing with a sickening thud. He moaned and was still.

“I think I owed you that” – Salmaninski gasped for air – “from something you did” – he grabbed at another breath – “a long time ago. It’s about time” – he coughed raspily – “I beat the shit out of you, whoever you are now.” His breath heaved through the sound system in thunderous exhalations. The great ruckus in the audience continued.

Salmaninski saw a large man, waving a badge in a leather wallet, climb on stage. “N.Y.P.D. Just cool it, okay?” the man said forcefully. He spoke into his cellphone, then added. “You’re under arrest.”

Some members of the audience cheered as other applauded, and a few rushed to the orchestra pit to help

Eastwind. "Don't move him, don't move him!" the man, an off-duty detective, shouted at them, and they pulled back. "An ambulance is on the way." He had Salmaninski in an arm-lock. Eastwind was bleeding at the nose, and someone pressed a handkerchief to it.

"You have the right to remain silent," the detective said, and Salmaninski gasped back, still amplified by the mike, "Yeah, that's what my students keep reminding me." As the cop recited the rest of his rights Salmaninski's knees buckled and he was allowed to sit on the piano bench.

Many of the audience were exiting, though a number stayed, waiting for Salmaninski to be led away, for the ambulance to arrive, waiting to see it finish.

Chapter Ten

Three Convalescent Dreams

In the coma, he was Ludi Vann again, in monologue.

"…wanted to be alone because I knew that the core of all of us is a great chasm, endless as it is black, reaching from the light of reason down into the original abyss creation leapt out of and preserved itself in as humus-beings. That was the meaning of 'alone' – no diversion, no forgetting, only the gaze into the chasm; to turn its bottomless depth into the truth of tones, *out of nothing*; to make something – not of nothing – but of its profundity. It was supposed to be my deafness that robbed me of sociable companionship; it was the chasm, it was long the chasm, it was Schubert's syphilitic despair without the infecting whore, it was dying the death.

"…the actual chasm itself the human person: corruptible, self-deceiving, the vanity of temporary immortality, pristine darkness of the true chasm distorted into a cellar where a temporal counterfeiting cranks out the falsified self, the presses of consciousness rolling under the glare of a naked, suspended bulb shedding artificial *dei*-light at sixty cycles per second, the exact rate at which the plate of the deceiving consciousness kisses the paper of the deceived consciousness in self-knowledge, eluding appearance…"

"It hum, you know, it moan, my frien'…"

"That's right, my friend. I have experienced the death of God and the failure of irony. I have learned in my time that every sigh is wind through unburied bones, the light at the end of every tunnel is only the reflection of the gleam in a horny eye, every future is the empty promise of a redeemed past – with all pasts sinking deeper into outer space towards black holes that would suck out the wound of an accidental happening, dress it in the blessing of oblivion: black hole, the cosmic cunt where all would be forgotten in re-entry, unknowing time-redemption, voided memory of the Alzheimighty.

"No. I wanted to be alone. Being with others makes you address the wrong questions with inappropriate answers.

"I wanted to be alone to compose. I saw the decomposition of my solitude into madness. I am Beethoven, I am Beastwind."

When he awoke from the coma, he found himself murmuring, "I was Beethoven. I was Beastwind. What name now goes with this persistent breath?"

* * *

Ann Yearly read in the *Times* about the melee and found out where Eastwind was being treated. She showed up at the hospital a few days later as Eastwind regained consciousness. He still fought fever, he still lapsed into listening to the strange voice of himself, but he was lucid in his waking hours.

He asked her to contact Roy about picking up his car, explaining what difficulties he might encounter because of the title-swap – and the left-turn signal; explain to him, he said with a wryness, that that defunct little device had a way with putting you in situations; tell him to look out for pacifist theoreticians of music. He asked her to see Polly about arranging things at the house during his stay in the hospital. Then the pain kicked in, and he rang for the nurse and more morphine.

"Sorry, Ann. Can you come back tomorrow?" he said in a voice tense with pain. "This thing is killing me right now."

She said she would, and kissed him on the forehead as she left. The nurse came in with the syringe, and he fell into disturbed sleep again.

* * *

In this dream, Eastwind was sailing a small boat in a stiff wind, noting the pleasure of driving forth so naturally, without a motor; a nice wake streamed behind the craft. But then the wind grew more intense, violent, omnidirectional. He tried to pull down the sails but the halyards were stuck around their cleats. The boat began yawing uncontrollably, then heeled over hugely, and he found it impossible to hold any kind of course.

In dream-urgency, Eastwind grabbed the VHF radio's mike and began calling the Coast Guard. "Hello, hello, this is the sailing vessel *Diabelli* asking for help. Mayday. S.O.S. Do you read me? Over."

An electronic voice answered. "We read you, *Diabelli.* What is your position? Over."

"My position? I have no idea," he answered in a jabber.

"No idea of a position? What if the issue is dodecaphony? Are you aware that you can find twelve different compass points? Over."

"Look, I'm in danger here. My ship is sinking."

"What tonality are we talking about, *Diabelli?* Over."

"It's all fully diminished sevenths in a minor key," he answered in a panic. "Tell me the key of the sea floor."

"Stand by, *Diabelli.* Let's see. Sea floor. Our charts are indicating F-sharp minor. Do you see three sharps beneath you? Over."

"I need help here! Can't you send a ship?"

"Sorry, *Diabelli.* Best we can do is send another sharp and hope for E-major. Do you want to try that? Over."

As Eastwind threw down the microphone the craft began to fall apart, gunwales flaking away, the sides crumpling. His ribs wracked him with pain as he fought to aim the boat ashore, but it was futile: the bulkheads began to appear, their structural cunning foiled by the roiling sea. The deck started falling away, and water began to engulf him. Then there was nothing but ribs, cracked and splitting. He sat like a living heart in an open skeleton whitening in the wash of the waves.

The boat went down as Eastwind reflected: it was so solid – and all the while it was so porous with this chance; it was so real and at the same time its disaster lived at its core, waiting for a stormy day. It was the truth whose lie lay at its center.

Like me, he thought as he was waking. Like me. Like me.

* * *

It was actually a few days later that Ann saw him. When she'd shown up the day after her last visit she was turned away; some sort of crisis had arisen then, but receded two days later.

Eastwind was glad to see her.

"You're better," she said. "They were worried about you, your doctor told me."

They talked awhile about the arrangements she had made with Roy and Polly. The car was at the Hamptons. He thanked her.

She told him she couldn't stay long because of needing to be at the city shelter in a while, and he reminded her that he would write a check for the homeless program.

"You'd better take it now," he said. "I think I'm getting out of the software business. I'll still get residuals, but it's all a big nothing now. Such a strange thing to have done. It's as if some cosmic pellet struck me and I reeled into this phony music thing. It's a shell I've abandoned."

"What will you do?"

He thought about this. "I'll get by. I'd sort of like to get back to… you won't believe this… I'd like to get back on the streets. Not homeless, though. Just… just in touch. Nothing's really meant much to me after those days."

"Maybe you could… work at the shelter," she said. "You'd be welcome."

Eastwind smiled. "Well, maybe I owe that back to you." He thought about it. "I could work there. But these broken ribs need some time to heal. It hurts just to shift positions in bed."

"I think they're charging Salmaninski with battery, aggravated battery, or something," she said. "And you could tell them about the letter fraud."

"I've thought of that before, but always hesitated," he said. "I'll have to decide. But you know, I miss Blind Boy. I miss Idiot Boy. I'd like to argue theology with The Professor, if I can find him. A new proof of God's existence."

"Oh my. Which is…?"

"It has to do with suffering."

Ann left when the doctor came in. The doctor said, "Tell you, software can be a pretty rough business. I've seen guys with their livers ripped out. You got off easy. But you're looking better here."

Eastwind laughed a little, then moaned at the pain that produced. After the doctor's examination he drifted into sleep.

* * *

The third convalescent dream sent him back to the stage at Carnegie Hall, where, somehow, Salmaninski was a game-show host and he the contestant. Both of them were wearing exaggerated nose bandages, though they were affable toward each other.

"So, my old friend here, guy I've known since he was Beethoven – ha ha – is with us tonight," Salmaninski was saying. "All right, you know the rules, right, Louie? For every wrong guess as to the identity of the Immortal Beloved, you gotta toss a marble onto the mat. Our producer's given you twelve, each with a note name on it. If you guess her, you win. But if we end up with twelve on the mat you gotta… Name That Tune! Are you ready, Louie?"

"Ready, Len."

"Okay. Here we go. Audience, please – no coaching. Louie, your first guess."

"Um," said the dream-Eastwind, "…Giulietta Guicciardi, the *Moonlight* maiden?"

"Off to a bad start." Eastwind tossed a marble. "Next guess?"

"Okay, how about Josephine Deym?"

"Another marble, Louie."

"Marie Bigot. I think he invited her for a carriage ride."

"You're right about the invitation. Pissed off her husband. Beethoven had a lot of 'splainin' to do. But she wasn't the Immortal Beloved."

Eastwind tossed another marble.

"Okay," Eastwind said, eyes looking toward the ceiling, "how about Giulietta Guicciardi's cousin… what's-her-name, Josephine Brunsvik?"

"Louie, you're doin' miserable here. Josephine Brunsvik was the name of the Deym dame before she married." Another marble hit the mat.

"All right, let's see. Julie von Vering?" Another marble. "Okay, okay. Therese Malfatti? Amalie Sebald? Marie Erdödy?"

Shaking his head, Salmaninski pointed to the mat and three more marbles landed.

"Dorothea Ertmann? Elise von der Recke?"

"No and no," said Salmaninski, and two more marbles hit. "That makes ten, Louie."

"Um… let me think. Okay, let me try Bettina von Arnim."

"Louie, for someone who was Beethoven you sure have a lousy memory." An eleventh marble hit the mat. "Last chance for us to… Name That Tune!"

Eastwind was perplexed. "But… those are all I can think of."

"Are you conceding, then?"

"I can concede?" Eastwind asked. "Is there a consequence for that?"

"Oh, you bet," replied Salmaninski. "There certainly is. We got only eleven notes here, and we'd have to play a game of marbles with them. And you wouldn't want that, because the object of the game is to end up at an even number; as long as you got an odd number, or an even number with me having an odd number, the game goes on. Isn't that right, audience?"

The dream audience applauded.

"Why is the goal an even number of marbles?" Eastwind wondered aloud.

"Because you and your self match. Like God, you are who you are. It's the perfect self-agreement of Two, it's mutuality, it's the hand-wounds of Christ," Salmaninski said. "A third keeps it from arriving. A third, an odd. Didn't you do a study on this with Antoine Lavoisier your head tutor? So we'd keep playing in perpetuity, wracking up more money for our sponsors. Each pass inside the circle would re-initiate an infinite loop; we'd live forever in a future of futures. It would be Ludi-Sisyphean." He paused and smiled a cheesy smile. "Of course that is precisely the definition of Hell."

In the dream Eastwind felt as if he were staring dumbly into space.

"But that's your option. So you wanna come up with that last name? You wanna tell us who your Immortal Beloved was?"

"Couldn't we just go with the eleven notes?" Eastwind asked. "What do we have so far?"

Salmaninski looked down, saying the names of the chromatic notes. "Every one but B-natural," he allowed.

Eastwind nodded a dream nod.

"Come on," Salmaninski said with a little menace to his voice, "try another gal in Beethoven's life, or concede."

"I won't concede. But I'm not tossing this last marble either," Eastwind said.

"Well, you just go ahead and be Mr. Hold-out. How do you like that, audience?" A concerted "boo" arose, with some hooting.

"As it turns out, I just happen to have another marble in my pocket here," Salmaninski went on. He pulled out a completely white one. "And since we need to put it in the row, let me toss this fake B-natural onto the mat and let it serve as the real thing."

Suddenly in the dream there was a piano and a chalkboard, and Salmaninski was looking at the row of notes on the mat and writing a melody in a key with two flats. "All right," he said when he had finished, "we got Reluctant Louie here, he's gonna… Name That Tune." He moved to the piano and played the melody.

Eastwind found something familiar about it. Salmaninski and the scene with the stage and audience began to fade, the melody alone sounding; eventually he began hearing it with the instrumentation of piano, violin and cello. The cello had it as the other instruments accompanied, then the piano took it. He awoke as he was noticing that the piano part was unusually simple.

"The fake B-natural. Supposedly the real thing," he murmured. The painkiller again set in, and he found himself listening to the voice of Roger McKane: "Beethoven wrote a little piece during his involvement with Antonie Brentano, a trio with a piano part for his Immortal Beloved's ten-year-old daughter, Maximiliane. The key was B-flat."

In his hazy condition, Eastwind contemplated those words. And his spirit plunged when it hit him: I changed it to B-natural just like I changed the Immortal Beloved to an unmarried woman. *To cover up having killed Brett Yearly.*

Chapter Eleven

Bline Boy

After his ribs had healed enough that he could leave the hospital, Eastwind visited his bank, got $5,000 in cash, and had a cashier's check for $100,000 made up. He drove his new old car into the city and went looking for Bline Boy down in the Bowery. Inelegantly dressed, he looked nonchalant as he sat on the sidewalk, back to a wall. It took several hours, but eventually he caught sight of the man, tapping his way in an easy rhythm.

He said, "Shia. Dere he be." It jarred him that he had reverted to his old speech patterns, but it felt right, too. "Bline Boy. Beebee. I back."

"Shia, tol' me you be back."

"Man, I be da proverbial badt penny. 'Cep' I got plenny goodt pennies widh me, like I tol' you, too."

"No shia? Goodt as you' wordt."

"You're fuckin' aye. Soldt my damn house and got more money outta dat."

"Shia. Why you do dat? Gotta live some damn where."

"I know, Bline Boy. But da place be like some sorta lavish tomb." For my dead soul, Eastwind thought. "Kinda a Taj damn Mahal widh, you know, like runnin' water 'n' servants. And like." In his mind Eastwind heard something like a section of a mutant Mass for the Dead:

Requiescat!
Requiescat, muvvah,
Requiescat in pace
Said *pace!*
  Tell the Apache!
  Tell 'em watch this space
  'Cause it's reportedly the case
  Geronimo's moved to Tallahatchee
  Where only coloreds and grammar
  Are still under the hammer –
Said *pace!*
Requiescat therein.

"You comin' back here?" Bline Boy asked, a little buoyed.

"Less jus' say I'll be aroundt. But looky-yeah, we gotta go to a bank, set up an account for you. Got a check for you, and some cash right now."

"So you Sandy Claws now?"

"Da damn Beethoven thing be over, Bline Boy. I tol' you. Sergeant Risperdal done been promoted to Captain. You be safe widh a lotta cash?"

"Giuliani done fix it up. Plus I got some pals look oudt fo' me."

"'Nother thing, Bline Boy. How about a dog – a seein'-eye dog? You can affordt one now."

The man thought about this. "A dog. Kin I name 'im 'Caney'?"

"Any damn thing you like."

"Where I get 'im? Da poundt?"

"Hell, no. Your poundt dog don' know lef' from damn right. You need a dog from a special college. They major in Traffic Lights, Stopping Before Doors, Crossing Streets, do a Man's Bes' Frien' practicum – like that," Eastwind said. "You doin' anything now?"

"Jus' takin' da day widh mah ol' frien'."

Eastwind took him to the Hyundai parked several blocks away, and they drove to the kennel the Lighthouse for the Blind had directed him to. They had only one dog available, they'd told him, adding that they had a huge waiting list – a statement which brought Eastwind to conceive of all the pools of darknesses that made up a sea of unknowing.

He led Bline Boy in, and they spoke to the trainer behind a counter who explained that all they would do that day was get Bline Boy and the dog acquainted. When Bline Boy had made accommodations for the animal, he could pick him up for good, but first would have to register for a tutorial with Blind Services. Eastwind said he would arrange that.

"They be no tes', now, see if I really be blindt," Bline Boy said.

"No test, sir," the young man answered, smiling. "We don't have any eye-charts for the blind."

"Dass goodt, 'cause I can't readt neither."

"But," said the man, amused, "I have to tell you that it might be a better idea to wait a while before picking him up. This dog could use a little more training. He still has obedience issues."

"Shia, dat da damn human story, obedience issues."

"See," the young trainer went on, "he wasn't raised in New York. Not even the North. Somewhere in the South. He could use some adjustment time. You might want to give him a month or so."

"I be raise' in da Souf. We prolly get along okay."

"Just so you know, sir. You can always bring him back."

"Whut his name?"

"We call him 'Pozzo,' but you can rename him if you want."

"I jus' call 'im 'Fido,'" Bline Boy said. "Don' know no 'Potso.' Whut kina dog he be?"

"He's part shepherd, part Rottie," the man said.

"Well, lessee kin we get along." Bline Boy turned toward the sound of barking and took Eastwind's shoulder as he leaned his cane against the wall. The trainer went ahead of them as the two walked toward the kennel door.

The kennel itself, with its wall of cages, was in the basement of the building; Eastwind led him to the landing at the top of the stairs. "Stairs here, Bline Boy. Step down." The young man, already at the bottom, was opening a cage. Bline Boy began slowly descending the stairs.

"Hey, there, Pozzo, old boy," the trainer was saying, ruffling the sandy-colored fur and fondling the ears of the dog. "Looks like you might be able to strut your stuff. Yeah, that's a good boy. What do ya think, boy? Can you guide this man?" He reached for a harness hanging above the cage.

Bline Boy was a quarter of the way down the stairs when the dog let out a growling roar and broke away in a dash at him. "No! No! Pozzo! Here, boy!" the young man yelled, then frantically thrust a slender silver whistle to his lips. The dog ran up the stairs and took the left calf of Bline Boy, who toppled over as Eastwind grappled with the animal, flailing at it with his naked fist. Bline Boy pitched down the stairs in a headlong roll that ended with a splintering crash. The trainer fell on the dog, then pulled him away.

Eastwind rushed to the bottom, saying, "Bline Boy, Jesus, Beebee!" He saw the blood forming a widening pattern under his friend's skull, and then he nearly froze in horror as he realized he'd just seen Bline Boy's dark glasses fly off and *his eyes* launch out of his head, one bounding down the steps with a "clack… clack!"; he suddenly understood they were glass eyes, and absurdly, when he reached Bline Boy, he desperately picked up the one that had landed on the step near the prostrate man.

He thought Bline Boy was dying. Eastwind raised his head and put a handkerchief to the scalp; shocked, he realized that the head he held was deeply crushed in the back of the skull. "Beebee… Beebee…"

He knew the trainer was calling for an ambulance. All he could do now was hold Bline Boy, try to keep him from losing blood. He peered at the glass eye in his grip, and drew back a little. On the white of it was an inscription almost too tiny to read without his glasses. Despite the urgency of the moment he wondered where in hell Bline Boy had gotten such a thing. Squinting, he read, The other eye is right. For a millisecond it occurred to him that this was an instruction to the wearer, but reason supervened in the awareness that it wasn't written in Braille.

"Bline Boy – don't die. *Jesus, you're not to die!* Everything was going to be all right with you!"

Eastwind gazed into the eye he held, and found himself drawn through its crystal cornea by what appeared to be swirling viscous fluid inside. He held his friend tighter, as if he could hold him from death and himself from absorption into the orb; but then knew himself inside the whirling cloud.

Suddenly it was the scene at the halfway house. He, as Ludi Vann, was ascending the stairs, opening the door to his room, glaring at finding Brett bent over at the lamp where the Martian emerged.

"Oh, hello, Ludi," Brett said. "I don't mean to intrude, but I thought it about time I took care of getting you that bulb."

Eastwind saw himself as Ludi keep glaring, then slowly say, "Hello, Karl."

"Hey, Brett, remember? A kindly Quaker. And part-time electrician, it looks like."

"I've known it was you a long time," Ludi said, with measured malevolence. "Nephew Karl."

"Come on, now, Ludi. You know me. We're friends."

"Everybody's somebody from before. You're Karl."

"Come on, Ludi." Brett would have moved but Ludi was blocking the doorway.

"I've made Belmont, too. I know who he is now. My angel helped me find him out. My Annie. And you're Karl," Ludi went on.

"Whatever," Brett said, realizing arguing was pointless.

"You betrayed me to your mother, you defiled your father, you married my immortal beloved!"

"Listen, I've got things to do. Why don't we talk about this later. That okay?"

"If it weren't for you she'd be mine."

Brett now stood in the doorway. "Now look, Ludi. What's this 'my Annie' business? You know, she *is* my wife," he managed to get out. "And we've been awfully good to you, wouldn't you say?" The two stared at each other. Brett then said, "You haven't been taking your medication, have you? Not swallowing it."

Ludi glanced down at the bottom drawer of the desk and saw that it wasn't quite closed.

"That's grounds for getting you out of here, you know that?"

"You'd take me from her? I wouldn't see *her?"*

"*Won't* see her. I just talked with Belmont on the phone. He said you weren't on your medication. He told me it was my choice whether we'd let you stay or not. And you've got to go."

Ludi looked away a moment, then came back with a raised fist and shook it in Brett's face. "Yeah, yeah, I know," Brett said. "Well, you'll just have to rage against your fate somewhere else."

The swirling fluid of the eye brought Eastwind into an agitated consciousness and he saw into the mind of the madman he had been. Ludi was aiming his fist with murder the target, but at once knowing that something was off, something wasn't right about it all; his agitation grew. "Tell me, O Godt, what to do!" Ludi shouted in his mind; Eastwind heard the words as an anguished prayer. The viscous fluid whirled faster and faster, and he saw Ludi looking for a sign, listening, wanting a voice out of a whirlwind, and finding nothing. And then Eastwind saw something that flabbergasted him:

Brett had backed off; suddenly, before Ludi's fist could strike, the man flew away, arms flailing as he leaned back into the air, landing on the steps, crashing his way down; lying dead, eyes turned back in their lids as if reviewing his life a final time.

Aghast, agape, Ludi slowly walked down the stairs and stood over Brett, seeing that only the whites of his eyes showed. In a moment he said to himself, he's dead, did… I kill him? Several notions crowded into his mind at once – that Ann was free for him now; that no one had heard the commotion of Brett's fall; that he was a murderer.

He thought, distinctly: can my madness support murder?

And then, without the slightest shift of mental gears, anguish overtook him at the next thought: I who have given birth to nine children who could rule the earth in the triumph of life and beauty… I have done this. He glimpsed a future darkened to eternity by the shadow of this day.

But no! *He* did this. *He fell.*

And Eastwind thought: God called me off, though I never heard his will or whistle.

He faded out of the eye, summoned by moans and the faint stirring of Bline Boy. "Jesus, don't die!" he said, "not you too!"

The young man, breathing hard, called from the top of the stairs, "There's an ambulance on the way. You need anything?"

"More cloth, a towel," Eastwind replied, surprised at his calmness. "Whatever bandages you have. I'm not having much luck with stopping the blood." The clerk rushed back into the office, where the dog was howling and moaning.

By the time the ambulance arrived and its crew rushed down the steps, Bline Boy was gone. Eastwind put the glass eyes back in the dead sockets and the dark glasses back over them, kissed him on the forehead, then pulled the sheet over his face.

"Take him to Bugg's" he said.

"Bugg's?" one of the EMT's asked.

"Bugg's Funeral Home. On West Forty-third."

"I know where it is," the other said. "But he's got to go to the coroner's first."

As Eastwind helped them move the body onto a stretcher, he said as an afterthought and a little absently, "It was his last request."

Chapter Twelve

Closing Cadences

The coroner certified the cause of death, and notified the police about the incident; the dog had to be destroyed. That was what Eastwind recounted to Idiot Boy, as they sat next to the body of Bline Boy on the gurney.

"The Lighthouse people wanted to know if his estate was going to sue," he told Idiot Boy. "I said I didn't know about his estate."

"His damn 'state went widh him. His 'state the inner-penetration o' touch 'n' soundt."

"Taste and smell, too."

"His four senses be walls of a room widdou' windows."

"They worried that I would sue."

"Shia, you wounn't sue."

"Not now," Eastwind said. "Not them."

"You thinkin' 'bout who show up tonight fo' the viewin'?"

"Man," said Eastwind, "I don't know any of his friends now. You don't either. I got his address from his wallet, went to the apartment house. No one there, so I left a note about the service. I'd like to find The Professor. He might remember him. But I don't know where to look."

"'Nouncement be in the paper. Bugg 'n' all. They show up they recognize 'im."

Eastwind turned his gaze to the face of his dead friend. The old pair of dark glasses covered the glass eyes. The white cane lay beside him. "Idiot Boy, did you know that he wore glass eyes under his shades?"

"Yep. Done got 'em a long time ago. After he move from 'Lanna. Nuthin' but empty sockets till he got the glassies."

"You ever see them – the glass eyes?"

"No. When I be knowin' 'im in the pass, never saw 'im widdou' his shates."

"One of them's very strange. Take a look at the left eye. Something's written on it. Something happened to me when I looked into it."

"Whut happen?"

"I… I think I found out what I wanted to find out from you," he said, considering how to put it. "About the Quaker."

"'Bout didt you kill 'im."

"Yeah. It all came to me, that day. I saw what happened."

"An' whut the eye tell you?"

"That I didn't kill Brett Yearly."

Idiot Boy turned to the face of Bline Boy and lifted the glasses. He squinted at the inscription on the left eye and muttered out loud, "'The other eye is… right.'" He added, "Pretty cool."

"I read that," Eastwind said, as Idiot Boy examined the right eye, "and I don't know why he would have that on it. He couldn't read it."

"But didt you look at the other one?"

"The other? There's something written on the other eye?"

"Looky-yeah. On the righ' one."

Eastwind went over, and putting on his reading glasses, barely made out: The other eye is wrong. He took off his glasses; his eyes cut down and to the side. In the back of his mind a tune with words began ringing in a voice that seemed distantly familiar:

Right is wrong and wrong is right
White is black and black is white...

"You know, Ludi Vann, I gotta fix him 'im up fo' this evenin'. Got to wash him."

Eastwind looked up and was silent a moment. "Would you let me help you?"

"Got a pair of gloves fo' you on the sink."

* * *

But they came. Eastwind scrutinized the coarse face of a raggedly-dressed white man who spoke to no one, and who went directly to the sandwiches Eastwind had had a caterer bring, along with a cooler of drinks, on the table at the back of the viewing room. He wondered if the man had even known Bline Boy, but whether he had or not it was okay with him. Another man, also white, youngish, made his way to the casket and shouted out, "He's dead!" His face had a severe tic to it, and his head jerked about; as he moved toward the cooler of drinks he shouted again: "A goner!" Eastwind surmised that the man had Tourette's Syndrome.

At first it seemed as though they were all street friends of Bline Boy he'd never known; then he looked at their faces more closely, allowing for the wearing down by time and grime, and thought he might have known some of them. He searched the wizened features of a later arrival, and aided by the diminutive stature of the man – recognized Hackensack the Dwarf.

"Hackensack!" he said. "Know me?"

"Un, no..." the man replied. "Ain't been called that forever."

"Fifteen years ago. A street-crazy who… well, I went by 'Ludi Vann.'"

The man's eyes grew large. "Yeah…!" he said after a second. "Is that you?"

"Well, I'm better now. But that was me. Bline Boy and I were pretty close."

"Right," he said. "Well, my voice ain't deepened any. Over the years." They both laughed.

He thought he recognized a tall and aged man, but his perception had momentarily fallen into a cognitive chasm that loomed as the clash between the man's lined, white-stubbled face and the jet black-dyed hair he sported, swept back into drooping wings.

"Darrell Jimmy," he said, and the man turned to him. "Remember Ludi Vann? Remember when we used to watch women together?"

"Ludi Vann," the man said, with a little awe, "you're white now? You're not out of your mind anymore? Where's your hair?"

"My wits strengthened when I lost my locks. Sort of the Samson thing in reverse."

"Delilahed," Darrell Jimmy deadpanned as he shook hands; Eastwind rolled his eyes in a look-away. The tall man went on, "Absolutely intriguing that appearance can mutate subject to the temporal condition…"

"Otherwise known as the ravages of time," Eastwind added.

"Precisely. Mutate and still belong to the same phenomenon. Or so it seems. The world is only appearance that has gravitated into the solidity of things…"

Eastwind found himself in an instantaneous reflection wondering what that said about the world. *Only appearance that has gravitated into the solidity of things.* He recalled the days when, both sane and mad, he had operated on the premise of such groundlessness. But for some time now he had embraced that abyss anew, entering through the back way, so to say, to find it not the means for manipulation or self-aggrandizement, but a void strangely benign, freeing. What he said to Darrell Jimmy was:

"I know. I know. But what does that have to do with women?"

"Why, everything," Darrell Jimmy chuckled. "I'm into crones now," he said, "bone structure. Skeletal promise."

"We sure dug them back in the day," Eastwind said, with a broad smile.

"Now they're about to get dug for," said Darrell Jimmy. "Though I'm still enamored."

Eastwind was surprised to see Salmaninski wander in, but then it made sense that he had come; he knew Bline Boy and "da Polecat" had known each other when the Beethoven years were on.

Salmaninski walked over to the casket and gave Bline Boy a once-over. He shook his head mournfully, then made eye contact with Eastwind. He ambled up to him and smiled wryly. A little sheepishly he said, "How's your nose?"

Eastwind thought of mentioning his ribs, but said instead, "Okay. How's your nose?"

Salmaninski chuckled a little. "Okay," he said. "The cops told me you're not pressing charges."

"Yeah," Eastwind said, taking a swallow of wine.

"But… *why?"*

"Let's just say I saw that the mountain had crashed into its valley," he said, "leveled to ground-zero. And I'm not doing anything about the letter you took and sold – the letter I wrote when I was nuts."

Salmaninski was aghast. "You… you know about *that?"*

"It was my investigators who interviewed you. According to the bill they sent me."

"You!" gasped the man.

"Salmaninski," Eastwind said, looking around to see that they wouldn't be overheard, "I'm the one who bought it. From Brixton's. I stipulated anonymity."

Salmaninski stared ahead, seeing nothing.

"For a lot of money, Leonard."

"And you're… you're not going to… take action?"

"No, Leonard. The right and wrong of it have left over something I can't figure out. In the kink and pith of things."

At sea with Eastwind's words, Salmaninski gave back a uncomprehending look. In a moment he said, "Okay, Ludi… Or I guess it's Louie, now," he added. "Whatever."

"But you might donate what's left of the money you got from it to the Society of Friends in New York."

"Ah, shit, Louie," the man said, "it's all about gone."

"That's okay too."

Salmaninski backed away, still baffled. "Okay," he said.

"Okay."

"Okay," he said again, and moved a little more.

"Okay," said Eastwind, and turned toward the others. Salmaninski left.

After a little while Eastwind saw a strange, stooped black man make his way into the room. He looked around, not recognizing anyone, then moved to the cooler where the drinks were; he poured himself some wine. It was the way he walked that got Eastwind's brain tingling, and then came the perception: The Professor.

"Professor!" cried Eastwind. "I was hoping you'd show up."

"Who you?" the man said, looking him up and down.

"I'm… I was Ludi Vann. In the old days."

"Shia… I 'member you. We both crazy then."

Eastwind couldn't resist. "Where're your signboards?"

"Done jettisonedt 'em. Excess baggage for an atheis'."

"You're an atheist now?" Eastwind was speechless. Then he said, "Shit. I wanted to talk with you about a new proof of God's existence."

"Nothin' to talk about."

"I thought you'd like to talk theology."

"I on my meds, Ludi. When I crazy I couldt talk Godt all day."

"Maybe later."

"No." Suddenly the man switched to a learned tone. "Later is always now in delay. And that now is – no."

* * *

After about half an hour Eastwind looked around and thought that he should say something about Bline Boy, but as he began moving toward where his friend lay Darrell Jimmy turned and moved ahead of him. Eastwind sat as his old acquaintance took a stand before the casket. The lankiness of his face, the gangly stance, the ill-fittedness of his clothes, seemed at that moment to define him anew for Eastwind – something along the lines of the square root of two in a Cubist mathematics. Darrell Jimmy looked around at the group, glanced back at the body of Bline Boy, then spoke:

"Bline Boy couldn't see. Nonetheless he stared into an abyss every waking hour, minute by minute. And what he saw was darkness staring back; his vision extended at least that far. But, let us ask, what precisely are the dimensions of darkness? Gentlemen, I put it to you."

The man with the shabby clothes and rough face spoke up. "How about a eulogy?" But Darrell Jimmy was oblivious.

"Lack, gentlemen, lack plays a significant role in answering that question. For in not being able to see others seeing him, he was denied the self-knowledge that comes from their gaze. He was not able ever to be that self so handily provided by the glare of others, for whom sighted people preen and strut, at whom we spit and scowl, visage wrestling visage. Past a certain point, Bline Boy no longer knew his own face in the mirror of society; the anchor of himself slipped in the silt of that unknowing. The structure of this failure of self-knowledge corresponded to that of a pit whose bottom was dropping out at the speed of night."

"Aah, drop out yourself!" from Hackensack, who had always hated D.J.'s diatribes.

"But we sighted people never know what others are really thinking; affection can be affected, cordiality can conceal. We become only the stuff of their stares in a similar unknowing. We are as in the dark about who we are for the world of others as he was. Thus did Bline Boy live the truth of our lives for us, just as Jesus, some say, died our deaths for us. His darkness was metaphysical."

"Mets! Physical!" from Tourette's man.

"But there was a corresponding outer dimension to the interior absence he lived. I ask you to ponder this."

"Jabbah, jabbah! Freak man!"

"What objective correlate to this inner lack was there for our decedent African-American?"

"You're nuts, man!" came from the shabby-looking guy.

"The answer is: his cane. His cane, gentlemen."

There was a momentary, more baffled silence.

"His cane. But in what way, you ask?"

"Shia, I ax you shut the fuck up," from The Professor. Eastwind sat immobile; the same old D.J., he thought. He realized he hadn't missed him.

"A positive object, constituted on its own, having no consciousness to torture it in the lack of knowledge of what it is for others. Having no subjectivity, gentlemen, it is a being frozen in objectivity…"

"Frost my nuts!"

"…such that, as cane, it attains to objective selfhood, to ipseity."

"'Tain to shit-aity!"

"Thus the inward slippage of self-lack was counterpoised by the outward stroke of cane-eity. Counterpoised and, let us note, counterbalanced, lest Bline Boy have been immobile. An inner darkness of infinite proportions opposed itself in the form of an outer cylindrical slenderness, white as it was finite."

Idiot Boy said, "Come on, D.J."

"But here we are called upon to think of what larger implications may obtain. I direct your attention to the fact that his cane *penetrated* space; that this penile instrument reached in and fertilized revelation, however crudely (blup! – don't go there; swish, okay, move ahead). This is how our defunct dark man knew the world. Space, the mother of all becoming, is the cunt-truth of the cosmos. Bline Boy Eddy was a man, no more, no less."

"Muthah*fuck*ah!"

"And so I end these observations with the justification for our search for pussy, gentlemen, our need to penetrate, and to my dying day I will honor the feminine – in my life now the flesh of women contends with its burgeoning contingency, their charms are droopy with use and time, but I have always… my dedication is such that…"

Eastwind got up and moved a step toward Darrell Jimmy.

"But for Bline Boy, it was only when someone, who's approaching me now, tried to replace caneity with caninity, I'm told, that the unity of these opposites was compromised, and, of necessity, dissolved. Here lieth the result of that dissolution: Bline Boy in formaldehydic transport, 'and all we mourn for.'"

The words bolted through Eastwind's heart, but they exited quickly and cleanly; the wound healed instantly. Darrell Jimmy sat down and Eastwind stood before the casket. He looked toward the small group of half a dozen. "Keep eating," he said, "keep drinking. Bline Boy wasn't your formal kind of guy." Tourette's man jabbered out, "Formal-*dehyde!*"

"I just want to say Bline Boy suffered. I suffered. We all suffered on the streets; maybe some of you are still there. I'd wanted to talk with The Professor here about the dreams I've had… strange dreams about God's suffering, dreams that have him in agony over having to be us, so as to be at all. But all that's probably nonsense…"

The shabby man shook his head in disgust. "Can we get a eulogy here?" he whined.

"Indeed," Darrell Jimmy added, "'More matter, with less art.'"

"Less *fart!*" from Tourette's.

Eastwind had thought of all the ways of trying to say what he wanted to say, ways that involved humans wandering in labyrinths that had God's secret design; he'd wanted to say something about God flooding the meadow of heaven with time to see who sank and who swam. He wanted to say that maybe the only meaning possible had something to do with suffering, that our suffering was God on the rack of time. We speak his silence, he'd wanted to say. But he found that it was he himself who was silent.

"Okay, okay," Eastwind said. "I guess all I can say now is that… that the darkness Bline Boy knew daily… *meant* something to me. I tried to save him…" His voice began to waver. "I tried to ease his suffering. I led him to the stairs…" His words started to crack, and he said, "I didn't know death would be a dog." He began to cry a little, and Idiot Boy handed him a handkerchief. "That's all I have to say," he said, clearing his throat and turning to his host, with Tourette's man going "Aw! Aw!" Eastwind said goodbye to Idiot Boy, then moved toward the lobby door, and when he reached it and it yielded to his bulk he heard the afflicted man shout, "Outta here! Outta here!"

Coda

Eastwind emerged to an unusually dark night that was relieved only as the lights of buildings still pressed patterns into the sky. The Professor came out and stood next to him on the sidewalk.

"I've had dreams about you," Eastwind said. "I guess I never got over your sign-boards."

"Man," The Professor said, "I never got over you' Beethoven gig. How you get over it?"

"Chemicals. Crystals of reason. Little lipids of lucidity."

"Me too," said The Professor. He became the professor, lecturing in a classroom: "Meister Eckhart used to pray to God to deliver him from God. Of course, he knew nothing of chemical therapy."

"Well, no more Beethoven for me. But I still love the symphonies, concertos, sonatas…"

"Shia," said The Professor, returning to his street persona, "they gotta car callt the Sonata now, know that?"

"Indeed I do, Professor. Drive one. It's rusting, been dented, rear-ended," he said, then began improvising. "License plate of zeroes run several times by the Despair

Detectives on the lookout for spiritual thefts, self-congratulations, bad faith…"

"But it get you 'roun'…"

"Gas gauge reads 'empty' even after filling up. Been ticketed by the Hallmark meter maids for parking on the edge…"

"Well," The Professor said, "I got a bumper sticker for it. 'God not dead prolly jus' comatose'…"

Eastwind looked into the night.

The Professor said, "I 'member somethin' 'bout you killin' a man, inna oldt days. Some Quaker guy. Not feelin' his oats now. You do that?"

"I don't know," Eastwind said, thoughtfully.

"Not knowin' not get you off the hook."

"No. The hook is a question mark."

"It punctuate."

"It punctuates."

"You servin' the sentence."

"I look to ellipses."

"Whatever," The Professor said, and swiveled his head to take in the night. He looked back to Eastwind. "Now you no longer Beethoven."

"No."

"They say you Eastwin' now."

"They say."

"So," the man said, "who you be?"

"To be perfectly frank," Eastwind said, aware of the pun, "I don't know that either. Anymore."

"Shia, Frank not a badt guy a be."

"To be perfectly rich," Eastwind added, "I'm full of the emptiness of myself."

"You know, Rich be a okay guy, too."

"My signature always seems a carbon copy these days. Original document can't be found."

A silence ensued.

Eastwind asked, “What did you do with your signboards?”

“Got rid of ’em long time ago.”

“You still walk like you’re carrying them. It’s how I recognized you.”

“I burnt ’em one night,” The Professor said, then switched to his erudite voice, “when humanism and theodicy had each other in a stranglehold.” He looked down the street. “Say,” he said, “you wanna fight? Mix it up right here and now?”

“No,” Eastwind answered, “I wouldn’t.”

“Gotta go,” The Professor said, and walked away.

Eastwind watched the stooped form go down Forty-third. Seeing all the street people he’d known before had, with the exceptions of Bline Boy and Idiot Boy, been a little disappointing, he reflected. Hackensack, Darrell Jimmy, The Professor, even Salmaninski – and he added Ludi Vann to the group – all gone. All over. All the *poesis* of personality, now the matter of memory; no more, no less.

He reflected that he had seen Bline Boy for the last time; Idiot Boy would address him to sepulchral eternity. And then Bline Boy seemed to be with him, talking, answering, bantering.

“Dat right, man. He box me up, send me one-way, Chrise-on-Delivery. Guaranteedt. But now, dat Frenchman – da three-blinker…”

“You mean Lavoisier? Da one who loss his headt?”

“He know sumpin’ ’bout first ’n’ thirdt. Da ultimate scene-makah.”

“’Bout eyelid-semaphore for alpha ’n’ omega.”

Bline Boy: He got da ocular twitch.
Eastvann: Da oracular bitch.
Bline Boy: Dat be da Sibyl.
Eastvann: Schuppanzigh’s fiddle.

Bline Boy: Playin' a tune.
Eastvann: Be a final rune.
Together (singing):
Oh, when dat ol' Augie blick his blick
You know it da endt o' da flick.

But this imagined camaraderie with his dead friend left him feeling more alone. He noticed how dark the night was, and beyond the buildings, how bright the stars were. They seemed to be distant fireworks, though he had no idea of what they might be celebrating. He made his way to the car.

His eyes, stung by the wintry air, had become moist, and when he looked up again the stars became strings of spectral fibers, reaching his eyes and at once back into the history of their light. "You know, Bline Boy," he said mentally, "there's a mystery to the distance between things you can't quite solve."

"No matter how fass you move."

"No matter how fast you move. Or the moves you make."

"Yep," his dead pal said, "it go fo' us too."

"True. Sometimes we invent the weirdest dances to draw up space…"

"Backin' 'n' fillin'."

"…sculptures of arcs conforming to the calculus of desire and regret…"

"But da distance, it still remai'," Bline Boy was saying.

Tell it, my brother, he answered in his mind as he caught the luminous tendrils stretching from the sky a last time. Stars and selves.